Praise for Ann B. Ross and

"Imagine Aunt Bee from the *Andy Grif[...]* [...] bone and confidence and drop her smack in the middle o[...] [...], rollicking plot akin to that of the movie *Smokey and the Bandit* and you have the tone and pace of Ross's entertaining second novel."

—*Publishers Weekly*

"Ross allows the reader to laugh gently at feisty, opinionated Miss Julia while thoroughly enjoying the view through her eyes. [For] readers who love Jan Karon."

—*Booklist*

"[A] hilarious adventure . . . as funny as the first book."

—*The Pilot* (Southern Pines, N.C.)

"*Miss Julia Takes Over* is Ann B. Ross's amiable sequel to her popular novel, *Miss Julia Speaks Her Mind*, a literary continuation in which Miss Julia once again finds her orderly world turned topsy-turvy. . . . Ms. Ross has a way of drawing us in with dead-on details. . . . You [...]!"

—*The Dallas Morning News*

Miss Julia Speaks Her Mind

"[...]utely loved this book! What a joy to read! Miss Julia is one of [...] delightful characters to come along in years. Ann B. Ross has [...] what is sure to become a classic Southern comic novel. Hooray [...] Julia, I could not have liked it more."

—Fannie Flagg

"[In the] radition of Clyde Edgerton's Mattie Riggsbee or that quirky [...] Jessica Tandy brought to life in *Driving Miss Daisy,* Ann Ross has created another older Southern heroine in Julia Springer, who is—as Southerners say—outspoken, but by whom? A late-blooming feminist, Miss Julia is no shrinking violet in this comic plot that tweaks stuffy husbands, manipulative small-town neighbors, snoopy preachers, and general human greed, but ends by endorsing the love and vitality that energize Miss Julia's sharp tongue and warm heart."

—Doris Betts, author of *The Sharp Teeth of Love*

"A witty tale . . . replete with charm . . . it is impossible not to like this book." —*Ft. Worth Morning Star-Telegram*

PENGUIN BOOKS

MISS JULIA TAKES OVER

Ann B. Ross, who has taught literature at the University of North Carolina at Asheville, is the author of *Miss Julia Throws a Wedding* and *Miss Julia Speaks Her Mind*, one of the most popular Southern novels in years. Though Ann Ross insists she's not Miss Julia, there are some undeniable coincidences: they both live in small Southern towns; they've both been involved in the usual social, civic, and religious organizations of their communities; and they were both brought up with a healthy respect for the proprieties of polite society. She lives in Hendersonville, North Carolina, where she writes full time.

Miss Julia Takes Over

Ann B. Ross

PENGUIN BOOKS

PENGUIN BOOKS
Published by the Penguin Group
Penguin Putnam Inc., 375 Hudson Street, New York, New York 10014, U.S.A.
Penguin Books Ltd, 80 Strand, London WC2R 0RL, England
Penguin Books Australia Ltd, 250 Camberwell Road,
Camberwell, Victoria 3124, Australia
Penguin Books Canada Ltd, 10 Alcorn Avenue,
Toronto, Ontario, Canada M4V 3B2
Penguin Books India (P) Ltd, 11 Community Centre,
Panchsheel Park, New Delhi – 110 017, India
Penguin Books (N.Z.) Ltd, Cnr Rosedale and Airborne Roads,
Albany, Auckland, New Zealand
Penguin Books (South Africa) (Pty) Ltd, 24 Sturdee Avenue,
Rosebank, Johannesburg 2196, South Africa

Penguin Books Ltd, Registered Offices: Harmondsworth, Middlesex, England

First published in the United States of America by Viking Penguin,
a member of Penguin Putnam Inc. 2001
Published in Penguin Books 2002

10 9 8 7 6

PUBLISHER'S NOTE
This is a work of fiction. Names, characters, places, and incidents either
are the product of the author's imagination or are used fictitiously, and any
resemblance to actual persons, living or dead, business establishments,
events, or locales is entirely coincidental.

Title page illustration adapted from a photograph
by Nancy R. Cohen, © 2001 PhotoDisc, Inc.

THE LIBRARY OF CONGRESS HAS CATALOGED
THE HARDCOVER EDITION AS FOLLOWS:
Ross, Ann B.
   Miss Julia takes over / Ann B. Ross.
      p. cm.
   ISBN 0-670-91026-0 (hc.)
   ISBN 0 14 20.0089 2 (pbk.)
      1. Widows—Fiction. 2. Women—North Carolina—Fiction.
   3. North Carolina—Fiction. I. Title.
PS3568.O84198 M574 2001
813'.54—dc21   2001017709

Printed in the United States of America
Set in Bembo / Designed by Carla Bolte

For Delin

Acknowledgments

Many thanks to Special Agent Chris Smith of the North Carolina State Bureau of Investigation for being generous with his time and expertise, as well as for an afternoon of cop tales that curled my hair. My thanks, too, to Steve Barkdohl, general manager of Andy Petree Racing, Inc. for a tour of the shop and a hauler. Special thanks also to Larry Parmalee, former NASCAR driver, now an instructor of beginning race-car drivers; and to John Lampley, a longtime sports-car driver whose favorite track is the North Carolina Speedway. All of these racing professionals revealed the nuts and bolts of a sport of which I knew little, and made, in the process, another racing fan. My thanks also to Greg Rummans, who listened to my ideas and laughed when he was supposed to.

Miss Julia Takes Over

Chapter 1

I declare, if it's not one thing, it's two more. Or, in my case, a half-a-dozen. Seems like everytime I turn around, there's something else to worry me half to death.

Feeling too antsy to sit still, I closed my checkbook and put it in the desk drawer. Who can balance a bank statement with troubles whipping around like the cold wind outside? March, I thought, with a shiver. We could do without it, if you ask me, yet the whole unpredictable month was still ahead of us.

I walked to the window and looked out at the gray morning, noticing the one, lone crocus poking up through the ice that lined the hedge along the side yard. If I'd had a poetic turn of mind, I might've seen it as a symbol of hope or of a brighter day coming or of some other such uplifting thought. But all I could do was wonder how the voles had missed it when they ate the rest of them.

I walked back to the fireplace and adjusted the flame in the gas logs that I'd had the good sense to put in after the last time we lost power in an ice storm. Be prepared, I always say, but nobody could be prepared for all the troubles and worries and problems that were piling up everywhere I looked. If we'd had a real fire, I'd've kicked a log.

Lillian stuck her head around the swinging door and called through the dining room. "You goin' to see Mr. Sam 'fore you eat, or after? I need to know 'fore I set lunch on the table."

"I can't be worried with him now. Lillian, I can't stand this.

Where is she?" I threw up my hands, just about at the end of my rope. "And I don't want anything to eat."

"Uh-huh, I hear you, but I already got it fixed." She propped her hands on her hips and announced in that bossy way of hers, "An' I don't know anymore'n you do about where she is, but somebody better be doin' something about it."

I knew who that somebody was. Me. Lillian'd been pushing me to do something ever since she'd come to work at seven this morning, while I kept hoping Hazel Marie would show up with a decent explanation for her overnight absence. I declare, it's a burden when everybody stands around, waiting for me to make everything right. Lillian, though, had been with me for so long that she didn't mind telling me what to do and when to do it. Half of what she said usually went in one ear and out the other. But not today, because I was either going to have to do something or pull my hair out, one.

But she wasn't through giving me instructions. "Go on over to Mr. Sam's an' see what he say. He countin' on seein' you, anyway."

"What can he do, laid up like he is with a cast up to his you-know-what? Serves him right, is all I can say, out there in a trout stream in the dead of winter."

"What's done is done," she said, "an' no use rantin' around about it. Now, come on in here an' get your coat."

With a click of my tongue, I followed her into the kitchen. "Well, he deserves to suffer the consequences, and I don't mind seeing that he does."

"Mr. Sam, he just want your help to see 'bout that home nurse the doctor say he have to have. It won't hurt you to go over there an' be sure she know what she doin', since he can't hardly do a thing for hisself with that leg hiked up all the time. He need you to lighten him up a little."

She moved a pan off the stove, while I stood there, feeling pushed and pulled a dozen different ways. I didn't have time to be entertaining Sam Murdoch, frittering away my day when I had so much to contend with right where I was, what with LuAnne Conover pestering me to death, moaning about Leonard and the state of their marriage, which as far as I could tell, had never been a model of conjugal bliss in the first place. And there was Brother Vernon Puckett, Hazel Marie's uncle—the sorry thing—calling on Pastor Ledbetter, as I'd seen with my own eyes that very morning when his low-slung, maroon and white Cadillac pulled into the church parking lot right across the street from my house. Now, I ask you, what could a self-proclaimed preacher of the airwaves have in common with a seminary-trained Presbyterian minister like Larry Ledbetter? Well, that had an easy answer. They'd both give their eyeteeth for a way to get their hands on the estate left by my lately deceased husband, Wesley Lloyd Springer. But, thanks to Sam and the State of North Carolina, Little Lloyd and I had it safely in hand.

But, worse than any of those worries, Hazel Marie Puckett, Little Lloyd's mother, had turned up among the missing, and I was about to jump out of my skin, not knowing which way to turn. I'd called every hospital in three counties, asking if an attractive, forty-year-old woman with professionally dyed blonde hair and a full charm bracelet on her arm had been recently admitted. The calls had told me where she wasn't, which was some comfort, but they hadn't told me where she was.

Lillian said, "You better quit standin' there, bitin' yo' lip like that. Go on over to Mr. Sam's an' see 'bout that home nurse woman, an' ask him what we ought to be doin' to find Miss Hazel Marie."

"Lord, Lillian, I'm of two minds about that. Sam always has good advice, but the doctor said not to worry him with anything. Make sure he gets his rest and don't agitate him."

I tapped my foot, thinking of how everytime I needed Sam Murdoch, he'd go and do something unforeseen and, in my eyes, just plain reckless. Take the time Wesley Lloyd passed so unexpectedly, and I was left with wills and bills and so-called financial advisers and grasping preachers and, as if that hadn't been enough, Wesley Lloyd's bastard to boot.

And where was Sam? Retired, that's where. And right when I'd needed his legal expertise the most. And here, history was repeating itself, since I'd have to bite my tongue about my current problems and be *pleasant,* of all things.

Well, give Sam credit, I thought, though at the moment I hated to. He'd come through for me, straightening out Wesley Lloyd's two wills so that neither Little Lloyd nor I had been stranded without a nickel to our names. Far from it, in fact.

And, to give Sam more credit, he'd handed me over to Binkie Enloe, as good a lawyer as any hoary-headed regular-type lawyer in town, and better than most. I can't help it if she carries on with Deputy Coleman Bates with no legalization of the situation anywhere in sight. I've gotten where I don't let things like that bother me. As long as she does my taxes right and gives me advice I can live with, I'm just not going to say anything about her private life. Although I do mention it, on occasion.

"Lillian," I said, as I reached for my coat, "I've tried my level best not to worry about what Hazel Marie's doing. I know, I know," I held up my hand to stop what I knew she was going to say. "You think it's none of my business. But it is. As long as she's living in my house, out of the kindness of my heart, I might add, I feel responsible for her. I think I have a right to know where she is, especially when she stays out all night long.

"Now, I don't think she'd do anything wrong, well, I mean, criminal. Well, I don't know what I mean." I stopped, remembering that Hazel Marie had lived in sin with my husband for ever so long, and it might've been a crime as well, for all I knew.

"The thing about it is," I went on, "Pastor Ledbetter's been instructing her in the catechism, since she wants to be a Presbyterian instead of a foot-washing Baptist or whatever she was, and now she stays out all night long with a man whose family nobody knows. Word will get around, Lillian, and that bunch of old men on the church session may refuse to write for her letter. It won't matter that she's never done anything like this before, or that she's doing it with a church employee, if that's what you can call Wilson T. Hodge." I sniffed at the thought.

Nothing would do but Pastor Ledbetter had to bring in an out-of-town fund-raiser to rouse the congregation into a pledging frenzy, since he couldn't raise any funds from me. And for what? Why, to get that family activities center built, that's what. You know, the one the pastor recommended I underwrite out of Wesley Lloyd's estate, seeing, as he'd said, that I needed some Christian financial guidance? Well, I'd put a lid on that as soon as he brought it up, not three days after the funeral, since I knew exactly where he'd guide it to. I didn't have any need for a gymnasium or a running track or a basketball court, nor did anybody else when all they had to do was join the YMCA. I ask you, how many times would I go over there and dribble a ball or lift weights?

"Lillian," I went on, with a sinking heart, "what am I going to tell that child when he gets home from school?"

"Well, I been wonderin' 'bout that, too," Lillian said, coming to the counter and leaning on it, "I thought his mama'd be in 'fore this or least, call an' say when she be here. It's gettin' on toward middle of the day, an' not word one from her. I thought maybe they be jumpin' the gun a little, havin' a early honeymoon like some folks do. But I don't know, Miss Julia, look like she have enough of it by now." Lillian looked up at the clock on the wall.

"You would think so. How long does it take to have dinner and see a show, even if they did drive to Asheville to do it? They've had more than enough time for decent people to do what they need to do. And I don't mean what you're thinking. They've been gone all night and half the morning, and I know something's bad wrong. We both know it's not like Hazel Marie to go off and stay gone, with neither hide nor hair of Wilson T. Hodge to be found, either. I've called his apartment so many times I'm sick of doing it, and he's not at the church, either, where he's supposed to be working."

"Yessum, an' that little chile just gonna be sick about it when he come home, an' she not be here. He know she don't have no sick friend like you tole him this mornin'."

"Well, what was I to do? You know how hard it is for me to out-and-out lie, and it was the only thing I could think of at the time. Should I've told him his mother was out all night without benefit of matrimony? She did that long enough with the child's father, which he doesn't need to know at this tender age.

"Oh, me, Lillian," I stopped and leaned my head against the door, overwhelmed with disappointment. I'd risked my name and reputation to take in my husband's paramour and the then nine-year-old result of their secret relations, and just look what had come of it. Two full years of my close supervision and exemplary influence didn't seem to've made a dent. "I declare, I thought Hazel Marie had given up such loose ways. I thought I'd shown her a more decent way of living and now, she's fallen right back into the gutter."

"You don't know that for a fact. Maybe they have a flat tire."

"Even I know it doesn't take this long to fix a flat, much less make a phone call." I straightened up, confirmed again in my first, unimpressed impression of Wilson T. Hodge, the man Hazel Marie'd chosen to have her first legitimate happiness with. I declare, I couldn't say much for her taste in men, and that included Wesley Lloyd Springer, too. But, if Wilson T. Hodge was her choice, I was trying to be happy for her. Even though I'd had my doubts about him from the first time he'd put a foot in my living room, smiling and standing too close and flattering me with compliments on my house, my furnishings and my own gracious self, as he smoothed that smudge of a mustache with a ring-laden finger. I don't trust people like that as far as I can throw them. He had thin lips, too.

I wouldn't've trusted him even if I hadn't known the line of work he was in. Lord, I didn't think it was right to pay somebody good money to raise more money. Something's wrong with the whole system when Christians have to be begged and pleaded with and finangled into pledging more than they can afford in order to build something they don't need in the first place. That'd been the reason I'd voted against hiring him, sight unseen, but they'd done it anyway.

"Maybe they have a wreck," Lillian said. "That car might be in the middle of Briar Creek, and nobody found 'em yet."

"Lillian! Don't say that! Besides, I've already put the Highway Patrol on alert and, besides that, Briar Creek is so shallow, you couldn't hide a go-cart in it, much less a full-size car. No, it's something else that's holding them up; I just don't know what it could be."

Hearing a gust of wind rattle the windows, I wrapped a wool scarf around my neck, readying myself for the icy blasts.

"I'd better go, if I'm going, but I won't be long," I said, picking up my purse and car keys. "If Hazel Marie comes in, give me a call, will you? But don't say anything to her."

"You don't have to tell me that. Not none of my business to say anything to that sweet woman." She turned away, folding the dishrag and hanging it on the faucet. "'Sides, you do enough for both of us, and she don't need to hear it twicet."

I rolled my eyes and opened the door. Stepping out on the side stoop, I wrapped my coat close against the wind and scrunched up in it. As I walked the few steps to the garage, I glanced out at the street and across to the church parking lot. With a start, I stopped, gasped and tried to catch my breath which had been snatched away at the sight.

Hurrying back to the door, I slammed it open and called, "Lillian! Do you know what he's done?"

"What? Who you talkin' about?"

"That preacher! That idiot preacher! Have you seen it? Come out here and look."

She came around the counter to the door, her run-over shoes flapping on her heels. "What in the world goin' on out there?"

Following me out, she squinched her eyes as I pointed to the church parking lot. There, directly across the street from my front porch, was a huge rectangle outlined by stakes and string. Little orange flags fluttered from each stake.

"You see it?" I demanded. "You see what he's doing?"

"I see it," Lillian said, "but I don't know what it mean."

"It means he's going to build that blamed building that's been on his mind ever since Wesley Lloyd passed, that's what it means. And look, Lillian," I said, grabbing her arm and pulling her along with me, "he's got it laid out right along the sidewalk over there. Do you know what that means?"

"No, I don't know what it mean, an' I'm freezin' out here."

"Well, just look! If he puts a wall along that string, what do you think we'll look out on from every window in the front of the house? A brick wall, that's what!"

"Yessum, but you have the street in between."

"I don't care about the street! He's putting that brick wall right in front of my eyes! It's vengeance, Lillian, that's what it is! I wouldn't build that building for him, so he's getting back at me by putting a wall right out in front, blocking my view, isolating me from my church." I was so mad, I could've wrung the preacher's neck if he'd been standing there. "I'm not going to have it! I tell you, I'm not. I'll have that vindictive man's head on a platter, along with the session's and every member of the congregation, see if I don't!"

"Well, jus' 'member you one of them members, so how you gonna do that?"

I jerked around and headed for the garage. "I'll think of something or, even simpler, I'll stop being a member. I'm going to see Sam, and I'm not going with nice, pleasant things to say to him, either. I don't care what the doctor ordered."

Chapter 2

I parked in front of Sam's large, white house with the floor-to-ceiling windows, bordered by Charleston green shutters. Then I stomped up the brick walkway, fuming at the nefarious ways of our pastor, and ready to demand that Sam do something about him.

"Mister Sam in the living room," James said, greeting me at the door as I crossed Sam's broad front porch.

That was plainly evident, since I heard laughter coming from the large room opening off the hall where we were standing. One deep rumble from Sam, and another lighter, almost infectious laugh from a woman. From the sound of it, Sam had taken a sudden turn for the better.

"That nurse," I said to James, "she's here already?"

"Yessum, she been here a while. She workin' on Mister Sam real good."

"I can tell," I said with a sniff, climbing off one high horse and getting ready to mount another one. I handed him my coat and scarf. "No need to hang them up. I won't be staying long."

I walked to the large arch that opened into Sam's living room and stopped in my tracks. All the worries that burdened my soul flew out of my mind as I saw what was going on. A fire blazed in the fireplace, warming the high-ceilinged room, filled with bookshelves and leather furniture. Sam sat in the big chair by the fire, his cast-laden leg stretched out on an ottoman. Everything was as it should be, except for the fact that he was bent over, half-naked and some curly-headed young woman was leaning over his back doing I couldn't determine what to him.

"Julia!" Sam called, looking up from what had to be a most uncomfortable position, though it didn't seem to be bothering him. "Come on in here. I want you to meet this angel of mercy. This is Miss Etta Mae Wiggins. Miss Wiggins, meet Mrs. Julia Springer."

"Pleased, I'm sure," Miss Wiggins said, continuing whatever ministrations she was conducting on Sam's back. Bright, cupid face framed with blond curls smiled at me. A face that would've been considerably improved with several layers of paint stripped from it. She wore one of those white pantsuits that nurses have so unprofessionally taken to, which do so little for most of them. This young woman, however, filled it admirably, if you admired tight fits.

"Miss Wiggins," I said with a formal nod of my head. I wanted it understood that I hadn't come to join in the kind of merriment they were obviously enjoying. "Don't let me interrupt whatever treatment the two of you are involved in. Sam, you asked me to come over and help you evaluate the need for a representative of the Handy Home Helpers, but it looks as if you've already made up your mind."

"So I have, Julia. But come on in and sit by me." He reached out his hand, which under other circumstances I would've taken. Sam was the kind of man that makes you feel comforted when you're close to him. Probably because he's a big man, full-chested and white-haired. Distinguished looking, I'd say, until you noticed his sparkling blue eyes that saw the humor in everything. That was the only thing I could hold against him, since I'm a woman of serious demeanor and intent.

"I'm glad to see you," he went on. "Miss Wiggins, here, is giving me a backrub to end all backrubs. Sit down, Julia, sit down."

I did, perching on the edge of the sofa near Sam's chair, but considerably ill-at-ease at the close proximity to his unclothed state.

Wiggins, I thought, watching her slather her hands with a floral-smelling lotion, nothing medicinal about it, and continue to massage Sam's back. I knew some Wiggenses. Knew *of,* that is, as did every resident of Abbot County. That family was known for as many less than stellar accomplishments as the Puckett family, of which Hazel Marie was a notable exception.

Miss Wiggins leaned over and whispered something in Sam's ear, making him shake with laughter. That was just so rude, to whisper in front of someone else. And Sam was as much at fault as she was, laughing without including me.

I stood up. "Well, I see you're busy with your therapy, so I'll be getting back. I do wish you'd called me, Sam, and saved me a trip in this weather."

"Don't go, Julia. You just got here. I want you to get to know Etta Mae. She's just what the doctor ordered, and has already done me a world of good."

That just put my back up. Obviously, all my help and care and concern since he'd gotten home from the hospital were not worth mentioning, since this little twit had come in for thirty minutes and canceled out everybody else. And *Etta Mae*? Since when had nurses allowed their patients such easy familiarity? This wasn't like Sam at all, who was as formal in his dealings with women of all ages as any well-bred Southern gentleman ought to be.

What had the young woman done to him? Just came into his home and within an hour had him laughing and chuckling and half-naked, rubbing her hands all over his back and around and under his arms and whispering things in his ear. It was the most unseemly kind of nursing I'd ever seen.

"Miss Wiggins," I said, as I stood up, "what is the condition of Sam's broken bone? Is the cast too tight? What about the itching that's driving him up a wall? What do you plan to do to make him more comfortable at night? He's hardly able to sleep with that heavy thing on him."

"Oh, don't worry about any of that; we're taking care of it," she said. Then, with a knowing smile, she went on, "Mr. Sam's not going to have any trouble sleeping tonight. Not after I get through with him." She ran her hands up around his neck, massaging the muscles with an indelicate kind of touching and rubbing. "You're gonna sleep good tonight, aren't you, you ole sweet thing, you."

My mouth dropped open. I expected Sam to put her in her place with that devastatingly polite way he had of cutting people down to size. But no, all he did was grin up at me, like, See, Julia?

I turned on my heel, having had enough of the spectacle. If that was the kind of service a home health care professional provided, then I wanted no part of it. And I was fuming because Sam couldn't see straight through her the way I could.

It was a settled fact that he had neither the time nor the interest to listen to my problems.

"If you need anything after Miss Wiggins leaves, you can have James call me," I said, heading across the room. "Although I doubt there's anything I can do for you."

"Julia," Sam said, straightening up and reaching for his shirt. Miss Wiggins helped him get into it, coming around in front to button it for him. A chore that he could've easily managed for himself. It was his *leg* that was broken. "Julia, don't go, we've hardly had time to visit."

"I'll come back when you're not so busy. How often do you plan to come, Miss Wiggins?"

"Anytime Mr. Sam wants me, I'll be here," she said, breezily. "All he has to do is whistle."

I could've smacked her. And Sam too, because he laughed with her, his eyes sparkling, as the brazen little snip took a brush to his hair.

"I'm gonna have you lookin' so handsome and feelin' so good that all the ladies in town're gonna be ringin' your bell," she said, leaning over him so that her bosom was practically in his face.

It was more than I could stand. "Sounds like you're going to be here all the time," I said, letting my feelings put an edge to my words. I couldn't help myself. "Maybe you should just move in."

"Why, I'd do it in a minute if he'd have me," she said, and part of what made me so mad was the fact that everything she said to me was really addressed to Sam. And he was eating it up. She reached down and smoothed his eyebrows. Then she had the nerve to say, "Any woman with any sense would grab this good-lookin' man and hold on to him as hard as she could."

Sam did have the grace to blush, but he liked it. Men just don't have any sense at all. Here was this little flirt, young enough to be his youngest daughter if he'd had one, flattering him without a lick of shame and he couldn't or wouldn't see through it. If this was what nursing had come to, it was time to reconsider the value of the whole profession.

If Sam needed flattery, which comes down to just plain lying, then I could do it just as well, and probably better. And it wouldn't cost him a dime. But you won't see me lowering myself to such a degree.

"Julia," Sam said, settling back in his chair after Miss Wiggins had buttoned his sweater and put an afghan over his knees. "Come on back here and talk to me a minute. I know you have something on your mind, and I want to hear it."

"Oh, it's nothing that won't wait until you have more time." I could be just as breezy as Miss Wiggins. "Just a few small matters like Pastor Ledbetter getting ready to build something in my front yard and Brother Vern sticking his nose in where it doesn't belong and LuAnne Conover about to leave Leonard after forty-something years and Hazel Marie off gallivanting all night long and nobody knowing where she is. Nothing at all to worry you with, since you're too sick to give a thought to what other people might be going through."

"Hazel Marie Puckett?" Miss Wiggins said. I gave her a glance that should've frozen her, but didn't. Most people know better than to enter a conversation that has nothing to do with them. But that didn't stop her. "I know Hazel Marie, and that girl's just had the hardest time. I heard she was living with you, her and that sweet little boy of hers. How's she doin' these days?"

Not wishing to discuss the hard time Hazel Marie'd had, especially since she'd had it with my husband, I pursed my lips and considered just ignoring her. But I was not one of those people who could be intentionally rude. "I don't know how she's doing right this minute since, as I said, she hasn't come home yet. Other than that, I guess she's doing fine. Sam," I said, turning to the one I wanted to talk to, "I don't know what to do. She went off with that Wilson T. Hodge, and you know what I think of him."

"Well, Julia, she's a grown woman, so I don't know that there's anything you can do."

"I'm worried about her. She's never done this before, and I don't care if she is thinking of marrying him. She ought not to be spending the night with him or anybody else. She has that child to consider."

Miss Wiggins looked from one to the other of us, her eyes as wide as the blue paint on them would allow. "That doesn't sound like Hazel Marie," she said. "That little boy's her whole life."

"Don't encourage Julia in her worries, Etta Mae," Sam said, as if I had to be calmed down and patted on the head. "Julia, Hazel Marie knows that Little Lloyd is in good hands with you. She's not going to be worried about him. For all we know, she and Wilson T. have eloped. They probably didn't want to go through that elaborate wedding you've been planning. I'd just not worry about it, if I were you."

"Well, you're not me. And don't start putting it off on me, either, implying that the plans I had for their wedding were not appreciated. I don't care if they elope or walk down the aisle of the First Presbyterian church with sixteen attendants, all I want to know is, where is she now."

"Give her a little more time, she'll be home. Now, Etta Mae, where's that special treat you promised me?"

"Right in the kitchen. It's some of my Granny's tea, and believe me it's just the ticket to young you up by about twenty years. Not that a fine man like you needs it, though. Miss Julia, would you like some? I've got plenty."

"No, I would not, thank you all the same. I have things to do." Better things, I wanted to say, but it's not my way to be sarcastic.

"I wish you'd stay," Sam said, but his eyes were on Miss Wiggins as she swished herself out of the room.

"You'll have to do more than wish," I said, half under my breath, as I headed into the hall, got my coat and left.

The temperature had dropped, although the wind had begun to slack off by the time I stood on his porch, wrapping my scarf around my neck and trying to get myself together. All I could think of was how history was repeating itself. First, Wesley Lloyd had cast an eye, as well as other things, toward a younger woman, now Sam was doing the same thing. Was it in every man's nature to discard a decent, upright and loyal woman in favor of any little twit who threw herself at him? I shook myself, not wanting to open up old wounds having to do with Hazel Marie who was now in different circumstances, thanks to my efforts. But it was hard, having just been a witness to how easily a man could be taken in. Even someone like Sam, who was as levelheaded as you could ask for. If he couldn't see past the makeup and the bouncing and jiggling and the flattery, then there wasn't a hope for any man alive.

Well, it was a settled fact that, like Wesley Lloyd, Sam couldn't be trusted. Better to know now, I told myself, than to find it out after the whole town was laughing behind my back.

A sudden gust of wind blew across the porch, making me shiver as I pulled my coat closer. But as cold as it was, I was steaming inside, knowing how close I'd come to making a fool of myself for the second time in my life.

And knowing that I was left to do everything by myself. As usual.

Chapter 3

"She jus' called, jus' this minute." Lillian had the side door open, waiting for me, as I hurried in from the garage.

"She still on the line?" I pulled off my gloves, throwing them on the table, as I headed for the phone by the refrigerator.

"No'm, she hung up 'fore you could get in here." Lillian was wringing her hands, so I immediately thought the worst.

"What'd she say? Is she all right? She's not hurt, is she?"

"No'm, yessum, I mean I don't know. Miss Julia, she jus' hang up in the middle. Well, not even in the middle, she jus' start in to talk, then she jus' quit. Of a sudden, she jus' quit an' the dial tone come buzzin' on."

"Well, what did she say? Exactly. Tell me exactly what she said." I glared at the telephone, willing it to ring again and tell us something.

Lillian sank down onto one of the chairs at the breakfast table. Taking a corner of her apron, she dabbed at her eyes.

"Lillian, I'm sorry. I didn't mean to jump on you. It's just, well, I guess I'm more worried than I thought I was."

"It ain't you," she said, leaning an elbow on the table. "You don't bother me none. I jus' scared to death for Miss Hazel Marie 'cause she sound so scared."

I took a deep breath to settle my nerves, and pulled up a chair beside her, slipping out of my coat. "Tell me," I said. "Just take it slow and tell me everything she said."

"Lemme see here." Lillian looked off into the distance, her hands folding and pleating her apron. "The phone ring. I pick it up an' say, 'Miz Springer's residence,' an' Miss Hazel Marie, she say, "Lillian, let me speak to Miss Julia, please, an' hurry. Please hurry.' She say it jus' like that, 'hurry. Please hurry.'"

"Oh, Lord," I said.

"Yessum, an' I say, 'She ain't here. She over to Mr. Sam's.' An' I try to say, 'She be back pretty soon,' or 'You can call her over there,' or some such, but she don't give me a chance. She cut in an' say, 'Tell her I need help. Tell her I'm at the big,' an' then that when it sound like she drop the phone an' that dial tone come on."

"She said she needed help? You're sure about that?"

"Sure as I'm settin' here. 'Tell her I need help,' that what she say. An' 'I'm at the big.' What you reckon she mean by that?"

"I don't have an idea in the world. But, I'll tell you this, Lillian, we were right to be concerned about her. She's in trouble of some kind, and it's that Wilson T. Hodge who's gotten her into it. I said from the first time I met him that he wore his shorts too tight. Nobody can be that upright and pious without trouble going on underneath."

"Bad trouble, sound like to me. These days, you don't never know what gonna happen ever' time you step out the door. Them UFOs is circlin' 'round all the time, first this way, then that, an' don't nobody know when they snatch somebody up."

"Lillian, for goodness sakes, Hazel Marie has not been snatched up in a UFO. Be practical." I jumped up and started pacing the kitchen floor. "We've got to do something. We can't just ignore a cry for help. And that's what it was." I whirled around and said, "Tell me again. She said she was at 'the big'? You're sure of that?"

"Sure as I can be. Ain't nothin' wrong with my hearing, and that what she said. 'Tell her I'm at the big.' But I don't know what 'big' she talkin' about, 'less it's that big ballfield at the high school where a UFO could swoop in an' swoop out 'fore anybody know it."

"Lillian," I sighed, "think of something else." I walked to the sink and gazed out the window, noting a few snow flurries swirling around the yard. "I need your help in figuring this out. What could 'the big' mean? That big movie house over in Asheville? No, no, forget that. They wouldn't still be at the picture show. Somebody's big house? A big store? That big intersection right outside of town? Wait, wait, let's back up. She had to be inside somewhere; that's where telephones usually are. Unless she was using an outside one. Do you know of any public phones on the side of the road anywhere? Did you hear any traffic sounds? Any background noises of any kind?"

"No'm, not nothing like that. It so quiet I hear her charm bracelet jingle one time. Miss Julia, I jus' think of somethin'. She kinda whisperin', like. Not so low I couldn't hear her, but not real normal, neither. An' she talkin' real fast, so I don't have time to tell her anything or ast her anything."

"Well, that settles it. I'm going to see Deputy Bates right now, and make him start looking for her."

I slung on my coat, which I'd barely had off, and grabbed my keys. "He's working days now, isn't he?"

"Yessum, Miss Binkie real glad about it, too, since he be home at night."

"Home," I grunted. "The man's home is supposed to be right up these back stairs, where he's paying good money to rent a room from me. But, I don't have time to think about that. I'm going to the sheriff's office and put this in their hands. With my supervision, of course."

"What about yo' lunch? You ain't had a bite since breakfast."

"I can't eat now, Lillian, I'm too upset. You go ahead, though, and I'll get something when I get back. Stay close to the phone in case she calls back. Grab it as quick as you can, as soon as it rings."

"Don't you worry. I'm gonna get me a plate and set right here beside it."

I was out the door and into the garage without stopping to see if Pastor Ledbetter had done any more stake-stringing. One thing at a time, I told myself, as I backed out into the street. I would take on the preacher when I had Hazel Marie well in hand.

There wasn't a parking place for citizens in trouble anywhere near the sheriff's office, so I pulled into one marked DEPARTMENT USE ONLY. I could make a case for my taking it, since I certainly intended to use the department.

The wind whipped my coat around my lower limbs, as I tackled the steps at the back of the courthouse. I held on to the metal railing, fearful of ice that might have accumulated on the worn concrete steps. It was one time I wished for fur-lined boots, instead of the slick leather-soled Red Cross oxfords I had on.

Closing the door firmly behind me, since I wasn't raised in a barn, I hurried over to a sliding glass window in the wall where a pony-tailed woman in a uniform was busy at a console of blinking lights. She had one of those wrap-around telephone sets on her head, leaving her hands free to do other things.

"I want to see Deputy Coleman Bates, please. Tell him Mrs. Julia Springer needs to see him right away."

She looked up at me, gave me a brief, I've-been-trained-to-meet-the-public smile and said, "He's out on a call right now. He should be back in about an hour. Can someone else help you?"

"No, I need to see him." My foot was tapping on the floor. The idea of him being out on a call tightened my nerves until I could feel them strumming. "Could you call him? Just tell him I'm here, and that it's urgent."

"Ma'am, I'm sorry, but he's answering a fairly urgent call already. You're welcome to wait, though, and I'll tell him you're here just as soon as I can get through to him."

I didn't want to be rude, that gets you nowhere, but I wanted to shake her. Instead, I turned and paced the waiting room or whatever the tiny space reserved for the public was. I'll tell you this, we needed better facilities for our law enforcement people and the public they were supposed to serve and protect. There wasn't a magazine or newspaper anywhere, not that I could've read anything, but it just didn't look good to have nothing available. Three metal chairs were against one wall, and one of them was bent. I walked back and forth, knowing that if Deputy Bates knew what was going on, he'd drop whatever he was doing and come zipping in to help me.

"Have you heard from him yet?" I was back at the window, drumming my fingers on the wooden ledge.

"No, ma'am, they're real busy with that call."

"You don't think you could just let him know I'm here?"

"No, ma'am, not on a call like this. You sure nobody else can help you?"

"Yes, I'm sure. No, wait. Maybe they can." I took a deep breath and my life in my hands. "What about Lieutenant Peavey? Is he available?"

"Well, he's monitoring the call Deputy Bates is on, but he's in the building. I don't know. . . ."

"Ask him. Please, just ask him if he'll see me. Mrs. Julia Springer, he knows me. Remind him about that kidnapping last year. No, maybe you better not. Just tell him I really need to speak to him before something awful happens."

She looked at me with a frown on her face, and began working some buttons and toggles, but not before sliding the glass closed so I couldn't hear her.

I guess Lieutenant Peavey did remember me, because it wasn't but a minute before a deputy came out and motioned me to follow him. We walked through a narrow hall into the inner workings of the sheriff's department. Deputies, male and female, passed in and out of the offices on each side, most of them nodding in a friendly, but distracted, way.

My guide knocked once on a closed door, then opened it for me. I walked in to face the man I'd lied to last year when Lillian, Hazel Marie and I had rescued Little Lloyd from Brother Vern's sticky grasp. And I'd lied with a straight face and without a qualm on my conscience. It had been necessary at the time, and I had no regrets now. I just hoped he hadn't figured out my part in the mess.

I declare, the day was dark and dreary, the wind blowing in snow flurries, and the temperature hovering in the low thirties, and there that man sat with his mirrored sunglasses on. Maybe he had an eye problem. I didn't know, but seeing myself reflected in those double mirrors put me off something awful. I almost forgot what I needed to say. Especially since I'd also almost forgotten how big he was, how silent and, well, suspicious his manner was. If you were a criminal, you wouldn't've wanted Lieutenant Peavey turning that big head in your direction while he waited for a confession that you couldn't wait to give him.

"Lieutenant Peavey," I said, edging near the front of his desk. "I'm Mrs. . . ."

"I know who you are." No change of expression, no welcoming smile, no nothing but that blank face and what I assumed were hard eyes behind his glasses. "What can I do for you?"

"Well, my friend, Hazel Marie Puckett, is in trouble and I don't know what kind or where she is or how to help her or anything."

"Puckett." Just like that. *Puckett,* as if that said it all.

"You need to understand," I said quickly before he could jump to conclusions, "that, even though she's a Puckett, she's not really one. I mean, she lives with me, her and her little boy, you remember him? He was the one that his great-uncle, Vernon Puckett, kidnapped? And you were looking for him, but he showed up at my house and, well, the two of them have been there ever since. Except for now, when she went out last night with Wilson T. Hodge, that fund-raiser from Charlotte who's been running all over town trying to drum up, . . . well, you're not a Presbyterian, so maybe . . . Anyway, she hasn't come home and it's been way too long and . . ."

"I remember a number of things about that episode last year."

"Well, but that's over and done with. And it worked out just fine, I wish you wouldn't bring it up, because this is something entirely different. Please, Lieutenant Peavey, I really need some help here."

"Have a seat."

I sank gratefully into a wooden chair that needed a cushion or padding of some kind. Lieutenant Peavey reached behind him to an open bookshelf, taking out a preprinted form and placing it before him on the desk.

"You have a missing person?"

"Yes," I said with great relief, "that's exactly what I have, or don't have. I mean she's missing and I don't have her."

"Let's hear the particulars. Name, age, date of birth, most recent address, Social Security number, where she was going, when you last saw her."

I started in telling him everything I knew about Hazel Marie which, as it turned out, was somewhat lacking in particulars.

"I'll get all that for you, Lieutenant, it's just that I was so worried about her that I didn't think to get her vital statistics before I left. I wanted the sheriff's department to start looking for her right away. I know she's in trouble; she said so herself."

"She said so?" Those mirrors aimed themselves at me, as he stopped writing. "When did you talk to her?"

"I didn't. Lillian did. You remember Lillian, she works for me?

Hazel Marie called, well, barely thirty minutes ago, wanted to speak to me but I wasn't there. I was over at, well, that doesn't matter. Anyway, she told Lillian that she needed me to help her and that she was at 'the big.' But we don't know what 'the big' is or where it is. That's what I need you to find out."

He folded the paper he'd been writing on. "Mrs. Springer, if you heard from her thirty minutes ago, she can't be classified as missing. Twenty-four hours before we can step in, unless there's evidence of a crime being committed, and it doesn't sound as if one has been."

I stared at him with my mouth open. Then I said, "You mean to tell me that you can't, or won't, do anything? Lieutenant, the woman's in trouble! She wouldn't've called, whispering and getting cut off, if she wasn't in desperate straits!"

"She's not hurt; she's not involved in a crime. . . ."

"You don't know that! I mean, she's not, I'm positive, but she could be the victim of a crime. Lieutenant Peavey, what does it take to get some help from this department?"

He stared at me for a good two seconds. At least, I guessed that's what he was doing; he may have been gazing over the top of my head for all I knew. "There are certain guidelines we have to follow, and this situation doesn't appear to meet them. You can let us know if something else occurs that would warrant our stepping in or when it's been twenty-four hours since you've heard from her but, for now, I'd advise you to wait it out. Nine times out of ten, a so-called missing person shows up sooner or later, and usually sooner. Now, why don't you go on home and see if I'm not right. Let me know if I can be of further help."

And with that, he rose to his full height, which was considerable, and indicated that the interview was over.

"But she needs help now!" I almost wailed. "How can I just go home and wait, while she's in peril or something?"

"Well," he said, with the hint of a smile at one corner of his mouth, which just about blew my fuse, "you can always hire a private investigator."

I got myself to my feet, and gave him a stare as blank as the ones he'd been giving me. "That's exactly what I'll do. When I'm paying somebody directly, without going through the tax commissioner, I guess I'll get my money's worth. Thank you for your time, Lieutenant, meager though it was. I'll just take care of this problem myself."

And I stomped out, my head held so high that I took a wrong turn and had to ask for help to get out of the place.

Chapter 4

"Has she called again?" A gust of wind practically blew me into the kitchen, but I hardly noticed. Slamming the door, I came out of my coat and hung it on a peg. "Have you heard from her?"

Lillian was sitting in the chair right under the wall phone, staying close to it as I'd asked her to. "No'm, it ain't rung since you been gone, an' I b'lieve I'll get up from here now, since you can help get to it if it do." She got to her feet and went to the stove. "Set down and tell me what them deputies doin' while I fix you something to eat."

"Just some soup, Lillian, if you have it. I'm not even sure I can eat that. And as far as what they're doing, it's absolutely nothing. Not one thing. They can't go against their guidelines, and Hazel Marie doesn't meet them. I declare, Lillian, I'm so undone I don't know what to do."

She turned, holding a pot in one hand and a Campbell's Soup can in the other. "You mean to tell me they not doin' nothin' to find that pore woman? I can't b'lieve Deputy Bates do any sucha thing."

"He's not. He was answering a call and unavailable to the likes of me. I saw Lieutenant Peavey. Does that tell you anything?"

"You mean Lieutenant Peavey what was ready to lock us up that time?"

"That's exactly who I mean, and he wasn't any more friendly or sympathetic today than he was then. Lillian, I didn't get a smidgen of satisfaction out of that man. Nothing we can do, he said. Then he suggested hiring a private investigator, which is what I'm just before doing."

"Why don't you then?"

"Well, I would, if I knew one to hire. I mean, it's not like going to Wal-Mart and picking out one of a dozen or so. Where are they located, I'd like to know. How do I get in touch with one, and how do I know he'll do a good job?"

"Oh, he do a good job, if you watch him like a hawk which I know you gonna do. I bet Deputy Bates know who you can get. Set down at that table, now, an' rest. You got yo'self all upheaved and nervous, an' you not gonna be doin' Miss Hazel Marie any good atall if you do yo'self in with all that worryin'. This soup be ready in a minute."

"Right. You're right. I've got to get myself under control here. But, I'll tell you, Lillian, it just makes me a crazy woman to need help and have everybody and his brother telling me there's nothing to worry about."

"That's not what I'm tellin' you. I tellin' you to get yo' ducks in a row, then do whatever it take to get done what you want done."

"Lillian, that's the best advice I've had all day. While you're fixing my plate, I'm going to put in some calls to Deputy Bates. He's not going to be able to turn around without somebody telling him to call Mrs. Julia Springer. If he ever gets away from whatever he's doing that's so important."

I called Binkie at her office, left my message for Coleman in case she saw him and cut her off when she started telling me that Hazel Marie would be home any minute. "Maybe so, Binkie," I told her. "But, in the meantime and in case she's not, I want to put some things in motion."

Then, I called Binkie's house, in case Deputy Bates got there before she did—he had his own key, I happened to know—and left a message on her machine. As much as I hate those impersonal things. Then, to be on the safe side, I called the sheriff's department again and left word for Deputy Bates to call me as soon as he came in. Surely the message would reach him at one place or the other.

After that, there wasn't anything to do except try to eat the soup Lillian had put before me, and worry myself sick with wondering how and what I was going to tell Little Lloyd. School would soon be out, and he'd be coming in here asking for his mother, and what in the world was I going to tell the child?

I put down my spoon and stood up. "Lillian, I can't just sit here, doing nothing. I'm about to jump out of my skin. I think I'll go on and pick Little Lloyd up at school. It's too cold for him to be walking anyway."

"It still a little early."

"Well, I may just get him out early. I want him home where we know he's safe. I declare, Lillian, I can't stand my family, such as it is, being spread all over creation." Of course, neither Hazel Marie nor Little Lloyd were my family in the strictest sense of the word, but they'd come to me in need and they'd repaid my efforts tenfold.

"What I gonna say if somebody calls?"

"If she calls, break right in and ask her where she is. We're at a loss until we know that. And if Coleman calls, tell him to come right over. Don't go into anything on the phone, because we don't want to tie up the line. I ought to be back here in fifteen or twenty minutes."

Braving the cold again, I left to pick up Little Lloyd. As I drove to Abbotsville Middle School, my mind was in a turmoil. Everybody—Sam, Lieutenant Peavey, Binkie—thought I ought to let things run their course. Not one person so far had felt the same urgency that I was feeling. Except Lillian. She and I knew Hazel Marie better than anybody else, and we knew she was in trouble.

Since I got there so early, I was able to park up close to the

main door of the school, without having a line of cars in front
me. I decided to wait for the bell to ring and not risk scaring the
child to death by getting him out early. So I just sat there, keeping
the motor running so I wouldn't freeze, and so it'd be warm for
Little Lloyd. Just sat there, thinking and stewing over what and
how much to tell him, and over the fact that nobody was as exercised over the situation as they should've been. The more I
thought about it, the more frustrated I felt. That's what happens
when you have to delegate duties to other people and then have
to sit and worry about them getting done. I squinched up my eyes
and tapped the steering wheel. One thing was for sure, though.
When you do it yourself, you *know* it'll get done.

As children began streaming out of the school building, I decided that I'd give Deputy Bates a chance to swing into action on
my behalf, or rather on Hazel Marie's behalf. And if he failed me,
I'd put a private investigator on my payroll and hound him till we
had Hazel Marie back where she belonged.

Seeing Little Lloyd hurry out with a crowd of children, I
leaned over and opened the door for him so he could crawl in,
that heavy bookbag swinging from his arm. I declare, he looked
so thin and pale that my heart clutched up in my chest. He was a
worrier worse than I was.

The first words out of his mouth were, "Has my mama come
home?"

"Let me get out of this traffic," I said, as the line started to
move with young mothers manhandling those clumsy-looking
sports vehicles which, if you happened to be behind one, you
couldn't see through, around or over. "We need to talk, Little
Lloyd, and I can't do it with all this going on around me."

His glasses started to fog up in the heat of the car. When he
took them off to clean them, his little face looked so pinched and
peaked that I reached over and patted him, though I'm not a
demonstrative woman by any stretch of the imagination. When

the traffic thinned out as cars peeled away in several directions, I took a deep breath and began.

"I've never tried to shield you from things that directly affect you, Little Lloyd, and I'm not going to start now." I told him of my and Lillian's concern, the lack of help I was getting every time I turned around, and his mother's phone call. In detail, because he was a sharp little thing and, if anybody could figure out *the big,* he could.

"What do you think?" I asked.

His lip trembled as he gazed straight ahead through the windshield. "Maybe she's gone to Raleigh."

"Raleigh?" That surprised me, but then I recalled that Raleigh was where she'd said she was going that day last year when she'd shown up at my door to drop off Wesley Lloyd's illegitimate child while she went to beauty school to learn the manicure business. First time I'd ever heard of either her or the child, so you can imagine the state my mind had been in. I was over that by now, considerably aided by the thought of Wesley Lloyd spinning in his grave at my taking them in like they were my own. Giving hardly a thought to the gossip in the town and in the church that my act of Christian charity generated, I'd been comforted by the fact that the gossip had been about him, and not me.

But now, I understood that in the child's mind, Raleigh was the place mothers go when they leave their children. "No, I think we can forget about that. Nobody but a politician would want to go there anyway. Besides, her call was a local. At least, there's no indication that it wasn't. If she had time to say 'the big,' she had time to say 'Raleigh,' so I think we can pretty well figure she's around here somewhere."

"Here we are," I said, pulling into the driveway at home. "Let's get in. Maybe Lillian's heard from her again, and maybe Deputy Bates has some word for us."

We hurried inside where Lillian met us at the door, her face sorrowful enough to tell me there was no news. She wrapped Little Lloyd in her ample arms and crooned to him as he buried his face in her apron.

"Come on now," I said, "let's have a snack and get ourselves organized. Little Lloyd, take off your coat and have a seat at the table. Lillian, something hot for this child, and for me and you, too. I'm going to try Deputy Bates again, there's just no sense in this sitting and waiting."

I couldn't believe it. When I called 911, because to my mind we certainly had an emergency, I was told to call the regular number. On top of that, when I did, I was told that Deputy Bates was still on that urgent call that was taking up his entire workday and then some, and he wasn't expected back for several more hours. I started to argue, but it was no use.

I hung up and turned to see Little Lloyd's peaked little face, blotched with worry and those unfortunate freckles he'd inherited from his father. His thin shoulders hunched over the table, as he waited for me to do something.

"Push up your glasses, Little Lloyd," I said, trying to make things as normal as I could. "And drink your hot cocoa. We have to keep up our strength, because I'm not about to throw in the towel yet. Not by a long shot."

He leaned over and took a quick sip from the cup without picking it up, a habit I thought I'd broken him of, but I didn't want to correct him under these worrisome circumstances.

"Miss Julia," he said, his magnified eyes gazing at me like I was his last hope. "Maybe we ought to go look for my mama, ourselves. I know we could do it, because you always say if you want something done, you have to do it yourself."

Well, that just put a spark to my logs. The child took to heart everything I ever said, which made all my efforts on his behalf more than worthwhile. He thought I could do anything I set my mind to, and I determined, then and there, not to let him down.

"You never said a truer word, Little Lloyd, and I thank you for reminding me of it."

I turned and dialed the same number again. "Let me speak to Lieutenant Peavey, please. Tell him it's Mrs. Julia Springer, and remind him that he said to let him know if he could do anything for me. And he can."

It took a while, but he came to the phone, sounding as if he hated doing it. "Lieutenant Peavey," he said and waited.

"This is . . ."

"I know who it is."

"Well, I need to know the name of a private investigator you'd recommend. Then I won't bother you anymore, you may be sure."

The line hummed for a few seconds, then he said, "If that's what you want, I'd recommend J. D. Pickens. He's got an office in south Asheville, not sure where. You can look him up in the phone book."

"I'll do that and, Lieutenant Peavey, I'm putting a lot of trust in your recommendation, and I expect you to stand behind it. Is this man the one you'd hire, if you were hiring?"

"No. I wouldn't be hiring one in the first place, but he's the choice if you are."

"I guess you're in a position where you don't have to go outside of normal channels when you need help," I said. "Seeing as how you have the whole sheriff's department at your beck and call. Some people, however, are not so fortunate. Thank you for your time."

He grunted and I hung up.

Chapter 5

When I told Lillian and Little Lloyd that Deputy Bates was out of the picture, at least for the foreseeable future, the boy hung his head so low it was practically on the table. I watched as his little shoulders began to quiver with the strain he was under and the tears began to flow.

Lillian went to him, hugging him close and telling him he needed to be loved on and she was the one to do it. I don't know if that helped, but maybe it did. Temporarily, at least. What the child really needed was his mama back safe and sound.

"Lillian, where's the Asheville phone book?"

"If it not in the drawer under there, I don't know where it is."

"Well, I can't find it," I said, pushing through the accumulated odds and ends in the catchall drawer. "Just one more thing to try my patience; nothing's ever where I need it, when I need it. I was counting on Coleman. I mean, if you know somebody on a personal basis in law enforcement, you'd think you'd get some personal consideration. Wouldn't you?"

"I think I know what he doin'," Lillian said, handing Little Lloyd a napkin to wipe his face.

I straightened up. "What? How do you know?"

"I know 'cause I called Willet who clean down at the sheriff's. He hear all they doin', though he ain't supposed to talk about it. I get this outta him 'cause I got something on him he want me to keep quiet about. Them deputies on a big raid down 'round

Jessup Mountain. They been plannin' it an' studyin' on it, an' checkin' on it ever since somebody broke in that racing man's place down east somewhere. It was in the paper the other day. An' today the day they goin' after somebody up here they think did it. So that's what Deputy Bates doin', an' why he can't come he'p us out."

"Well, thay Lord," I said. "What kind of raid? Did Willet say?"

"No'm, he don't say. He only hear so much, you know, when he sweepin' round their feet."

So that's how Lillian knew so much of what went on in town. The people who swept and mopped and emptied trash cans in the shops and offices all over town heard and saw what the shakers and movers were doing. I smiled at the thought.

Giving up on finding the Asheville book, I flipped through the yellow pages of our thin directory, surprised to find a listing for private investigators. And sure enough, there was The Pickens Agency, J. D. Pickens, P.I., as big as life.

I glanced over at Little Lloyd, who had his hands clasped between his knees. He was a nervous child even under the best of circumstances, what with biting his nails and blinking his eyes and just being jittery by nature. His nerves acted up on him a lot, in spite of all my efforts to calm him down and teach him to take life as it comes, the way I did.

His face was pale and drawn, those freckles standing out like new pennies. "Sit up straight, Little Lloyd, and take heart. I'm going to get us some help and get something done about this situation. I declare," I went on, "it's a shame when you have to do everything yourself."

As I reached for the phone, it rang under my hand. Hoping it'd be Hazel Marie again, we all looked at each other before I snatched it up and answered it.

"Julia," Sam said, "how about you and Little Lloyd coming

over and having supper with me? James has made a roast that I'll
be eating on all week if you two don't help me put a dent in it
tonight."

I bit my lip to keep from making a sharp remark about that
woman who'd been all over him earlier. Instead, I glanced over at
Little Lloyd's miserable face and said, "I'm afraid I can't make it,
Sam, since I still have a number of things to do. But Little Lloyd
could use some cheering up. Why don't I send him on, and I'll
pick him up after you've had supper?"

"I'll miss you, Julia. I have a lot to talk to you about."

Uh-huh, I thought, and I don't want to hear it. But I didn't say
it, just thanked him and hung up.

"Little Lloyd," I said, feeling the need to reassure him and give
him some hope. "Sam wants you to come over and have an early
supper with him. So run on over and I'll pick you up a little later.
Now before you start worrying again, I want to put your mind at
rest. I'm going to call this private investigator and we're going to
find your mother. You can count on it."

The boy started up out of his chair, obedient as always, trying
on a pitiful-looking smile as he rubbed his eyes. "I knew you'd
think of something, Miss Julia. You always do what you say you
will."

Lord, when a child puts his trust in you, it can scare you to
death. Or at least, it ought to.

After getting Little Lloyd off, with instructions to go straight to
Sam's and wait for me to pick him up, I dialed the number of the
private investigator. A man answered, taking me aback since I
thought I'd have to go through a secretary or two.

"Mr. J. D. Pickens, please."

"You got him."

"Oh. Well, this is Mrs. Julia Springer, over in Abbotsville? And
I'd like to employ you to find a missing person, and don't tell me

she's not missing just because she called this afternoon to tell us she needed help."

"Whoa, back up there a minute. You got a missing person who called to say she's in trouble?"

"That's right. And Lieutenant Peavey, he's the one who recommended you, won't do anything, and Deputy Bates is too busy, and we are quite understandably at the end of our rope, here."

"Well, you've come to the right man. Let me look at my appointment book."

"No, I don't want an appointment," I said quickly, fearful of being put off for days. "I need to see you right away, today."

"You're in luck, then. I'm between cases right now, but it's pretty late in the day. How 'bout first thing in the morning?"

"That won't do, Mr. Pickens. How am I and Hazel Marie's little boy, to say nothing of Lillian, going to sleep one more night without something being done? What about right now? I could be at your office in thirty or forty minutes."

"Can't do it that quick."

I thought I might break down as Little Lloyd had done and start some crying myself. It is just so frustrating to have to push people to do what you want them to do.

"Tell you what," Mr. Pickens said. "How about meeting me halfway? Say in a couple of hours, about six or so? I've got some things to do here, then I'm going to La Casa Roja for supper. You know where it is? Right off the interstate at the Delmont exit?"

Relief flooded my soul. "I'll find it. Now, Mr. Pickens, I need to know one thing before we go any further. Just how good are you at your job?"

There was a moment of silence, then I heard what sounded like a strangled cough. "Mrs. Springer, I'm like the Canadian Mounties; I always get my man. Or woman, as the case may be. You won't find a better P.I. in the area."

Well, that wasn't saying a whole lot, considering the area, but I let it go with some throat-clearing of my own.

"Then I'll see you about six, and I thank you, Mr. Pickens."

"Thank *you,* Mrs. Springer."

It was like a burden rolling off my shoulders to know that we now had somebody who was going to find Hazel Marie. The fact that I'd detected a note of relief in Mr. Pickens's voice hardly registered at the time. Maybe he needed the work.

"We've got us some help," I said with a lightened heart, as I hung up the phone and turned to Lillian who'd been following my side of the conversation with nods of her head. "We're meeting Mr. Pickens at a Mexican restaurant at six o'clock tonight, although I'd just as soon have regular food here before we go. I don't think my system can take that spicy stuff, nor Little Lloyd's either. At least he'll have a decent meal in him before we get there."

"That man say he gonna find Miss Hazel Marie?" Lillian asked.

"He said he always finds whatever he's looking for, which I hope is not a blatant overstatement. But I'll be there making sure he works at it. Now, Lillian, we need to get together everything we know about Hazel Marie. Lieutenant Peavey asked me questions I couldn't answer, so I want to be ready for Mr. Pickens. I'll need her birth date, well, I know that but I don't know the year. I'll need a picture of her; there ought to be several good ones in Little Lloyd's album, and anything else you can think of."

Trying to think of all we needed to do, I sank into a chair and put my head in my hands. "Lillian, I hope to goodness this works. Now . . . ," I stopped as the front door bell interrupted me. "Who in the world is that?"

"I'll get it," Lillian said, heaving herself up. "But I know it not Deputy Bates. He always come in back here."

"No, keep your seat, Lillian. I'll see who it is and get rid of them. I don't have time for drop-in company today."

When I got to the door, I wished I'd pretended not to be

home. LuAnne Conover stood there looking as pitiful as she could be, a Kleenex wadded up in her hand and her eyes red and overflowing.

"Oh, Julia," she wailed as I opened the door and before I could say a word. "I'm at my wit's end. I don't know what I'm going to do. I just can't stand it anymore."

I sighed and opened the storm door. "Come on in, LuAnne, before you freeze. Come sit by the fire a minute before you go home. Sorry I can't visit with you, but I have to be somewhere in a little while."

Instead of taking the hint, she took off her coat, dropped it on the sofa and plopped down in one of the Victorian chairs by the fire. She opened her purse and took out a handful of fresh Kleenex, and I knew I was in for another long session.

As I took the chair opposite her, she blew her nose and said, "Julia, I don't know what I'd do without you. If I didn't have you to talk to, I think I'd go crazy."

"What about Pastor Ledbetter? Aren't you talking to him?" The pastor had recently taken a course in pastoral counseling and, since he was now an expert with a framed diploma on the wall to prove it, he'd make an appointment at the drop of a hat. I'd had to caution him on several occasions about mixing psychology in with the catechism sessions he'd been having with Hazel Marie.

"Well, of course. I've just come from the church but, Julia, you're a woman and you know what I'm going through and another man, even if he is a preacher, just can't understand this kind of misery. Oh, Julia, I don't know where I've failed. I've tried my best, you know I have."

I sighed and did a little eye rolling since she was wiping her own and didn't see me. "LuAnne, it seems to me that Leonard needs some counseling too. I mean, he's part of the problem, or maybe the whole problem. Get him over at that church, either by himself or the two of you together."

"You don't understand!"

"You just said I did."

LuAnne's little birdlike hands ripped that Kleenex to shreds. "I mean I haven't told you everything. See, Julia, it's like this." She stopped, took a shuddering breath, wiped her eyes again and went on, "I don't know if I can tell you."

"That's all right," I said, beginning to rise from my chair in the hope that she would too. "We can talk when you feel more like it, and when I . . ."

"But I've got to tell you. I have to tell somebody; it's driving me crazy." And I had to wait out another sobbing fit, checking my watch as she kept on.

"It's Leonard," she wailed.

"I know that," I said with as much sympathy as I could muster. I mean, she'd been complaining about Leonard for the last six months and, if he'd been my husband, I'd've been complaining about him long before that. But he'd been her choice, not mine. "What's he done now?"

"It's not just *now.*" Her voice rose, and I wondered if she was going to get hysterical on me. Frankly, I didn't think Leonard deserved that kind of emotion. "This has *been* going on. And on and on, till I can't stand it any longer."

"Well, LuAnne, I know it's hard to have a retired man underfoot all day, every day, but there ought to be something he could do that'd get him out of the house and give you some time to yourself."

"That's not it!" She put her head on her knees, crumpling up on herself as she gave way to gulping sobs. I thought to myself that all I'd heard for these many months was how Leonard made every step she made, tagging along on her heels like a puppy. She couldn't go to Velma's to get her hair done without Leonard going along too, much less to the Winn-Dixie where he questioned everything she put in her grocery cart.

"Well what is it then? I declare, LuAnne, I can only go on what you tell me, and that's what you've complained about ever since he retired. Now, if it's something else, let's hear it or at least, tell the preacher. If you're inclined that way." Though I wouldn't be.

"Oh, Julia, I *have* told him." She sat up, her face streaked with tears. "In so many words. And he says it's up to me to get Leonard over it, and I've tried everything I know to try, and nothing does any good."

"What in the world is wrong with Leonard?" Other than having no life, I wanted to add, but didn't. Leonard was as dull as dishwater, having been a civil servant all his life, which tells you everything you need to know.

"Oh, LuAnne," I said with sudden understanding of her distress, "don't tell me Leonard's got some terrible disease."

"That's exactly what I'm telling you, and I don't think I can handle it any longer. I've *suffered,* Julia, you just don't know."

I hated to hear it, but I couldn't help but wonder why she was the one doing the suffering and not the one who was afflicted.

"I'm so sorry," I said, and I was. I'd never thought much of Leonard, nor had Wesley Lloyd, but I felt for LuAnne. "What does he have?"

"Oh, Julia, he has . . ." She stopped, looked around and back over her shoulder to be sure we were alone. Then she leaned forward, took a breath and whispered, " . . . *e.d.*"

Chapter 6

"E.d.?"

"Yes," she whispered fiercely, "and it's a terrible affliction. It affects the wife just as much as the man. No, even more than the man, take my word for it. Julia, I've tried everything I know to try, read those books the pastor gave me, which didn't even *mention* this problem since they're Christian books and, besides, I need more than prayer in this case. I've been on my knees a million times, and nothing works. But the worst thing is that Leonard is not the least concerned about it, says he's too old and set in his ways to try anything new, in spite of the fact that I spent a fortune at Victoria's Secret."

"E.d.?" I knew that every new disease or condition got shortened to its initials these days, but this was a new one on me. I tried to figure it out. Esophageal displacement? Eating disorder? Environmental disease? Educational deficit?

"Yes, and I can't live with it any longer. Julia, I've made up my mind. I have to divorce him and find a life for myself."

Well, I couldn't blame her, but it seemed to me a little late to be looking for a life. I mean, she'd put up with Leonard for more than half of the one she'd had, why get fed up now?

She dabbed at her eyes again and went on, "Pastor Ledbetter said that was the worst thing I could do and he couldn't recommend it, because it's a sin. But, either way, Julia, I'm running into sin. If I stay, I can't get Leonard to do anything and the pastor says that's my fault, too."

"I don't understand. How can this e.d. disease be your fault? You didn't give it to him, did you?"

"Of course not!" She glared at me, outraged at the question.

"Then how'd he get it?"

"Well, I don't know! But it's certainly not my fault, I don't care what the pastor says."

"LuAnne, I hate to admit this since you think I know what e.d. is, but I don't."

She jumped up from the chair and, tiny as she was, towered over me. "You don't know what it is! How can you give me advice when you don't know what you're talking about? I declare, Julia, I thought you were a better friend than that."

"Don't jump on me, LuAnne Conover." I stood up too, and did a little glaring of my own. After all, I hadn't been the one demanding help and advice. "I don't happen to keep up with the latest medical news, not being interested in it myself. In spite of having it crammed down my throat every evening by Peter Jennings and the like. Now, sit down and tell me what it is."

The air seemed to go out of her, and she sank back into the chair. She covered her face with her hands and whispered, "Leonard is experiencing, well, I've got to be brave and just say it." She drew a long, shuddering breath and said, "*erectile* dysfunction. Just like Bob Dole, but without his courage to do something about it."

I stared at her, while unwonted mental pictures of Leonard's problem and LuAnne's efforts to solve it flashed in my mind, along with images of what I'd seen in Hazel Marie's Victoria's Secret catalog that came by mail, which I made sure Little Lloyd never got his hands on.

As these unseemly pictures revolved in my mind, I was beginning to get about half mad at the nerve of her, telling me more than I ever wanted to know about things better left unsaid. All I could think of for a minute was the certainty that Pastor Ledbetter would have had the same pictures in his mind. No telling what kind of sermon we'd be getting, come Sunday, but I knew he'd be stirred to a rouser.

"LuAnne," I said, with my hands on my hips, determined to draw the line. "I don't want to hear any more about it. I'm your friend, but there are some things that friends shouldn't be privy to, and this is one of them."

"Julia, you've got to help me."

"What in the world can *I* do?"

"I don't know," she wailed, throwing her head back against the chair. "I just know that I can't go on like this! He follows me around all the time, crowding me and getting in my way, wanting to know where I am every minute of the day, but, Julia, he never *touches* me! He gets in the bed and turns over, and that's it!"

I covered my ears and turned away. "Don't tell me any more. I don't want to hear it."

"Well," she said, drawing herself up straight, "Looks like you don't have the time of day for me, but I guess I shouldn't've expected any help from you, what with having so much going on in your own house." She cut her eyes at me, looking to see how I'd take this bolt from the blue. "People talk, you know and, if I were you, I'd put a stop to what's causing it."

Before I could get into it with her and find out what rumors were currently making the rounds, Lillian stuck her head around the kitchen door, and I was never so glad to see anybody in my life. "Miss Julia," she said, "I sorry to innerrup', but you got that meetin' an' you gonna be late, you don't get started pretty soon."

"Thank you, Lillian," I said with some relief. "LuAnne, I'm sorry, but I have to be somewhere. Look, why don't you give this some thought before you do anything you'll regret. And I'll think about it too, then we'll talk. I hate that I have to hurry you out, but this is just not a good time for me."

I held her coat, giving it a little shake to get her moving, and finally she did. "I really expected more from you than this, Julia. But if you can't spare the time." She sniffed.

Lord, I couldn't tell you the amount of time I'd already spared for that woman, listening to her and sympathizing with her, and all that time she'd kept me in the dark as to the real problem. And after hearing the real problem, I wished I was still in the dark.

"I'll talk to you later, tomorrow maybe," I told her with a pat on her back as I opened the door. "We'll come up with something, don't worry."

I closed the door behind her and leaned against it. Here I was telling somebody not to worry, when that's what everybody'd been telling me. Lot of help that was, and I knew it. But when you can't or, in some cases, won't offer any help, what else can you say? And what in the world had she meant about something going on in my house and people talking, telling me such a thing when I'd been the prime subject of gossip for years on end?

Well, LuAnne was going to have to take second, maybe third, place on my list of worries. I had an appointment with J. D. Pickens, P.I., and more important things on my mind than Leonard Conover's husbandly duties. Or lack of same.

"You better come on in here and eat something 'fore you take off to see that private man," Lillian said, holding open the kitchen door.

I followed her and, glancing at the clock, said, "I don't have time to eat. I declare, Lillian, some people have problems I didn't even know existed."

"Ain't that the truth. But we got enough of our own. Now, eat this sam'ich I fixed for you or yore stomick gonna be growlin' so you won't hear what that Mr. Pickens got to say."

I knew it was the truth, so I began to eat, not even taking the time to sit at the table. I still had to go by Sam's and pick up Little Lloyd, since I wanted him with me to watch the exit signs while I watched the traffic. I didn't like driving at night, not being accustomed to it and, regardless of how much of it I'd had to do lately, I still got nervous when I had to do more of it.

"I think I better go with you," Lillian said. "I don't like you an' that chile out toolin' round by yo'self at night."

"We'll be all right," I said, though I wasn't as sure as I sounded. "Besides, Hazel Marie might call again, and I'd feel better if you were by the phone. Do you mind staying late, and I'll run you home when we get back?"

She frowned, but then nodded in agreement. As I reached for my coat, the front doorbell rang. We both looked at each other, wondering who else was interrupting our evening plans.

"I'll see who it is," I said, slipping into my coat. "Whoever it is will see I'm on my way out and won't stay long."

"It good an' dark out there," Lillian said, "an' it ain't no time for people to be ringin' no doorbells." She stopped and looked at me with her eyes getting bigger. "Maybe it some word on Miss Hazel Marie. I'll go with you."

So we both went to the door, Lillian hanging back behind me. We both gasped out loud when I opened the door and saw a sheriff's deputy standing there with his hands full of thick papers.

Hazel Marie, I thought, and I hung on to the door, as Lillian reached for my arm. Bad news always comes in a dark blue uniform, and this one was topped by a round face with a sandy fuzz above his lip, looking more like a high schooler selling magazines than an officer with news of our worst fears.

"Yes?" I quavered, not even able to ask him in as I'd ordinarily have done.

"I need to see a . . . ," he glanced at the papers, "Hazel Marie Puckett. Is she here?"

It took me a minute to realize that if he was looking for her, he couldn't be there to tell us what we didn't want to hear. "Ah, no, not at the moment," I said, my mind working overtime, trying to figure out why he was looking for her and why he didn't know she was missing. I straightened up and got myself back together. No need giving anything away until I knew just what was what.

"No, officer," I went on, "she's not here at the moment. May I help you?"

He shifted his feet, then said, "Well, ma'am, maybe so. I have to serve these papers on her."

"Papers! What *kind* of papers?" I squinched up my eyes at him and demanded, "Is Lieutenant Peavey behind this?"

"Ah, no, ma'am," he said, giving me a look like he thought I'd lost my mind, "I don't believe he had anything to do with this. It's usually a neighbor or a relative with an interest in the child who comes in and files a complaint."

"You're telling me that somebody has filed a complaint against Hazel Marie? Why? Who would do that when she's done nothing wrong? I never heard of such a thing in my life! You ought to be ashamed of yourself!"

"Ma'am," he said, taking a step backward, "this is pursuant to, ah, let me see, chapter seven of the Codified Juvenile Code of the North Carolina General Statutes. It doesn't always mean anything's wrong; the law says that anybody who's concerned about a child's welfare can ask the court to look into it. But, see, that's what the summons is for, so the complainee can come in and state their case. Then there'll be a hearing and a judgment handed down. That's the law, ma'am, and, well, that's all I know, except I'm supposed to pick up a . . . ," he studied the papers again, "minor child, Wesley Lloyd Puckett. Is? . . ."

"What are you talking about!"

"Ma'am, I've got instructions to take this child into protective custody. See, it's right here." He opened up an official-looking document and held it in front of my face. "It's called a snatch-and-grab order, and I'll need to take him with me."

My mouth dropped open, and so did Lillian's. I couldn't believe what I was hearing.

"Young man," I said. "What is your name?"

"Uh, Jim," he said. Then, as his face turned red, he corrected himself, "I mean, Deputy Daly."

"Well, Deputy Daly," I said, pushing the document away, "that child is not here and neither is his mother. And if you think you're going to be doing any snatching and grabbing around here, you can just think again. Now you just take those papers right back where you got them and tell them they have a nerve to be serving papers on an old woman. And after dark, too!"

"Well, ma'am," he said, shuffling his feet, "we know this is their legal residence and, if they're not home, I'll have to ask you to accept the summons. Hazel Marie Puckett will have to appear within ten days and, I'm sorry to upset you, but I'll have to take the child as soon as I can, since the complaint has to do with his welfare. Judge's orders, straight from the clerk of court. When will he be home?"

Lord, my mind was in a whirl, trying to think what to do and what to say. And what not to. Lillian's hand gripped my arm tighter and tighter, and I was glad of the support.

While I tried to think of something to put him off, Lillian chimed in. "That chile spendin' the night with a frien'. We don't know who it is, 'cause his mama, she know, but she ain't here. I 'speck she be home 'bout midnight, she out on a date with Mr. Wilson T. Hodge. You know, that man what works for the Presbyterium church over there."

"Oh, well, okay," Deputy Daly said, and I could've hugged Lillian for coming up with some church-related credentials for Hazel Marie. And not even lying too much about it, either. "Well, I'll just leave these papers with you, ma'am, and ask you to see that she gets them. Somebody'll be back for the boy first thing in the morning."

"He goin' straight to school from his frien's house," Lillian said, with a straight face, "so he won't be here then. It be 'bout three o'clock tomorrow 'fore he be home."

"Okay, if we don't get him from school, we'll be back then. Sorry to disturb you so late, but these papers just came through and we have to serve them." He held out the documents, which I took because I didn't know what else to do.

As soon as I closed the door behind him, I leaned against it and said, "What in the world is going on?"

Lillian said, "Look at them papers an' see if they tell us anything."

I did, and they did. "Brother Vern!" I yelled. "Lillian! It's that money-grubbing, television-preaching country fool, Vernon Puckett, Hazel Marie's uncle, who's behind this! Can you believe it! He's signed a complaint against Hazel Marie, claiming that it's in the best interests of the child that he be granted custody."

"How can he do such a thing?"

"It's easy!" I shrieked, ready to pull my hair out at the thought of gullible judges and magistrates and clerks of court. "Didn't you hear that deputy standing there, quoting chapter and verse? Anybody with an ax to grind can do it! Looks like, in this state, all anybody has to do is walk in and swear up, down and sideways that a child is in peril, and they'll snatch up the child and issue a summons for the parent to appear and answer the complaint."

"Well, but she can't answer no complaint if she not here."

"I know that! But *see*," I shrieked, unfolding the document with a flip of my wrist, "it says right here that the child's circumstances require the sheriff to place him in protective custody! That makes me so mad I could spit. The child's in better circumstances than he's ever been in his life, and it's the circumstances that *I've* provided that's in question!" I stopped to catch my breath, then nearly sunk to my knees. "Good Lord, Lillian, this is absolutely the worst time in the world for this to happen. Do you reckon? . . ." I stopped again, my eyes narrowing as things began to fall into place. I grabbed Lillian's arm. "Listen, Brother Vern was over at the church to see Pastor Ledbetter this very morning. I *knew* I should've gone over there to see what was going on. You know what it could mean, don't you?"

"No'm, 'less them two up to something."

"That's it, exactly. Though I can't imagine Brother Vern and my pastor in cahoots about anything. Unless, *unless,* Pastor Ledbetter knows Hazel Marie's missing, and Brother Vern knows it, too. But how could they? It doesn't make sense, but I know that man would take any advantage he could to jump in and try to get Little Lloyd and his inheritance away from us. But whatever he knows or doesn't know, he's pulling the same stunt he tried last year, only this time he's using the law to do it. And Pastor Ledbetter," I went on, squinching up my eyes till I could hardly see through them, "he'd help the devil himself to get that blasted building built. It's a conspiracy, that's what it is. Lillian, what are we going to do?"

"Better call Mr. Sam and Miss Binkie, first thing. Then worry 'bout the next thing."

"Yes. No. Wait a minute, let me think. All these papers are official, no mistake about that, signed and sealed and everything." I shuffled through the papers again, hoping to spot a technicality, though I'm not sure I'd've recognized one. "Binkie's an officer of the court, or some such thing, so she'll have to do what the court tells her to do. And, as for Sam, I don't know what he is now that he's retired, but you know him. He wouldn't go against the law for anything." I stopped and thought for a minute. "If he knew he was going against it, that is, but he's got his mind on other things, so I'm not going to bother him. I'll handle this myself."

"What you thinkin' 'bout doin'?"

"I'm thinking two things," I said, looking off in the distance as I got my mind together. "First, I have to meet with Mr. Pickens and get him started on finding Hazel Marie. She's got to get back here to answer this complaint. And second, I'm thinking that we have to keep Little Lloyd out of sight of any and all sheriff's deputies. And that includes Coleman, too. I declare, Lillian, I'm surrounded by people who won't do anything but follow the law to the letter."

"'Cept me."

We smiled at each other, knowing that it was up to us to keep Little Lloyd out of the clutches of Brother Vernon Puckett. Which meant hiding him from the Law, as well.

Chapter 7

"I'm going to Sam's and pick up Little Lloyd," I said, heading for the kitchen to get my purse and keys. "Then we'll go meet Mr. Pickens and get him started looking for Hazel Marie. In the meantime, let's be thinking what we can do with Little Lloyd to keep him out of sight till his mother gets home. Then, we'll get Binkie on it to answer that fool's complaint with a complaint of our own."

"What kinda complaint you gonna make on him?"

"I don't know. Something, harrassment or fraud or maybe for trying to get at Little Lloyd's inheritance under false pretenses. There ought to be something we can get him on. But I'm not going to worry about that right now. Lillian, the thing is, well, just think, you and I have no legal claim on that child and, if his mother's not here to make her appearance, the court'll grant custody to the next of kin. Which means . . ."

"I know what it mean," Lillian said. "It mean we got to find Miss Hazel Marie and we got to hide Little Lloyd so good, not nobody find him till we want him found. I can hide him at my house."

I stopped the pacing I'd been doing, thinking she'd hit on the perfect solution. But then I reconsidered. "No, it stands to reason they'd come looking there, since everybody who knows us knows how much that child means to you. Besides, it'd be hard to keep him hid, since he's likely to stand out a little. We'll have to think of something else—maybe LuAnne would keep him. No, that won't work; she's got her own problems and it wouldn't do to put a child in that situation." I did some more hand-wringing, then pulled myself together. "But right now I have to get out of here or Mr. Pickens'll think I'm not coming. At least, Little Lloyd'll be safe for a little while."

"I be thinkin' what to do with him while you gone, maybe something'll pop up. But, Miss Julia, he got to go to school. How we gonna manage that?"

"I'm not going to worry about it. He can miss school without it doing any damage. He's so far ahead of the others, his absence'll give them time to catch up. Besides, what good will one day of school do, when it'd just mean being taken out by a bunch of deputies? I declare, I never heard of sending the sheriff to pick up a child who's never done a wrong thing in his life. I say, snatch and grab! I'll tell you one thing, if we ever get all this straightened out, I'm going to do a little snatching and grabbing of my own. And Brother Vern's going to be first in line."

I pulled on my gloves and turned my collar up. "I've got to go, Lillian, before somebody else rings the doorbell with more bad news. We shouldn't be but an hour or so."

"You watch that weather out there," she said. "It feelin' like the North Pole with that wind scurryin' around."

I waved and headed for the car.

———

When I pulled in at Sam's, I determined not to give him much more than the time of day. Even though I'd've given anything for his help, I just couldn't trust him. If Sam knew that Little Lloyd was being sought by the sheriff, he'd try to talk me into doing the right thing. According to his lights. But I knew better. And on top of that, I was still mad at him for the spectacle he'd made of himself with that Wiggins woman. Perky, was what she was and, believe me, perkiness can get old in a hurry.

But if Sam thought it'd bothered me, I aimed to put his mind to rest. There's nothing like an old fool, and he was welcome to his foolishness, as far as I was concerned.

When James opened the door, I spoke and hurried on into Sam's living room where a table had been pulled up over his cast-laden leg. He and Little Lloyd were hunched over it, putting a puzzle together.

"Julia!" Sam said, smiling with what at any other time I would've taken as pleasure at seeing me. "Come on in here. We need help with this puzzle, and you're just the one we need."

"I don't have time for puzzles, Sam. I've got enough of my own to deal with. Get your coat, Little Lloyd, we have to get on home."

"What about . . . ?" he started, but I cut him off.

"All taken care of. Now come on, you still have some home-work to do."

He began to shake his head, both of us knowing his homework had been done at school, but at my squinch-eyed look, he sub-sided and went for his coat. He always got my unspoken messages, since our minds worked so much alike.

"What's your hurry, Julia?" Sam said, as if he thought I had nothing better to do than entertain him. "Looks like you could spare a minute to cheer up an ailing man. Have a seat over here by me."

"Ailing man, my foot," I said. "I had some pity for you up un-til I saw how that so-called nurse cheered you up without half trying."

"Why, Julia," Sam said, his eyes twinkling like he'd just discov-ered a secret. Except I didn't have one, so there wasn't a thing he could discover. Then he laughed a little and held out his hand to me. "Come on over here. You know I like a mature woman, one who understands me like you do."

"*Mature* just means old, and I don't understand a thing about you, Sam Murdoch, so don't be trying to flatter me. I'm not in the mood for it."

"Well then, what *are* you in the mood for?"

"Not a thing you have to offer. And you needn't smirk at me like that. I have to get this child in bed, so we'll be going." I started out to the hall, but felt bad leaving on that note. Turning around, I said, "I have a lot on my mind today, Sam, which I'd like to share with you. But I don't have time tonight."

He didn't like it, but I was too busy worrying about the long arm of the Law to linger in his house. Besides, it wouldn't hurt him to have a few of the feelings I'd had that morning.

Little Lloyd was quiet as we got in the car, and so was I as I drove through town watching for patrol cars. Who knew but what the sheriff had roadblocks out for us? But probably not, because nobody but Lillian knew we were going anywhere.

Little Lloyd suddenly sat up and looked out the window. "Where're we going, Miss Julia? We've already passed our house."

"Yes, you and I have an appointment with Mr. J. D. Pickens, P.I. at a Mexican restaurant, of all places. If we like his looks and his manner, we're going to hire him to find your mother."

"Tonight? Right now?" The child swung his head toward me, his face lit up in the glow of the dash lights.

"We certainly are. So let's just hope he's up to the job. And, there's another thing you need to know, but first I want you to help me watch where we're going."

He sat up in his seat as far as the seat belt would let him, eager now that I'd put some things in motion. I hated to tell him the latest in the Brother Vern saga, but I had to. He needed to know what the scoundrel was up to, so I told the child how we had to keep him out of sight so he wouldn't be snatched and grabbed.

"Now, just remember," I cautioned as I finished the sorry tale, "nobody knows this but you and me and Lillian. Well, the sheriff does, and all his deputies, which means Coleman, too. That's why I didn't want to say too much to Sam, because he'd probably feel obligated to obey the Law and turn you over to them. Anyway, all we have to do is keep you out of sight until we locate your mother. Then we'll call Binkie and put that great-uncle of yours in his place."

"I don't know why Brother Vern would want to do something like this," Little Lloyd said, his shoulders hunched over with worry. "He never has acted much like he wanted me around."

I heard the fear and confusion in his voice, and took a chance at releasing one hand from the wheel to pat his arm. "Who knows what that man is thinking," I said, although I well knew what was on his mind. He was thinking dollar signs, now that Wesley Lloyd's estate had been probated or whatever it was that had to be done to it. "But you'll be safe with Lillian and me, because we're going to take care of you. Now, put your mind on this Mr. Pickens and help me decide if he has what it takes to locate your mother. But let me caution you, Little Lloyd, let's not say anything to him about Brother Vern and his complaints and summonses. The fewer who know we're hiding from the Law, the better. Don't you think?"

"Yessum," he said, slumping back in his seat. "It'd be better not to confuse him, so he'll keep his mind on finding my mama."

"First things first, right?" Then in an effort to cheer him up, I added, "And when she's home, we're going to cook Brother Vern's goose."

"I sure hope so," he said with a sickly smile. Then, proving he'd learned something in Sunday school, he added, "He's been a thorn in our flesh long enough."

"Watch for the Delmont exit," I reminded him, squinching my eyes against the glare of headlights as we merged onto I-26. "I know about where it is, but everything looks different at night, so give me plenty of warning before I have to come off this thing."

The interstate was as busy as it ever was in the daytime. Big trucks, little trucks, loud trucks and every kind of automobile whizzed past us, but I stayed right under the speed limit, not wanting to be the cause of an accident.

Little Lloyd navigated as well as he did everything else, being the steady and reliable child that he was. I often thought he resembled me in many of his attributes, even though we weren't a lick of kin. Environment plays a heavy role, don't you know.

"That's it, right over there," Little Lloyd said, pointing at a former steak house at the end of an exit ramp on our right. The place was lit up with neon signs and red, blue and green Christmas lights strung across the front and in the trees along the side of the parking lot. As soon as I parked and shut off the motor, I could hear Mexican music being piped outside. No telling what it'd be like inside.

"I hope he's already here," I said. "I'm in no mood to sit and listen to that squalling while we wait for him."

We walked across the parking lot along with several other patrons, most of whom had arrived in pickups and blacked-out vans. Not quite the clientele of the Abbotsville Country Club, but most of them had children with them, so I took some comfort in that. In spite of the fact that I heard talking in Spanish and English and some combination of the two, making me feel like a foreigner in my own county.

"I don't have an idea in the world what Mr. Pickens looks like," I said to Little Lloyd as we waited in line for one of those smiling Mexican men who worked there to seat us.

"Why don't we just ask for him?" the boy said, showing again that he was smart as a whip. "I'll bet he's left word at the desk for us."

That proved to be so. The man at the desk knew just who we meant when I mentioned Mr. Pickens's name and, even though I didn't understand a word he said on the way, he led us to a booth along the back wall. A man, neither young nor old, but about the right age to've had a little experience in the world looked up at us with eyes as black as sin. He had a head full of black hair and what looked to be an equal amount under his nose. I took his measure when he stood as we walked up. I appreciate any courtesy I can get from a man, and gave him a preliminary gold star for making the effort.

Mr. Pickens was one of those men who don't look as tall as they actually are because of their thick chests and wide shoulders. Lots of black hair on his arms, which I couldn't help but notice because the sleeves of his white shirt were rolled up. A quick association flashed through my mind, as I wondered about the likelihood of his chest being similiarly arrayed.

I flushed, furious again at LuAnne because of the thoughts she'd put in my head. I don't ordinarily entertain such intimate matters. I mean, at my age you'd think my mind would've long put such thoughts to rest. But Mr. Pickens was one of those few and far between men who generated some sort of male hormone into the air around him, which was mixing in with Old Spice, of all things. Considering the trouble that aromatic mixture had gotten me into one time before, I determined to keep my distance.

"Glad to meet you," Mr. Pickens said, as I introduced myself and Little Lloyd, and received a firm handshake and a gleam of white teeth from under that bristly brush. "Slide on in." He motioned to the booth.

Little Lloyd scooted in opposite Mr. Pickens and I followed him on the torn plastic. Looking into Mr. Pickens's black eyes, I tried to determine just what kind of man he was and whether he possessed the qualities to help us. I didn't want any fly-by-nighter who would take my money and do nothing.

Saying that he'd just ordered, he handed us a menu that had been propped against a napkin holder.

"We've eaten," I said, waving it away, "but you go right ahead. Mr. Pickens, I want to know one thing right off."

"Let's have it."

"What are your qualifications for this job?"

He leaned across his forearms as they rested on the table and looked me straight in the eye with the most serious expression on his face. "Listen, hon," he said, "I'm the most qualified man you'll ever meet. I know this business backward and forward, inside and out. I was with the Charlotte-Mecklenburg Police Department for ten years and the Atlanta PD for four before that. I've worked vice, missing persons, crimes against property, homicide, you name it. Had my own agency for going on eight years now, and what you're looking at is the most experienced and the dead-level best private eye in the business. Bar none."

I appreciate a high degree of self-confidence as much as the next person, but it's been my practice to withhold judgment until I see some results. So, I discounted the bragging he was doing without letting it irritate me as much as it ordinarily would've. I was still hung up on that "hon" he'd thrown at me.

Before I could straighten him out on the proper term of address when speaking to me, the waitress sat a huge platter of strange-looking food before him. Then she put down a frosted glass and a full pitcher.

My back stiffened at the sight. "Mr. Pickens, would that pitcher contain an alcoholic beverage?"

"It sure would." Glancing up at the waitress, he said, "How about another glass, darlin'?"

"No." I held up my hand. "No, thank you. I don't care to partake." And I didn't care for him partaking either, if the truth be known. If he was a bad drinker, then Lord help us, but I was at my wit's end and had to use what was available. But I didn't like it. Nor did I like the undue familiarity he was exhibiting to every woman within earshot.

"Do you good," he said, winking at Little Lloyd as he poured the frothy stuff into the glass. "Put hair on your chest, too."

I reared back in the booth, dismayed at how he'd picked up on some of my earlier unwelcome thoughts. "Mr. Pickens," I said, "we're not here to discuss masculine hair patterns, and I'd appreciate it if you wouldn't mention such matters in front of this child."

"Sorry," he said, with another wink at Little Lloyd. Then he started in on that conglomeration of cheese, beans and I-don't-know-what-all on his plate. "Why don't you go ahead and give me a run-down on your case."

So I did, although I'd've hardly called Hazel Marie a case. I handed him her birth certificate, Social Security card and a picture. He gave considerable attention to the last-named item, while I told him all the details of our concern. During my recital, he ate and shot occasional sharp glances at me from those black eyes of his. Almost putting me off worse than the way he was steadily emptying that pitcher.

Chapter 8

After he finished his meal and paid the check, he ushered us out of the booth. The tip he left for the waitress indicated a generous, but somewhat profligate, nature. I'd have to watch that, too.

When we walked out of the restaurant, I pulled Little Lloyd's cap down over his ears. The temperature had dropped considerably while we'd been inside, and both of us huddled in our coats as we stepped out onto the porch. Mr. Pickens didn't seem bothered by the cold, braving it with only a black and white tweed sport jacket. His hand on my back as we negotiated the few steps to the parking lot felt like a heating pad through my coat.

"Where're you parked?" he asked.

"Right over there." He walked us to the car, earning another gold star in my mind.

Before opening the car door, he stood for a minute studying Hazel Marie's picture in the glow of the Christmas lights. It was one of those so-called glamour shots that she'd had done at Wilson T.'s insistence. I'd gone with her to the studio in the mall and watched while they gave her a makeover, undressing and draping and back-lighting and airbrushing her like she was a model or something.

The picture didn't give a hint of the shape she'd been in the time she'd come to my door, all bruised and battered and bleeding. She'd had a hard life all the way around and had needed a firm hand, which I'd given her. That hair, for instance, had been bleached to within an inch of its life. I'd taken her to Velma, who'd conditioned it and put on a softer color than the brassy yellow it had been. And I'd introduced her to a better make of clothes than she'd been able to afford with the pittance Wesley Lloyd had made available to her. She still wore her dresses way too short to my mind, but that seemed to be the style, so I hadn't said too much about it.

Hazel Marie was a pretty little thing, even though she didn't much think so herself, and was remarkably improved since I'd had those two lost teeth replaced for her. Skinny, like Little Lloyd, with thin arms and legs. But uncommonly large in the chest area. You know the type. She'd taken the eye of every widower and single man and, I'm sorry to report, several of the married ones in the Presbyterian church and, I'll tell you the truth, it'd been something of a relief to me when Wilson T. came along and took her out of the running, so to speak. Even though I wouldn't've given two cents for him or the kind of work he was engaged in.

"Nice," Mr. Pickens said, giving the picture an uncommonly long study. Then, smiling at Little Lloyd, said, "I see where you get your good looks, sport."

Little Lloyd ducked his head, smiling at the compliment, but I began to wonder if Mr. Pickens knew the truth from a hole in the ground.

"Regardless of how she looks," I said, anxious to keep his mind on the subject, "can you find her for us?"

"Oh, yeah," he said, as he finally slid the picture back into its envelope. "I'll need to keep this awhile. First thing in the morning I'll run a credit check, see if she's used a credit card anywhere. Then I'll run down this 'big,' whatever it is. We need a starting point, and that looks to be the obvious one. Unless," he said, looking up with one of those sharp glances, "you know what movie they were going to see?"

"I don't have a clue, neither knowing nor caring what those

Hollywood types do. Little Lloyd, did she say what they were going to see?"

"No'm, she just said they were going to Asheville to eat and see
a movie." He stopped, thought for a minute, then said, "She
doesn't like action movies much. But Mr. Hodge does, so I don't
guess that helps, does it?"

"You never know," Mr. Pickens said. "Tell you what I'll do. It's
about the same time now that they would've gone to the movies
last night, so the same people ought to be working tonight. I
think I'll make the rounds, show 'em this picture, and see if anybody remembers seeing her."

My heart lifted at his willingness to get right to work, and I felt
some better about my choice of private investigator, in spite of his
drinking habit. I'd have to watch that and nip it in the bud as soon
as I had him on my payroll. At least, though, he hadn't given me
a song and dance about waiting around, doing nothing, until
Hazel Marie showed up on her own.

"Excuse us a minute," I said, turning Little Lloyd by the shoulder and walking a few steps away.

Leaning down to the boy, I whispered, "What do you think?
Should we hire him or not?"

Little Lloyd craned his neck around me, giving Mr. Pickens a
thorough going-over. Then he nodded and said, "Yessum, I guess
we better. But he sure does like that beer."

The child and I thought so much alike, it lifted my heart. I
smiled and gave him a pat. "We'll just have to keep an eye on him,
and him away from it."

Walking back to where Mr. Pickens was waiting, I said, "I take
it, then, that you're willing to take the case?"

"You bet. Shouldn't take more than a day or so to find somebody that looks like this." He waved the picture-holding envelope. "She's the type that sticks in your mind."

I wasn't sure of the healthiness of his motive in looking for Hazel Marie, but at that point I figured I'd take what I could get.

"Now," he went on, "we need to settle the matter of my fee. It'll be sixty dollars an hour, plus expenses, with a three-hundred-dollar retainer."

"My word."

Little Lloyd looked up at me with a worried frown on his face. He knew how careful I was with my money, and I expect he figured I wouldn't stand to be soaked for that much. It gave me pleasure to reassure him.

"You're awfully expensive, Mr. Pickens," I said, not wanting the man to think I threw money around any which way. "But," I said, with a long sigh, "if that's what it takes to get this boy's mama back, I guess I'll have to put up with it. Unless you want to give us special rates, seeing as how Hazel Marie's looks will make it so easy for you."

He threw his head back and laughed out loud. Then he gave my arm a squeeze. "I like your style, hon. I'll have to watch what I say around you, won't I?" Then he got all businesslike. "But no, no special rates, other than the fact that you're getting the best in the business for just your average cost."

"I'll believe it when I see it. Or rather, when I see Hazel Marie safe and sound. In the meantime," I said, opening my pocketbook, "I want you on the job. So I'll give you your retainer right now so you can get started."

I thought it'd hurt to write a three-hundred-dollar check made out to a perfect stranger but, when it came down to it, I went ahead and wrote it for five hundred.

"This is to ensure that you'll be working just for us. I don't want you frittering away your time with any other clients," I said, handing him the check. "I want results, Mr. Pickens and, if you're as good as you say and you find Hazel Marie before this money runs out, I'll expect a refund."

I think his eyes twinkled in the red and green glow of the Christmas lights, but I couldn't be sure. I was sure that his eyebrows went up when he saw the amount on the check.

"She's as good as home right now," he said. "Count on it." He folded the check and put it in a billfold that was curved from being sat on. "I'll check in with you every day but, if something breaks, I'll let you know right away."

"That won't do," I said. "You can't expect us to just sit home twiddling our thumbs, waiting for word from you and never knowing what you're doing. We're going with you and, when this boy has to be in school or otherwise occupied," I said, thinking of how I had to keep him hid, "*I'll* be with you."

"Uh-uh," he said, shaking his head. "That's not the way it works."

"That's the way it'll have to work, if you work for me, Mr. Pickens. I know how people are. They take your money and when it suits them, they might get around to doing the job they're hired to do. Well, I'm not having that. I want to know what, when and how you're conducting my business, and I want Hazel Marie home before something awful happens to her." I saw, or maybe felt, Little Lloyd take a deep breath at what I'd said, and I felt bad about scaring him. But it had to be said in no uncertain terms so Mr. Pickens would see that I meant business.

"Look, hon," Mr. Pickens said, as he put his hand on my arm, rubbing my sleeve up and down. "I know you're upset, but what I do is not something either of you ought to be involved in. Investigative technique is a specialized subject, and I can do a better job by myself. That's why I left the Charlotte PD and Atlanta before that, too many people looking over my shoulder. Trust me. I can do the job."

Well, I've never trusted anybody who felt it necessary to say "trust me," so I was even more determined to keep my eye on him. I stepped back out of rubbing distance from his hand and said, "Mr. Pickens, the matter is not up for argument. I've hired you and you've taken my money, so accept the terms. We're going with you."

"No," he said, having the nerve to point a finger in my face, "you're not."

"Yes, we are."

"Uh-uh."

"How does a bonus sound?"

He studied me for a minute, undoubtedly adding up figures in his mind. "What're we talking about here?"

"I'm talking about a sizable one, say, a forty-hour week's worth if you find Hazel Marie within twenty-four hours. It'll go down for every day after that, but I won't expect a refund from the retainer."

"You drive a hard bargain."

"Not as hard as I'm going to drive you."

He turned those dark eyes on me, considering the proposition for several seconds. Then he said, "You'll slow me down."

When they start to give, you know you've won. "Not for a minute, Mr. Pickens. We'll be a help to you, you'll see. I want you to earn that bonus, and you'll feel good about yourself when you do. Now, we've still got a couple of hours before Little Lloyd's bedtime, so where do we go first?"

He looked off into the distance and shifted his feet. Then shaking his head, he said, "I still don't like it. It won't work and, if you're right, and she's in danger, where does that put you and the boy?"

"Right behind you, Mr. Pickens. If you're as good as you say, I'm sure you'll protect us." I sighed then, realizing what he was up to. "I'm disappointed in you, Mr. Pickens. You're just trying to soak a poor widow woman but, if that's what it takes, so be it. I'll double the bonus."

He did a double take. "Double? Well, why didn't you say so.

Hon, for two weeks' income for a day's work, I'll take you, the boy and anybody else you want to drag along."

That told me all I needed to know about J. D. Pickens, P.I., right there. He wanted money, or needed it, one, and when I saw the dented and rusted car he was driving, I knew he was in bad financial shape. I smiled at the sight, figuring I had his number and sure that he'd do things my way. I was in the catbird seat, which was where I intended to stay until Hazel Marie was safe in her own home. Well, my home, but what difference did that make?

Chapter 9

"We'll take my car next time," I said, trying my best to find a comfortable position on the rump-sprung bucket seat. I wasn't even sure the door was closed tight, which was one reason I was hanging on to the armrest.

Mr. Pickens just grunted and stomped down on the gas pedal. The outside of the car might've looked like a bent-up tin can, but there was nothing wrong with the motor.

Little Lloyd, belted in the backseat, said, "I like this car, Miss Julia. It's a Firebird."

"Well, whatever it is, it needs some body work."

Mr. Pickens ignored our discussion of his vehicle, keeping his mind on the highway and weaving in and out of the the traffic, as we headed for Asheville and the four most likely movie houses. I'd wanted to follow him in my car, but he'd said no. That wasn't all he'd said, following it up with the comment that if I was bound and determined to go with him, I could just do it, because he couldn't be bothered with having another car trailing him. Which, he'd added, couldn't keep up with him, anyway. I believed him, having now been witness to and passenger in a tire-squealing, oil-burning, nerve-racking, high-speed car ride.

"Are we speeding, Mr. Pickens?"

He glanced at me in the light of the dashboard and oncoming cars, one hand on the wheel and the other on the gear shift. "Make you nervous?"

"Certainly not." I made a conscious effort and released the

armrest. "I'm just worried about Little Lloyd. I wouldn't want him to be in a wreck."

"I'm okay, Miss Julia," Little Lloyd said. "I like to go fast."

I immediately took that as a critical comment on my own careful driving, but decided to let it pass with only a sniff. Mr. Pickens's mouth twitched as he swerved to pass another car that was poking along at the speed limit.

"We'll start with this one," Mr. Pickens said, turning into a south Asheville mall with a double movie house at the far end. He slowed down enough to avoid arrest as he maneuvered through the parked cars.

Parking the car in the fire zone right in front of the ticket booth, he got out of the car without a "be back in a minute," or a "kiss my foot" or anything else.

"Wait, we're coming, too," I said, but I don't think he heard me as he slammed his door and walked off. "Come on, Little Lloyd."

We followed as quickly as we could, coming up behind Mr. Pickens as he shoved Hazel Marie's picture through the opening in the glass booth. A thin, washed-out-looking young man wearing a white shirt, black bow tie and a maroon vest gazed at Mr. Pickens like he couldn't understand a simple question. Pimples dotted the young man's face, as did patches of beard that his razor had missed.

"Huh?" he said.

"Have you seen this woman?" Mr. Pickens said again. "She was here last night about this time. The man she was with probably bought the ticket, but you might've noticed her."

"Well," I chimed in, wanting to get the facts straight. "We're not sure she was at this picture show, but she could've been."

The ticket seller swung his eyes from Mr. Pickens to me and back again. "Uh-uh, I ain't seen her."

Mr. Pickens glared at me, jerked the picture back and grabbed my arm. Pulling me away from the booth, he leaned right down in my face and said, "Look, when you're questioning somebody, you don't give them an out. Which is exactly what you just did. He hardly looked at the picture, much less gave it any thought before you let him off the hook."

"Well, I'm sorry."

"Sorry won't cut it. Now get back in the car and stay there." He punctuated the order with a pointed finger in my face. Then he headed for the double doors leading inside the movie.

"Hey!" the ticket seller yelled, leaning down to call through the slot. "Hey, mister, you got to buy a ticket."

Mr. Pickens swung back and leaned down himself. "I'm not going in to see the movie. I'm going to see if anybody working inside has seen this woman."

"It don't matter," the ticket seller said. "Anybody goes through the doors has to have a ticket. That's the policy."

Quick as a flash, Mr. Pickens's hand went to his inside coat pocket and came out with a wallet. Flipping it open and flapping the badge pinned on it in the ticket seller's face, he said, "Police business."

As the doors closed behind Mr. Pickens, I shivered in a gust of wind that scattered popcorn boxes across the sidewalk.

"I guess we better get back in the car, Little Lloyd," I said, my hand on his back. In spite of the cold and the dressing down Mr. Pickens had given me, I was beginning to feel somewhat pleased with myself, all things considered.

"Little Lloyd," I went on, as we settled in our seats, "I think we've made a good decision by hiring Mr. Pickens. I tried my best to get some official help through official channels and couldn't get to first base. But, without even knowing it, we've gone and hired our very own private policeman. You saw that badge, didn't you?"

Little Lloyd looked over the seat at me, frowning and twisting his mouth. "I'm not sure he's a policeman, Miss Julia. I don't think policemen have their own businesses."

"Well, I'm not going to worry about the details. He seems to know what he's doing and, what's more, he has the wherewithal to do it. Bundle up back there; I don't want you catching cold."

By the time Mr. Pickens came out of the warm theater, the car felt like the inside of a refrigerator. We should've gone in with him, whether he liked it or not.

"Did anybody recognize her?" I asked as he swung into the driver's seat.

"No. I'll try another one."

After pulling out onto the city street and turning toward downtown, gearing down with a roar at each stop light, he finally turned to me and said, "Let's get something straight. *I'm* the one doing the questioning." And he had the unmitigated gall to take his hand off the gear shift and point that finger at me again. "Remember that."

"Mr. Pickens," I said, drawing myself up to face him down, "you point that finger at me one more time, and you'll draw back a nub."

He cut his eyes at me, then started laughing. At *me*. I took immediate offense, as anybody would've who'd been both reprimanded and laughed at but, with an admirable act of will, I decided to let it go. At least, he now knew where I stood when it came to being on the receiving end of orders. Lightheartedness in a man, especially in a man who's supposed to be working, didn't ordinarily inspire a great deal of confidence from me, but then, active hostility between us wasn't going to be of much use in finding Hazel Marie. So I relented enough to manage a smile to let him know there were no hard feelings.

But he had to learn who was in charge. When we got to the Northside Cinema, I told Little Lloyd to stay in the car while I marched myself in right behind Mr. Pickens. In spite of the fact that he stopped dead, put his hands on his hips and glared at me.

"I just want to learn how it's done, Mr. Pickens," I said, as pleasantly as I could. "From an expert, so to speak."

He rolled his eyes, then turned without a word. I trailed behind him and watched while he showed Hazel Marie's picture to the ticket seller—this one was a bald man who was sweating inside his glass booth—then followed him inside.

"Don't say a word," Mr. Pickens said in a low, commanding tone as we went into the lobby.

The smell of popcorn filled the carpeted area, and had drawn several patrons from their seats. Mr. Pickens waited while the young girl behind the counter sold buttered and nonbuttered, Cokes and candy. When the last lanky teenager turned toward the curtained doorway, sucking on his drink as he went, Mr. Pickens went to the counter. I stood back, as ordered, and observed. I learned a lot but I wasn't exactly sure what it was.

"How you doin'?" he began, leaning one hand on the counter and smiling like the ponytailed, earringed girl before him was a good friend instead of someone he'd never seen before. "I wonder if you could help me out, and I just bet you can."

She smiled, but it was a little on the tentative side, I thought. "Well, I'll try."

Mr. Pickens didn't say anything for a minute, just stood there smiling at her, taking her in with his eyes. And the more he did, the broader her smile became. I didn't know what he was communicating to her, but she liked whatever it was. "I bet you see a lot of people come through here," he said. "They probably all run together and you don't remember any of them."

"Well," she said, raising her arm to twirl the ponytail and, Mr. Pickens couldn't help but notice, to pull her sweater tighter. "Some of 'em kinda stand out in your mind. But mostly, it's just 'I want this,' 'I want that.' Why?"

"Reason I asked, I'm a private investigator and . . ."

"You are? Cool."

"Yeah, and I'm looking for a woman. . . ."

"Oh, yeah?" She laughed and leaned across the counter toward him. "You better watch yourself with that line, you might get one."

Mr. Pickens laughed, too, and slipped Hazel Marie's picture out of his pocket. "Looks like I'd be in luck, if I wasn't working. Too bad, but I might get back this way sometime soon and see if I can find me one. Unfortunately, I have to look for this one tonight." He held the picture in front of her, and it took a few seconds for the little twit to look away from him and give it some attention. "Maybe you saw her here last night?"

"Uh-uh. I don't think I seen her."

"Think hard," he urged as she continued to shake her head.

"I might reco'nize her if I seen her again but, like I say, it's mostly 'Gimme this,' 'Gimme that' around here and I don't have time to look at faces. Well, you know, unless it's somebody like you that comes up to talk. I prob'bly won't forget you."

"I won't forget you, either," he said, putting away the picture and handing her a card. "Here's my phone number. If you see her or happen to remember anything from last night, will you call me?"

"I sure will. I might even call if I don't remember."

Giving her a last throb of the heart, he grinned at her and whispered something that made her blush. The whole thing put me in mind of Sam's unseemly behavior with the Wiggins woman. Disgusting, if you want to know the truth.

Before I could say anything, he turned and breezed past me, on his way outside. With me tagging along behind him.

In the car again, I said, "Well, that was certainly instructive. I can see why you wouldn't want anybody around to witness a display of your investigative technique."

"Honey gets more flies than vinegar, or haven't you noticed?"

The car took off with a jerk and we were speeding down the street before I could answer. When I caught my breath, I said, "You were certainly spreading enough of it around in there."

He glanced over at me and, with a lopsided smile, said, "Keep watchin', hon. You might learn something."

I turned my head and looked out the side window, biting my lip to keep from teaching him a thing or two.

We made stops at two more large cineplexes, as they call those places these days, with me learning little more from Mr. Pickens's techniques than he'd already demonstrated.

"Let's try one last place," he said, throwing the car in gear and taking off so fast that the seatbelt tightened up on me.

The car careened down the streets, as he headed it right downtown, then brought it to a screeching halt in front of a dilapidated marquee with half its lights out, announcing that we were at the Adult Art Cinema.

"Where are we?" I asked, looking around at the empty sidewalk and dark store windows, several of them boarded up. It wasn't a part of town I was familiar with and, from the looks of it, I didn't want to know it any better.

"You don't want to go in this one," Mr. Pickens said as he opened his door. "Trust me."

"I've seen picture shows before, Mr. Pickens," I said, determined to show him that I was up for whatever it took. Opening my door to follow him, I told Little Lloyd to stay in and lock the doors.

I was right behind Mr. Pickens as he approached the ticket seller, an unhealthy-looking man who hardly listened to the questions, for staring so hard at me. I guessed he wasn't used to seeing a lady in that part of town. As Mr. Pickens went through his questioning ritual, I took note of the posters and nearly lost my breath.

I plucked at Mr. Pickens's coat to get his attention, and whispered, "Mr. Pickens, do you know what kind of shows they put on here? Hazel Marie would never come to something like this."

"You never know," he said, turning to me with a know-it-all grin that made me want to smack him. "I told you to stay in the car."

And he headed into the lobby, with me right behind him. Well, what else could I do?

I stood right inside the doors, fearful of taking another step, while Mr. Pickens went up to an usher who was looking through one of the magazines he had for sale. I wouldn't for the world mention what all was on the covers of those magazines but, believe me, they were a poor substitute for popcorn and Milk Duds.

"How you doin', Harry?" Mr. Pickens said, as he pulled Hazel Marie's picture from his pocket. I started to snatch it out of his hand, not wanting anything about her associated with what I was seeing.

But before I could do anything, it hit me that Mr. Pickens was showing an unnerving amount of familiarity with this Harry person, smiling and joking with him. What kind of man would patronize such a place? And drink beer, too? I backed up against the door and clutched my pocketbook with both hands, wondering what I'd gotten Little Lloyd and myself into. All I could do was pray that Mr. Pickens would hurry up and finish so we could get out of there.

"Ready?" he said, grabbing my arm and pulling me along with him as he hurried outside.

"More than," I said, trotting to keep up with him, anxious to shake the dust of that wicked place from my feet.

Chapter 10

By the time Mr. Pickens took us back to the Mexican restaurant where my car was parked, I couldn't say much for my first private investigative experience. And said as much to him.

"That's part of it," he told me as he parked beside my car, "and I warned you before we started. Knocking on doors, asking questions, stakeouts where you just sit and watch, going over and over the same things until something breaks, that's what an investigation is. When I was with the Charlotte-Mecklenberg PD, I cleared more cases than any other detective because I've got the patience for it."

He cocked an eye at me, as if to say I didn't.

"Give me your address," he went on, without a "please" or "do you mind" or anything else. He certainly liked to give orders, I'll say that for him. "I'll be over first thing in the morning to take a look at her room, see if there's anything that'll tell us where she might've gone. In the meantime, I want you to be writing down everything you can think of about this Hodge she went off with. Any ideas about him?"

"You don't want to hear the ideas I have about him," I said with a twist of my mouth. "I've never trusted a man with a mustache. . . ." I stopped, staring at the bushy thing under Mr. Pickens's nose, and corrected myself, ". . . with a *thin* mustache. The first place to start, though, would be with Pastor Ledbetter, who thinks the sun rises and sets in him, and knows him better than anybody. Leave that little matter to me, Mr. Pickens. I'll handle the pastor."

"Okay, but I'll need Hodge's full name and date of birth so I can track his credit card usage. I may want to interview your preacher, too."

"Feel free anytime you want to tackle him. But I warn you right now, the man'll likely hit you up for a donation to his building fund if you give him half a chance."

"Huh," he said, echoing my sentiments exactly.

I shook my head then, thinking of the time I'd wasted that day worrying myself sick instead of doing something. "I declare, Mr. Pickens, I should've started making some inroads on Wilson T. before this, learning as much about his background as I could. All I can tell you is that he's been missing all day, too, if unanswered phone calls are any indication. He has a temporary apartment in Abbotsville while he's working for our church, although his permanent address is in Charlotte, I believe. I don't have that address or phone number, but I've called his local number a dozen times today, and he's not there. He hasn't been at the church, either. I'm convinced that he's the reason Hazel Marie is missing, but I don't want you considering any romantic eloping nonsense. She wouldn't do that to Little Lloyd and me, and she wouldn't be gone these twenty-four hours without letting us know something." I stopped, then told him what I really thought. "I might as well admit it. I've had my suspicions of Wilson T. Hodge from the first time I laid eyes on him."

"What's your problem with him?" Mr. Pickens asked, his eyebrows raised.

"He's a church fund-raiser. Does that answer your question?"

He nodded. "Oh, yeah."

His quick grasp of the situation gratified me, and I decided Mr. Pickens ought to have a little more background on Hazel Marie.

Turning toward the back seat, I said, "Little Lloyd, jump on out and get in our car. I want a word with Mr. Pickens before we go."

When Little Lloyd had crawled out from behind my seat, I pulled the door to and told my new employee about my husband and Hazel Marie, their dozen or so years of illicit communion that I'd known nothing about although the whole town had and the result of that communion who'd been riding in his back seat. I told him how it'd just about killed me when I'd learned what Wesley Lloyd had been up to all those years at the same time he'd been an elder in the church and a dominating force at home and in his business.

"Everybody was amazed when I asked Hazel Marie and Little Lloyd to live with me, but I wanted to show the town that I could rise above the common crowd. And by that time we'd been through so much together, getting Wesley Lloyd's two wills straightened out and rescuing Little Lloyd from Brother Vern and nursing Hazel Marie back to health that, well, I'd just gotten used to having them around. Besides, that child needed a firm hand and a decent home, which I've been happy to provide." I stopped and thought for a minute. "Maybe another reason I took them in was to get back at Wesley Lloyd. His reputation meant everything to him, and I guess I wanted everybody to know what he really was. I'm not proud of that reason, Mr. Pickens, but I'm an honest woman."

I waited for him to say something but, when he didn't, I went on. "I can't say I blame Hazel Marie for taking up such a life and bearing a child out of wedlock. Well, maybe I did at first a little, but she was young and impressionable, and, well, you had to've known Wesley Lloyd to understand the situation."

"Good-looking man?"

"Oh, no. No, I can't say much for his looks. He was a man of will, I guess you'd say. Able to make people do what he wanted them to. Maybe that's why Hazel Marie and I took to each other so well; we'd both put up with him longer than we should've. Anyway, he's out of the picture now, and I hardly ever think of her and him together anymore."

He was impressed or, maybe, stunned at my Christian forbearance and said as much. Well, what he said was, "I hadn't figured you for the forgiving type, Mrs. Springer."

"I can't take much credit," I told him, "since it was easy enough with Wesley Lloyd in the ground. If I'd learned what he'd been up to while he was still around, it would've been a different story, let me tell you.

"Now you know the background," I went on, "but don't let the fact that she and the boy are not my blood kin slow you down. I've invested a lot in those two, my reputation in town, for one thing, since everybody thought I'd lost my mind by taking them in. I intend to prove them wrong. So, if Hazel Marie has gotten herself into headline-making trouble—since I don't trust Wilson T. Hodge as far as I can throw him—I want to get her out before anybody knows about it." I stopped, mortally tempted to tell him about Brother Vern's latest effort to disrupt our lives, and how I had to hide Little Lloyd from the sheriff. Then I decided that the better part of discretion was to find out a little more about Mr. Pickens's views on law and order before trusting him to circumvent them.

"I'll find her," he said, giving me one of those smouldering looks again. "Count on it."

"That's what I'm doing, Mr. Pickens." And after hesitating a moment longer, tempted again to tell him everything, I bade him good night and got in my car. With my lips still sealed.

———

Little Lloyd and I didn't make much conversation on the way home. Night driving usually takes up most of my concentration, and he seemed tired and subdued. I tried to interest him in making a list of all we knew about his future stepfather, but I couldn't get much out of him. And the more I thought about it, the more I realized that we didn't know a whole lot about the man. He was from Charlotte, the so-called Queen City of the South, and he was part of a fund-raising organization that sent its employees all over the country when pastors needed outside help to pry money out of their congregations. He was what I called a typical salesman: an overly polite arm-twister and instigator of guilt. Wilson T. was selling Pastor Ledbetter's dream of a church complex that he could point to and say, "Look what I built." The pastor wanted the entire block filled with buildings, monuments to family values, family recreation and family fun.

Well, whoever heard of church being fun? That wasn't why I went but, if it had been, I certainly wouldn't've gone to the First Presbyterian Church of Abbotsville to find it.

As we came into town, my nerves began acting up on me again. All I needed was to see a patrol car, and I'd've probably gone through the roof. I glanced over at Little Lloyd as we crossed Main. He had his head leaning against the door and, at first, I thought he'd drifted off. I turned down Polk and slowed considerably, peering at the few cars parked along the street. If the sheriff had my house staked out, I wanted to know it before I drove in. Lord, I'd gotten nowhere in coming up with a safe place for Little Lloyd, what with going to one picture show after another with absolutely nothing to show for the effort, so all I could do was take him home again.

As I inched the car along, looking right and left for cars with light bars on top, he straightened up with a long sigh.

"Tired?"

"Yessum, a little." He slumped back in the seat and said, "I sure wish my mama was home. I'm getting real nervous about her."

"I am, too. But maybe Lillian's heard from her while we've been gone." I hated to give the child false hope, but I had to keep us both going. "Here we are."

As I turned into the driveway, relieved that no blue lights were flashing my way, I noticed lights on in the pastor's suite of offices over at the church. Another Building Fund Committee meeting, I supposed. Then, with a sudden flash, it occurred to me that it was a good time to check again on the whereabouts of Wilson T. Hodge. Maybe the pastor had heard from him or knew where he was.

Lights were on in the back of my house where I knew Lillian was holding down the fort and waiting for the phone to ring.

"Let's get inside, Little Lloyd," I said, stepping out of the car. "It's cold enough out here to freeze."

"Y'all find her?" Lillian had the back door open before we got up the steps.

"No'm, we went to all the movie houses, but nobody's seen her," Little Lloyd said with enough despair to wring my heart, as I followed him inside. "Has she called again?"

"No, honey, but y'all come on in here an' tell me about that private eye man."

"Little Lloyd," I said, smoothing down his hair that was full of electricity from the cold. "You tell Lillian about Mr. Pickens and how he goes about his investigating." Giving him a pat, I looked up over his head. "Lillian, they're having a meeting at the church, so I'm going over there to see if anybody's heard from Mr. Hodge. Now, while I'm gone, I want you to get this child in bed, but do it without turning on the lights in his room. I don't want anybody knowing he's home. Wait a minute, though. I just thought of something." I thought it through for a minute, then said, "We never know when Coleman'll show up to spend the night in his room, so maybe Little Lloyd's ought to stay empty. If Coleman takes a mind to look in on him, we don't want him to find anything. What do you think, Little Lloyd?"

He started wringing his hands in that nervous way of his, so I took one of them in mine. "I think," he said, "that I don't know where I'm going to sleep."

"Why, with me, of course. You don't mind, do you?"

"No'm, I guess not."

"Well, see, I know it's not the best solution, but Coleman would never open the door to my bedroom. He's too much of a gentleman, even though he is a deputy. Nobody but me and Lillian will go in there, so you'll be safe till I can figure something better or till your mother gets home. Which Mr. Pickens has assured us will be very soon. Lillian'll get you in bed, and I'll be back in a minute or two."

He started taking off his coat, then turning to me, he said, "I don't want you to get in trouble because of me."

"Lord, child, don't you worry about that. If the sheriff wants to put an old woman in the Atlanta Pen for taking care of her own, well, just let him try. We'll put him on *60 Minutes* and he couldn't get elected dogcatcher after that."

He gave me a quick smile, making me want to grab him and hold him close. Instead, I gave his arm a little squeeze and hurried outside.

I wrapped my coat around me against the cold and headed across the street. Just as I approached the back door of the church, several men walked out, some lighting cigarettes and others talking together as they went to their cars. Most of them nodded at me and all of them looked surprised to see me going into the church at that late hour. Gallivanting around after dark was not a customary practice for me. I hurried inside, not wanting to engage in conversation in which I knew my reasons for being abroad would be questioned. It was none of their business.

Heading for the pastor's office, I could hear the rumble of his voice as he spoke to a few stragglers from the committee. When he saw me, I saw the surprise on his face.

"Miss Julia, what're you doing out this time of night? Is anything wrong?" He came over to me, and I was pleased to note some evidence of concern over my welfare. The pastor had generally avoided my path ever since that episode last year when he'd tried to have me declared mentally incompetent, with the intent of getting himself appointed my financial guardian. Don't you just hate it when somebody thinks they know what's good for you better than you do, yourself? I hadn't had much use for him ever since.

"I need a few minutes of your time, pastor. I won't keep you long; I know you want to get home."

"Come on in here, then," he said, leading me into his dark paneled office as he said his last good-byes to those who were leaving. "Have a seat, Miss Julia, and tell me what I can do for you."

"I'm not going to stay that long," I said, refusing the chair he pointed to. "I need to know one thing. Was Wilson T. Hodge at your meeting tonight? It was the Building Committee, wasn't it?"

"Yes, it was. Now, Miss Julia, I know that you haven't yet come around to supporting our efforts for the Lord, but I hope you'll give it a lot of prayer and reconsider your position. The Lord has blessed you with considerable gifts, and it is our privilege to return those gifts to him. Whatever you give will come back to you sevenfold."

"That may be, pastor, but I don't need any more than I already have. So getting back more than I give is not an argument that cuts any ice with me. But I'm not here to discuss your athletic building or whatever it is, nor the means by which you plan to erect it, nor *where* you plan to erect it which is practically in my front yard. I'll take that up with you at another time. Right now, all I want to know is, was Wilson T. Hodge present tonight?"

"He's in Charlotte for a few days so, no, he wasn't here. But if you want to discuss your Building Fund pledge with him, I'll be glad to make an appointment for you and he'll see you as soon as he gets back."

The man had a one-track mind, and I didn't have the time or

the energy to derail him, so I said, "When do you expect him back?"

"Sunday, at the latest. But the fund-raising drive continues apace even when he's not here. I'll tell you, Miss Julia, the committee is highly enthusiastic, though I know you and a few others were against our decision to bring him in. But professionals can do so much more than we can on our own. And Mr. Hodge is a true professional, just gets us all so spirit-filled and eager to erect that building for the glory of the Lord. It'll be a witness to everybody in the community."

"I'm sure it will be, pastor," I said, but refrained from mentioning just what it would be a witness to. "But to get back to the subject I'm interested in, when did you last speak with Mr. Hodge?"

"Why, just this morning, early. He called from his car phone to say he was needed for a few days at his Charlotte office. He assured me he'll be back by the Sunday morning worship service. You can speak to him then, if you want."

"He called you this morning?" So, where was Hazel Marie while he was doing this calling?

"Yes, he always let's me know when he has to leave town. Why? Is there a problem I can help you with?"

I glanced around his office, suitable for any business executive but hardly appropriate for the pastor of a church that couldn't support itself without holding auctions, bake sales and car raffles, wondering how much I should confide in him. He had not proved to be a solid rock on which I could stand in the past, but I could see no harm in planting a seed of worry in his mind. Especially since I knew Brother Vern had visited him that morning, and two more unlikely conspirators you'd never find anywhere.

"My problem is this, Pastor. Wilson T. Hodge and Hazel Marie left to go to Asheville yesterday evening for dinner and a movie. At least, that's what he said. Hazel Marie still hasn't come home, and it's been more than twenty-four hours and we don't know where she is. Now you tell me that Wilson T.'s gone to Charlotte, and that he called without saying one word to you, me or anybody about where *she* is. I want to know what he's done with her. That's my problem, and I want some help from you in tracking him down."

He lost his soothing, ministerial manner then, and began making excuses. "I, well, surely, you're mistaken. Wilson T. is as fine a man as I've ever known. He wouldn't just . . . Maybe he brought her home and she went off with somebody else before coming in?"

I had to lean against his desk, in an effort to keep myself collected as he began to lay blame on Hazel Marie. "That's the most foolish thing I've ever heard. Now, let me tell you another thing, Pastor," I went on with renewed vigor. "I know that Hazel Marie's uncle was over here today, because I saw his car, which can't be mistaken for anybody else's. And after that visit with you, the fool apparently went crazy and instituted legal proceedings that require Hazel Marie's presence. So I need an explanation from you as to what's going on between you and Brother Vernon Puckett, and I need an explanation from Wilson T. as to what he's done with Hazel Marie. And if I don't get them, I'm going to raise a hue and cry in this town the likes of which it's never seen."

"Well," he said, consternation spreading over his face as the possiblity of rumors and gossip floating around about his Christian fund-raiser, as well as about his connection to Brother Vern, occurred to him. "Well, well, I'll be upfront with you, Miss Julia. I asked the Reverend Puckett to come by. Ecumenism is a big thing now, you know, and I thought, since he's had so much experience raising funds, that he could give me some pointers. I've been worried that some few of our members, like you for instance, haven't responded to our building fund drive as I'd hoped. And that means, of course, that the total hasn't, well, *isn't* where I expected it to be. In fact," he stopped, fingered the Bible on his desk, looking somewhat pensive, "it's way off. But the Lord always provides, so I know it'll work out."

"Let us hope so," I said, although I never minded giving the Lord a hand now and then. "But what I want Him to provide right now is Hazel Marie's whereabouts."

The pastor drew himself up and went on. "Well, as far as Ms. Puckett is concerned, I expect you misunderstood the situation. I mean, are you sure she went out with Wilson T.? He didn't mention her when he called. I don't want to distress you, but from the talk that's unhappily come to my attention, I understand that she's quite popular around town."

"*Talk?* What talk?"

"Now, Miss Julia, you understand," he said in the patronizing way he had that just burned me to a crisp, "that as a man of God, I don't engage in gossip or the passing on of rumors. It is my duty, and her uncle feels the same way, to issue a caution when certain actions of certain people give rise to untoward talk."

"I don't have an idea in the world of what you're talking about." And if he'd had an idea of the head of steam I was building up, he'd've backed off right then. But no, not him.

"I'm just saying that our church members have to be like Caesar's wife. And Ms. Puckett even more so, given her past history which you, of all people, know so well. Understand me, now, I'm not saying anything against her; it's been my privilege to instruct her in Presbyterian theology and she's been an apt pupil. But, Miss Julia, you know that where there's smoke, you're likely to find some fire. The Reverend Puckett said as much just this morning and he knows her better than anybody. He's deeply concerned about some of her more recent activities that've given rise to rumors and gossip."

"Stop right there," I said, holding up my hand. "I'm not about to let you or that unprincipled uncle of hers slur Hazel Marie's name. I don't know who else you've been listening to, but you ought to know by now that Brother Vernon Puckett would do and say anything to get his hands on Little Lloyd and the funds Wesley Lloyd left him, and I'll tell you right now that's not going to happen. I'll have you know that Hazel Marie's conducted herself better than Caesar's wife ever hoped to do. Although I don't know what a dead Roman has to do with it. She hasn't gone out with anybody but Wilson T. Hodge since she's been in my house, so if you need to caution anybody I'd recommend a word to him." I took a deep breath and barreled on. "And, I will remind you that the only reason she went out with him in the first place was because he was said to be a church-going man and a committed Christian. By *you,* Pastor. So you can take comfort in the fact that at least one person in your congregation listens to you, and believes what you say. Now look what's come of it."

"Okay, okay. I'll tell you what I'll do," he said, quickly backpedaling from throwing off on Hazel Marie when I brought up Wilson T. again. "I'll call his Charlotte office first thing tomorrow. I was planning to do that anyway, since there's this other little matter concerning the fund's balance I need to talk with him about. Nothing for you to worry about, but at least we'll know something."

"No, we won't. All we'll know is whether he's in Charlotte or not. And I'll tell you one thing, he better *not* be there, going about his business like nothing's wrong. If Hazel Marie's in trouble, he better be in the same trouble. The idea of a man taking her out and leaving her somewhere! One thing you need to know, Pastor, I intend to track him down and get some answers. And to that end, I want his Charlotte address and his date of birth. Social Security number, too, and anything else that's on his job application form."

"What? Why? I can't give out that information."

"You can either give it to me," I informed him, "or you can give it to Lieutenant Peavey or the private investigator I've hired."

Consternation wasn't the word this time. Pastor Ledbetter's face went white at the thought of a police search for and an investigation into the man he'd backed, pushed, praised and recommended to his congregation. If Hazel Marie was suffering from town gossip, without a reason in the world for it other than Brother Vern trying to besmirch her any way he could, then just wait till word got around about Wilson T. Hodge and his shifty ways.

"Miss Julia, please," he said, his hand raised to ward me off, "let's not do anything rash."

"Oh, Pastor, you know me. I never take a step without knowing where my foot's coming down."

The pastor gave me the information I wanted, albeit reluctantly, and I left him in a discomfited state of mind and went home. I was quite pleased that my investigative technique had gotten some results, contrary to some other techniques I'd recently observed. Which I fully intended to mention to Mr. Pickens.

Chapter 11

I hurried back across the parking lot, watching out for the pastor's stakes and strings so I wouldn't break my neck, and thinking to myself that it was past time for him to get a call to another church. It'd been my experience that the Lord never called a preacher to a smaller, less affluent congregation than the one he was in, it being plain that the Lord believes in progress and upward mobility as much as any American. But would you ever get a preacher to admit to such a thing? No, you wouldn't. I've heard preacher after preacher in my day get up in the pulpit and with a long face and sadness dripping from his words announce that the Lord had called him elsewhere. He acts as if it's a matter of great regret to him, as if he's making a huge sacrifice to obey the Lord's leading and accept a call to a larger church and a bigger salary. Have you ever noticed that?

I decided then and there that if Pastor Ledbetter kept on at me to contribute to a monument to his pastorate and if he didn't relocate same from in front of my house and if he said one more word against Hazel Marie, I was going to see if I couldn't arrange a call from the Lord. I knew some Presbyterians in a large church down in South Carolina who were looking for a preacher. A note to the effect that Pastor Ledbetter might be open to a move should do the trick. I might even be open to contributing to the salary they were offering, just to get him away from here. If I could get away with it.

When I opened the kitchen door, Lillian started up from her

chair with a face as long and mournful as the ones I'd been thinking about.

" 'Bout time you got yo'self back here," she said. "I been worriet sick."

"What's going on? Have you heard from her?" I took off my coat and hung it up. "Little Lloyd gone to bed?"

"Yessum, he already down, an' I hope don't no deputies an' the like try to come an' get him. An', no'm, I ain't heard from Miss Hazel Marie, but I heard from somebody else."

Tears welled up in her eyes, and my heart skipped a beat. "Who? What's happened, Lillian?"

"Deputy Bates, he come by not long after you left. An' he say he know you been lookin' for him, an' I tell him Miss Hazel Marie missin' an' that's what you want with him. He say he already heard that an' he got somethin' important to talk to you 'bout, an' him an' that Lieutenat Peavey want to see you down at the sheriff's at eight o'clock in the morning an' it have to do with Miss Hazel Marie."

"Oh, dear Lord." I took hold of the counter and hung on to it. "What in the world does that mean? Did he say?"

"No'm, well, kinda, but he say he have to talk to you. I mean, he real businesslike, come to the front do' an' all, an' he jes' say it serious."

"Wait a minute, let me get this straight. Was Deputy Bates looking for Little Lloyd like Deputy Daly was?"

"That's what I thought, an' I was gettin' scared, 'cause I don't know I can tell Deputy Bates a bareface lie. But he didn't ast, an' I didn't bring it up. He say he need to talk to you 'bout Miss Hazel Marie."

"Oh," I gasped, patting my breast, "what could he want to talk about? What if she's in jail somewhere? And Brother Vern found out about it and that's why he filed for custody? But no, how would he know something before the sheriff, and Lieutenant

Peavey didn't know a thing this afternoon." I grabbed a dish towel and started wringing it worse than Lillian ever had, my heart pounding. "But I'll bet you money that Brother Vern knows Hazel Marie can't answer that summons. Why else would he pounce right at this time?" I stopped as a chilling possibility filled my mind. "Oh, Lillian! We could lose that child just like we've lost his mother. He could end up in an orphanage or living in that Cadillac of Brother Vern's, being carted around from one revival to the next." I felt the blood drain from my head as I clutched at the counter again to keep from falling into a dead faint.

"You jes' stop that," Lillian said, grabbing my arm. "This ain't no time to be weakin' down on us. Don't matter what Brother Vern knows or don't know, what we got to do is keep Little Lloyd safe somewheres. Then we can find out the rest of it." She gave my arm a shake. "You hear me, now."

"Yes, you're right. I'm all right now." And I was, knowing that it was entirely up to me, and I determined to be entirely up to it. I took a deep breath. "What I have to do is brace myself for whatever Lieutenant Peavey and Coleman have to tell me, and figure out what kind of story to tell them if they straight out ask me where Little Lloyd is."

"If they got something bad to tell you 'bout Miss Hazel Marie, you gonna be so done in you not be able to tell 'em anything."

"Well, that's true," I said, with some relief that I wouldn't be put on the spot with maintaining a lie. Then I sank down in a chair. "Oh, my word, Lillian, I don't want to get out of it that way. No, no, I'm not even going to plan for that. I'm going to get my story straight and stick to it." I straightened up with a new thought. "I know! I'll tell them Little Lloyd went with Wilson T. and his mother to the movies, and he's been missing as long as they have. That'll do it."

"Then they gonna ast you why you didn't say so when you reported his mama missin'."

"Oh. Well, I'll think of something. Which brings me to the problem of thinking of something, or some*where,* to really hide him. We can't keep him here, with me planning to be gone all tomorrow with Mr. Pickens. Who knows, Brother Vern could get a search warrant and snatch him out of here." I rubbed my forehead as all kinds of dire possibilities roiled around behind it. "Lillian, I'm beginning to get an idea."

"What kind you gettin'?"

"I'm getting an idea of putting that child where nobody'll think to look, and if I can manage it, Lillian, I'm going to lie through my teeth about it. Although I don't think this kind of thing is really a lie, do you? I mean, when you're doing it for somebody else's good?"

"I don't know 'bout that, but it don't worry me none. Where you gonna put him?"

"I better not tell you. I don't want you to be in a situation where you have to lie, too. The less you know, the better."

"You don't think I can lie as good as you?" She glared at me like I'd insulted her. Maybe I had.

"That's not it. I just thought you'd rather not have to lie about it. I mean, Lillian, when that Lieutenant Peavey looks at you through those dark glasses of his, well, it makes you want to beg him to let you confess."

"Well, you right 'bout that. I tell you what, don't tell me now, but if I ast you again, you go ahead an' tell me."

"Count on it, as Mr. Pickens says. And that reminds me, he'll be over here early tomorrow morning to go through Hazel Marie's things, just when I have to be in Lieutenant Peavey's office. Give him this information on Wilson T. that I just finagled out of the pastor," I said, handing her a sheet of paper where I'd copied down Wilson T.'s personal statistics. "And let Mr. Pickens look wherever he wants to except in my room, where I want you to keep Little Lloyd, and don't let Mr. Pickens leave till I get back."

"How I gonna keep a grown man around if he want to go?"

"Tell him the truth, Lillian, which is always the best policy." She frowned at me. "You know what I mean, it's the best policy except in cases where it's better not to. He'll need to know whatever I find out, though, since it has to do with Hazel Marie, and she's the one he's looking for. Just don't say anything to him about Little Lloyd's problem."

"You want me to hide Little Lloyd from him?"

"Yes, pretend he's in school. It shouldn't even come up, if you don't say anything. Let him assume the child's not around."

"Look like you don't trust him too good."

"Oh, I do. It's just that I don't know how *legal* he feels he has to be. I'm sure not going to keep a secret from Sam and Binkie and Coleman, and then tell a perfect stranger who might turn right around and hand Little Lloyd over to the sheriff. I've got to feel Mr. Pickens out first. If he's like me and you, he'll keep a secret no matter how illegal it is. But if he's not, well, we'll keep him in the dark, and do what we have to do by ourselves."

"Well, I hope you figure out what it is we have to do by ourselves. And do it before mornin' comes which, if you ast me, ain't too long in comin'."

"You're right. You are staying over, aren't you?"

"I'm not about to leave with all this goin' on. I already got that cot made up in the spare bedroom."

"Lillian, for pity's sake, use the bed. You don't need to be pulling your back out, sleeping on a cot. Now let's turn these lights off and go on up."

After I made sure Lillian would sleep in the bed by taking the covers off the cot, I went into my room. I looked down on Little Lloyd, all scrunched up on the far side of my bed, and felt the anger well up in me at the idea of Brother Vern getting his greedy hands on the child. He didn't want him for any other reason than the money Wesley Lloyd had left, and I didn't see how in the world any judge wouldn't see that right off the bat.

I tucked the covers up around Little Lloyd more tightly and smoothed his hair down where it stuck up in the back. He moaned a little in his sleep, dreaming, I guessed, of all the troubles piled on top of him.

I stood by the side of the bed and silently promised him that nobody was going to take him away from his mother or, if she couldn't be found—which made my heart sink—from me. I'd take the both of them to Canada or even to Timbuktu if that's what it came down to.

Chapter 12

I declare, I didn't think I'd be able to sleep with another person in bed with me. I'd gotten so used to sleeping alone since Wesley Lloyd had been put to rest in the Good Shepherd Memorial Cemetery, that I doubted I'd get any rest at all. Having the bed all to myself made getting into it something to look forward to. Not having the covers jerked off or being kicked during somebody else's nightmare or made to suffer through hours of ear-splitting snores seemed to me to be one of the blessings of widowhood. I'd said as much to a more recent widow of my acquaintance, trying to show her the bright side of her situation, and she'd said none of that had ever bothered her because the cuddling she got more than made up for it.

I wasn't able to judge one way or the other, since Wesley Lloyd had never been the cuddling type.

I crawled into bed beside Little Lloyd, and he hardly stirred. I lay there for a while, fuming over Brother Vern and Pastor Ledbetter and worrying about Hazel Marie. And then switched to wondering what Lieutenant Peavey and Coleman were going to pile on me the next morning, and trying to get all my stories straight in my mind. Laying part of the burden before the Lord, I told him that he was just going to have to look out for Hazel Marie by himself, while I made sure of Little Lloyd's safety. When that was taken care of, I'd be happy to take up Hazel Marie again.

To that effect, I began going over what we needed to do to keep the child occupied while Mr. Pickens, or whoever else dropped by, was in the house. Schoolbooks, I thought, and sat bolt upright in the bed. Lord, his schoolbooks were in his room, which if anybody noticed, especially that sharp-eyed Mr. Pickens or Lieutenant Peavey, or Coleman for that matter, they'd know the boy was neither in school nor had he spent the night with a friend.

I got up and put on my robe and slippers, shivering in the cold since the furnace automatically cooled down during the night hours, and slipped across the hall to Little Lloyd's room. I dared not turn on a light, for fear that Deputy Daly or somebody was watching, but there was enough glow from the church's safety lights and the street lamp for me to make my way to his desk. I gathered up his books and notebook and backpack, and tiptoed back across the hall. I slid them all under my bed and had my robe halfway off when I thought of something else.

I hurried as quietly as I could past the room where Lillian slept, and crept down the stairs. Feeling my way into the kitchen, I took the boy's coat and toboggan cap off the hook by the door, and carried them with me back up the stairs.

Back in my room with the door shut, I hung them in my closet, then sat down for a minute to decide if there was anything else out in plain view that would give away his whereabouts.

There was. I went back across the hall to his bathroom and got his toothbrush, comb and a washcloth that was still damp, and took them with me. And while I was at it, got a change of clothes for him for the next day. Lord, when you set out to lie, you have to think of every little thing.

When I finally crawled back into bed, I didn't think I'd sleep a wink, what with having traipsed all over the house in the dark and having Little Lloyd mumbling and moaning in his sleep and having so many worries on my own mind.

But I did. In fact, I got a good night's sleep, which just goes to show that your conscience won't bother you if you know you're in the right.

———

I was ready to leave for my meeting with Lieutenant Peavey and Deputy Bates by seven-thirty the next morning. Lillain fussed at me for not eating any breakfast but, I declare, I was too nervous to risk putting anything on my stomach. Coffee was all I could stand, and even that was sloshing around in a threatening sort of way.

"Now, Lillian," I said, smoothing on my gloves. I'd dressed with extra care that morning, wearing a fox fur hat and one of my Sunday woolens under my new winter-white cashmere coat with a fox fur collar. It was the kind of ensemble that LuAnne called a CCC—country club, church and cemetery outfit. One that was suitable for all the ceremonies of life, and I figured that being summoned to a conference at the sheriff's department qualified for ceremonial attire. Besides, I wanted Lieutenant Peavey to know I was somebody he shouldn't be messing with, although not much had stopped him in the past. "Be sure and see that Little Lloyd stays behind closed doors. And don't let anybody in the house but Mr. Pickens. I don't care who comes to the door."

"How I gonna know who he is?" She was spooning grits onto a plate for Little Lloyd. A tray with a glass of milk and a plate of biscuits waited on the counter.

"You won't have any trouble recognizing him," I said, as I pinned my hat on more firmly. "Just look for a big, black mustache and he'll be behind it. Besides, Lillian, he'll have identification, and he drives a beat-up black two-door car with a loud motor. You can't miss him. He's one of those men who take up a lot more space than their size justifies. Although he's big enough to begin with."

She grunted, frowning at my description, then wiped her

hands on a dish towel and came over to the counter where I was standing. "What you reckon that lieutenant and Coleman gonna tell you 'bout Miss Hazel Marie? I'm jes' so worriet, I can't hardly think what kinda news they got. An' after I get so roiled up 'bout that, I start worryin' 'bout them wantin' to take Little Lloyd."

"I know what you mean, and I'm sick about it too. But I can't put off facing them any longer. At least we'll know what we have to contend with." I took a deep breath and headed for the door. "We have to depend on each other, Lillian, and I'm depending on you to keep Little Lloyd hidden and to keep Mr. Pickens here till I get back. Be sure and give him that information I got from the pastor, so he can start tracing Wilson T. Well, I'm going now. Wish me luck."

"Yessum, and me too. We both gonna need it."

———

Coleman came out to the pitiful waiting room at the sheriff's department to meet me. He touched me on the arm to draw me aside before we headed for Lieutenant Peavey's office, and said, "Lillian told me last night about Hazel Marie. Have you heard anything from her yet?"

"Not one word. Oh, Coleman, I am so worried."

He frowned, glanced down the hall and apologized for not being able to meet with me the day before, saying he'd been on a raid. Then he said, "Things're getting messy, Miss Julia. I wasn't here when Brother Vern came in yesterday, but I heard about it. Everybody's talking about how he went to the clerk of court's office, demanding immediate action, saying that Hazel Marie's not caring for the boy and that Lloyd needed to be in protective custody. Then he came over here to see that we served the papers right away." He stopped and looked straight at me. "Then I heard that you'd come in yesterday to report Hazel Marie missing. That was not good news, Miss Julia, because it gave Brother Vern's claims credibility. At least, a judge might see it that way. I hate to tell you this, but you'll have to give up the boy temporarily. At least until his mother gets back to answer the complaint and prove her fitness as a parent, which we can all testify to. Where is Lloyd, anyway?"

"He spent the night with somebody," I said. Which was as true a statement as I'd ever made.

"We'll be picking him up this morning. I'm just as sorry as I can be about it, but we're required by law to do it when a complaint like this is made. Now, Miss Julia, don't get upset. Once Hazel Marie appears before the judge, the whole thing won't amount to a hill of beans. She's just got to get back here for the hearing. And, ah, that may present a problem, which is what Lieutenant Peavey wants to talk to you about."

Lord, I'd never seen Coleman so serious in my life. What was coming through to me was that, without Hazel Marie, Brother Vern could have Little Lloyd impounded in his care. All I could do at the time was clutch my pocketbook to my bosom and try to temper my pulse as the blood pounded in my head. I nodded at Coleman, unable to get a word out, and followed him on down the hall.

Knocking once on Lieutenant Peavey's office door, Coleman opened it and waited for me to precede him. I did, to be greeted by the lieutenant who, to my surprise, stood and welcomed me. He gestured to the chair in front of his desk and asked me to be seated. I did, as Coleman took a chair at the side of the desk.

The three of us sat for a few moments waiting, it seemed to me, for somebody to open the show. I certainly wasn't going to do it, since I'd been the one summoned and, besides, I'd come of my own accord the day before and gotten nowhere for my trouble. Not to mention the fact that Lieutenant Peavey's unexpected courtesy was scaring me to death.

"Mrs. Springer," Lieutenant Peavey began, "you reported a Hazel Marie Puckett missing yesterday."

It wasn't a question, but I answered it anyway. "I did."

"Have you heard from her?"

"Not since the telephone call I told you about and which you said indicated she wasn't missing."

He squirmed just a little in his chair. "Well, just to refresh my memory, you reported that she went off with a," he paused to consult a folder in front of him, "Wilson T. Hodge on Wednesday night and, other than the phone call, you've not seen or heard from her since. Correct?"

"Why? Have you found her?" My heart began to thud, as I waited to be told that she'd been found in a condition I didn't want to think about. Then, just as I thought I was beginning to hyperventilate, I reassured myself that Coleman wouldn't've let me learn of it this way. He'd have come to the house and stayed until I got there. He'd have been there to comfort Little Lloyd and me. Or certainly he'd've prepared me for the worst out in the hall. No, I told myself, they haven't found her; this little meeting had to be about something else.

"No, we haven't found her," Lieutenant Peavey said, scanning the papers in the folder again. "A coupla questions, Mrs. Springer, before we get to her whereabouts. First off, when was the last time you saw her?"

"Night before last. She left to go to dinner and a movie with Wilson T. Hodge." I thought I'd already told him that.

He wrote something on his paper, then, without looking up, asked, "She a race fan?"

"What?"

"Does she go to the races? NASCAR races? Make a little bet now and again?"

"I should say not!" If I could've sat up any straighter, I would have. "Hazel Marie's a fine, Christian woman who neither races nor gambles. What in the world makes you ask such a question?"

He and Coleman exchanged glances, then he said, "Deputy Bates, here, has something to show you. Deputy?"

Coleman took a small plastic bag from the side of the desk, opened it, and spilled a tiny gold something or other out on the desk in front of me. "You recognize this, Miss Julia?"

I bent down to look at the thing, glanced up at the worried frown on Coleman's face and wondered if mine was giving anything away. "What is it?" I asked, playing for time.

"Looks like a charm from a bracelet," Coleman said, "or maybe a pendant from a necklace. Could it be Hazel Marie's?"

I wasn't ready to commit myself, not knowing where they'd found it nor what its presence in their possession meant to Hazel Marie's welfare. I wished Mr. Pickens or Binkie or Sam was there to advise me but, as usual, I was left to take care of everything myself.

"I'm not sure," I said, reaching out to touch the little thing with my finger, turning it right side up. Yes, there was the opal on the top of the miniature baby shoe. "Where did you find it?"

Lieutenant Peavey shifted in his chair. I gasped with a sudden thought. "You didn't find it in a wreck, did you? Oh, Lord, Coleman, it didn't come from some poor woman so mashed up in a wreck that you couldn't recognize her?"

"No, no, Miss Julia," Coleman said, reaching out to hold my hand. "Don't think that. It didn't come from a wreck, and it wasn't taken from a body. It was found in a warehouse that we raided yesterday, along with some incriminating evidence of a crime that was committed in another jurisdiction. We're just trying to trace the owner of this, hoping for a lead."

"Well," I said, keeping my expression as neutral as possible and pretending that the thought of Hazel Marie being in the midst of incriminating evidence had not shaken me to my core. It was a settled fact that I'd never admit recognizing the charm as the one

I'd given Hazel Marie to commemorate Little Lloyd's birthday last October. She loved the clash and jangle of the charm bracelet I'd started for her soon after the two of them moved in with me. "You're on the wrong track then. Hazel Marie's not the criminal type, but I know a few who are. What kind of evidence are you talking about, and who does it incriminate?"

"Whoever owns this." Lieutenant Peavey was bad for giving short answers. He stared at me through those dark glasses like he could see right into my mind and read the thoughts that I was trying to keep from him. "All we need to know now is, do you recognize it as belonging to the person you reported missing?"

"I didn't exactly *report* her missing," I corrected him. "I *told* you she was missing, but you refused to make a report."

"Look," he said, hunching those huge shoulders over the desk. "I need some straight answers. This thing," he poked it with a finger twice as wide as the charm, "was found in a warehouse at Jessup Mountain in the southern part of this county, along with some pieces of computer disks that were stolen a few days ago from a well-known NASCAR driver down in Rockingham. Now, the Rockingham deputies notified us that they'd found a monogrammed baseball cap at the scene of the crime that was apparently left by one of the thieves. That cap points directly to the race team who had their shop set up in the warehouse here, which means somebody in our jurisdiction was involved in, or knows something about, the Rockingham theft. Namely, the owner of this trinket."

"Wait," I said, acting confused and trying to put him in the same condition. "Are you saying that this," I pointed at the charm, "was stolen in Rockingham? Or found in Rockingham? Or that Hazel Marie lost a cap? Why, she doesn't even own a baseball cap."

"No, that's not what I'm saying." Lieutenant Peavey looked peeved. He hiked himself up in his chair and spoke slowly and deliberately. "Look, Mrs. Springer, we're dealing with two racing teams." He counted on his fingers, so I'd be sure to follow him. "One is a big, famous operation in Rockingham, and that's the one that was robbed. The other team has two shops, one in Rockingham and one here at the Jessup Mountain warehouse. We found this thing," he pointed to the charm, "in the warehouse *here,* along with some broken computer disks that'd been stolen from the first shop *there.* The Rockingham sheriff found a cap in the shop that was robbed, and that cap had the logo of the team located here. You following me? They're connected in some way, is what I'm saying."

I tried to look addled, which wasn't hard considering my state of mind. Lieutenant Peavey frowned, then carried on. "Whoever owns this trinket," he said, "may know something that will lead to an arrest and the recovery of the other stolen goods. You reported a woman missing during the very time the warehouse was being raided and, if you can identify this as hers, it'll give us a direction to go in."

I was stunned, to say the least. I looked at Coleman, hoping for a little help and he responded.

"Miss Julia, you need to understand," he said, in a calming sort of way. "This is big. The disks and some other valuable stuff was stolen from Jerry Johnson. You ever heard of him?" I shook my head, unable to speak. "Well, he's a big-name NASCAR race driver, and he's got friends all over. The media's giving it a big play, especially since something we *didn't* recover is important to his career."

Things were taking a turn that I didn't at all like. I couldn't understand why the loss of this Jerry Johnson's material goods was getting more concern than my loss of Hazel Marie, nor how her charm had turned up where crooks had hung out. I needed to get home and place it all in the hands of my own investigator.

"If this thing," Lieutenant Peavey said, poking the charm again, "belongs to the woman you reported missing, then she's a suspect and we need her in here for questioning."

"A *suspect?*" I shrieked, jumping up from my chair. "Now see here, Lieutenant, I'm not going to sit here and have you accuse a woman who's not here to defend herself of a crime. The woman's in trouble, and all you can do is try to connect her to some criminal activity, when all she's done is not come home when she should've. Through no fault of her own, I am convinced."

"Miss Julia," Coleman said, standing with me and putting an arm around my shoulders. "That's not what we're doing. I'm concerned about Hazel Marie too, and all we want to know is whether she might've been at a place where evidence of a crime was found. She could've been there weeks ago and lost it then. She's not being accused of anything. We just want to question her and try to find some answers."

I stepped away and pulled myself together. "Well, that may well be, but I can't go so far as to definitely identify the charm as hers. The fact of the matter is, half the women in town own jewelry of this nature."

Lieutenant Peavey sighed like he was tired of fooling with me, and said, "We know that, Mrs. Springer, but half the women in town haven't been reported missing. Do you know of any reason this Hazel Marie Puckett would've been at the Jessup Mountain warehouse?"

"I do not." That was one question I could answer with assurance. "It's not hers, if that's all you have to go on. She was with Wilson T. Hodge when she left my house, and a man like that wouldn't be caught dead in a place where he might get his hands dirty."

I stopped and bit my lip again. "You didn't find him dead, did you?"

"We didn't find anybody, dead or otherwise," the lieutenant

said, as if he hated to admit it. In fact, it looked as if it was all he could do to keep from grinding his teeth.

"Well, Wilson T. Hodge's the one you ought to be looking for. Find him and you'll find Hazel Marie. Although, I don't know what she could tell you about this." I waved my hand toward the charm, as if it didn't start my heart pounding every time I looked at it.

"Well, we're going to get to the bottom of it," he snapped. And this time I heard his teeth scrape together. "One way or the other. Now tell me more about this Hodge. Where can we locate him?"

"I wish I knew. According to Pastor Ledbetter of the First Presbyterian Church, Mr. Hodge is in Charlotte but, as far as I'm concerned, he better not be. But the pastor can tell you more about Wilson T. Hodge than I can, and I know he'd be happy to assist you."

It couldn't hurt to spread the lieutenant's attention around a little. I sank back into my chair and leaned my head in my hand. "This is so upsetting," I said. "I'm sorry I'm not being much help to you, but so much worry . . . I'm not as young as I once was and I'm not handling all this too well." I sniffed, and rummaged in my pocketbook for a Kleenex.

Coleman was immediately solicitous, leaning over me and telling me not to worry. Lieutenant Peavey, when I peeked at him, didn't seem impressed.

Chapter 13

"I think I'd better go home now," I quavered, holding on to Coleman and rising to my feet. "I have these weak spells, don't you know. The medication helps a little."

The only medication I was on was an aspirin every now and again, and a dose of Metamucil when I needed it, but they didn't need to know that. Especially since Coleman was worried enough to offer to drive me home. I hated pulling the wool over his eyes, but I had to get out of there before Lieutenant Peavey asked any more questions. I didn't quite make it.

"Mrs. Springer," Lieutenant Peavey said, standing to his full height. "Sorry you're not feeling well, but there's one more thing. Ms. Puckett's son, where is he?"

I stopped and leaned against Coleman, afraid to turn around and face the man. "Right at this minute, I don't know, Lieutenant," I whispered shakily. "But I'm sure I can put my hands on him later today. Let's hope so, anyway."

I felt Coleman stiffen. "Is Lloyd missing too? Why didn't you tell me?"

Lord, I hated to lie to him, and I tried my best not to. "I kept trying to reach you yesterday. I wanted to talk to you, and oh, Coleman, you just don't know."

Lieutenant Peavey frowned. "You didn't say anything about a missing child yesterday."

"You didn't give me a chance," I snapped. Then, afraid I'd

given myself away, I wiped my eyes and whispered, "I wasn't sure. I assumed he was in school, but . . . Oh, Coleman, I don't know how I can bear up under this strain." I cried as best as I could manage.

Lieutenant Peavey frowned some more and when he finally spoke, I detected some concern in his voice. "You know we have a court order to remove the child." He thought for a little, then went on, "Maybe that's why they're both missing."

"I don't think so, Lieutenant," Coleman said. "Miss Julia reported Ms. Puckett missing before her uncle filed the complaint."

"You're right, Coleman," I said before the lieutenant could respond. "She went missing Wednesday night, and Deputy Daly showed up at my house with his papers late yesterday. According to him, the complaint had just been made, so she couldn't've known about it. And, Coleman, that deputy said he was there to snatch and grab Little Lloyd. Can he do that? Are you going to let him do that?"

I heard Lieutenant Peavey make some kind of irritated noise down in his throat. "That's a term that shouldn't've been used. Deputy Daly is new on the force, so just ignore what he said. But a complaint's been filed, so we're obligated to pick up the child. He'll be held in protective custody until his mother appears to present her side. Then a judgment'll be rendered."

A hot flame surged through me at the idea of North Carolina laws that let a conniving you-know-what like Brother Vern make unfounded claims and tear up all our lives. I made an effort to control myself so Coleman, who was still letting me lean against him, wouldn't notice. "Lieutenant Peavey," I said, as pitifully as I could, "how's his mother going to answer anything if she can't be found?"

Lieutenant Peavey wouldn't let go of anything, in spite of my weakened condition. He shrugged just enough to make me want to smack him. "That's a problem, from her viewpoint, but we're responsible to the court. He'll be picked up as soon as he's located, with or without his mother."

Coleman nodded, but I could tell he wasn't happy about it. He knew how much Little Lloyd meant to me and Lillian, to say nothing of his mother. I scrunched up my shoulders and headed for the door, wanting out of there before I heard any more distressing news.

"Mrs. Springer," the lieutenant said, stopping me again just as I thought I was on my way. "What about the private investigator you asked me about?"

I didn't know what to tell him, so deep in lies by that time that I didn't know which end was up. So I hedged. "I have an appointment with him this morning." Which was the absolute truth.

"You don't need to do that, Miss Julia," Coleman said. "Let us take care of it. We'll find them both, and quicker than any private agency can."

"Well, if you think you can," I said, letting him think whatever he wanted to. "I just know that Lieutenant Peavey recommended a Mr. Pickens, and I know Lieutenant Peavey wouldn't steer me wrong. I was just doing what the lieutenant seemed to think was the best thing to do, but if he's changed his mind, I'll talk to Mr. Pickens this morning."

With that, I finally got out of the office and headed toward the front door. Coleman followed me, offering a ride, concerned about my condition, telling me they'd do everything they could, and that I didn't need to worry myself.

Hah, was all I could think, but didn't say. Coleman had a good heart, but he was a signed and sworn deputy sheriff and, as such, limited by the law. I was neither.

Thanking him, I assured him my car was near and that I could make it home all right, and that I had complete trust in the Abbot County Sheriff's Department.

Alone in my car at last, all I could think about was whether Mr. Pickens was waiting for me at the house. I needed him worse than I had at anytime before.

———

I hurried into the house through the kitchen door, having left my car half off the driveway in my agitation. Lillian was setting a plate of hot cinnamon rolls before Mr. Pickens, who was sitting at the table with a cup of coffee in front of him. They both turned to me as I entered.

"Mr. Pickens," I cried. "I'm so glad you're here. I've got news, and you need to do something about it right away."

I hung up my coat and went on before either of them could speak. "Lillian, pour some more of that coffee and sit down with us."

I pulled out a chair and plopped down, wondering where to start. Mr. Pickens just waited, watching me from under his black eyebrows.

While I tried to get my breath, he reached across and patted my hand. "Take it easy, hon. Don't get yourself in a tizzie; just tell me what you found out."

To my mind, I had enough reason to get into two or three tizzies, but I let it go and told them about the charm that the police had found.

Mr. Pickens frowned, and Lillian asked, "Was it Miss Hazel Marie's?"

"Of course it was. Don't you remember, I had it custom made with Little Lloyd's birthstone. They found it at that warehouse they raided, which turned out to be a place of racing criminals, so I didn't let on that I recognized it. And, Mr. Pickens, it was *broken*. I mean, the little gold link that held it to her bracelet was pulled apart." I grasped the edge of the table, wanting him to reassure me. "That doesn't mean what I think it does, does it?"

"Let's don't jump to conclusions," he said, sounding too calm to suit me. "It could mean that it'd been loose and just dropped off there. It could mean that she snagged it on something and it fell off by itself. It could mean a lot of things but, if you're sure it's hers, it does mean that she was there at some time, but not necessarily in the past few days."

"No, she was there recently, I just know it. Because, if she'd lost it before this, she'd've said something about it. She loved that charm. She'd've turned the house upside down, crying and looking for it, wouldn't she, Lillian? So, no, Mr. Pickens, she had to've lost it sometime since she's been gone. The problem is, I can't for the life of me figure out what she'd've been doing with a racing team down in the southern wilds of the county. I mean, there's nothing down there but woods and thickets and dirt roads. And hunters and marijuana patches. Oh, Lord," I moaned, thinking of men with rifles and machetes, and I didn't know what all.

"Thay Lord," Lillian said, sinking into a chair. "What that pore woman doin' down there with them mean folks?"

Mr. Pickens hunched over the table, twirling a spoon while he thought about it. At least I hoped he was giving it some thought. He glanced up at me, and said, "No reason at all for her to be down there? She's not into racing?"

"I should say not. Lieutenant Peavey asked the same thing. I don't know what she could've been doing in such a place. In fact, I don't know what *anybody* would be doing there."

"Peavey didn't tell you anything else? Why the cops raided the Jessup Mountain shop in the first place?"

"Well, now that you mention it, he did. Not that I understood it all, but he said there'd been a theft from some big-time race-car driver in Rockingham, and one of the thieves lost his cap. In a hurry to get away, I guess. But some way or another, that cap pointed to the Jessup Mountain racing team, which is why the Rockingham deputies told our deputies to raid the place. All of which culminated in finding Hazel Marie's charm, along with some broken computer disks that'd been stolen, too. And from that little coincidence, Lieutenant Peavey called Hazel Marie a suspect and wants to question her. Can you believe that?"

"Jessup Mountain," Lillian said, slowly rising from her chair. "I jes' think of something." She walked over to the counter by the refrigerator and picked up the morning paper. "Look at this here," she said, holding out the front page.

And there it was, making headlines: DEPUTIES RAID RACE SHOP, with a grainy picture of a large low-slung building with a sign over the door that I couldn't make out. Lillian spread the paper out on the table so Mr. Pickens could read it with me. I skimmed the article, leaned back in my chair and said, "Well, I never."

But Mr. Pickens read every word, the frown on his face growing deeper and more solemn. "Jerry Johnson," he said, almost to himself. "How 'bout that."

"Yes, they mentioned that name. He's the one the thieves stole the disks from, although why anybody'd go to the trouble of breaking in for those things, I wouldn't know. Hazel Marie certainly wouldn't, I can tell you that. Some other things were stolen from him, too, but they didn't say what."

"Says here," Mr. Pickens said, as he ran his finger down the article, "there was some heavy-duty vandalism, and a lot of tools and equipment were taken. Those disks you're talking about had chassis set-up data on them."

"What that mean?" Lillian asked.

"Well, see, all the NASCAR speedways have different lengths, degrees of banking and so on. You have to know what they are so you can calibrate the amount of rpm's, horsepower and torque in your engines to conform to each track. Like, for instance, you'd need high horsepower and low torque for the Atlanta Speedway, but high torque and low horsepower for Bristol."

Lillian and I looked at him like he was speaking in tongues.

I shook my head, not a bit interested in mechanical engineering. "That's all well and good, but it doesn't have a thing to do with Hazel Marie. I mean, I'm sorry this Jerry Johnson, whoever he is, had his disks stolen. But he can buy more where they came from, whereas she can't ever be replaced. I can't understand why everybody's so exercised over his problem, putting it in the newspaper and all, and not even raising an eyebrow about Hazel Marie being missing."

"Look here," Mr. Pickens said, pointing to a paragraph. "Jerry's quoted as saying the theft and vandalism were done to cover up something else, but he doesn't say what. Listen to this, 'When I come in and found what they'd done, I knew the sorry rascals wanted to knock me out of the points race. But I know my fans're behind me, and they can count on my Number 17 truck being in Phoenix, come next weekend.'" Mr. Pickens shook his head and said, "Poor ole Jerry. He'll be climbing the walls over this. But I'll say this, Lieutenant Peavey's right. There is a connection between your lady and what happened to him. Got to be, if her charm and his disks were found at the same place."

"I don't like the sound of that," I said. "Mr. Pickens, Hazel Marie wouldn't steal a thing if her life depended on it. Would she, Lillian?"

"No'm, she wouldn't. But Mr. Pickens got a head start on them deputies, 'cause he know that charm belong to Miss Hazel Marie, an' they don't. Lieutenant Peavey, the only reason he ax you questions about her is 'cause you tole him she been missin', an' I 'spect he axin' 'bout everybody else missin' in town, too."

"I hope you're right, Lillian," I said, knowing there couldn't be that many more people missing from Abbotsville. There were a gracious plenty of thieves, though, so Lieutenant Peavey had his work cut out for him. I hoped it'd keep him busy enough to forget about Hazel Marie. "Mr. Pickens," I said, leaning toward him, "do you know this Jerry Johnson person?"

"Yeah, I know Jerry." Mr. Pickens gave me a crooked smile. "Have for years, ever since I did a little dirt-track racing back in my younger days. He's a good man, and other teams'll help him get ready for the next race. I'd like to help him, too, and maybe I can. We've got a missing woman and he's had a theft, and we know they're tied together."

"That's fine, if they are," I told him, somewhat troubled by his admitting to having been a racer himself. I didn't see that as exactly a high-class recommendation, but I didn't say anything. "Just as long as you don't get your priorities mixed up. Your first concern, Mr. Pickens, is Hazel Marie, and I don't want you to forget it."

"I'm not likely to," he said, with a wry twist of his mouth. "But it won't hurt us to do what we can for Jerry. He's special to a lot of people, including the governor and some state senators. Wouldn't surprise me if he decided to run for office one of these days."

"Well, that's real interesting," I said, having heard as much as I cared to about Jerry Johnson. "But I can't see what any of it has to do with Hazel Marie. Especially this NASCAR thing everybody seems to be mentioning. What is that anyway?"

"Winston Cup?" he said, raising his eyebrows. "Busch Grand National?"

"Sorry." I shook my head. "I neither smoke nor drink."

He flashed me a quick grin, shaking his head. "Your education is sadly lacking, Miss Julia. You don't mind me calling you that, do you, hon?"

"I don't care what you call me, but now is not the time for

niceties. Let's get serious here." I realized with a pang how quickly time was passing, and I'd still not done one thing about hiding Little Lloyd. I stared hard at Lillian and lifted my eyes to the ceiling, trying to ask her how he was doing. She frowned at me and mouthed, "What? What?"

I gave up, and said to Mr. Pickens, "I think it's time for you to be doing something."

"Don't rush me. I'm thinking. Which means I'm doing something." He ignored my skeptical look. "I've not been able to track them, since neither of them has used a credit card in the past twenty-four hours. And there's nothing in her room that tells me anything, no ticket stubs, no match covers, no letters, no diary or notes of any kind."

"I could've told you that. What's next?"

"I'll get in touch with Jerry, get some details on what happened to him. Then I'll run another credit check on her and Hodge to see if there've been any charges for gas or hotels since I last checked. And I want to feel out some contacts I have in the local law enforcement, as well as the SBI. The paper says the state boys were in on the raid, too."

"Oh, my goodness, that's right. Lord, if the state is looking for Hazel Marie, she's really in trouble. Lillian, I don't think I can stand this."

"Me, neither. But that jes' mean we got to get her outta their way. I don't want them puttin' her down in that Raleigh jailhouse no more'n you do."

"Don't even think it! Mr. Pickens, I assure you, Hazel Marie is not a criminal, and she doesn't know how to race. If she is mixed up in this NASCAR outfit, it wasn't her own doing." I stopped, thinking of all the possibilities. "It had to be Wilson T. Hodge who's got her involved. If she is, which I don't believe for a minute."

"Okay," Mr. Pickens said, "don't ruffle your feathers. I'll find her. Then we'll see what her legal situation is."

"That's exactly what I want to hear. Let's find her and get her out of the situation, legal or otherwise. And do it before the sheriff or those state boys you know can do it. We're counting on you, and it's time you got started on it."

"You want some more coffee?" Lillian asked him, as she reached for the coffee pot.

"No, he doesn't," I said. "Mr. Pickens, you need to get a move on. The time for sitting around thinking is over."

I stood up, reaching for my coat, ready to accompany him on his search for Hazel Marie. He opened his mouth, probably to say I couldn't go, but he didn't get a chance. The front doorbell stopped us all in our tracks.

Lillian and I stared at each other, both of us thinking of the endangered child upstairs.

As the bell sounded again, Mr. Pickens looked from one to the other of us. "You gonna get that?"

"Look and see who it is, Lillian," I said. "But don't let them see you." She headed for the dining room to peek out the window, wringing her hands as she went.

While we waited, I noticed Mr. Pickens's raised eyebrows at our strange behavior, so I said, "I have a friend who drops by and pesters me with her problems. I just don't have time for her this morning. If it's her, we'll just sneak on out."

Lillian pushed back through the swinging door, the whites of her eyes showing. "It's that Lieutenant Peavey and Deputy Daly standin' out there, big as you please. What we gonna do?"

I needed something to hold on to. I clasped the back of the chair, my knuckles white with the strain. Deputy Daly had called in the big guns to help him pick up a sweet, innocent child. I declare, it didn't seem fair.

"Good," Mr. Pickens said, getting to his feet. "I'll talk to Peavey, see what else they have. And let him know I'm working the case, too."

"Sit down, Mr. Pickens," I managed to say. "I have a proposition for you."

Chapter 14

"Mr. Pickens," I went on, gripping the back of the chair hard enough to snap the thing in two, "I don't have time for arguments or explanations. I want you to go on ahead and take Little Lloyd with you. Lillian, run up the back stairs and bring Little Lloyd down that way. Bundle him up good, but hurry and don't make any noise."

She took off, moving faster than I'd given her credit for being able to do.

Mr. Pickens's black eyes followed her, then he turned them on me. "What's going on?"

"I'll explain later. You just take the child to your office and wait for me there." I started out of the kitchen, wanting to smash the bell and whoever's finger was mashing it so hard. "But don't leave until I get those two out there in the living room, so they won't see you. And be quiet about it."

"Wait just a damn minute," Mr. Pickens said, stopping me as I reached the swinging door. "You're not sending that boy with me. I've got things to do."

I heard Lillian's shoes flopping on her heels in the hall upstairs, and knew she was herding Little Lloyd down to the kitchen.

"Watch your language, Mr. Pickens," I said. "The deputies're here to pick up that child, and I'm not going to let them. And you're going to help me and, if you can't see your way clear to protecting a poor, innocent child, well, let it be on your head.

Now I want you to sneak Little Lloyd out to your car, and keep his head down till you're out of town."

"Hold on," Mr. Pickens said, holding up his hand like he was stopping traffic. "I need more than that. Just what're you getting me into?"

Little Lloyd entered from the back stairs, Lillian right behind him, both of their faces showing the strain. Little Lloyd had one arm through his coat sleeve, with Lillian trying to get the other one on him.

"Little Lloyd," I said, ignoring Mr. Pickens for the moment, "you're going with Mr. Pickens. He'll look after you till I can get there. Hurry now." I crossed the room to the back door and eased it open, looking out to see if any other deputies were sneaking around, while the doorbell kept on ringing. "Lillian, go let them in, but keep them in the living room."

"What I gonna tell 'em?"

"Tell them anything. No, wait, tell them I'm indisposed, but you'll go upstairs and see if I'm able to get out of bed. But take your time doing it. That'll give Mr. Pickens time to get Little Lloyd out of here and into his car."

She shuffled off toward the front of the house, calling, "I'm comin', I'm comin'."

Mr. Pickens was still shaking his head, standing there acting as stubborn as a mule. "Taking care of a child is not in my job description. I want to know what's going on."

Well, he just made me so mad. When you employ someone, you expect them to do as they're told. "Truancy, Mr. Pickens," I snapped, saying the first thing that popped in my head. "That's what's going on. The boy's not in school as you can plainly see, and the reason is, he's worried sick about his mother. And instead of looking for her as they ought to be doing, those deputies out there are piddling away their time on such as this. Now, help us out here or return my check."

We glared at each other, with the sound of Lillian opening the front door trickling back to us, and I wondered if I'd gone too far. I didn't want my check back; I wanted Mr. Pickens to do what he was told.

"Look," I said, trying a different tack in spite of the urgency of the moment. "If the boy's cited for truancy, his mother'll have to answer for it. And as you've noticed, she's not here to do any answering. So I'll have to do it for her, and that'll take up time I need to help you find her."

"That's not a bad idea," he said. "Because I'm telling you right now, I'll do what you hired me to do but I'm not going to have you and the boy tagging after me every step of the way. Are we clear on that?"

I steamed for a minute, then decided that it'd be better to let him think he was winning a round. "Very clear, Mr. Pickens. But do this one thing, and I'll come get him as soon as they leave. Then we'll let you find Hazel Marie."

"I'm holding you to that," he said, pointing a finger at me, which made me want to wring it off. But then he turned to Little Lloyd. "Come on then and let's go. Miss Julia, I hope you know what you're doing. I don't want to lose my license for aiding and abetting."

He winked at Little Lloyd, who'd been standing there trying to follow what was going on. I didn't think it necessary to explain to the child the story I'd given Mr. Pickens. He knew why the deputies were looking for him, and I gave him credit for understanding why we didn't need to tell Mr. Pickens what he didn't need to know.

Just as I was shooing them out, Little Lloyd glanced at the newspaper on the table, then stopped on a dime. He reached for it and, pointing at the picture, said, "I know where that is. Mr. Hodge took me and my mama down there one time. Left us in the car while he went in to talk to his cousin. My word, Miss

Julia," he went on, sounding more like me than I did myself at times. "It says it was raided."

"Cousin?" I said.

Mr. Pickens leaned over the boy's shoulder to look again at the picture. "Hodge's cousin owns it?"

"Yessir, and I wanted to go in to see the race trucks, but Mr. Hodge said kids weren't allowed. I know it's the same one 'cause, see, you can just make out THE BIGELOW MOTORSPORTS CENTER right there on the sign, and that's where we went."

Mr. Pickens and I looked at each other, both of us saying "The *big,*" at the same time.

"That's it, Mr. Pickens," I said, relieved and agitated at the same time. "That's what Hazel Marie was trying to tell us. Now you've got something to get your teeth into. So get on out of here and do it."

"It's a start, anyway," he said, still studying the picture.

Voices from the living room drifted back to us, reminding me of our current crisis. I was about to jump out of my skin by that time, so anxious to light a fire under Mr. Pickens that it was all I could do to keep from smacking him out the door.

"You've got to go, Mr. Pickens," I said. "I'll meet you at your office as soon as I've handled the situation here, and we can figure out what to do next."

To my great relief, Mr. Pickens put a hand on Little Lloyd's back and moved toward the door. "My car's on the side street, so we'll go 'round the back of the house. But I hope you understand that I can't do any work if I have to baby-sit."

"Oh, for goodness sake. Little Lloyd's not going to hold you up. It's you who's doing that. Now, go on so I can take care of those two out yonder."

I closed the door behind them and hurried up the back stairs, grateful that I'd changed my mind about giving my room to Hazel Marie. I'd fixed up a bedroom for her downstairs, since it wasn't appropriate for her to be on the same floor as Coleman even though he had eyes only for Binkie and spent most of his time with her. You can't be too careful these days, and I'd not wanted to give anybody cause for talk.

By the time I got to my bedroom, I could hear Lillian calling me as she came up the front stairs. I didn't know what to do, whether to undress and get in bed or just sling a robe over my clothes.

"Miss Julia," Lillian whispered, as she poked her head around my door, her eyes wide with apprehension, "they say they got to look through the house, see if Little Lloyd be here. And they got a warranty that say they can do it."

"A search warrant?" I couldn't believe they'd go that far, which plainly meant that Lieutenant Peavey had not believed me when I'd let him think Little Lloyd was missing too. The idea!

"Oh, Lord, Lillian, quick, look around and see if there's anything that'll give us away."

"His pajamas," she said, pointing to them on my bed.

Footsteps sounded on the stairs, and we gaped at each other. The nerve of them, just taking over my house like it belonged to a common criminal.

"Go," I told her. "Go stop them. Hold them up as long as you can. Tell them I'm sick and they can't come in here."

She left, while I grabbed the pajamas and threw them in the hamper. Looking around the room, I could see no other evidence of Little Lloyd's night there. Then, fearing they'd do more than glance around, I stooped and pulled out the child's books and backpack from under the bed. Taking them with me, I went into the bathroom and put all of Little Lloyd's things in the linen closet, stacking my Charisma Supima cotton sheets over and around them. Then I locked the bathroom door. From inside.

I put the lid down on the commode and sat on it, my hands shaking and my heart racing. I can't stand to hang a gown and robe in full view on the back of a door, but this was one time I wished that's where mine were. I could've undressed with time to spare, but mine were in the clothes closet where I couldn't get to them.

I sat there scared to death, wondering if they'd break down the door and come into a woman's most private place. I could follow their voices and heavy footsteps as Lillian led them across the hall to Little Lloyd's room, then down the hall to Coleman's room. Which he hardly ever used since he'd taken up with Binkie. In fact, it seemed the only time he used it was when he was so starved for a decent meal that he'd show up at my house. Binkie couldn't boil water.

I heard the deep voices and heavy footsteps come toward my room, with Lillian's lighter voice warning them that I was sick as a dog and might be catching. I closed my eyes and held my breath, going over in my mind the things in my room that might draw their attention. Thank goodness, neither Lillian nor I had had time to make my bed. That should prove I was sick.

As I heard them enter the bedroom, I held on to the toilet seat with both hands.

Lillian tapped on the bathroom door. "Miss Julia? You have some gentlemans to see you."

Lord, Lillian, I thought, no gentleman would insist on visiting a woman while she was on the toilet.

I took a deep breath and, in a pitiful-sounding voice, said, "Who is it?"

"Lieutenant Peavey," Lieutenant Peavey said, standing right outside the door. "Sorry to disturb you, Mrs. Springer, but we have a warrant to search the house for the Puckett child."

"Well," I quavered, "he's not in here."

There was a moment of silence, and I wondered what was going on in Lieutenant Peavey's mind. He'd already proven to be the suspicious type.

"Lieutenant?" I called weakly.

"Ma'am?"

"I'm sorry I'm not able to help you. I wasn't feeling well when I left your office, and now it looks like I've picked up that intestinal flu that's been going around. Lillian's just getting over it, but it's gone through both of us like Sherman through Georgia. I hope you don't get it from us."

"Uh, well," he said, as I heard him back away from the door, "I guess we'll have to take that chance. I'll give you a minute, but we have to inspect that room."

I moaned softly, like I was being ravaged by an internal spasm, and said, "Step out in the hall, lieutenant, and I'll do my best to get off this thing."

When I heard them move out of the bedroom, I flushed the commode and dashed for the bed, dress, sweater, shoes and all. Pulling the covers up to my neck, I weakly called them to come back in.

Lieutenant Peavey strode in, glanced at me with a muttered "sorry to bother you," and went into the bathroom. In which he found absolutely nothing that wasn't supposed to be there, even behind the shower curtain. Deputy Daly watched from the hall, clearly uncomfortable at this invasion of a sick woman's privacy. I could tell he'd been raised better than Lieutenant Peavey, who had no such qualms. Or manners, either.

On his way out of the bedroom, Lieutenant Peavey said, "We'll try the school. But if the boy shows up here, you're required to turn him over immediately."

"Yessir," I mumbled, shivering under the covers. "If I'm able."

Then I closed my eyes in relief, as they turned and went down the stairs. When I heard the front door close behind them, I got up and straightened my clothes.

Chapter 15

I met Lillian on the stairs as I was going down and she was on her way up.

She took my arm and said, "Let me he'p you on down."

"Lillian, for goodness sake, I'm not sick."

"Well, you sho' sounded like it. Didn't sound like no playactin' to me."

"Good. Maybe it convinced them too. You're sure they're gone?"

"Yessum, I watched 'em till their car went right on outta sight towards Main Street."

"Good," I said again, relieved that we'd slid past that problem. Now I could turn my attention to Hazel Marie. "Lillian, I'm going on over to Mr. Pickens's office. Thank goodness he's located in south Asheville and out of the sheriff's jurisdiction. I'll just keep Little Lloyd with me all day, and he'll be out of their sight. And their minds, too. I hope."

"What you gonna do with him when you have to come home?"

"I'll worry about that when the time comes. Or maybe," I said, stopping to think through an earlier thought I'd had, "maybe he can stay with Mr. Pickens. Yes, that might do it."

"That Mr. Pickens, he don't act too happy 'bout takin' care of him."

"Making Mr. Pickens happy is not high up on my list. Anyway,

I better get on over there, so we can figure out where Hazel Marie is."

As soon as we reached the kitchen, I didn't stop, just headed straight for my coat, ready to get on the road.

Lillian said, "What I gonna tell them deputies, if they come back again? You s'posed to be sick in the bed."

"Tell them I've gone to the Emergency Room. Nobody could find anybody in that place. Lillian, I'm gone. I'll let you know if we learn anything."

I was halfway out the door when the phone rang. I stopped, fearing it was more bad news but hoping it was Hazel Marie again. Lillian hurried to it, jerking the receiver off before it could ring again.

"Miz Springer's residence," she said, then stopped, listening as the frown on her face deepened. Then her face brightened, and she jumped with excitement, "Yessum, we will. We sho' will."

I hurried over to her, as she thrust the phone at me. "Hello? Hello?" Nothing but static on the line. "Who is this? Hello?"

Then I heard a recorded voice telling me to hang up the phone. I jiggled the receiver, but it did nothing but get me that loud, annoying noise that means a phone is off the hook.

"Lillian, who was it? There wasn't a soul on the line."

"It was Miss Hazel Marie callin', least that's what the operator say. She say, do we accep' a collect call from Hazel Marie, and I say we will, then you take the phone and that's all I hear."

"Oh, Lord, why can't she stay on the line long enough to tell us anything?" I sank down in a chair, just about undone with how close we'd come to learning where she was. "Lillian, was there any hint of where she was calling from?"

"No'm, I done tol' you everything I hear."

"Then I know what to do," I said, picking up the phone again. "I saw this on *The Rockford Files* a long time ago, but it ought to still work." But it didn't. The operator could not be wheedled, cajoled or threatened into telling me anything about where the collect call had originated. I'd get it on my bill at the end of the month, if, she said, the call was actually connected.

"That just beats all," I said, slamming down the phone. "Well, this is where Mr. Pickens can start earning his money."

I dialed his office number, hoping he'd had time to get there but ended up having to leave my message on a recording, which I mortally hate dealing with. I told the machine to tell him to get busy and trace the call we'd received, using whatever special methods he had to get the information, and that I was on my way and would expect some results by the time I got there.

Complaining half under my breath about people who slow-poked around and weren't where they were supposed to be, I finally got on my way to Mr. Pickens's office.

It took me thirty minutes to get to south Asheville and almost another thirty to find his office, which was located in a strip mall between a beauty supply house and an insurance office. A covered sidewalk ran the length of the several shops and offices that faced the highway. When I pulled in and parked, I was relieved to see Mr. Pickens's semblance of a car nearby. I didn't care how much Little Lloyd admired it, it was one step above a rattletrap to my mind and I hoped I'd never have to set foot in it again.

To that end, an idea occurred to me, one that would kill two birds with one stone—keep me from having to ride in it and put Mr. Pickens in my car with us. I wasn't sure how to do it, but Jim Rockford had done it plenty of times so it couldn't be too hard.

Locking my car, I surveyed the area, taking special note of the lack of pedestrian traffic and how close together the cars were parked in front of the shops and offices. Then I slipped between the cars and stooped down beside a front tire of Mr. Pickens's car. Using a ballpoint pen from my pocketbook, I began letting the air out of the tire. Deciding that method would take forever before any evidence showed up, I found my nail file and used a rock to hammer it in between the treads. By the time I got it done, my lower limbs were so stiff I could hardly get back up.

But I did, holding my head high so no one who might be watching would dream that a woman of my caliber could do what I'd just done. Turning toward Mr. Pickens's office, I noted the large window that faced the arcade and the chipped black and gold paint on it that spelled out THE PICKENS AGENCY. Underneath in smaller letters, I read PRIVATE INVESTIGATIONS & DISCREET IN-QUIRIES.

The only thing that could be said for the looks of the place was that at least he didn't operate out of the trunk of his car. As I opened the door and stepped into the unlit reception area, I stood and took it all in. Furnishings can tell you so much about the person who chooses them, but I didn't much like what these were telling me. The whole place was paneled in dark wood, so the first thing I did was reach over and open the blinds. Then sneezed from the dust. One of those nubby-fabric upholstered sofas and a matching chair—you know, the kind with wide wooden arms—took up most of the space. An end table with a brass lamp that I'd seen advertised in a Kmart ad, an artificial tree that looked like nothing that'd ever grown in nature over in the corner, and a magazine rack with gun and car periodicals in it made up the rest of the furnishings. With a decor like that, it was no wonder no one was waiting to see him.

Following the narrow hall off the waiting room, I stopped in the door of a small office in the back. Glancing in, I was pleased to see that it, at least, looked as if some work at some time had been done in it. A large wooden desk, which Mr. Pickens sat be-hind, just about filled the room. File cabinets were lined up along one wall, and a narrow table extended the desk to hold a com-puter and various books. Another table near the door where I stood held a coffee maker, mugs, a bag of sugar and an empty Krispy

Kreme doughnut box. Various plaques, pictures, diplomas and framed official-looking certificates and citations hung wherever there was space on the wall. In contrast to the piles of paper, folders and other odds and ends on all the surfaces in the room, the material on the wall was perfectly aligned and carefully hung. Mr. Pickens had obviously taken a great deal of care to document the progress of his career.

A radio on top of a file cabinet played something that passed for music and, just as I stuck my head in, Little Lloyd asked Mr. Pickens when he thought I'd get there.

"I'm here now," I said, walking into the office, "and I'm glad to see the two of you here too. I tried to get you earlier, Mr. Pickens, when I thought you'd had plenty of time to get here." Mr. Pickens frowned from behind his desk. I'd already figured out that he didn't take criticism too well, even when it was meant for his own good.

"We stopped for a Hardee's biscuit, Miss Julia," Little Lloyd said, his face alive with excitement. "And guess what, we got your message about Mama calling you, and Mr. Pickens used his police contacts and a telephone operator who's a friend of his, and now we know where my mama is!"

I put a hand on the door to steady myself. "Where?"

"Have a seat," Mr. Pickens said, waving at the only unoccupied one in the crowded space. "I traced that collect call to a truck stop off I-85 just east of Gastonia."

"My word," I said, collapsing into the chair. "What could she be doing at a truck stop? And in Gastonia, of all places? That's the murder capital of the state. Is she still there? Did anybody see her?"

"Hold your horses," he said, infuriating me. "I've talked to some of the people working there, and one of the waitresses may've seen her about an hour ago. But don't get your hopes up; she'll be long gone by now."

"Did they say who was with her? She couldn't've been by herself. Whoever's with her won't let her complete a phone call. Mr. Pickens, I declare, we've got to do more than just sit here discussing the matter."

"I've been doing plenty, don't you worry."

"He has, Miss Julia," Little Lloyd confirmed, twisting in his chair as he excitedly defended Mr. Pickens. "He just talked to Jerry Johnson, you know, *the* Jerry Johnson. They're real good friends, and Mr. Pickens put him on the speaker phone so I could hear him, too. And we were right, it was somebody from Bigelow Racing who lost his cap when they broke in. BMC was what was on the cap that the thieves dropped. BMC, Bigelow Motorsports Center, Miss Julia, and Jerry said that was the only race team with those initials, plus my mama said "the big," so we know it's them."

Mr. Pickens reared back in his patched executive chair and propped a foot on an open drawer. "Yeah, that's the way it's shaping up. Jerry and Bigelow've been rivals in the Craftsman Truck Series for years. Not that Bigelow drives; he's an owner, but he's put one driver after the other in his trucks, and none of 'em ever comes close. So Jerry's convinced that Bigelow's behind it to keep him out of the Chevy Trucks 150 at Phoenix that's coming up next weekend. Then right after that is the California Truck Stop 250 at Mesa Marin. If Bigelow can keep Jerry out of both of them, he'll be so far behind in points, he'll never catch up."

"Jerry, Jerry, Jerry," I said, pursing my lips. "I've heard all I want to hear on that subject. Besides, this Bigelow's gone to a lot of trouble for very little return, it seems to me. You've already said that other teams'll help Jerry out, and he said he'd be ready to race anyway, so what has Bigelow accomplished?"

"There's something else going on that Jerry doesn't want publicizied. It'll ground him, for sure, so he's pretty broken up over it."

I rolled my eyes. I had just about lost all sympathy for this Jerry

Johnson, whose problems were taking first place in everybody's mind, except mine. "Back to Hazel Marie, Mr. Pickens. What's the agenda? From what we now know, she's with this Bigelow crowd against her will or she wouldn't be calling for help, which makes sense since Wilson T. has a kin connection there. So we can figure that *he* got her involved with Bigelow, right? And now she's called from Gastonia, so where're Bigelow and Wilson T. taking her, and where is she now? That's the question."

Mr. Pickens sat up suddenly, his foot coming down on the floor and the springs of his chair squeaking. "That *is* the question. Jerry, if you'll pardon the mention, said Bigelow has another place outside of Rockingham. Near Jerry's, in fact. I'm figuring Bigelow was using the shop in Abbot County to get his trucks ready for Phoenix, because he didn't want to hang around Rockingham after stealing Jerry blind. But when he found out about that cap one of his team dropped, he'd know the sheriff'd show up, so he had to pull out fast, taking whoever happened to be there with him. Looks like Hazel Marie might've stepped in at the wrong time."

"Huh," I said. "I don't buy that. It was Wilson T. who put her in it."

"Probably." He nodded, agreeing with me for a change. "Hazel Marie's call came from Gastonia, which is on the way to Rockingham, so he's headed back that way. I don't know why, though, since he's well known around there. I'm wondering why he didn't just go on to Phoenix, even if he'd be a few days early for the race."

"Maybe his trucks aren't ready," Little Lloyd said. "Maybe he has to have some equipment that's in Rockingham."

"Could be," Mr. Pickens said. "Now, the question is, do I head for Gastonia and Rockingham to look for them, or do I fly to Phoenix and wait for them."

"That's no question, Mr. Pickens," I said, not at all liking the way his mind was working. "You'll go to Gastonia and on to wherever they went after that. There's not going to be any flying and sitting around waiting for them to show up. We don't know what indignities Hazel Marie's suffering, so I want you right on her heels every step of the way."

"Okay, I was just waiting for you to get here so I could leave. Now, I want you to take this boy home, and wait till you hear from me."

"No sir, that's not what we're going to do. We're going with you."

"No, you're not. I need room to operate, and . . ."

I held up my hand and rode right over him. "Don't give me any excuses or reasons why not. Little Lloyd and I can't just go home and wait, now that we definitely know she's in with a bunch of thieves. How can you expect us to do that?"

"I don't care how you do it. You're not going."

"We'll just see about that. Come on, Little Lloyd." And taking his hand, I sailed out of the office and got us in our car. Cranked it and sat there waiting for Mr. Pickens. If we couldn't go with him, we'd go behind him. He'd be glad to see us when his tire started wobbling. If, that is, I could keep up with him.

Mr. Pickens came storming out of the office, his face as dark as a thundercloud, and didn't even look at us. He got to his car, the keys dangling from his hand, and stopped as if he'd run into a clothesline. He stared at his front tire like he couldn't believe what he was seeing, then he squatted down to get a closer look. He stayed that way an inordinately long time, his head bowed over.

"What's wrong with him?" Little Lloyd asked. "I'll go see if he needs anything." He reached for the door handle.

"Stay in the car, Little Lloyd," I told him. "Mr. Pickens is learning that pride goeth before a fall, and we'll be right here when he's ready to be helped up."

As I revved my motor, pretending not to notice Mr. Pickens's plight, he stood up and glared at me across the hood of his crippled car, his mouth as tight as a zipper. Breathing hot and heavy, he barreled over to my car and jerked my door open.

"I'm driving," he said, in a tone I didn't want to argue with. "Get in the back."

"Little Lloyd . . ."

Mr. Pickens pointed at Little Lloyd. "Sit still." Then he pointed at me. "You. In the back, and no back talk."

I got out, pushed up the seat and crawled into the back, telling myself that the owner of a car ought to know how it rides from behind the driver.

I gathered my coat around me and buckled the seat belt. Little Lloyd glanced back at me from between the two front seats wondering, I was sure, why I'd let Mr. Pickens take the wheel without a word of protest.

"Push up your glasses, Little Lloyd," I said, as Mr. Pickens backed the car out with a jerk. My head snapped back, and I opened my mouth to tell him to watch what he was doing.

I closed it again upon seeing his fierce glance in the rearview mirror.

Deciding not to comment on his driving, I took refuge in pleasantries. "Something wrong with your car, Mr. Pickens?"

Chapter 16

We got to Gastonia in something under two hours, taking back roads and overtaking every vehicle on the road. I'd bitten my tongue a hundred times to keep from saying anything. My restraint had little visible effect on Mr. Pickens, however, because he drove like one of those NASCAR racers he'd been talking about. My little car had never had a hand like Mr. Pickens's on it, but it didn't seem to mind. We zoomed down the highway like we were the only ones on it, and it was all I could do to keep from mentioning highway safety tips to him. I refrained, though, because he didn't seem to be in the mood for conversation. Little Lloyd took his cue from me and, other than a few glances my way and some at our silent driver, didn't open his mouth the whole way.

So I held my peace and the armrest, nervously telling myself that we were on a mission of mercy. Sometime soon after we'd started, Mr. Pickens had adjusted the front seat, sliding it back and cramping me up something awful. I didn't even say anything about that, figuring that was one way I could give him room to operate.

I'd seen truck stops from the highway as I'd passed by, but I'd never been in one. When Mr. Pickens took an exit ramp and pulled into Smiley's, it was like going into a new world. Well, not exactly new, but different. We threaded through parked tractor-trailers, some just sitting there rumbling and emitting diesel smoke, others way over to the side, empty and still, while several were hooked to gas pumps or air hoses. Cars and pickups were parked closer to the restaurant that advertised real good home cooking. Somehow I doubted it.

Mr. Pickens parked with a jerk and opened his door. "Stay in the car," he said and, slamming the door, headed toward the restaurant.

"Well," I said to Little Lloyd, "I don't know about you, but I've about had enough of taking orders and being treated like I'm in the way. Don't you need to use the rest room, Little Lloyd?"

"Yessum, I do. But he told us to stay here, so he might not like it if we get out."

"The man can't be that insensitive. And we might not have another chance anytime soon. Let's go."

I'd never seen a restaurant quite like it. As soon as we walked in the door, passing several men on the way out with toothpicks in their mouths, I just stopped and looked around. A long bar faced us with men on stools, their wide shoulders hunched over their plates, and along each side of the door there were booths filled with a few women and a lot of men. I didn't know who'd raised the majority of the men in the room, but somebody hadn't taught them to take off their caps when they came inside.

The din of deep voices ordering the meatloaf, the loud laughter of half a dozen waitresses, and the clatter of forks, knives, pots and pans filled the long room. Over it all some cowboy singer on the jukebox was wailing away about blowing smoke rings in the dark, which is a good way to kill yourself.

"There's a coupla empties at the counter, hon," one of the waitresses said as she passed with plates in her hands and stacked along her arms. "Better grab 'em quick."

She didn't wait for a reply, which was just as well. I'd never eaten perched up on a stool, and I didn't intend to start.

Looking around, I noticed Mr. Pickens leaning over the end of the counter to our right, talking with a frowzy blonde waitress at the cash register. She was smiling and leaning right back at him. Another incidence of the professional investigative technique he was so proud of.

I touched Little Lloyd's shoulder and nodded toward the left where the room took an angle. A large sign indicated that rest rooms, showers and beds were in that direction. Lord, I thought, I didn't want to eat there, much less sleep in the place.

About that time, Mr. Pickens turned and saw us. He straightened up, scowling something awful. I pointed toward the rest room sign and, not giving him the chance to stop us, proceeded toward it. But not before I saw the waitress touch his hand to bring his attention back to her. Which he was quick to do. The man was a caution when it came to women.

We walked the narrow aisle between the counter and the booths, dodging waitresses with pencils stuck in their hair, and cowboy boots stuck in the aisles. We passed between shelves of toiletries, snacks and truck magazines, and racks of postcards and keychains. In a nook off the room we found the rest rooms, the doors to the men's and the women's facing each other.

"Go on in," I said to Little Lloyd. "I'll wait by the door till you come out. But don't sit down."

"No'm, I won't. I don't have to."

I waited by the door to the men's room, ready and willing to go in after him if something untoward happened. While I waited, I noticed two telephones for public use hanging on the wall between the rest rooms. Hurrying over, I knew from Mr. Pickens's call tracing that Hazel Marie must've been in that very spot, using one of them. We were close to her, I could feel it, and I began to read all the numbers and notes that were written on the wall. Some of the writing was just doodles, while some lonesome somebody had left a string of phone numbers, but more than you might imagine was most unsuitable for reading. And in a public place, too.

Little Lloyd came out and walked over beside me. I hoped he wasn't tall enough to see some of the worst. He studied the phones and said, "She might've called from here."

"I think she did, and I've been reading the wall, thinking she might've left a message. But I don't see a thing she could've written. You don't need to look, I've checked them all.

"Now, you wait right here while I go to the ladies'. Don't go anywhere and don't talk to anyone. I'll be right out."

It didn't take me long, because I never liked to leave Little Lloyd alone in a strange place and because the room wasn't fit for lingering. I adjusted my hat in the mirror, then went out drying my hands on a Kleenex, since all they'd had in there was one of those hot air devices that never dried anything.

"Miss Julia, look," the boy said, his eyes sparkling behind his glasses. He held out his hand for me to see. "I found it and it's Mama's. I know it is."

I leaned down for a closer look, and he was right. It was another tiny charm from Hazel Marie's bracelet, a thin gold disk with her initials on it, plain as day.

"Oh, my goodness. Where'd you find it?"

"In that phone." He pointed to one. "I checked the coin return on both of them, and found this just laying in one."

"Then she was certainly here, and not long ago or somebody would've already found it. And, Little Lloyd, *she* put it there herself. It couldn't've fallen off or been torn off, and end up where you found it."

"We've got to tell Mr. Pickens." And the boy hurried off, with me close behind to find our expert investigator who hadn't wanted us along.

We turned the corner at the end of the counter, and I wanted to cover my ears from the caterwauling on the jukebox. I mean, whoever heard of anybody thinking such as that about a tractor?

Then I stopped in my tracks. Mr. Pickens was nowhere to be seen.

"Oh, Lord," I said, clutching Little Lloyd's shoulder, "he's gone off and left us."

"He's right over yonder," the boy said, pointing toward the last booth.

I could've sagged with relief. Believe me, you don't want to be stranded at a truck stop with a ladies' room in the state that one was in.

Marching toward Mr. Pickens, I could see him sitting with that same waitress he'd been all over before. The woman's hard life was plain as day on her face, but that hadn't stopped her from pretending otherwise. I declare, if I'd lived that hard I wouldn't've drawn attention to the fact by dying my hair, painting my face and wearing my pink uniform half unbuttoned. She leaned across the table, eating Mr. Pickens up with smiles and eyelash fluttering, and he was encouraging her for all he was worth.

I hadn't yet figured out whether playing up to every woman he met was a calculated method of investigation or whether he just couldn't help himself.

I came to a halt beside the booth. "Mr. Pickens, Little Lloyd found . . . are you *eating*?" I couldn't believe it. Here, the boy and I had been finding clues, while the one being paid to do so was idling away his time with a hot roast beef sandwich and a truck stop strumpet.

"This lady thinks she saw Hazel Marie. And I couldn't refuse a hot meal on the house while this sweet thing tries to remember who was with her. You and the boy'd better get something too. To go, because I'm not waiting on you." And he had the nerve to dangle my keys in front of me, then turn his attention back to the woman.

I turned my back on him, but not before hearing her ask if I was his mother. That just burned me up. For one thing, I didn't like such an uncalled-for assumption of my age and, for another, I hoped she didn't think I'd've raised such an out-and-out womanizer as Mr. Pickens was turning out to be.

Placing a rush order at the counter for two grilled cheese sandwiches and two chocolate milk shakes, I was too mad at Mr. Pickens to feel ill-at-ease as I stood next to a driver on a stool, who was spooning up chili practically in my face.

"Miss Julia," Little Lloyd said, "aren't we going to tell him what I found?"

"He's too busy for us right now. We'll get our lunch and go on out to the car. He doesn't know it, but I have an emergency key in my purse. If he's still hanging on that woman when we're ready to go, we'll just leave him."

Little Lloyd frowned, making his glasses slide down his nose. "I don't think we ought to do that."

I sighed. "Well, he's about stretched my patience to the breaking point."

When our lunch came, I took the bag and swung past Mr. Pickens's booth, Little Lloyd right behind me. I shook the bag in front of him and said, "We've *paid* for our lunch and we're ready to go. And you might be interested to know that we've found a clue. So whenever you're ready . . ." Hoping he'd pick up on my subtle hints about his behavior, I left before he had time to open his mouth.

I had a good mind to sit in the front seat and put Little Lloyd in the back, but decided I wasn't ready for an all-out confrontation. As we unwrapped our sandwiches, Mr. Pickens came out and took his seat under the wheel. Just like it was his own car.

"So what's the clue you found?"

"This." Little Lloyd held out his hand, showing him the charm. "I found it in one of the telephones by the restrooms."

Mr. Pickens picked it up and held it, examining both sides. "These her initials?"

"Yessir."

"Okay, hold on to it." He handed it back to the boy. "It confirms what we already know. That waitress thinks the woman she saw was with a man, tall, well dressed in an overcoat, not your run-of-the-mill truck stop patron."

"That had to be Wilson T.! What else did she say?"

"She thinks there were several other men with them, but she's not sure. They didn't all come in together, just one or two at a time. But she got the impression that they knew each other. Now, we're going on to Charlotte, and if it doesn't suit you," he said, angling the rearview mirror to look at me, "that's too bad."

"I thought you said we were going to Rockingham, wherever that is. Although we're not exactly prepared to go anywhere for any length of time." Thoughts of no toothbrush or change of underclothes, and Lillian worrying about us were getting all mixed up with some relief that Little Lloyd'd be safe from police custody for a few more hours. "I just want to know what we'll do in Charlotte."

"You mean, what will *I* do in Charlotte. What you'll do is sit in the car and wait for me."

Mr. Pickens cranked the car and pulled back out on the interstate, edging and twisting and scooting in and out among those long-haul trucks, barreling toward the Queen City.

I intended to change Mr. Pickens's plans about who would do what. But not before he got us off that eighty-mile-an-hour highway.

Chapter 17

We passed the airport on our right, with me ducking as a huge plane took off over the highway. Mr. Pickens swerved off the interstate onto a ramp that led to a broad avenue into the city. At every traffic light, he studied a piece of paper, then checked the street signs.

"Is that a computer map?" Little Lloyd asked.

"Yeah. Got it before we left."

"I can call out the directions for you, if you want me to."

"Okay." He handed the map to the boy. "Don't get us lost."

Since Mr. Pickens was sounding a little more amenable to friendly intercourse, I decided to join in. "Little Lloyd's a good navigator, you don't have to worry about him. I expect, though, that we'd both like to know where we're going."

I didn't think he was going to answer, then he said, "To Wilson T. Hodge's house. I got the address while we were waiting on you this morning. Gastonia's too close to Charlotte to pass up a chance to check it out, and it's on the way to Rockingham."

"Well I declare, Mr. Pickens. I commend you for thinking ahead."

"That's what I'm paid to do."

I subsided, since the man couldn't even graciously accept a compliment. Besides, we were entering an area of the city where large, well-kept houses took my eye and attention. Beautiful homes and tree-lined avenues gave off a sense of ordered lives, causing me to reflect on my own confused and agitated state during the last several days.

At least, though, I comforted myself, Mr. Pickens was obeying the speed limits and Little Lloyd's directions. We turned into an area bounded by a tall brick wall, passing through an open iron gate onto curving lanes between rows of two-story townhouses.

"Real good security," Mr. Pickens noted, as we passed an un-guarded guardhouse. "But fine for us."

I was pleased to note his use of the plural pronoun, including his passengers for a change. Mr. Pickens drove slowly in and out the maze of similar-looking houses with neat, well-kept minia-ture yards, looking left and right for a house number. The place looked empty to me, with few cars on the street and garages tightly closed.

"Does anybody live here?" I asked, wondering at the lack of children in the yards and pedestrians on the broad sidewalks.

"Oh, yeah. It's got the look of hard-hitting go-getters who're all at work. I hope."

"There it is," Little Lloyd said, pointing to one that looked no different from any of the others, except for the number over the door.

Mr. Pickens parked two doors away from the townhouse that Little Lloyd had indicated, then he turned in his seat to look at me. "Stay in the car, and I mean *stay in the car*. I don't care what kind of reason you think you have, I don't want to see either of you put a foot outside this car. Are we clear on that?"

"Well, of course. You don't have to use that tone of voice; a pleasant suggestion's all that's needed."

He rolled his eyes, then got out. We watched him walk back down the sidewalk and up the several steps to the door of number 218. Interested in learning more of his investigative technique, I carefully watched him, seeing nothing more unusual than a man ringing a doorbell.

"What do you reckon, Little Lloyd?" I asked the boy, who was also craning his neck to watch. "You think Mr. Hodge is in there, and'll just open the door and tell him everything we want to know?"

"No'm, I don't think he's home."

"Then this was a wasted trip. Seems to me that Mr. Pickens could've accomplished the same thing with a telephone call. Now we've wasted all this time when we could be halfway to Rockingham."

"Look! He's going in. Somebody must be home. Oh, I hope my mama's there. I'm going to see."

He had his hand on the door handle. "Wait. Don't get out yet. Let's wait till Mr. Pickens calls us. I don't want to upset him any more than he already is."

The fact of the matter was, I didn't know what would be found in the house and I didn't want Little Lloyd to be the one finding it.

"Look, Miss Julia!"

I did, and Mr. Pickens was crossing the yard toward us, not running, but moving with purpose. He opened Little Lloyd's door and said, "Both of you, out. Hurry, but don't run. No telling who's watching. We're going in for a visit, so act like it."

I started to ask if Mr. Hodge was in there, but a broad hand on my back didn't give me a chance. Mr. Pickens urged us up the steps and into a showplace of a living room. And when I say showplace, that's what I mean. It looked as if it'd been copied from a magazine, lots of chrome and glass and leather, with shiny, waxed floors and little indication that anyone had actually lived in it.

Mr. Pickens closed the front door and walked up so close to me that I could feel the heat he generated. His metabolism must've been working overtime. "Now, listen to me. This is important unless you want to spend the night in jail."

I gasped, and Little Lloyd whimpered. "What's wrong?" he asked. "Is my mama here?"

"No, nobody's here, but there will be in about two minutes. The house has a security system that I set off when I jimmied the door. It's a silent alarm, so the police or some guards'll be coming to check it out. I want you two to look like you're here legitimately. Tell 'em you're visiting Hodge from out of town, and you didn't know how to turn off the alarm. Tell 'em, well, tell 'em anything. Wing it, but calm 'em down so they won't look upstairs."

"Where're you going?" I asked, happy to be of service in his investigation. He'd just proven again that he lacked moral qualms when the circumstances, such as a locked door, dictated. I mentally congratulated myself again for hiring him, although he was certainly hard to get along with.

"Up there somewhere." He pointed to the stairs. "Just make 'em think you're supposed to be here, and get rid of them."

He took the stairs two at a time, leaving us standing there looking at each other.

"Quick, Little Lloyd," I said. "Take off your coat and let's find the kitchen."

Throwing my coat on a chair, I hurried to the kitchen, hoping I could find a prop or two, and Little Lloyd followed me.

"See what's in the refrigerator," I said, opening cabinets and finding a glass and a cup and saucer.

"Not much in here," he said, his head stuck in a Sub-Zero. "Here's a Coke."

"Take this glass, then, and pour some in it. Wait, pour some in this cup, too. Now hurry back to the living room and make yourself at home." I filled what looked to be a brand new kettle with water and put it on the stove, turning the eye on low. Then finding a tea bag in a cannister, I bobbed it in the soda pop in my cup, squeezed it out and left it on the saucer—a practice that I don't ordinarily condone. The dark liquid wouldn't've fooled anybody, so I diluted it with water until it looked vaguely tea-colored.

By the time I got back to the living room, I saw a car with a large decal on the door pull up at the curb and two guards in gray uniforms get out.

"Find a magazine, Little Lloyd, and be looking at it."

I put my cup and saucer on a small glass and chrome table beside a chair, then noticed the pilot light on under the logs in the fireplace. I leaned down and turned it on. A nice fire sprang up, and I thought we'd set the stage as well as we could, given the circumstances.

The doorbell rang and, with a concerned glance at Little Lloyd, I started to answer it before they took it in their heads to break the door down. "Little Lloyd, you're my grandson, and Wilson T. is your uncle, okay? He knew we were coming to visit and gave us a key."

"What if they ask you for it?"

"I won't be able to find it. Trust me, people expect the elderly to be absentminded."

I opened the door to a thin uniformed man with slumping shoulders and a protruding abdomen. He had a thin mustache, stained teeth and a squinty-eyed look.

"How do you do?" I said, as friendly as I could be. "If you're selling something, we don't want it."

"You the owner?" He said it like he was expecting trouble, harsh and suspicious sounding.

"No sir, I'm not. Mr. Wilson T. Hodge is, but he's not here right now. Still at work, I suppose. Why, what's the trouble?"

"The alarm went off here, which means that somebody's in here who's not supposed to be. Mind if I look around?" And he pushed past me, just as his partner, a heavier, younger version, came around the corner of the house.

"Oh, well, it's just us. Wilson T.'s my sister's son, and my grandson and I have come from up in the mountains for a visit. He didn't tell us about an alarm system, just gave us a key. Oh, you mean that thing on the wall that keeps on blinking and beeping? I declare, I wondered what that was. We don't have such things up where I come from, don't even need them."

The both of them stood looking around, noticing Little Lloyd sitting on the leather couch with a magazine in his lap and a Coca-Cola in his hand. The fire added a nice, homey touch. The younger one kept hiking his right hand to his hip, like he wished there was a gun and holster there instead of a ring of keys. I don't know what they'd've done if they'd found a real crook in the house. Yelled for help, maybe.

"Could I offer you some refreshments, officers? There's some soft drinks and tea, if you'd care for anything."

"No, ma'am," the younger one answered, shifting his eyes to his partner to see what he wanted to do next. His partner was shifting his eyes around the room, looking for clues, I guessed. "Mind if we look around? Just to be sure everything's okay?" He moved toward the kitchen without waiting for my permission. The older one went toward another downstairs room that I had yet to visit.

"Why, go right ahead. Little Lloyd and I just got here and, I declare, that bus trip was enough to do me in for a week. We're just waiting for Wilson T. to get here so we can go back to the bus station for our bags."

Little Lloyd gave me a worried look as we heard them opening and closing closet doors and wandering through the house. He cocked his head toward the second floor, frowning, as we both wondered how well Mr. Pickens was hidden.

"Everything looks okay," the older guard said, as he came back through the living room. "You say you had a key? And the door was locked, no evidence that somebody had come in before you?"

"That's right. Locked tighter than Job's hat band. You just wait till I get my hands on Wilson T. for not telling us about that alarm. I'm just so sorry to've bothered you, making you come out here for nothing. But I'll also tell him how good you are at your job. I declare, it makes me feel as safe here in the big city as I am in my own home. I commend you both," I said, as the younger one came in just in time to be included in what I was laying on thick. "I wouldn't be surprised if Wilson T. doesn't write a letter of commendation, recommending a bonus or a raise in pay. He'll be so pleased when I tell him how pleasant and efficient you've both been."

There was a noticeable easing of tension between the two of them as I buttered them up good.

"Well, we'd appreciate that," the older one said. "And looks like everything's under control here, so we'll be on our way."

The younger one cocked his head and raised his eyebrows toward the stairs, so I quickly reached for my pocketbook. "Could I interest you gentlemen in a little something for your time, since I know you don't have it to be wasting on an old woman who didn't know any better than to interrupt your regular work?"

I held out two twenty-dollar bills. They looked at each other, each waiting for the other to reach for them. I wouldn't've dared do it if they'd been real officers. I know a bribe when I see one. But they didn't, or didn't care if they did.

I saw them off, each twenty dollars richer and pleased with themselves for conducting such a rewarding investigation.

I closed the door and leaned against it, marveling again at how easy private investigation was turning out to be.

Chapter 18

"Mr. Pickens?" I called from the bottom of the stairs. "You can come down now. They're gone."

"Hold your horses," he called back. "I'll be through here in a minute."

The man was enough to make a preacher cuss. I wanted out of there before those guards decided to take another look. Besides, it was plain that Hazel Marie was not in the house, and searching for her was our first order of business.

"Let's straighten this place up," I said to Little Lloyd, "and be ready to go when he is."

I stuck the things we'd used in the dishwasher, hoping they'd give Wilson T. a turn when he saw them, and turned off the stove and the gas logs. We put on our coats and sat down to wait.

"Miss Julia," Little Lloyd said, "I don't see a Bible anywhere. Reckon he's even got one?"

I glanced around at the coffee table where a large display book lay, and at a set of chrome bookcases where a pitifully few books were arranged with some awful-looking knickknacks. I'd never been able to understand the taste of some people.

"Maybe it's by his bed. But you'd think a man in his business would have more than one, wouldn't you?"

"Yessum, that's what I was thinking."

Mr. Pickens appeared in the door, having come down the stairs without making a sound. "Let's go." And he headed for the front door.

We scrambled after him, with me getting more and more put out with him. He could've at least told us what he'd been doing upstairs and what he planned to do next. But no, he had that car cranked before I could squeeze into the back seat. You'd think he'd've had the courtesy to commend us for fooling those guards, but he didn't have a kind word for us.

"It does beat all, doesn't it, Little Lloyd," I said, as Mr. Pickens drove out of the area and back onto a broad street, heading away from the way we'd come. "I mean, here we were, unwanted and ignored, yet wasn't it a good thing that we were around to save somebody's bacon when that somebody needed us?"

Little Lloyd peeked around his seat, a smile on his face, and nodded. Mr. Pickens had the child too intimidated to speak his own mind and agree with me. Then I looked up and saw the hint of a smile at the corner of Mr. Pickens's mouth. His mustache might've been tickling him, though, for all he let on.

"Little Lloyd," I went on, "would you be so good as to ask Mr. Pickens where we're going now?"

"Mr. Pickens . . . ," Little Lloyd started.

"We're going to Jerry's."

"My Lord, why?" I asked, leaning forward as far as the seat belt would let me. "It's getting dark and no time to be visiting old friends. We need to find Bigelow's place."

"Look," Mr. Pickens said in that tone of voice he used when he wanted no argument, and which I was getting real tired of hearing. "You two take a nap or something, and let me think this through."

"Think what through?"

"What I found in Hodge's home office."

"What'd you find?"

"Mrs. Springer," he said, sounding tired and put upon. "Give it a rest."

"Well," I said, sitting back and huffing to myself.

By this time we were leaving the city, getting out where the traffic was thinner and the strip malls were interspersed with small, brick residences waiting to be bought out. I put my head back against the seat, determined not to speak to Mr. Pickens again. Let him see how he liked my silence when it came time to be paid.

He picked up speed when he got on a highway headed east. Then he reached over and turned on the radio, twisting the dial until a country music station came on loud and clear. I rolled my eyes, which I was sorry he couldn't see, and resigned myself to listening to that squalling for I-don't- know-how-many miles. I'd just stay quiet and let him alone, and I managed to do that for a good long while. Then I thought he needed reminding that he had passengers to consider.

"I guess if you take it in your head to drive all the way to the Atlantic Ocean, you'd let us know, wouldn't you?"

Mr. Pickens's shoulders slumped. "I knew it. I just bet myself that you couldn't stay quiet for ten miles."

"That being the case, why don't you just tell us what you're thinking about, and maybe we can be thinking about it too? If I had something to engage my mind, I wouldn't feel the need to interfere with your mental processes." Whatever they are, I thought to myself.

"Hush a minute," Mr. Pickens said, reaching for the radio dial.

Before I could let my displeasure be known at being hushed, he turned up the sound and we heard a plaintive, country voice fill the car. "This is Jerry Johnson speakin' to all my fans out there and askin' for your help. You all know about the damage done to our shop and how it's put us behind for Phoenix. But we're gonna make it, I promise each and every one of you. It sure would help us out, though, if y'all would help the police track down that sorry bunch and get back what all they stole from me. We just got a few more days before the Chevy Trucks 150, so I'm askin' if anybody knows anything, you'll call your local law enforcement or call me direct at 1-800-Go-Jerry. I'm offerin' a reward that'll knock your socks off, pit passes for the rest of the season and no questions asked. He'p me out here, all you racin' fans. I 'preciate anything anybody can do, an' you won't regret it."

Mr. Pickens turned the radio down, shaking his head. "Poor ole Jerry. He's got a real problem."

"Poor ole Jerry, my foot. Keep your mind on Hazel Marie, Mr. Pickens, and forget about Jerry Johnson's problem. Now, tell us what you're thinking about."

"All right. All right." Mr. Pickens reached into his breast pocket and brought out some folded papers. He handed them back to me. "It's all tied in together, like I thought. That's the motive, right there."

I unfolded the papers and studied them for some time. "I can't make head nor tails out of this stuff. Looks like a list of races, for one thing."

"Right. A list of possible entries in the Bud Pole next weekend, too."

"That doesn't mean a thing in the world to me."

"Qualifying laps for the race the next day."

I rolled my eyes, sick to death of hearing about the racing world. I now knew more about it than I'd ever wanted to know, and didn't understand the half of it.

"Well, where's that motive you mentioned?" I shuffled through the papers, picking up ticket stubs and a small, black notebook as they fell to my lap.

"Right there in your hand," Mr. Pickens said, as he swerved the car into the fast lane and kicked it into overdrive. I'd done more gasping since he'd been behind the wheel than I'd ever done in my life. And the day wasn't over.

"These things?" I managed to say, holding up the stubs. "What are they?"

"Betting stubs," he answered. "And from the looks of 'em, your Wilson T. Hodge hasn't had much luck betting on Bigelow's drivers."

"Betting?" Little Lloyd asked, his eyes wide behind his glasses. "Mr. Hodge bets on races? Why, he works for the church; he's not supposed to be placing bets."

"You got that right," Mr. Pickens said, although I detected a hint of sarcasm in his voice. "But from the looks of that little notebook, he's expecting his luck to change at Phoenix."

I flipped through the notebook, glancing at such unintelligible notations as NAPA 250, Powerstroke 200 and Ram Tough 200. What was intelligible, however, was the dollar sign on a number of breathtaking figures beside each notation. "My word," I said. "Does this mean what I think it does?"

"Probably, but it's hard for me to know what you're thinking." Mr. Pickens had a smart mouth on him, and I glared at the back of his head. "Check out the Phoenix entry."

"I don't see Phoenix."

"Look at Chevy Trucks NASCAR 150," he said. It was a mystery to me how he got Phoenix out of that, but I found it and nearly lost my breath.

"Ten thousand dollars! Has that idiot bet ten thousand dollars on a *race*!"

"Looks like it. See the check mark beside it? Probably means called in and placed."

Little Lloyd's mind was way ahead of mine. He said, "I bet that's 'cause he figures Jerry won't be there, don't you, Mr. Pickens?"

"Right." Mr. Pickens nodded. "So I figure Hodge knew they were going to put a crimp in Jerry's chances."

"Don't bet, Little Lloyd," I admonished him, anxious to curb any bad habits before they took root. "And I agree that it looks like Wilson T. has been in on it from the start. That sorry thing.

What I want to know, though, is where did Wilson T. get this kind of money. Working for a church is not one of your better-known high-paying jobs."

"He may be placing bets for Bigelow," Mr. Pickens said. "NASCAR officials keep too close a watch on the teams for them to risk it themselves. Then again, Hodge may have money of his own."

"Shoo," I said, waving that thought away. "Wilson T. Hodge doesn't have a pot to . . . Oh, my goodness, Pastor Ledbetter! Oh, my goodness!" I started patting my chest with my hand, unable to put the awful thought into words.

"What is it, Miss Julia?" Little Lloyd turned in his seat, his face a picture of worry. "Are you all right?"

"I just remembered something. The pastor said something last night. Something about the building fund not being as full as it ought to be. Oh, Mr. Pickens, you don't reckon Wilson T.'s embezzled church funds, do you? And Hazel Marie's involved with him. Oh, Lord, I knew it, I knew that man was as crooked as a snake."

"No, you didn't, Miss Julia," Little Lloyd said. "You liked him at first."

"That was just good manners, Little Lloyd." I leaned up and tapped Mr. Pickens on the shoulder. "We've got to hurry, Mr. Pickens, this is getting worse by the minute."

"I'm doing the best I can. It's rush hour, and every damn fool in the city's on the streets."

I pursed my lips at his language, but I was too busy studying the implications for Hazel Marie to reprimand him.

"I'm gonna stop up here in a little," he went on, "and find a phone. I need to put Jerry in the picture, so if you two need a rest stop, you'll have ten minutes."

"I could use a stop, and I expect Little Lloyd could too.

Though I hate to take the time for it. We might think about getting some supper pretty soon, too. It's getting dark, Mr. Pickens,
and we're a long way from home."

"Nothing would do but you had to come along, so don't complain to me."

"I'm not complaining, I'm just reminding."

I think he growled, so in an effort to make him feel better, I
said, "If you need to use a phone, why don't you use the one in
the car?"

The car swerved as he jerked his head around toward me. "You
have a car phone? Why didn't you tell me?"

"You didn't ask."

He said an ugly word under his breath that nearly raised the
hair off my head. Then, "Well, where is it?"

"I don't like that kind of talk, Mr. Pickens, and I'm not going
to warn you again. Look in the console."

But by that time Little Lloyd had gotten it out for him. "I
should've told you, Mr. Pickens; I just didn't think."

"Let me have it first, Little Lloyd," I said, reaching between the
seats. "I need to call Lillian, and Mr. Pickens shouldn't talk on the
thing while he's driving, anyway."

That got me a rearview mirror glare that I pretended not to see.
"Hurry up, then. I need it."

Little Lloyd showed me how to turn the power on, and I dialed
home. When Lillian answered, I could hardly get a word in edge-
wise as she castigated me for being out of touch so long.

"Where you been? Where're you now? Why don't you let me
know something? I been settin' here, worryin' myself sick all day.
Have you found her? When you be home?"

"Lillian, Lillian, wait, let me catch up here. We're on the highway, outside of Charlotte on our way to see Jerry Johnson . . .
Well, I don't know, but Mr. Pickens seems to think Mr. Johnson

can help, although it's hard to tell what Mr. Pickens thinks half the time." And I did a little glaring of my own at the back of that black head in front of me.

Then Lillian told me something that gave me a start. "Deputy Coleman Bates come by this afternoon, an' he set an' talk for a long time. He say he figure you done take Little Lloyd off some- wheres, though that Lieutenant Peavey don't 'spect nothin' like that yet. An' he say it be better if you bring that boy on home an' face the music, an' it got to be done real soon. Time runnin' out, but he say he don't think no judge gonna grant custody to any- body but his mama, but runnin' from the Law ain't no way to handle it." She took a deep breath. "I think I got all he say. But, Miss Julia, he worriet 'bout you an' the trouble you lettin' yo'self in for, an' he want to help but he say his hands're tied up, long as you don't show up with Little Lloyd like you 'sposed to."

I turned away from the front and lowered my voice, not want- ing Mr. Pickens to hear this line of discussion. "Doesn't Coleman know we're looking for the child's mother?"

Mr. Pickens looked up in that mirror he was so fond of and said, "Don't stay on the phone forever. I need to use it."

"Have patience, Mr. Pickens," I said, then whispered into the phone, "Now, Lillian, we're not exactly running from the Law, even though it might look like we are. We're dealing with two separate things here, and Coleman needs to understand that."

"I don't think he do," Lillian said. "They all mashed together in his mind, seem like. Anyway, Mr. Sam been callin' off and on all day long, an' he get that home nurse to bring him over here, too."

That got my back up in a hurry. "What! Why'd he do a thing like that?"

"He jus' see if I doin' all right by myself, an' see have I heard from you. He real upset, not knowin' where you are an' what you doin'."

"Well, just let him be upset. The idea, bringing that woman

into my house." I gripped the phone as if my life depended on it, trying to hold on to my temper. That Sam, out running around with a tempting woman who'd stop at nothing. I knew her type, and Sam was doing nothing to put a stop to it. You can't trust anybody these days, especially a man you find yourself thinking about too much.

Lillian broke into my thoughts. "You still there?"

"Just thinking. Lillian, call him tomorrow and tell him I don't need his worry or his concern. Tell him I hope he's enjoying himself."

"I'll do no sucha thing. All he want to do is help us out, an' the least you can do is be nice to him."

Mr. Pickens chimed in again, "Hurry up back there; you'll use up all the power."

"Oh, hold your horses. Not you, Lillian. Mr. Pickens thinks everybody ought to jump on his say-so." I turned even further into the upholstery and whispered, "Now, listen, don't tell Sam about Little Lloyd's trouble. Since he's taken up with that woman, no telling what he's likely to do, and remember to let Lieutenant Peavey think that the child's with his mother, and that I'm sick, and remember not to tell Coleman too much."

"I don't know can I keep all them stories straight, but one more thing. Miz Conover, she come over all upset an' cryin' this mornin', an' I hope you know what her trouble is, 'cause it don't make no sense to me."

"To me, either," I said, thinking that I was glad to've missed that visit. "Call her, if you don't mind, and tell her I'll be in touch as soon as we get back. You didn't tell her what we're doing, did you?"

"No'm, but she get mad when I told her you not here. She don't ax no questions, jus' say it a fine time to be out of town when yo' friends need you."

I sighed. LuAnne couldn't allow anybody but herself to have

trouble on their hands. "I'll make it up to her when we get home. Anything else?"

"Yessum, yo' preacher, he come over an' he don't want to say too much. But he go all the way 'round Robin Hood's barn tryin' to find out if I know anything about that Mr. Hodge. He worriet about that man, I could tell, an' yo' church, too. He pale as a sheet, eyes flittin' about everywhere, mumblin' 'bout Miss Hazel Marie, an' when she be home, an' church financials, an' I don't know what all. Then he kinda come to hisself an' say he sure Mr. Hodge be in Charlotte doin' the Lord's work, an' he worriet that you might be slanderin' him."

"Slandering who? Him or Mr. Hodge?"

"Mr. Hodge, I think he mean."

"I'll tell you this, Lillian, I'm going to do more than slander Wilson T. Hodge if we ever find him. I have to hang up now; Mr. Pickens is having a fit, and him driving, too."

"Well, one more thing happen you not gonna like."

"Thay Lord, what else?"

"Somebody call on the telephone, wantin' to speak to Little Lloyd. When I say he not here, that somebody say real mad like, 'Well, where is he?' He say that boy 'sposed to be here an' he say Miss Hazel Marie, she messin' with fire, leadin' the Lord's anointed into sin an' he ain't gonna set by an' do nothin' an' he have a good mind to sue somebody. He don't say who he is but, Miss Julia, I think it be that Brother Vern. He hang up 'fore I get it outta him."

"My Lord." I sat there, running up the phone bill, trying to make sense of it all. "What in the world was the man talking about? Wilson T.'s nothing but a hired fund-raiser, and how any-body could call him the Lord's anointed is beyond me. And, for his information, Hazel Marie's not leading anybody into sin; it's the other way around. I declare, Lillian, the man's crazy as a loon." I started to say that's what happens when you get so wrapped up in the Gospel that you start judging everybody but yourself, but I didn't, since once I got started on that subject, I wouldn't be able to quit.

"I'll straighten him out when we get home. Lillian, it sounds like you're holding things down real well, and I thank you for it. Just keep on like you're doing, and I'll let you know if, I mean when, we find Hazel Marie. I'd put Little Lloyd on, but I'm afraid Mr. Pickens would cut a flip. We'll see you soon."

I punched the off button and said, as pleasantly as I could, as I handed the phone over the seat, "Here you go, Mr. Pickens. Your turn now."

He took it out of my hand, without a word, and turned the car into the parking lot of a McDonald's, which I would've bypassed if it'd been up to me. But I figured by that time I'd better keep my preferences to myself.

"You two go on in," he said. "And don't linger."

As we got out of the car, he began dialing without telling us another word about what his plans were. I was about fed up with his behavior, and hoped Little Lloyd wasn't taking any lessons in unacceptable conduct from him.

I stuck my head back in the car, thinking that I'd show him I could be nice, even if he couldn't. "You want us to bring you something?"

"No, I do not."

"Well, no need to be rude, Mr. Pickens. It's most unattractive. Come on, Little Lloyd, let's leave him to sulk by himself."

Chapter 19

By the time we got back to the car, Mr. Pickens was just finishing with his telephone call, but did he tell us what he'd learned? No, he did not. But I'd brought him the biggest Big Mac on the menu, thinking he'd be in a better mood if he had something on his stomach.

He unwrapped the thing with a nod of thanks, which was certainly insufficient, and set his coffee in the cupholder. Then he cranked the car, backed out and steered us out on the highway, all with one hand.

"Where're we going now?" I ventured to ask.

"I told you. We're going to Jerry's."

"You just talked to him, didn't you? Going to see him'll just delay us that much longer. It's Hazel Marie we need to be looking for, I don't care how much sympathy you have for your friend."

"Give me some credit here," Mr. Pickens said, wadding up his hamburger wrapping like he wanted to do the same to somebody. "Jerry knows Bigelow, knows where he lives, knows where he hangs out, knows what we need to know. That's why we're going to see him. I hope that meets with your approval."

I studied on that for a minute, wondering why Mr. Pickens had such a prickly temperament. Poor upbringing, probably. All I was trying to do was keep his mind where it was supposed to be. As I looked out the window at the darkening streets, the car lights and street lights coming on, it seemed to me that his mind was working out what to do with the passengers he hadn't wanted along in the first place. I wouldn't've put it past him to be planning to dump us off for the night while he went off on his own. And if that's what he was thinking, he was going to have another think coming because I didn't plan to let him out of my sight.

"Maybe Jerry Johnson can help us, Miss Julia," Little Lloyd said. "He's real famous and knows a lot of people." Then turning to Mr. Pickens, he asked, "Do you think he'd let me see his racing truck?"

"You bet, sport," Mr. Pickens answered. "You can see his shop, meet his team, sit in the truck, whatever you want."

Huh, I thought, sounds like Mr. Pickens is planning to stay awhile. Which meant we'd be staying, too.

"If you're not going to look for Hazel Marie tonight, Mr. Pickens, I'd as soon stay at a Holiday Inn."

He ignored me.

"I can't wait." Little Lloyd bounced in his seat, as the two of them continued to discuss a matter foreign to me. "He won at Homestead-Miami last year. I saw it on ESPN. Did you see that, Mr. Pickens? Did you see it when he made contact with the wall and spun out? He came out of it and poured on the power, fish-tailed around the turn and took the lead again."

"Yeah, and he's right on up there this year."

"How many points does he have so far?"

"Beats me. I used to keep up with him, but I've lost track here lately."

I'd had enough of being left out. "What're we talking about?"

"Jerry Johnson's run for the championship, Miss Julia," Little Lloyd said, craning his head around the front seat. "You know, his standing in points."

"Well, no, I don't know, but I'll take your word for it. And at the risk of repeating myself, I'd prefer to go to a motel, unless Mr. Pickens plans to drive home tonight. Which I don't think he ought to do since he's been on the go all day long, and ought to be tired. Besides, I think we ought to find Bigelow's place and see if Hazel Marie's there or not."

Mr. Pickens said, "Give it a rest, hon. I'm working on it." Which had to suffice because that's all I could get out of him.

It'd been dark for a good while by this time, although it wasn't that late, and we'd quickly driven through and out of the little town of Rockingham. All I could see was flat country, farmland, sandhills and pine trees that were typical of that area of the state. As far as I could tell we were going south on a straight, two-lane road, with nothing between us and South Carolina but more of the same. It made me nervous.

"Mr. Pickens," I said, "I need to know exactly what you have in mind. May I remind you that you're in my employ, and I'm requesting an accounting from you."

He glanced in the rearview mirror. "Got you worried?"

"Why, no. I generally enjoy tooling around in strange places after dark with somebody I hardly know at the wheel."

He may have smiled, but who could tell since he did it so infrequently. "Jerry knows the area, and he knows the racing circuit. If this Bigelow has a place to hole up, Jerry'll know it. And he can give us some background on him."

"Well, that makes sense then. I declare, Mr. Pickens, you have a good mind for your business and, if you'd just tell me what you're doing, we'd get along so much better. That's just my opinion, though."

"I figure you'd have something to say regardless of what I come up with, and I'd as soon not have to put up with your arguments until I have to."

"Why, Mr. Pickens, when have I argued with you?"

"When have you not?"

"Well, don't expect one now. You're doing just fine, and as long as you don't expect me to get in something that goes around in circles on a racetrack, I'll put up with whatever you decide on."

"We'll see," he said, giving Little Lloyd another sideways grin.

"Miss Julia," Little Lloyd said, "I wish you and Mr. Pickens wouldn't fuss at each other so much."

"Don't let us worry you," I said, reaching up to pat him. "Mr. Pickens doesn't pay attention to me anyway. Everything I say just rolls off his back, although he'd do well to listen to me on occasion."

Mr. Pickens grunted, which I decided to take as agreement. Then he said to Little Lloyd, "Watch for a turnoff up here pretty soon. It's a state road, so there ought to be a sign."

When we came to it, Mr. Pickens turned left onto an asphalt road that led between nubby pines crowding up on each side of the road. Weeds grew in the ditches and, in the dark with only our headlights to see by, it seemed as if we were traveling through a tunnel. There wasn't a streetlight or a glow from a house or any other indication of human habitation. I couldn't for the life of me figure what a race-car, or race-truck, driver would be doing so far off the beaten path. It gave me an awful lonesome feeling, especially at the thought of Hazel Marie in some similar place without a friendly face around her. At least I had Little Lloyd and, I guess, Mr. Pickens, who could be as friendly as you please as long as he was getting his way.

Soon, though, after several twists and turns in the road, a bright glow ahead lit up the countryside. Mr. Pickens turned through a gate in a chain-link fence onto a large paved area. Pole lights made the place clear as day, and I could see a huge low-slung building in the center with a sign that read JERRY JOHNSON RACING on it. Several cars were parked in front and on the side of the building, and I caught a glimpse of a huge tractor-trailer in the back.

"End of the line," Mr. Pickens said, as he parked close to the front door of what looked like an office entrance. "Everybody out."

Before we got to the door, it swung open and a skinny back-woods-looking man with a head of straw-colored hair and a matching bushy mustache bounded out, grinning to beat the band.

"J. D.!" he yelled. "Where the hell you been, son? Man, you showed up just in time. Get on in here an' let me look at you."

Lord, the man was loud, making me want to step back out of range of what was coming out of his mouth. He was a picture, too, wearing blue jeans so tight that I wondered if he'd given a thought to the damage they could do. A wide belt with an engraved buckle rode low on his thin hips, and a bright blue silk shirt made in the Western manner was tucked neatly into his pants. Cowboy boots, a large gold watch on his wrist, and several gold chains around his neck rounded out his outfit. I don't ordinarily trust men who wear necklaces but, if he was willing to give us some help, I'd be willing to make an exception. Although when I caught sight of a tiny gold ring in his ear, I nearly reconsidered.

His lined and weathered face creased in a wide grin as he led us through a narrow hall with an office on either side, then through another door into a cavernous space littered with parts and carcasses of pickup trucks, tools, rolling carts and various pieces of machinery.

"Look at this, would you?" he bellowed, giving Mr. Pickens a whack on the back. "Man, we oughta been smokin' with the new sponsors we got, JR Landscaping's handin' out money right and left, there wasn't nothin' too good for us. But take a gander at it now. It's just a flat mess; they musta took a ballpeen hammer to everything in here." His voice caught in his throat at the outrage he was feeling.

I couldn't see it, myself. The place looked pretty much like every other garage I'd ever seen, although bigger and considerably cleaner. I'd give them that.

"Hey, boys," Mr. Johnson yelled. "Look who's here! Got us some real help now."

Several men in white coveralls disengaged from under hoods and axles and came over, smiling and wiping greasy hands on the cleanest rags I'd ever seen. They swarmed around Mr. Pickens, grinning and smacking him on the back. That seemed to be the normal method of greeting, and I determined to keep my distance from all of them, not wanting to be pounded half to death.

Little Lloyd and I hung back while Mr. Pickens shook hands all around, asking how everybody was and, in general, enjoying the welcome he was getting.

I heard one of them say, "What you been up to, J. D.? Drinkin' the whole state dry?" I figured right then that Mr. Pickens's dissolute character was well known to them.

Mr. Pickens finally turned to us, saying, "Jerry, I want you to meet Mrs. Julia Springer, and this is Lloyd Puckett." He gestured toward us, just as I was wondering when he was going to take notice of the one who was footing the bill.

Jerry Johnson whirled around and came bounding over to us, his hand outstretched. "Glad to have you," he bellowed, "real glad to have you folks. Hey! I know a Southern gal when I see one. Bet they call you Miss Julia, don't they?"

I gave him my hand in greeting and almost had it wrung off. "Some do," I said. "Mr. Johnson . . ."

"Jerry! Call me Jerry! Hell, 'scuse me, ma'am, last time I got called Mr. Johnson, it was a judge doin' the callin'!" Then he offered his hand to Little Lloyd, who shook it just like I'd trained him to do. "How do? You like racin'? Look around all you want, Floyd, there's lots to see."

"Lloyd," Little Lloyd corrected him, but he seemed dazed to be in the presence of this loud-talking, seemingly famous personage. I don't think he cared what name he was called.

"We got a lounge over yonder," Mr. Johnson yelled, making me wonder if he thought we were all deaf as posts. "Come on and take a load off. We'll lift a few and get ourselves caught up. J. D., I got trouble you won't believe, son, and I hope you can help us out here. Come on, Miss Julia, honey, you look like you could use a little."

He swung an arm around Mr. Pickens's shoulders and motioned for me to come with them. I followed, but kept my distance, not wanting to lose my hearing and not sure of what he was offering. Coffee sounded good, since it looked as if our bedtime was nowhere near. He led us to a corner room with couches, easy chairs, a television set and racing magazines open on the tables.

I glanced back at Little Lloyd, but he'd been taken in hand by the mechanics and seemed intently interested in what they were showing him under the hood of one of the garishly painted, though dismantled, trucks.

As I made my way to a chair, Mr. Johnson pulled out three bottles of beer from a refrigerator, handing one to Mr. Pickens and setting another one in front of me. That just did me in. Did I look like somebody who'd drink that stuff?

"I don't care for it," I said. "Thank you all the same."

"Oh, you want a glass?" Mr. Johnson was instantly solicitous. 'Scuse me, I wasn't thinkin'. I'll get you a glass."

"No, thank you. A glass won't change the contents, though I appreciate the offer. I'm a Presbyterian, Mr. Johnson."

"That a fact? Well, I'm a Baptist myself, but lemme get you a soft drink. Don't want you to break no rules or nothin'." And he laughed in a good-natured, but ear-shattering, way.

Mr. Pickens was having nothing to say, just sitting there with a self-satisfied smile on his face with that brown bottle in his hand. It seemed to me that he'd follow my lead and turn his back on temptation, but before I knew it the both of them were opening two more bottles. I sat stiffly, registering my disapproval as best as I could, but it didn't seem to affect them one way or the other.

Just as I nudged Mr. Pickens to get down to business and engage Mr. Johnson's interest in our problem, Mr. Johnson began to regale us with his own.

"J. D.," he blared, "I swear to God, you couldn't of showed up at a better time. Man, I need some help real bad."

"Nothing's changed since we talked?"

"Not a blamed thing." Mr. Johnson bowed his head and, I won't swear to it since that's not my way, but his eyes seemed to get wet and glittery. My heart went out to him, knowing as I did, what it was like to suffer a loss.

"Don't look like I'm ever gonna get it back," Mr. Johnson went on, shaking his head in sorrow. "Might as well hang it up, as far's my driving's concerned. I guess I'll go ahead and send the crew on to Phoenix, then we'll light out for Mesa Marin, but it'll just be goin' through the motions. We had to buy more power tools, and then we begged and borrowed some setup disks. You know, I got the best fabricator and engine man in the business, and they was able to get a truck halfway ready to run, but I'm gonna have to put a young driver in it. Won't be me, that's for sure, even though everybody's countin' on me. I swear, J. D., I won't hardly be able to hold my head up anymore, settin' on the sidelines watchin' my Number 17 JR Landscapin' GMC truck come trailin' in like a cow's tail."

"Hey, don't be giving up so quick," Mr. Pickens said with a great deal more concern than he'd been showing me. "You've still got a few days before the Phoenix race and, now that I'm here, we'll track down Bigelow and get you set."

That deserved a comment from me, if anything ever did. "Mr.

Pickens has a lot of self-confidence, Mr. Johnson. You may have noticed that."

"I sure do need some from somebody," Mr. Johnson said, hanging his head low and modulating his voice to a normal level. Clearly, he was powerfully moved. "Any kind of confidence I ever had is flat gone. I tell you, J. D., I've had bad dreams about even climbing in that truck. I hate to admit it, never thought I'd get so dependent on anything in my life. I'm thinkin' I ought to just pull on out now. All I can see is my Number 17 truck comin' in dead last, embarrassing myself and my whole crew. Or something even worse. No way in the world I'm not gonna go down in points, and that's just gonna kill me. Here I got a world-class pit crew and a A-number one sponsor, and not a lick of luck to go with 'em."

"Jerry," Mr. Pickens said, leaning toward him, "I know you put a lot of stock in that lucky charm of yours, but that's not what makes you win races."

Lucky charm? I thought, frowning. It beat all I'd ever heard to listen to two grown men talking about lucky charms.

"I know it don't make no sense," Mr. Johnson said. "But like I told you on the phone, once something like that gets in your head, all you can do is go with it. If you got it, which I don't since that's what Bigelow was after all along. Everything else he did was just to cover up."

Mr. Pickens frowned, commiserating with his friend, while I wondered how a grown man could be so superstitious as to be undone over a charm like the ones Hazel Marie had been dropping like bread crumbs along her trail. But, of course, you could never tell about a man who wore as much jewelry as Mr. Johnson did. Some people I knew had lucky coins or four-leaf clovers that they thought brought them good luck, and most of them church-going people too. I even knew one man who carried a buckeye in his pocket every day of his life. Not that it'd done him any good, since his place of business burned down and he was arrested for arson.

I tried my best to be patient and sympathetic to Mr. Johnson's plight but, let's face it, Hazel Marie was more important than finding a piece of jewelry or an Indian-head nickel or whatever it was. Even if it meant losing a race or two, which I couldn't bring myself to believe would happen in the first place. I'd always believed that luck was a matter of grit and determination, to say nothing of your basic character traits and willingness to work for what you wanted. But I didn't share my thoughts, being a visitor and all.

I did get concerned, though, that Mr. Pickens would let himself be sidetracked and would put his mind on Mr. Johnson's minor problem to the detriment of what he was hired to do. I began to tap my foot, impatient to get to our business.

Even though I was agitated enough to jump out of my skin, Mr. Pickens went right ahead and promised again to help Mr. Johnson find his lucky charm. Then, to my great relief, he said, "But I've got Miss Julia's case to wrap up first. Although one might well wrap up the other. Here's how I see it."

And Mr. Pickens began to tell Mr. Johnson how he'd put together my missing person with Mr. Johnson's missing trinket. He told him what the Abbot County deputies had found in Bigelow's shop, which didn't include any people to rescue or crooks to arrest. Then he told him about our stops in Gastonia and Charlotte.

"Looks like they headed back this way," Mr. Pickens said. "I'm figuring that from the Gastonia connection, as well as what I found in Hodge's townhouse. Show him, Miss Julia."

I dug the notebook, papers and ticket stubs from my pocketbook and handed them over.

"Well, I be dog," Mr. Johnson said, as he shuffled through them. "I knew Bigelow had a hand in stealin' my lucky charm from the cap somebody lost. But I thought it was just to put me outta the runnin', seein' as how he's always wanted to beat me. I can't stand him an' his underhanded ways, an' he can't stand me. But I sure didn't know he was up to his neck in gambling. This here's big money, son."

"We still don't know if he's in it," Mr. Pickens said. "Those bets may just be Hodge's doing." Then he went on to tell Mr. Johnson about Hazel Marie and her connection to Wilson T., as well as about the charms we'd been following, and how we needed to know whatever Mr. Johnson could tell us about Bigelow and where he might be.

Mr. Johnson kept quiet, listening and tipping up his bottle and nodding his head. When Mr. Pickens wound down, Mr. Johnson nodded again and leaned forward in his chair, his arms resting on his knees.

"Ole Bob Bigelow used to be big in street stocks. Did a lot of drivin' when he was a young man. Daddy knew him. Never liked him much, though. He was mixed up in all kinda stuff on both sides of the Law, so they say. But whatever you're lookin' into now, he ain't in it. Kicked the bucket 'bout ten year ago. He left a bunch of kinfolk, though, an' all of 'em into racin' of some kind. Coupla 'em drive on the monster truck circuit, some in the Daytona Dash, an' this, that, an' the other, all tryin' to work up to the Busch and Winston Cup Series. On my back, too. An' you might be interested in this. Hodge is the name of one side of the family, but the worst of the whole lot is Bobby Bigelow, Jr., who took up where the ole man left off, and that's who you're lookin' for. I'll tell you one thing, he's meaner'n a snake. Puts on a good front for NASCAR officials, but he'll do whatever it takes to win. And what he's done to me is a good example of it."

"Yeah, well, now we know how far outside the Law he's willing to go," Mr. Pickens said, emptying his second bottle and getting up to help himself to another one. I frowned at him but he didn't notice. "It looks like they want to take you down and make some money on it, too. Hodge is one of them, maybe the one assigned to place the bets even if he didn't take part in the break-in. I found phone numbers and addresses for both Bigelow shops in his house, and some other stuff that puts him right in with Bigelow. But," he went on, nodding his head at me, "my main concern is finding the woman 'cause it sure looks like she wants to be found."

"It do, don't it? Dropping all them clues like she done. I hate to say this," Mr. Johnson said, in what for him was a subdued kind of way as he looked at me, "but they's some rough folks back in these parts. So I'd like to he'p you, and maybe find my lucky charm too. Besides," he went on in a normal tone, which for him was just below a bellow, "I don't like the idea of them tryin' to fix NASCAR races. Us drivers have a reputation to uphold with the fans. That kinda stuff puts us all in a bad light."

"We don't like what they're doing to NASCAR, either," I said, although I'd never lose a wink of sleep over it. But I was determined to nip in the bud any further display of self-pity about his loss. First things first, I always say. "And that little boy out yonder is just worried sick about his mother, to say nothing of myself. I'd be so grateful for any help you could give us in finding Hazel Marie."

"Okay, here's the scoop. Bigelow's place's about twelve miles west of here if you got wings, twice that on wheels." And he began telling us how you go so many miles and take a right at Junior's Stop and Shop, then a left at old man Whitaker's place, then you take a right on a dirt road that was easy to miss if you didn't know what you were looking for. He stopped and took a deep breath. "I might better go with you. You don't want to tangle with him by yourself."

"Let's go, then," I said, gathering my coat and purse and thinking it was about time we did something besides talk.

Mr. Pickens and Mr. Johnson looked at each other, nodded in unspoken agreement, then Mr. Pickens said, "Not tonight. I want to check in with the local sheriff, see what they've come up with, and be sure we won't be stepping on an operation they've already got in place. First thing in the morning, okay?"

"Yeah," Mr. Johnson agreed, "it'd be better to go on to my house for the night. If Bigelow's Abbot County crew cleared out up there like you say, they'll be joining up with the team at his shop here. We'll probably need a little help to handle 'em. And I'm like J. D., I don't wanta to mess with anything the sheriff's got goin'."

I didn't like it, but far be it from me to interfere with the Law.

Chapter 20

"Mr. Pickens," I said, fastening my seatbelt as we prepared to follow Mr. Johnson to his house. In spite of the fact that I'd made my
sleeping preferences so clearly known. "Why does that gentleman
talk in such a loud manner? Does he think we're all deaf?"

"No, but he is." Mr. Pickens switched on the headlights and
pulled out behind Mr. Johnson's fancy red car that Little Lloyd
was so taken with. "Or all but. He's been around racing all his life,
driving, and testing and building engines. The noise is something
else. You ought to go to a race sometime and see for yourself."

That was a suggestion that didn't warrant an answer, so I turned
to another subject. "Well, tell me this. What in the world would a
race-car driver be doing with a lucky charm? I mean, I know men
have taken to wearing earrings and necklaces and such, but a
charm bracelet? I'm surprised a man would admit to such a
thing."

"It's not that kind of charm," Mr. Pickens said. "Tell the truth,
not many people know what it is since he keeps it pretty close to
his chest." That seemed to tickle him, but he didn't share the joke
with us. "I know a little about it, but I'm not at liberty to tell anybody. Client confidentiality, you know," he said, with a glance in
the rearview mirror. "But it's not unusual for drivers to have
something they consider lucky, like a special pair of driving shoes
or something. I know one driver who has to have a pat on the
back from his crew chief right before he starts his engine. He can't
stand it if the chief forgets. But Jerry, well, he really believes his

charm not only helps him win, but it keeps him safe. He doesn't want anybody to know how much he depends on it, and the fact that he admitted as much to us, shows how it tears him up to be without it."

"Well, I never," I said.

"How'd whatever it is get to be lucky?" Little Lloyd asked, while I hoped he wouldn't be influenced by hearing so much about such superstitious beliefs. Pastor Ledbetter would say it was all of the devil, but I couldn't help being somewhat interested in the answer, myself.

"All I know is that Jerry had it with him when he was running in the Pronto Auto Parts 400 a few years ago. Somebody made contact as they were coming off turn two going wide open, bounced Jerry off the wall and flipped him three or four times. Threw the engine two hundred feet one way and the transmission into the infield. About all that was left was the bent-up frame with Jerry still strapped in. Worst thing I ever saw, but he came out of it like a, well," he stopped and grinned, "like a charm. Banged up pretty good, but it's a wonder it didn't kill him. Ever since, he's been convinced that something his wife gave him that morning was what kept him alive." Mr. Pickens stopped again, giving us time to absorb what he'd said. "'Course," he went on, "the wife's long gone, but he's still got that lucky charm. Or did, up until now."

"What a remarkable story," I said, unable to comprehend such dependence on a material item. "Pitiful, though."

Mr. Pickens didn't answer, so I sat back in the corner of the back seat, contemplating our next moves.

"Mr. Pickens?"

"What?"

"If Mr. Johnson's lucky charm is such a big secret, how would anybody know what to steal?"

"That's the kicker," Mr. Pickens said. "Bobby Bigelow, according to Jerry, is one of the few who knows what it is. Saw Jerry putting it on under his Nomex one time, that's a driving suit to you. That's one reason he kept it under lock and key from then on."

I thought about this for a while, feeling the car sway through the turns on the back road. And wondering where Hazel Marie was and what she was doing.

"Mr. Pickens?"

"What now?"

"Well, we now know where this Bigelow garage is, but what're we going to do about it? I mean, it's possible that Hazel Marie is there, isn't it? Or that somebody there knows where she is? I still think we ought to go right out there and do some investigating."

"We are. First thing in the morning."

That didn't make sense to me. The best time to sneak around and see what somebody was up to was in the dead of night, and I said as much to him. And Little Lloyd agreed with me, which should've decided it once and for all. But it didn't.

"Look," Mr. Pickens said, and I prepared myself for another lecture on investigative techniques. "I know what I'm doing, so just let me do it."

"Well, it seems to me that going to some stranger's house and spending the night is not doing much of anything. And I hope you're not going to let yourself get diverted by Mr. Johnson's loss. I mean, I sympathize and all that, but who knows what Hazel Marie's going through right this minute? I say let's go on and try to find her."

"I do, too," Little Lloyd said. "They might take her somewhere else by morning. My stomach gets all knotted up, just thinking about it."

"Both of you, listen to me," Mr. Pickens said, as he turned into the yard of a house with four large pillars along a front porch. I had Hazel Marie so much on my mind that I couldn't give the place the attention it deserved, but it crossed my mind that the racing business must pay real well. Mr. Pickens parked the car on the horseshoe drive and turned in his seat to face me. "I need to make some phone calls, check in with the local sheriff and the Abbotsville Sheriff's Department, then talk to some of my buddies on the Charlotte-Mecklenburg force. See what else I can come up with on this Hodge character. I don't want to go out there blind, not knowing how many's out there or what I'll find. I'm going to get your lady back for you, but I don't want to put her in danger when I do. And Jerry's gonna be a help, not a hindrance. Now does that explain anything to you?" Then turning to Little Lloyd, he said, "What about you, sport? You all right with this?"

"Yessir, I just want to find my mama. My nerves're getting real bad, I'm so worried."

"I know you are, but you get a good night's sleep and we'll find her tomorrow."

It seemed I'd heard that promise before. Still, his reasons for delaying made sense, so I contented myself with following him out of the car and into Mr. Johnson's house.

It was a sight. I didn't know who his decorator had been, but whoever it was ought to've been ashamed of herself. I'd never seen such a conglomeration of styles in the furnishings, lots of cowhide and leather and animal heads, along with crocheted pillows and afghans. Embroidered samplers and Bible verses were framed and hanging on the walls in between racks of guns. There were braided rugs on the floor and a huge stone fireplace taking up most of one wall. A lot of money had been spent to so little effect, other than to unsettle a woman of taste like me. Still, Mr. Johnson was a gracious host, offering food and more drink, which Mr. Pickens was foolish enough to accept, and showing Little Lloyd and me to our rooms off a hall that overlooked the two-story living room.

Lying in bed sometime later, unable to close my eyes, I could hear Mr. Pickens and Mr. Johnson talking, especially Mr. Johnson. But the house was so large that I only heard bits and pieces. As best as I could make out, they were making phone calls and working at Mr. Johnson's computer, whose programs and Internet access Mr. Pickens had been pleased to discover.

I turned over for the dozenth time, wishing for daylight and wondering how Little Lloyd was resting in the next room. Knowing I wouldn't sleep a wink with Hazel Marie weighing so heavy on my mind, I dropped off before I knew it.

———

I got up the next morning to a cold, overcast day from the dreary looks of Mr. Johnson's yard from my window. And from the looks of my face and hair in the bathroom mirror, I needed a croker sack over my head. It just doesn't do to go off without hygienic aids and clean step-ins. Thank goodness, I had a comb and face powder in my pocketbook.

I hated to face the day feeling and looking frowzy and disheveled, but you do what you have to do. This was the day we were going to find Hazel Marie or, barring that, at least make a raid of our own on another Bigelow warehouse or shop or garage, or whatever it was. To that end, I was eager to get started and wondered why I wasn't hearing Mr. Johnson's braying voice downstairs.

It struck me that the both of them had imbibed so much the previous night that they were still laid up in bed, sleeping it off. "If that's the case," I mumbled to myself, "I'm going to take a broom to both of them."

I went next door and got Little Lloyd moving, telling him to do the best he could with his teeth and urging him to hurry.

As I went downstairs to find out the plan of action for the day, the silence in the big house put me on edge. I wandered through the downstairs rooms, noting the empty bottles just left out to smell up the place. And the more I wandered the madder I got. There wasn't much I could do to straighten out Mr. Johnson; he wouldn't be under my influence long enough. But Mr. Pickens was another story, and I was determined to let him have some choice words on the matter of drinking on the job.

Although the truth of the matter was, he didn't need to be indulging at any time. That stuff just eats up your stomach.

By the time Little Lloyd came downstairs, looking a good deal worse for the wear as I did myself, I was getting more and more agitated. I took my comb to his hair, which was sticking up every which way, not that it did much good.

"Run back upstairs, Little Lloyd," I told him. "See if you can find Mr. Pickens and Mr. Johnson and get them up. Tell them we're ready to go."

By that time I'd taken to wringing my hands, trying to calm my nerves and not let on to Little Lloyd how upset I was. The house had an empty feel to it, and I was beginning to suspect that the boy and I were the only ones in it.

My suspicion was confirmed when Little Lloyd came back down, his formerly sleep-glazed eyes now wide with worry, and said that they weren't in any of the beds. I knew what'd happened as soon as I opened the front door and found my car sitting where we'd left it and Mr. Johnson's car missing in action.

"They've gone, Little Lloyd! They've gone to look for your mother and just left us here." I stomped back inside, so outdone I could've wrung Mr. Pickens's neck if I'd had my hands on him. "I can't believe this! He knew we wanted to go, knew I wanted to get my hands on Wilson T. and that Bigelow, too. And what has he done? Waited till we were asleep and snuck off just to keep us from going. I've a good mind to get in our car and go home without him! Just strand him like he's stranded us. That'd show him!"

Little Lloyd was watching me rant and rave, his face screwed up with worry. "Let's don't do that, Miss Julia. We have to wait for him. If he finds my mama at Bigelow's, he'll bring her back here."

Well, of course the child was right. But that didn't make me feel better about any of it. Mr. Pickens had me where he wanted me—out of his hair and stuck where I was. I didn't like it one little bit.

"How long have they been gone, I wonder? Did you hear them leave? I didn't either. I didn't hear a thing, just slept like a log while Mr. Pickens—I know it was him—planned this sneaky, underhanded and totally unwarranted maneuver to keep us from going. Just had to do it himself, that's all it was. I'll tell you, Little Lloyd, egotism is a terrible affliction and I hope you take a lesson from this."

"Yessum, I will." The child was wringing his hands by this time, and I realized that I wasn't being much help in easing any of his worries.

"Are you hungry?"

"No'm, not much."

"Let's go to the kitchen anyway. Mr. Johnson can just treat us to some coffee."

We headed for the kitchen, a huge tiled room with every labor-saving device known to man. Which didn't do me a bit of good, since I didn't know how to work most of them.

When I got the coffee going, I turned to the boy with a sudden thought. "I know what we can do."

"I don't think we ought to, Miss Julia. We ought to stay right here and not go off anywhere. They may be on their way back right now, and have my mama with them." Little Lloyd had begun to pick at a hangnail, a sure sign of his distress. I took his hand and put it in his lap.

"No, I wasn't thinking about going off anywhere. We have to stay here, as Mr. Pickens well knew, because he was careful not to discuss his plans in my presence. No, I was thinking of calling Lillian again. You didn't get to talk to her yesterday, and maybe it'll keep us from worrying about what Mr. Pickens is up to."

He brightened at that, and looked around for a phone. "Will Mr. Johnson mind?"

"I don't care if he does. Well, on the other hand, maybe you ought to call collect. You know how to do it?"

"Yessum, I think so." He headed for the telephone on a far counter, while I poured coffee for both of us. While he spoke to an operator, I rummaged through the cabinets and refrigerator, looking for some little something to eat.

As soon as Little Lloyd got through to Lillian, I heard her shriek all the way across the room. Little Lloyd jumped off the stool he was sitting on, his face white and drawn, as he held the phone out to me.

"Something's happened, Miss Julia! She wants to talk to you." I snatched up the phone. "What? What is it? Lillian, slow down and tell me."

I listened, my hand clutching Little Lloyd's shoulder as he bit at his fingernail. We were both trembling, frightened at what couldn't be anything but more bad news, considering the run of bad luck we'd been having. I put my arm around the child and hugged him close, as much for my own comfort as his.

"What!" I jerked upright at Lillian's news. "Is that all she said? Tell me again, Lillian, tell me exactly what she said."

Lillian took a deep breath, ending with a quiver in it. "She say he takin' her to Phoenix, I think is what she say, an' she don't wanta go nowheres but home."

"Phoenix! Why?" But I knew why. It had to be for that blasted race next weekend.

"Miss Julia, I don't know an' I don't get a chance to ast her 'cause I break in an' say 'Where you at now?' an' she say she locked up in a RV goin' all over creation, an' now she parked in a field somewhere I never heard of."

"In a *field*! Where?" Lord, if we'd finally gotten the specifics but couldn't understand them, we'd be no better off than having no word at all.

"I don't know, Miss Julia, I jus' tellin' you what she say an' she talkin' real fast, sayin' she parked at the, let me see, I wrote it down, at the North Carolina Speedway an' they leavin' for Phoenix soon's they do some kind of practicin', so you got to hurry."

"Lillian, none of that helps me at all. The North Carolina Speedway could be anywhere in the state, and we can't search everywhere. Did she say anything else?"

"No'm, she kinda screeched then an' I hear some awful fumblin' an' mumblin' on the line an' the phone get hung up real hard. I jus' been worryin' something awful, 'cause I didn't know how to call you, so it a good thing you call me."

I nearly sagged with the thought that I'd only thought to call her to give Little Lloyd something to do besides jiggle around from one foot to the other. And with the thought that if we'd gone with Mr. Pickens, we wouldn't've called at all. Some things do work for good, even those you don't expect to.

"Hold on, Lillian. Little Lloyd, you have any idea where the North Carolina Speedway is?"

He put a finger to his lips, frowned in concentration and said, "No'm, but I know how to find out."

He ran out of the kitchen, and I quickly told Lillian we were hot on the trail and would be back in touch. Following Little Lloyd, I found him hunched in front of Mr. Johnson's computer. The thing was dinging and changing pictures, and I marveled at what they were teaching children in school these days.

I watched over his shoulder and whispered, "What're you doing?" Afraid to disrupt what was going on on the screen.

"Going online," he said, which didn't help. "Hold on a minute. Mr. Johnson's got NASCAR in his bookmarks. There it is. Now I'll just hit tracks and scroll . . . got it! Now, click on North Carolina Speedway and check the directions to it. Miss Julia! Look, look! We're practically at it. Ten miles from Rockingham. See that, on Highway One, ten miles from town. We can be there in no time."

Well, modern conveniences are wonderful, and that is a fact. Of course, you have to have somebody who knows how to make them work, and Little Lloyd knew more than I ever would.

But even with this new information, I began to wring my hands again. "That Mr. Pickens! Gone, just when we need him! Should we wait here for him or go look for her ourselves?"

Little Lloyd turned off the computer and swiveled around in the chair. He squinched up his eyes as he thought about our dilemma. "No two ways about it, Miss Julia, we've got to go. They've been moving all over the place and, if we wait, they may take her off somewhere else." He shivered. "Like Phoenix."

"You're right. Get your coat and let's go." Then I thought of another problem. "We can find Highway One, I have no doubt, but will there be signs to that speedway? How will we find it?"

"It's pretty big, Miss Julia. I don't think we can miss it. If you're willing to try, I'm willing to help."

The child's confidence was a comfort to me and I told him so. "Little Lloyd, you are a wonder, and I don't know what I'd do without you." Which brought to mind the danger waiting at home for him, and my redoubled determination not to have to do without him. "Let's go get your mama."

Well, the change in that child was nothing short of a miracle. Life came back to his eyes and color to his cheeks. And the jiggling turned into jumping, which I had to caution him against. Although I felt somewhat like doing it myself.

"Oh," he said, gloom settling on him again. "What if she's gone again by the time we get there?"

"One thing at a time, Little Lloyd. Let's just get there, then we'll see what else we have to worry about." It ran through my mind that here I was, doing everything myself. Again. And even with a private investigator on the job. But then, that's the burden an industrious person such as myself has to bear.

We scurried around, getting our coats and my pocketbook, and pinning on my hat with my heart pounding at the thought that they might take Hazel Marie across the country before we could get there. Lord, I didn't know the way to Phoenix and didn't want to learn.

But as anxious as I was to leave, I took the time to write Mr. Pickens a note, thinking as I did that it'd serve him right if we just left without telling him a thing, just as he'd done to us. But I'm a considerate person, and didn't want to put that kind of worry on him. Still, he needed to be taught a lesson.

So I wrote:

Gone to NC Speedway, 10 miles north of R., which is where H.M. is, parked in a field in somebody's RV and not at Bigelow's place as you have now ascertained for yourself. Will call you as soon as we find her. If you're back from wherever you went. Hope Mr. Johnson can get you somewhere to meet us before we go on to Abbotsville, since he's so willing to take you places. My kind regards to him for putting us up for the night.

There, I thought as I signed my name, that'll fix him. Maybe Mr. Pickens would think twice the next time he decided to leave us behind.

Chapter 21

Thank goodness for the extra car key I kept in my purse, just as the manual recommended, for Mr. Pickens had known better than to leave the one he had. As if that was going to stop me.

But I had to admit to a few qualms about going off without him, even as I was pulling out of the driveway. I'd never liked doing unto others what they'd done unto me, although given the circumstances I had no choice in the matter. Hazel Marie needed us, and there was no telling when Mr. Pickens would get back. We surely couldn't be expected to sit around waiting on him while she was in danger.

"Let's hope we can find the place without spending all morning looking for it," I said, shivering in the cold car. "This weather's looking worse all the time."

Little Lloyd stopped biting his fingernail and put his mind to the directions he'd written out.

"Turn right when this road dead-ends, go back to Rockingham and look for Highway One. I don't think it'll be hard to find; it runs right into town." I declare, the child was smart as a whip, working computers, reading maps and doing all the things I didn't have time for. He wiggled in his seat, glanced at the speedometer, and revealed a bent for tact. "We might ought to hurry. What if she goes off again before we get there?"

"It won't be her doing, if she does. I tell you, Little Lloyd, that Wilson T. has a lot to answer for."

He nodded. "Bigelow, too," he said, biting his lip, because the thought of his mother being under somebody's thumb wasn't at all a comforting thought. It wasn't to me, either. But I strengthened my resolve by picturing Wilson T. and Bigelow and everybody with them at the mercy of Mr. Pickens. No, in the hands of Lieutenant Peavey made a more satisfying picture. That'd fix them, if they survived what I planned to do to them.

I grasped the steering wheel with both hands, seeing from the corner of my eye Little Lloyd wringing his, and knew that worry nagged at him, as well. I pushed on toward Rockingham, noticing with a sinking heart that a little rain was spitting against the windshield. I put the wipers on intermittent sweeps, and hoped the rain wouldn't get worse.

Neither of us had much to say, exchanging frowning glances as we entered the small town and started looking for highway signs. I continued to be concerned about the weather, what with the heavy clouds and freezing temperature. There was little chance of the rain turning to snow this far south but, up around Abbotsville, it'd be a different story.

"Those clouds look threatening, Little Lloyd. I just hope this rain doesn't freeze on the streets. But let's worry about one thing at a time. Once we have your mother with us, we'll manage whatever else comes our way."

"I wouldn't be so nervous if I knew she'd still be there. What if she's gone off again? You reckon she has?" Before I had to express my own worry on that score, he sat up and pointed to a sign. "There it is. Turn there, Miss Julia. Now it's just ten more miles."

I nodded, drove through the town as fast as I safely could and headed north toward Hazel Marie. Lord, I was beginning to wish Mr. Pickens was with us. And I was also about to worry myself sick over just how we'd get her away from people who didn't want to let her go. As much as Mr. Pickens could outrage me, I could've used some of his high-handedness in facing a bunch of thieves and crooks. But, as you've noticed, he was off on a wild goose chase while we were solving the case.

"Look!" Little Lloyd pointed ahead to our right. "There's the speedway!"

I gasped at the size of the thing. "My stars, it looks like a stadium."

"It kinda is, Miss Julia. Oh, I hope it's open. It's not a race day, so what if we can't get in? Look, there's a road. Turn right there."

I headed the car toward the huge structure, entering a parking area the likes of which I'd never seen except around a Wal-Mart. But this one was a sandy field with paved access roads running through it, and it was all but empty, with just a few cars and pick-ups inside a fence up near the stadium where the back of the bleachers rose up to a monstrous height. From the expanse of the parking area, racing must've been a popular spectator sport. Or else the owners were the optimistic type. A gate stood open, I was glad to see, and I drove right through it.

"I had no idea the thing would be this big. How in the world are we going to find her?"

"Go on around, Miss Julia. Maybe the parking lot is the field she was talking about."

But it wasn't. We went all through that sandy parking lot and there wasn't a recreational vehicle to be seen. And not much else, if the truth be known.

"Miss Julia!" Little Lloyd yelled, making me jump.

"What!"

"It's the *in*field! That's what she was talking about. It's got to be, or else they're gone. Oh, please, Miss Julia, let's try the infield."

"Well, I'm perfectly willing if I knew where it was."

"It's inside the track, you know, where pit row is."

Not knowing a pit row from a corn row, I said, "Just tell me how to get there."

"Keep going around," he said, leaning toward the dashboard to see better. "There ought to be a tunnel somewhere that'll take us under the grandstand and the track."

"Tunnel," I said, not at all liking the sound of that.

"There it is! Look, right down there. Drive in, Miss Julia, and we'll come out in the infield."

I hesitated at the mouth of one of the tunnels, reassured by the lights inside. Then I looked up at the back of the seats that towered over us, and lost my reassurance.

"You sure?"

"Yessum. This is the way all the transports and the fans' RVs go to get inside. Go ahead, Miss Julia, let's take it."

As I gingerly nosed the car into the passageway, Little Lloyd suddenly cried out, "Wait, wait, we're going in the out!"

"Too late," I said, thoroughly committed with no room to turn around. And I certainly wasn't going to back out. "I'll toot my horn."

I'd always thought tunnels were dark and narrow, but this one was plenty wide enough for my car. I caught my breath, though, when the tunnel took a downward slant and I realized what all was on top of us. But then, we were on an upward ramp and daylight, such as it was on a cloudy, threatening day, showed us the way out. I stopped as soon as we emerged, taking in the several acres of a grassy oval with paved drives threaded through it and several low block buildings scattered around. I looked up and around, marveling at the racetrack that curved and banked around us and the rows of bleachers stretching above our heads.

"You think we ought to be in here?" I whispered, awed by the immensity of the place.

"Look!" he shouted, pointing toward the buildings on the oval inside the track, "there's some people down there around that tractor-trailer. I bet they've been doing some practice runs."

I saw several men in coveralls closing up the back of the trailer, then I caught a glimpse of a beige recreational vehicle on the far side of it.

"There's one of those things she said she was in," I said. "You see it? I'm going to drive on up there, if I can manage it."

"Drive on the apron, Miss Julia. That's the level area at the bottom of the track. See it? Oh, I hope my mama's in that Winnebago."

"You watch for her, while I maneuver this thing."

I eased the car onto what Little Lloyd had called the apron, which would be a surprise to Lillian, and drove sedately toward the tractor-trailer and the RV. As we drew closer, the men stopped what they were doing and watched us. I smiled and gave them a little wave, like we were tourists just passing by. Or the queen out for a drive.

I followed the curve of the infield, leaving the men still staring behind us. We drove around to the far side of the oval, with Little Lloyd twisting around to keep the RV in sight.

"How should we do this, Little Lloyd? If we knew for sure that she's in that Winne-whatever, we could drive right up to it and knock on the door. But if she's been moved to one of those buildings, we'd've given ourselves away."

"I know what we can do, Miss Julia," he said, bouncing up in his seat. "Hit the panic button and, wherever Mama is, she'll hear us."

"Hit the what?"

"This," he said and reached over to smack the large, red button in the middle of the dashboard. Then his little hands flashed here, there and yonder, twisting and turning knobs, and flipping switches all around and on the steering wheel. Well, that car kicked up a fit like it was in mortal agony, lights flashing and horn blaring and windshield wipers flapping, carrying on the likes of which I'd never seen nor heard.

"Thay Lord!" I said, coming to a halt, so unnerved I didn't know what to do.

"Don't stop! Keep going, but slow so she'll see us."

The child seemed to know what he was doing, so I followed directions and drove slowly on around the apron, drawing about opposite to where the RV was parked in the infield. The cover-alled men had come around the tractor-trailer, trying to see what was wrong with us. Well, a lot of car horns get stuck, so I just looked straight ahead and pretended I didn't notice the racket we were making.

"There she is!" Little Lloyd screamed, jabbing his arm in front of my face and pointing to the infield. He unbuckled his seat belt, and crawled between me and the steering wheel so he could lower my window and scream, "Mama! Mama!"

Thank goodness I was going slow or we'd've wrecked right there. I was finally able to get the child off me so I could see where I was going. Quick-thinking as always, Little Lloyd reached up and slid open the sunroof. Then he climbed onto the console and stood there, his head and shoulders sticking out of the top of the car, waving his arms and yelling to his mama. And here came Hazel Marie running across the grass, no coat, hat or gloves to her name. The RV door stood open behind her, and Wilson T. Hodge was bounding down the steps after her.

Hazel Marie screamed, "Miss Julia! Lloyd! Wait, I'm coming!" She ran for all she was worth, but Wilson T. was closing fast. The men on the far side of the field watched, then a few trotted off to join the chase.

"Hold on, Little Lloyd," I said, jerking the wheel and giving it the gas. We bounced onto the grassy field, the back wheels sliding a little before they grabbed and held.

I headed for Hazel Marie, lights still flashing and horn blaring loud enough to wake the dead. She ran toward us, screaming, her hair tangling in the wind and cold sprinkles of rain, and the dress she'd left home in three days ago flipping up around her you-know-what. Wilson T. looked beyond her and saw us coming. He put on a burst of speed and almost caught her. She swerved, then turned and swatted at him with her fist. As he grabbed at her again, she reared back and landed a kick that slowed but didn't stop him.

"Oh, hurry, hurry!" Little Lloyd screamed.

I was doing the best I could, trying to decide what to do first, get Hazel Marie or run Wilson T. down. As I swung the car between the two of them and skidded to a stop, Hazel Marie made the decision for me. She grabbed the door handle on my side and flung the door open.

"Miss Julia!" she screamed and leapt into the car, across the steering wheel and my lap, reaching for Little Lloyd as he tumbled back down into the car.

As Wilson T. stretched out his hand for the passenger door, I stomped on the gas, in spite of the fact that I couldn't see anything but Hazel Marie's bottom. She was wedged between me and the steering wheel, with her legs dangling out the open door.

"Get in!" I yelled, trying to drive by feel. The car bounced and swerved and skidded on the field, with Wilson T., first dodging, then chasing us. "Lordamercy, Hazel Marie, I can't see!"

She wiggled on across just as the car hit the pavement of the racetrack and we bounced back onto the oval. Crying and gasping and screaming, she ended up on top of Little Lloyd, while I slowed enough to get my door closed.

"Get us out of here!" Hazel Marie yelled. "Hurry, Miss Julia, hurry."

"Oh, Lord," I said, as I saw the RV trundling across the field toward us, and Wilson T. running alongside it until he could grab on and swing up inside. "They're after us. How do we get out of this place, Little Lloyd?"

"The tunnel! Find the tunnel."

I didn't have time to look, for the RV was coming fast. There was nowhere to go but around the track, so that's where I went. I didn't know those big, lumbering vehicles could go so fast but, before I knew it, the RV was right on our bumper.

"Speed up! Speed up!" Hazel Marie yelled, looking back at the thing filling our rear window. "It's Bigelow and he'll run us down!"

Well, I wasn't going to have my little car smashed to smithereens by the likes of him, not after having survived Mr. Pickens's driving. I mashed down on the gas pedal, feeling the car gather itself, then shift into a heretofore unused gear. It took off like a rocket and, before I could get a deep breath, we were zooming down the straightaway with that RV close behind and the first curve coming up fast.

"Go low, Miss Julia!" Little Lloyd screamed, trying to see the track from over his mother's shoulder. "Go low into the turn!"

That's what I was trying to do, aiming for the flat apron that we'd cruised so sedately only a few minutes before at—my Lord!—sixty-five miles an hour! I felt the car tilt as we went into the turn. Then we were slung up on the banked track, like we'd been snapped out of a slingshot. The next thing I knew we were whipping up on the bank, headed for the wall.

Hazel Marie shrieked. Little Lloyd screamed bloody murder.

"Turn it, oh, turn it!" Little Lloyd yelled.

Well, I'd been driving on crooked mountain roads for most of my life and, when you've seen one hairpin curve, you've seen them all. Although not ordinarily at this speed. I gave it some gas as we flew up into the turn, nudged the wheel just a little as the tires dug into the curve, and that little car whizzed by the wall with room to spare. Not much, I admit, but a miss is as good as a mile.

Then we were zooming down the opposite straightaway, edging toward eighty, and I risked a glance in the rearview mirror.

The RV was coming on, but it'd lost ground on the turn, which didn't surprise me at all. Those things are top-heavy, don't you know. I managed the next two turns pretty much the same way, but the wall on that end seemed a whole lot closer.

"Look!" Hazel Marie yelled, pointing across the infield. "Oh, no, they're pulling the tractor-trailer across the track!"

"Find the tunnel!" Little Lloyd yelled, flailing the arm that wasn't pinned under his mother.

"One more of these turns and I'm heading for the field. Look for the tunnel so I'll know where to go."

The RV had pulled right back on our rear bumper as we headed into the next turn, and I didn't think I could go any faster. Not, and keep the car from flying off into the grandstand.

Holding on to the wheel for dear life and feeling the car swing up on the banked curve, we heard the most awful banging and scraping and sliding and skittering.

"They're shooting at us!" Little Lloyd screamed.

"Oh, Lord!" I screamed.

"No, they've wrecked!" Hazel Marie yelled, craning her neck to look back. "Look! They blew a tire and slammed into the wall!"

I slowed somewhat and looked back. The RV was on its side, sliding along the bank with its top scraping the upper retaining wall. Smoke billowed up around the tires, and pieces of chrome and glass were flying along the track. The back end began to slue toward the apron, still sliding along the track.

"Oh, my Lord," I said, and poured on the power to get us out of the way. The thing was coming after us on its side about as fast as it had when it was upright. Then I looked ahead to see the tractor-trailer pulling across the straightaway. "Hold on!"

I was too close to the monster to stop, so I twitched the car into the remaining space between the truck grill and the wall, getting a glimpse of the driver's open mouth as we whizzed through. Hazel Marie and Little Lloyd screamed their heads off.

"Look for the tunnel!" I yelled, turning off the track and skidding onto the field. "I'm all turned around; help me find the thing!"

"There it is!" Hazel Marie screamed, her partially denuded charm bracelet jangling on her arm as she pointed ahead of us. "Right down there!"

I saw it then, and headed for it with hardly any let up in the speed. As we dashed across the field toward the tunnel, I caught a glimpse of Wilson T. and Bigelow climbing out of the RV. It had come to rest on the apron, lying on its side with wheels still spinning and smoke roiling around it. Bits and pieces of metal and tire treads were strewn in its wake on the track.

I aimed for the opening of the tunnel and hit the down ramp hard. The car leveled out at the bottom, then bounced up on the up ramp, popping out of that place like a piece of toast from a toaster. Lord, I was glad to see something besides a paved oval in front of me.

I headed for the highway as fast as I could, having had my fill of racetrack driving. There wasn't much traffic, which was both a good and a bad thing. Good, because we could make better time, and bad, because those idiots behind could overtake us. But not in the RV, I thought, with some satisfaction and a great deal of relief.

"Close that hole in the roof, Little Lloyd," I said, as I punched the button to run my window up. "It's freezing in here."

Chapter 22

He did, then reached around his mother and stopped the racket the panic button had started. The quiet was a welcome relief from the spectacle we'd been making of ourselves. I wiped a hand on my coat, marveling that I was able to break the grip I'd had on the steering wheel. As I slowed to normal speed on the highway, I noticed that ice had begun to collect on the sides of the windshield where the wipers had swept it.

"This stuff's freezing," I said, as my blood pressure jumped a notch. I'd just run a road race that hadn't worried me half as much as the thought of driving home on icy roads. "You'd think the weather'd know it's March, and not January, wouldn't you?"

But Hazel Marie and Little Lloyd weren't paying attention to my problems. They were busy carrying on over each other.

"Lloyd! Baby, oh, sweetheart!" Hazel Marie cried, as the two of them wrapped themselves around each other, crying and squeezing and laughing all at the same time. "Where'd you come from? How'd you find me? Oh, my goodness, I'm so glad to see you!"

Then as they untangled themselves and Little Lloyd climbed between the seats to get in the back, Hazel Marie turned to me. "Oh, Miss Julia, I've never been so glad to see anybody in my life. How'd you know to come out there? I called Lillian but she didn't know how to get you. It was like a miracle when I looked out the window of that RV and saw your car. I couldn't believe it. Seemed like I'd just managed to slip and call Lillian on Wilson T.'s cell phone."

So I told her how we'd followed the trail of gold charms she'd laid out along her way, and that we'd been at a certain Jerry Johnson's place, at which time Little Lloyd interrupted to tell her that it was *the* Jerry Johnson of some little racing fame. Before she got too impressed, I went on to tell her how the same Jerry Johnson had helped Mr. Pickens sneak off and leave us in order to rescue her from Bigelow's local garage where, as it was plain to see, she had not been.

Instead of immediately putting to rest our fears about her safety the past few days, she said, "Who is Mr. Pickens?"

"Mr. J. D. Pickens, the private investigator I hired to find you."

"You hired a private investigator? Oh, Miss Julia." Tears welled up in her eyes and, before I knew it, she leaned over the console and hugged me. An intimacy I'd never much cared for and had avoided whenever I was able to. Especially when I was trying to drive.

"I can't believe you'd do that for me," she said, her voice breaking as she wiped her eyes.

"And why not, I'd like to know? You think I'd just let you go off and never hear from you again, with this child mourning you the way he's done? To say nothing of Lillian and, well, me? Nosirree, that's not the way I operate."

"Look!" Little Lloyd yelled. I nearly had a heart attack, thinking Bigelow and Wilson T. had confiscated one of those pickups we'd seen and come after us. But Little Lloyd was waving and flapping his hands out the side window. "It's Jerry and Mr. Pickens!"

I caught the flash of Mr. Johnson's red sportscar as it whizzed past us, headed for the speedway. So they'd found my note and were riding to the rescue. Somewhat late, I might add.

"Look at that!" Little Lloyd was kneeling on the back seat, looking out the rear window. "He's doing a one-eighty!"

I glanced in the rearview mirror in time to see Mr. Johnson's car skid into a turn that slung him around in the opposite direction. Then he was coming up fast behind us.

Just as the red car filled the rear window, Mr. Johnson swung out beside us, cruising at our speed. Mr. Pickens rolled down his window and had the nerve to point his finger at me, then at a gas station up ahead. I pursed my mouth at being given orders again, especially since we'd been doing so well without them.

As Mr. Johnson spurted on ahead and pulled in at the gas station, I decided that the better part of wisdom was to do what I was told. So I turned in and stopped beside them. It wouldn't hurt to have their help, since I doubted Bigelow and Wilson T. were through with us.

Mr. Pickens got out, leaving Mr. Johnson in the car with his arm crooked on the rolled-down window, watching us. The motor of his car rumbled, as he waited beside the road. The storm clouds on Mr. Pickens's face, as he approached us, were worse than what was overhead. He came to my side of the car and, as I lowered the window, he put his hands on his hips and said, "What the hell you think you're doing?"

"Your job, Mr. Pickens, and watch your language. This is Hazel Marie Puckett who, as you can see, is no longer in the clutches of criminals."

He leaned down to glare across at her, and did it a good long time. She gave him a sweet smile. "Glad to meet you."

He grunted, took another long look, then said to me, "Get in the back. I'm driving."

"I'll have you know . . ." I started.

"The roads're icing up." He cut me off, opened my door and waggled his hand for me to get a move on. I did, crawling into the back seat with Little Lloyd, fuming at Mr. Pickens's reassumption of the driving responsibilities. I don't know why all the men on the face of the earth think they're the only ones who know how to drive.

"Look!" Little Lloyd screamed in my ear. "It's them! They're following us."

Sure enough, a white pickup truck slowed as it came abreast of the filling station. Three men in the cab looked us over, taking in my car and Mr. Johnson's, then spurted on out of sight.

"Oh no," Hazel Marie said, sliding down in the seat. "The one in the middle was Wilson T. He's still after me. What're we going to do?"

"Don't worry, Mama," Little Lloyd said, with more confidence that I had. "Mr. Pickens and Jerry will take care of us."

Mr. Pickens gave the child a quick smile. "Hold on a minute," he said, and went over to consult with Mr. Johnson.

When he came back, he slid behind the wheel without a word as to what they'd concluded. He just reached over and turned on the defroster, which I'd forgotten about in all the excitement, glanced at Hazel Marie in her Wednesday night date dress, and said, "Cold?" Then he jacked up the heater and pulled out behind Mr. Johnson's car.

As I sat steaming in the back seat, I began thinking of how much catching up we needed to do with Hazel Marie. Questions flooded my mind, but the atmosphere in the car wasn't conducive to detailed interrogation. At a stoplight in Rockingham, Mr. Pickens came out of his coat and handed it to Hazel Marie. She was shivering, even though the car was warm. I'd had my mind on too many other things to've noticed her miserable state. I declare, Mr. Pickens could make me mad enough to spit, then do something so nice that I had to somewhat reevaluate my opinion of him. Although he undid me again because he kept flicking his eyes in Hazel Marie's direction, instead of keeping his mind on his business.

Of course, I was familiar with Hazel Marie's effect on men in general and, by now, familiar with Mr. Pickens's propensity for women in general. Hazel Marie would have to be cautioned about him, although you'd think she'd've learned her lesson by now. I leaned my head back for a minute, feeling worn out from keeping him in line, to say nothing of all the perils to life and limb we'd so recently been subjected to and that I'd had to overcome on my own.

Then I straightened up. "Where're we going, Mr. Pickens?"

"Back to Jerry's."

"Do you think that's wise? Don't you think those men in the truck recognized Mr. Johnson and that souped-up red car of his? And Wilson T.'d certainly know my car. He can put two and two together as well as the next person. Besides, Hazel Marie needs to get home, and that's where I think we should go."

He gave me a quick look in the rearview mirror from those hot black eyes and said, "I know what I'm doing, so let me do it."

I sighed, because here we were, going at each other again. The man just would not brook a question, much less a more than reasonable suggestion.

Then I thought of something else. "If you think we're going to fiddle around here while you help Mr. Johnson find his lucky charm, I remind you that your job for me isn't over till we get Hazel Marie home." Hazel Marie glanced back at me, then at Mr. Pickens, wondering, I was sure, at my forebearance of his intolerable behavior. Little Lloyd kept reaching up to touch her, making sure she was safe.

"Have you noticed the weather?" Mr. Pickens asked, with an unattractive touch of sarcasm. "It's worse to the west of us."

I gave up and concentrated on his driving. The streets through Rockingham were getting slushy, and we passed a wreck in which the two drivers were standing out in the freezing stuff while they examined the damage.

"Be careful, Mr. Pickens," I said, as I felt our wheels slip when we pulled away from a stop sign.

"You want to drive?"

"Well, no, I don't believe I do."

"Then let me do it."

"I'm happy for you to. I'm just pointing out the road conditions."

He reached a hand back and, to my surprise, patted my knee. "Don't get yourself in an uproar, hon, I'll get us there safe and sound. We'll wait out the road conditions at Jerry's, where I doubt Bigelow would want to show his face. Then we'll get you all to Abbotsville. That sound like a plan to you?"

"It does, and I thank you for letting me know what you have in mind. You're always thinking, Mr. Pickens but, I declare, I wish you'd remind me of it every now and again."

By the time we got to the asphalt road that led to Mr. Johnson's place of business, Mr. Pickens had the car in low gear, steering carefully and more slowly than he was accustomed to doing. Mr. Johnson in his colorful car was inching along in front of us. I noticed the trees hanging over the road, beginning to sag with ice, while our tires crunched on the road.

I thought of something else to worry about. "What if Mr. Johnson loses power? We'll freeze to death out here in the country."

"He's got a generator. Now, listen to me, hon, you're paying me to do the worrying and I wish you'd let me do it. Believe me, I can do it better by myself."

"He probably can, Miss Julia," Little Lloyd said, adding his reassurance to Mr. Pickens's.

So I decided to let him. Unless I thought of something he might've forgotten.

Mr. Pickens followed Mr. Johnson as he turned into the lot at the Jerry Johnson's Racing place of business. Hazel Marie sat up and looked around, holding Mr. Pickens's coat around her shoulders.

"Wait'll I come around," Mr. Pickens said. "I'll walk you both to the door. It's not iced over yet, but there'll be slick spots."

But Hazel Marie and Little Lloyd got out on their own, holding on to each other as they made their way to the entrance, where Mr. Johnson waited for them. I managed to get across the front seat and hold on to the door until Mr. Pickens got to me.

"Hold on," he said, putting an arm around me. "We don't want to break anything."

I must say that steadying myself against his strong arm made walking on ice a comforting experience. Hazel Marie had missed something by not waiting for him, but young bones can afford to take chances.

Mr. Johnson stood, grinning, at the door. "Here comes Wonder Woman!" he bellowed, his voice bouncing off the walls. "I swear, Miss Julia, you're so good at finding things, I'm about ready to hire you, myself! Get on in here where it's warm and tell us how you found this good-lookin' woman. Was Bobby Bigelow there? Didn't see anything of mine, did you? Hey there, Little Boyd, thought you'd gone off and left us. You're one heck of a detective, and I'm ready to put you to work."

Little Lloyd softly corrected the name he'd been called without making an issue of it. Like me, he always appreciated hospitality in any form he could get it.

I declare, Mr. Johnson was more wound up, if possible, than he'd been before. I wondered if he needed medication, but of course worry does that to some people. Even though I didn't personally hold with superstition, I could understand his anxiety about his lucky charm. Lord knows, I'd suffered enough anxiety over Hazel Marie to sympathize with anybody who'd lost anything, especially something he believed, against all scientific evidence, would keep him in one piece on the racetrack. Now that I'd had some racing experience, I knew that he took his life in his hands every time he got in one of those cut-down trucks he had in his garage. I'd've found another line of business, if it'd been me.

There was only one mechanic in the garage, a man Mr. Johnson called Curtis, as we passed through on the way to the lounge. He waved at us and said he'd put the coffee on.

"I guess I've lost my mind," Mr. Johnson said, ushering us into the lounge, "but, with this weather, I sent most of the crew on ahead to Phoenix. I'm hopin' against hope, J. D., that you'll find my charm and make the trip worthwhile. If it don't turn up, I'm just gonna set down and bawl."

Hazel Marie looked at him with a frown on her face, not understanding where he was coming from. Mr. Johnson did take some getting used to.

As I headed for the coffee pot, Mr. Pickens assigned himself to take charge. "All right, Miss Julia, let's have it. How'd you and the boy know to go to the speedway?"

"Well, it was like this. Hazel Marie called Lillian this morning and told her she was in an RV, parked in a field at the North Carolina Speedway. Then we happened to call Lillian right afterward and found that out. Then Little Lloyd looked up directions to it on the computer. After that, it was simple. Too bad you had to go off somewhere and miss it all." I ignored his mumbling about needing to check out Bigelow's house and shop. "Mr. Johnson," I went on, "I hope you don't mind us using your electronic equipment, since it was in a good cause."

"Not a-tall!" he yelled, a wide grin on his face. "Wish I could've seen their faces when you showed up at the track."

"You should've seen us!" Little Lloyd broke in, loud enough to rival Mr. Johnson. "Miss Julia outran them all! When we got Mama in the car, they came after us in the RV, but she went around that track like Bobby Labonte!"

"That a fact?" Mr. Pickens said, his eyebrows raised halfway up his head. Skeptical, was what he was.

"Yeah! They spun out and wrecked on the number four turn, but we just kept on going!"

Mr. Johnson, though, was so astounded, he almost spilled his coffee. "Y'all lapped the track?" he bellowed. "Why, that thing's got a twenty-five degree bank on the third and fourth turn, and just about as bad on one and two."

"Yessir, we did!" Little Lloyd had to stop and get his breath. "And Miss Julia didn't wreck or anything!"

Mr. Pickens tried not to be impressed, but I knew he had to be. "Now, Ms. Puckett, Hazel Marie," he said, "we all want to know what happened to you."

Hazel Marie huddled up in his coat, as she took an easy chair and warmed her hands on the coffee cup I gave her.

"First off," Mr. Pickens said, "tell us about this boyfriend of yours."

"He's not my boyfriend!" she snapped, surprising me with this show of spirit. And relieving me of any lingering concern about having a church fund-raiser in my family.

"Sorry." Mr. Pickens favored her with one of his smiles, but it didn't register very high on her scale.

"Hazel Marie," I said, hitching up in my chair. "Tell us where you've been for the past two days and three nights. We've been out of our minds with worry, and you don't even know the half of it. Sheriff's departments all over the place have been looking for Bigelow and Wilson T., and you along with them and, on top of that, Mr. Johnson, here, is losing his livelihood because of those two. And something has to be done about it. So start off, and don't leave anything out."

She put a hand up to her forehead and rubbed it, shaking her head. "I didn't know what was going on, Miss Julia. It all happened so fast. When Wilson T. came by for me," she looked up, confused, "when was it? Wednesday night. We were halfway to Asheville when Wilson T. got this call on his cell phone. He turned around real quick, told me he had a business emergency he had to take care of, and off we went to his cousin's garage at Jessup Mountain. Well, when we got there, all these men were scurrying around, working on a racing truck. And Bobby Bigelow was in the offices, packing up files and papers and so on. Stacking them in boxes, like he was moving. He and Wilson T. talked and seemed to argue a little. I wasn't paying much attention, except I heard them say something about meeting in Phoenix and then going on to California. I kept telling Wilson T. that I was hungry and we were going to miss the movie if we didn't hurry up and leave. I couldn't understand why we had to be there in the first place. I mean, according to Wilson T., it's Bobby Bigelow's business, and he just enjoys being on the sidelines of a race team."

She stopped and looked up at Mr. Pickens, who told her something she didn't know. "The sheriff raided the place the next day. Bigelow must've known it was coming."

"Raided?" she whispered, then seemed to put two and two together. "That's why they got in such a hurry later on and, maybe, why Bigelow was so mad that Wilson T. had brought me along. See, something was wrong with their racing truck. The mechanics kept working on it while Bigelow and Wilson T. loaded the vans with the office stuff. Well, it got way up in the night and no sign of us leaving, and I started looking for a phone but they'd been packed up. I was real mad by that time and would've walked out if we hadn't been so far back in the woods."

"You were there all night?" I asked, recalling my own restless night. "What did you do all that time?"

"Begged to go home most of it," she said, frowning at the memory. "Wilson T. kept putting me off. Said he had to help Bobby and he'd take me home when the crew left. But they were still working on that racing truck, running the motor and tinkering with it, and Bobby Bigelow getting more and more upset and nervous. I finally dropped off to sleep on a couch for a while, and woke up when I heard Bigelow and Wilson T. arguing something awful out in the shop. Bigelow was mad because the race truck still wasn't right. Said they'd have to take it back to Rockingham where there was better equipment. See, I think they were planning to go on to Phoenix that night, and now they couldn't. Anyway, he gave Wilson T. some things to keep safe for him, and told him that they all had to stick together. And, and, he said that since they had to stay in the state longer than he'd planned to, they couldn't afford to let me tell anybody where they were. That's when I got scared and finally found somebody's cell phone and called home. And that's when they locked me in the RV, and that's when I knew I was really in trouble." She stopped again, her eyes getting bigger as something dropped into place. "Jerry Johnson!" She turned her big eyes on him. "That's *you*, isn't it? I heard them talking about you; you're the reason they didn't want to come back to Rockingham. Bobby Bigelow said he didn't want to see you until you were nothing but a blur in his driver's rearview mirror."

Mr. Johnson jumped up from his chair, so agitated he could hardly speak. A phenomenom, in itself. "I knew it! I knew they was trying to get at me." He whirled around and faced Hazel Marie. "Did you see anything that belonged to me? My lucky charm's missin', and I know they got it."

She leaned back away from his booming voice. "No, I don't know what they had. They loaded up their computers and boxes of papers, and what looked like rags and junk to me."

Mr. Johnson smacked his fist into his hand. "Thieves! That's what they are, just low-down, sneakin' thieves."

"As far as charms are concerned," Hazel Marie went on, "I do believe some are lucky. When Wilson T. snatched the phone away from me, I pulled one off my bracelet and threw it under a counter, hoping somebody'd figure out what was happening to me. And then there was that second one I left when we stopped at Gastonia where I tried to call again. I'd sure like to have them back, in case I need them again."

"I've got one, Mama," Little Lloyd said, plunging his hand in his pocket. "See, it's the one you left in the phone, and Deputy Bates has the other one. They worked just the way you wanted and led us right to you."

"Oh, I'm so glad to get it back," she said, the remaining charms on her bracelet clashing together as she reached for it. "I hated to pull them off, but I didn't know what else to do. Bigelow was so awful to me, I was scared to death of him, and he made Wilson T. watch me like a hawk. I was so mad at Wilson T. because he wouldn't stand up to him, just did everything Bigelow told him to and not taking up for me at all. Then I got him into big trouble. Bigelow was so mad he threatened to lock him up with me when I managed to make those phone calls." She smiled, pleased with herself. "More than once, too. I declare, Miss Julia, Wilson T.'s not real bright. I don't know why I hadn't noticed it before, dang his hide. Don't listen, Little Lloyd."

"No'm, I won't." Little Lloyd smiled, a dreamy look on his face, as he hung on her chair and every word out of her mouth.

"Why, that sorry thing," I said. "And he kept you locked up in that RV all this time?"

"Just about. We left Jessup Mountain right after I managed to call home, and they drove way out of the way, down into South Carolina on back roads. They were in sort of a convoy, with the RV, a transporter and a couple of cars. It took forever to get to Gastonia, where I begged Wilson T. to let me out for a little privacy. That's where I got to a phone again. Then we went somewhere out in the country around here, but they kept me locked up while they worked some more on the race truck. This morning, they decided they needed to do a practice run before leaving for Phoenix, and that's why we went to the speedway. Wilson T. let me out of the back room of the RV to walk around up front, and when he was watching them practice, I got his phone and called Lillian. When Bigelow found out that I'd made another call, he told Wilson T. that he was going to make him eat that phone if I got hold of it again. That's when you got there, Miss Julia, and just in time, 'cause they were ready to leave, and I might've never gotten home then."

"Yes, you would've," Mr. Pickens said, those dark eyes centered on her. "I'd've found you no matter where they took you."

I rolled my eyes, but neither of them noticed.

Chapter 23

While we absorbed Hazel Marie's story, drank coffee and kept an eye on the weather, Little Lloyd wandered out into the shop, fascinated by the open hood of a race truck. He came back into the lounge, his eyes shining, and went over to Mr. Johnson. "Jerry, Curtis said I could ride with you in your Number 17 truck sometime. I sure would like that." Then, unable to contain himself, he reverted to proclaiming my driving skills again. "After going around that track with Miss Julia, I wouldn't be scared. Y'all should've seen her."

"It was nothing," I said, waving my hand. "Just a couple of turns around the track that we managed just fine. Though I can't say the same for Bigelow and Wilson T. Hazel Marie," I went on, getting to my feet. "I think we need to use the ladies'. Where is it, please, Mr. Johnson?"

He pointed toward the front of the building. "Go out in the hall, second door on your left."

I got to my feet, saying, "Come go with me, Hazel Marie." As I left, with her right behind me, I heard Little Lloyd begin again to give the details of our racetrack adventures, his voice high with the thrill of it all. There wasn't a sound from Mr. Pickens or Mr. Johnson all through his recitation but, as we went into the ladies' room, I heard Mr. Johnson yell that he had a good mind to put me in his truck at Phoenix. Fat chance, I thought. I didn't care to ride in a pickup, much less drive one.

As soon as we got the door closed, I sat Hazel Marie down and told her of the latest course of action by Brother Vern and how she now had less than ten days to answer the complaint he'd filed.

"Lillian and I've been keeping Little Lloyd out of sight so Lieutenant Peavey and Deputy Daly can't implement their snatch-and-grab order," I told her.

Tears welled up in her eyes, while her mouth tightened with anger. "Why can't Brother Vern leave us alone? Why's he doing this, especially now, with all this other mess Wilson T.'s got me into?"

"I don't know. But I'll tell you this, Brother Vern went to see Pastor Ledbetter Thursday morning, telling him that he'd been hearing uncomplimentary talk about you, and the pastor implied that he'd heard much the same. Now, wait, Hazel Marie," I cautioned her, as she started up at my news. "Don't get upset. You know how bad Abbotsville is for gossip. If nothing's going on, somebody'll make something up. But don't you worry, we'll put a stop to it. Anyway, that very afternoon Brother Vern filed his complaint, claiming to be acting in the best interests of the child, of all things." I studied on it for a minute, squinching up my eyes with the effort. "You know, I've been wondering what the pastor knew and when he knew it. He was awful worried about Wilson T.'s whereabouts and what was in, or *not* in, the building fund."

"He thinks Wilson T. embezzled the building fund? Oh, Lord, Miss Julia, how'd I get mixed up with such a man?" She buried her face in her hands.

"We don't know for sure that any money's missing, but we do know that Wilson T. put down a big bet on the Phoenix race. Ten thousand dollars' worth. Mr. Pickens picked the lock at his townhouse and found all sorts of incriminating evidence."

"Gambling! He's into gambling, too? What did I ever see in him? Here, he's as good as kidnapped me, brought Brother Vern out of the woodwork to threaten Lloyd, helped that sneaky cousin of his steal from Jerry Johnson, and all because he wants to *gamble*! I swear, I'd take his head off if I had my hands on him."

I smiled at the thought of Hazel Marie, as quiet and shy as she was, taking anybody's head off. "Well, the first thing we have to do is get you home, and how I'm going to drive up the mountain in this weather, I don't know. One more thing, Hazel Marie, no-body knows about the peril to Little Lloyd but Lillian and me. We didn't know who we could trust, so we've kept it to ourselves. That means that Mr. Pickens doesn't know squat about it, so don't let on. For all I know, he'd turn him over to the sheriff, and I don't want to take a chance on his willingness to evade the Law. Although he's certainly done so when it suited his purposes."

"Then we'd better leave before it gets any worse out there," she said, standing up and pulling Mr. Pickens's coat tighter. "I have to get home, so Binkie can help me fight off Brother Vern. Oh, Miss Julia, you'll testify for me, won't you? If it comes to that, I mean."

"You don't even need to ask. And it won't come to that. All we have to do is show up that thorn in the flesh for what he is, and prove that the child's best interests lie right where he is. I don't care what kind of gossip Brother Vern's passing on, you're a de-cent woman and everybody knows it."

Tears started streaming down her face. "I don't know what's wrong with me. I have the worst luck with men. Seems like the wrong kind just pick me out of a crowd, and I don't have enough sense to tell them apart." She stopped and looked at me, her face downright ashy-looking. "Oh, I am so sorry. I didn't mean to throw off on Mr. Springer. I know you don't want to talk about him, and I don't either, and I wouldn't hurt you for the world, Miss Julia. It just seems like I keep getting fooled by the likes of Wilson T. Oh, not that Mr. Springer was anything like him, but then there's Brother Vern who just waits for a chance to make trouble. And I've tried to live a good life, especially since you've been so good to us. I just try as hard as I can to make you proud of me, but nothing works out the way I want it to."

Well, it took me a second or two to figure out what to say to her. She was right, I didn't want to discuss Wesley Lloyd with her. It wouldn't've done either of us any good, but I had to admit that from her point of view he'd been a mighty poor pick. From mine, too, come to think of it. And I could see that she'd had bad luck with the men in her life, at least the ones I knew about. But I couldn't let her get down in the mouth, thinking she had some kind of curse dogging her when it came to men. That'd be as bad as Mr. Johnson putting such store in a lucky charm.

"Why," I said to her, "you just stop putting yourself down like that. I'll admit you've had bad luck so far, and I'm not excluding Mr. Springer. But you're not the only one as far as he was concerned. Your problem is that you've let the men do the picking. I say it's time you did some picking of your own. Take a hand in your own life for a change and things'll start looking up in the romance department."

Before she could agree with me, we heard the front door open and somebody walk through the hall, calling in a low voice to Curtis. I peeked out the bathroom door and nearly had heart failure. "It's Wilson T.!" I whispered. "I can't believe he'd just walk in like nothing's happened."

Well, that little woman, who was as sweet and agreeable as anybody could want, built up a head of steam right in front of my eyes and stormed past me through the door.

She came to a stop in front of Wilson T. and let him have it. "What're you doing here? You followed us, didn't you?" she demanded, her fists clenched by her side and her body trembling, she was so mad. "Well, it won't do you any good, because I don't want to see your sorry face again. So just go on back where you came from."

I stood by the bathroom door, waiting to see if Bigelow or any of his crew were coming in behind him, and wondering where Mr. Pickens was.

Wilson T., looking somewhat bedraggled from his vehicular accident, said, "If you've got it, Hazel Marie, just hand it over, that's all I'm asking. I never meant for you to get mixed up in this, but I've got to have what you took from Bobby."

"I don't know what you're talking about."

"Yes, you do." He took a step toward her, but she stood her ground. "Listen, I don't want to hurt you, but I've got to have it. Bobby made me come over here, and I can't go back without it. You know how he is. So give it here and I'll be gone."

"You're going to be gone, anyway, because I don't have anything of his. And you've got a nerve, just walking in here and acting like you didn't lock me up and lug me all over the state like a sack of potatoes!"

Wilson T.'s mouth tightened as he glared at her, doing a little fist-clenching, himself. I saw Curtis standing beside the truck he'd been working on, then he glanced out a back window as Mr. Johnson and Mr. Pickens passed by. I could see them talking, gesturing at the weather, completely unaware of the tense situation inside. Little Lloyd peeked out of the lounge, his eyes big at the sight of his mother and Wilson T.

"Be that way then," Wilson T. said. "We'll see what you say when Bobby gets hold of you. Let's go." He grabbed her arm and pulled her toward the door.

Before I could make a move, Little Lloyd streaked across the garage and made a flying leap for Wilson T.'s back, his arms flailing like a windmill. "Don't you hurt my mama! You get away from her!"

I got myself in gear and clutched a handful of Wilson T.'s overcoat, trying to pull him away from Hazel Marie. He shoved Little Lloyd aside and shook me off, neither of us slowing him down in his rush for the door, pushing Hazel Marie before him.

"Stop!" I yelled. "Mr. Pickens! Help!"

I grabbed the back of Wilson T.'s collar, pulling it tight enough to choke him, while Little Lloyd latched on to his leg. Hazel Marie screamed, as she twisted and turned, trying to break his hold.

Wilson T. shook his leg, sending Little Lloyd sprawling, and swatted at me. He pushed Hazel Marie against the wall, where she got enough purchase to slip his grasp. She turned and kicked and pounded on him, screeching at the top of her lungs, "Don't you hurt him! Leave my baby alone!"

His face red as a beet from the hold I had on his collar, Wilson T. grabbed her and shook her until her head flopped back and forth. "Give it here," he yelled, gasping for breath. "I know you've got it. Give it to me!"

I turned loose of his collar, took a firm hold of my pocketbook and started swatting him over the head with it. Wilson T. kept yelling, "Where is it!" and Hazel Marie screamed and scratched at him, while Little Lloyd kicked and hollered, "Don't you hurt my mama!" I yelled for Mr. Pickens, adding my two cents' worth to the din, at the same time getting in a particularly well-aimed whack, the jar of Metamucil in my pocketbook coming in quite handy as it clanked against Wilson T.'s head.

He released Hazel Marie and threw back his arm, sending me slamming against the front door. Before I could catch myself, my feet slid out from under me on the waxed floor and I flopped down on my backside with my legs spraddled out in a most shameful fashion. Sitting there slightly dazed with the suddenness of it, I felt myself being slid across the floor as the door was pushed opened behind me.

Mr. Pickens came barreling in, leaving me crumpled up between the door and the wall. I heard Mr. Johnson come at Wilson T. from the opposite side, yelling, "Dog bite it, leave that woman alone!" as he snatched Little Lloyd out of the fray. Mr. Pickens swung Wilson T. around and pushed him against the wall hard enough to put a dent in it. He had his hands more than full with Hazel Marie, though, because she kept going after Wilson T. She flew into him like a banty rooster, scratching and clawing at him, yelling, "I've had enough of you! You, you sorry excuse for a Christian! You're gonna regret the day you got me in this mess!"

"Hold on, hold on here," Mr. Pickens said, grabbing her around the waist from behind and holding her close.

"Turn me loose! He's got it coming and I'm gonna give it to him!" She tried to wiggle free of Mr. Pickens, but he had a good hold on her, which was probably the only thing that saved Wilson T. from serious injury.

My land, I thought as I struggled to stand up, having to turn over and hike my rear end up in the air so I could push off with my hands. It's the knees that go first, you know, and mine needed all the help they could get. But I wasn't worrying about my own ungraceful climb to my feet, being awed and amazed at Hazel Marie's display of fighting spirit.

She was wound up like a top and, if not for Mr. Pickens's arms around her, she'd've torn into Wilson T. again.

"Hold on now," Mr. Pickens said. "Let's get this straightened out. Who is this, anyway?"

"Wilson T. Hodge, that's who," Little Lloyd yelled.

"Bigelow's jackass is more like it," Hazel Marie said, struggling in Mr. Pickens's grasp.

Mr. Johnson switched his head around and let out a yell that echoed around his shop. "Bigelow! Is that egg-suckin' dog around here?"

Wilson T. didn't get a chance to answer. Hazel Marie balled up her fist and swung with all her might, landing a good one right on his nose. Wilson T. grabbed at his face and added his bellow to Mr. Johnson's. He looked ready to tear Hazel Marie limb from limb, and might've done it if Mr. Pickens hadn't put a hand out to hold him back. Mr. Pickens pulled Hazel Marie out of arm's reach, trying his best to calm her down.

Mr. Johnson noticed me hanging on to the door knob, trying to straighten myself up and catch my breath. He came over, bellowing right in my ear, "You all right, lady? Hurt anything?"

"Why, no, Mr. Johnson, thank you for asking. But I think I'd like to sit down for a minute."

He grabbed a chair, swung it behind me and shoved it against my knees, yelling, "Set it on down and rest yourself."

Wilson T. had pulled himself together by this time, and had regained some of his take-charge manner. "I don't know who you gentlemen are, but all I'm trying to do is get back something this woman's stolen."

Hazel Marie strained against Mr. Pickens's arms, trying to get at Wilson T. again. "You crooked, lyin', underhanded son of a . . . of a biscuit-eater!"

Mr. Pickens's eyebrows shot up at Hazel Marie's command of the language, and Mr. Johnson roared, "Whoa!" Then glaring eye-to-eye with Wilson T., Mr. Johnson bellowed, "You with Bigelow? You one of them thieves that robbed me? Huh? Huh? I want my lucky charm back and my disks and tools, and I want compensation for vandalizing my shop! J. D., you better call the cops, before I take somebody's head off here."

Wilson T. jerked away from him and straightened his suit coat down in an effort to regain his dignity. "I don't know anything about your shop problems. I was in Abbotsville up until yesterday, and I can prove it. Hazel Marie," he said, turning to her, "come on with me, and you can give Bobby's property back to him. I don't care what you do after that."

"What? What! I don't have anything to give to Bobby!" Hazel Marie was still so mad she could hardly catch her breath. "Get that through your thick head, and don't try to weasel out of anything.

You may not've robbed anybody, but you took me off in that RV and wouldn't let me go."

"That was all Bobby's doing. You'll recall that he wouldn't let me leave, either. So if he's in trouble with the Law, it has nothing to do with me. I'm just a messenger here, trying to get back what you took from him. Then I'm washing my hands of it all."

Hazel Marie squirmed in Mr. Pickens's arms, trying to get at Wilson T. again. "Okay, okay," Mr. Pickens kept saying, trying to get her under control. Then to Wilson T., "She says she doesn't have what you're looking for, so leave it alone."

"I'm warning you . . . ," Wilson T. started, but that was the wrong thing to say to Mr. Pickens, as I had earlier learned.

Mr. Pickens handed Hazel Marie over to Mr. Johnson, who was frowning with the strain of trying to hear what everybody was saying. Then Mr. Pickens stepped up and got right in Wilson T.'s face. "Warn me again."

Wilson T. shriveled up at Mr. Pickens's challenge, to say nothing of his manly presence standing four-square and ready in front of him. I drew in a breath, hoping I wouldn't have to be a witness to an all-out dog fight. Which if it came down to it, Mr. Pickens would fix Wilson T.'s little red wagon good. There'd be a mess to clean up, though.

Wilson T. stared across Mr. Pickens's shoulder, unwilling to meet his eyes, and said, "I just want what belongs to Bobby. Make her take it back to him, and we're through here."

Mr. Pickens gave a short laugh. "*Make* her? Man, you don't know women. I'm not about to make her do anything."

I'd known all along that Mr. Pickens was a good man at heart.

Wilson T. then tried another tack. "Look," he said, finally meeting Mr. Pickens's eyes in an effort to talk man-to-man. "I have to warn all of you. She's taken something that belongs to

Bobby, and it's valuable. You don't want to tangle with him, because well, let's just say that he'll get it back one way or another."

"What're we talking about here?"

"*She* knows. Hazel Marie, you don't know what you're letting
yourself in for."

Hazel Marie's eyes blazed at him, as she tried to jerk herself
away from Mr. Johnson. "I didn't know what I was letting myself
in for when I met you, either! Get your sorry hide outta here, and
I hope you and Bobby Bigelow rot in jail for the rest of your
crooked lives!"

"Where is that sneakin' thief, anyway?" Mr. Johnson bellowed,
turning Hazel Marie loose and rushing at Wilson T. "Tell me
where he is."

"I don't know!" Wilson T. cringed against the auditory on-
slaught. "I swear I don't know. He told me to get back what she
stole from him, and that's all I know."

"I didn't steal anything from him!" Hazel Marie cried, as Mr.
Pickens grabbed her again.

"Where's Bigelow?" Mr. Johnson blasted the air like a thunder-
clap. "Where is he?"

"I don't know, I tell you," Wilson T. said, holding his arms in
front of his face, scuttling away from Mr. Johnson's screwed-up
face and blistering voice. "He's gone on ahead before the
weather. . . . I'm supposed to go back to Abbotsville, the church,
you know, my work. But I have to get back what she stole, please,
that's all I know."

"You lyin' *thing,* you," Hazel Marie yelled. "Get outta my
sight!"

"Good idea," Mr. Pickens said, keeping her uncommonly close
to him. "Pack it in, Hodge. You may not've had anything to do
with the robbery here, but the Abbot County sheriff'll want to
talk to you." Then he spoke softly to Hazel Marie, "Come on
now, it's over for now."

She went docilely enough, except for spitting at Wilson T. as she passed by. Mr. Pickens kept hold of her arm as he led her toward the lounge. Mr. Johnson got up in Wilson T.'s face again and, in his usual forceful manner, told him to take a hike and tell Bobby Bigelow that he was going to whip him to within an inch of his life. If Bigelow was ever man enough to face him, instead of sneaking into people's garages to tear up jack and steal what didn't belong to him.

Wilson T. made haste to leave, and I comforted myself with the thought of Lieutenant Peavey putting him on the hot seat when he got home.

"Come on, Little Lloyd," I said, putting a hand on his shoulder. "I declare, your mother made me so tired just watching her that I need to sit down awhile."

"She was something, wasn't she?" A note of pride filled his voice, and it warmed my heart to hear it.

Chapter 24

We got to the lounge in time to see Hazel Marie fling herself away from Mr. Pickens and stomp across the room to a chair. She flopped down, crossing her arms in a huff, still seething and steaming.

Mr. Pickens stood over her, his hands on his hips. "Man, lady, warn me before you get mad at me." He shook his head in admiration, a smile playing under his mustache. "You about put a permanent crimp in him."

Hazel Marie cut her eyes up from under her brows to give him a glare. "I would've, too, if you hadn't stopped me."

He laughed, earning himself another glare.

"I need to get home," she said.

"I'm working on it," he told her, but before he could let us in on his plans, Mr. Johnson came bounding in.

"What was that Hodge feller lookin' for, anyway?" he yelled, as Hazel Marie cringed from the blast to her eardrums. "Think it could've been my lucky charm? Ma'am," he said to Hazel Marie. "Did you see either of them with it?"

"No." She shook her head. "I didn't see anything like that. All I saw were disks and papers, and tools and motors and a lot of junk that didn't mean anything to me. The only charms I know anything about are the ones I dropped along the way."

Mr. Johnson just stood there with his head sinking lower, about overcome with the thought of it all. "J. D.," he said, slowly shaking his head, "I swear, son, if Hodge and Bigelow don't have it, where could it be? I was sure countin' on you gettin' it off of them."

"Mr. Johnson," I said, "it seems to me you're putting too much importance on something that can't possibly measure up to your own talent and knowledge and experience. I think your problem's all in your mind, and you ought to rise above it. Mind over matter, you know, even though I don't ordinarily hold with that Christian Science belief since I go to the doctor whenever I need to. But I think you ought to buck up and quit letting some little superstitious thing put you off so bad."

Mr. Johnson looked at me like I was crazy. "Ma'am, I 'preciate your advice, but I know it ain't no use me drivin' without it. I've tried it, didn't want to lean too much on superstition, like you say. But every time I drove without it, something bad happened. One time in the Powerstroke 200, this was a while back before I knew how bad I needed it with me, I blowed an engine. Very next race, I made a pit stop and went back out with loose lug nuts. Then on a qualifying run at the Texas Speedway, a Bigelow driver made contact when I was goin' high and he spun me into the wall. Tore everything all to hell and back, includin' my leg and collar bone, a coupla ribs and my truck. Took me out for most of the season. Man, I come outta what was left of my truck, hardly able to stand up, but I waited on the track till that driver come around again and throwed my helmet at him." He took a deep breath, reliving the experience. "Ever since I've had my charm, though, it's been clear sailing. I know it's superstitious, but that don't mean it don't work. Every time I have it with me, I blow the doors off everything on the track. And that's a fact.

"And now," he went on, looking down at the floor and shaking his head again, "just when I'm leadin' in points and got the championship all but sewed up, an' ready to move up full time in the Winston Cup series, this has to happen. I been racin' more'n twenty year an' never been closer than I am now. J. D., they used to call me the Mark Martin of the Craftsman Trucks, 'cause I couldn't win the big ones. But I showed 'em last year, comin' in first three times, and this year I had a chance to do it again, and win on points, too. But there won't be no victory lane for this ole dog now. Might as well stay home, and let the young drivers have it."

"Don't give up, Jerry," Little Lloyd said. "Your fans are behind you. We're all pulling for you."

"Aw, that's real nice, Little Boyd," Mr. Johnson said. "I 'preciate it, but speakin' of fans, I got to ask each and every one of you not to let on to anybody about my lucky charm. I mean, people know I got one, but I'd never live it down if they knew how much I depend on it. I never wanted anybody to know and they wouldn't of, if that danged Bigelow'd kept his hands to himself. So don't nobody tell anybody, okay?"

"We can't, Jerry," Little Lloyd reminded him. "We don't know what it is."

"Well, it ain't much, I don't mind saying. Nobody but me'd look twice at it." He took a deep, shuddering breath and went on, "I'm just worried to death about the shape it's in by now. It was about wore down to a nub already, and it won't stand no rough treatment." He shook his head, overcome with his loss. "Thought it'd last a few more years anyway, and me and it'd retire together."

While Mr. Johnson bemoaned his pitiful situation, Mr. Pickens had commenced pacing back and forth by the window that looked out over the back of the garage. He glanced out of the window now and then, checking the weather, his hands rammed in his pockets while he enjoyed a few minutes of silence from Mr. Johnson. It concerned me that Mr. Pickens might be giving too much attention to Mr. Johnson's lost lucky charm, seeing as how he still hadn't gotten Hazel Marie home, which was what he'd been hired to do.

But, after watching him for a few minutes, I saw that he'd not forgotten her at all. In fact, the way his eyes kept glancing her way, sweeping all up and down her, I had to worry that he'd get distracted from his job in another way entirely.

I walked over to him and, lowering my voice, said, "Mr. Pickens, we need to work something out. I've got to get Hazel Marie home to straighten out some legal problems, which have nothing to do with our current ones, and she's got to do it as soon as she can or something awful will happen. We can't afford to fritter away any more time. The clock is ticking, Mr. Pickens. If you have a mind to take on Mr. Johnson's problem to the extent that you have to linger here, we'll just be on our way now."

He studied me for a minute with that penetrating gaze that almost unnerved me. "You looked out the window lately? It's a mess out there."

"Well, I know it but, between Hazel Marie and myself, we'll just have to manage. We can't afford to get iced in here for several more days. I'm telling you, you don't know what's at stake. I've got to get Hazel Marie home."

He frowned. "You mean there's more to this than Bigelow and Hodge?"

"There certainly is."

"Well, what?"

"If you must know," I said, edging closer to him and lowering my voice, "it has to do with her uncle, who's trying to get custody of Little Lloyd. He's sworn out a complaint against her, and at the most inopportune time, as you can see. And all because he wants the little bit of money in the child's educational fund." That's all I was willing to tell him of Little Lloyd's inheritance. Neither he nor anybody else needed to know that the fund would've educated every child in Abbot County, and then some.

Mr. Pickens twisted his mouth, making his mustache jump around, as he gave her another long look. "Interesting woman."

"Believe me, Mr. Pickens, if you find her interesting, you

don't have a chance in the world of having any of it returned until she attends to the problem at home. That ought to be incentive enough for you." I hated to encourage him, knowing how susceptible Hazel Marie was to a man's attention, and knowing how quick he was to give it, but I had to use what I had.

"Won't give me a second thought till then, huh?"

"That's right. I know her, and what she's facing is going to take all her time and attention. Think about it."

"Oh, I am, and looks like I'm just gonna have to get you home one way or another." He smoothed his mustache with a thumb and forefinger, then touched my shoulder. "Tell me this, was she serious about Hodge?"

"Doesn't matter whether she was or not. She's certainly not now. I'll tell you this, Mr. Pickens, Hazel Marie's not had much luck when it comes to picking men. As you can see, she's in bad need of cheering up, and you're as good as anybody I've ever seen in that department. So, I'd appreciate it if you'd use some of those winning ways of yours in the service of a good cause, just to make her feel a little better. But it's to be only a temporary measure; I don't want you leading her on with false promises like she's already had too many of. But you're so good at what you do, I know you'll know how to handle it. I declare, Mr. Pickens, you certainly have a way with you when it comes to women."

Lord, I was laying it on thick, and he was eating it up, believing every word I said. What man wouldn't, since they all think they're God's gift? But he needed a spur or maybe a whip to get us on home, and I wasn't above giving him whatever it took to get us there. Meanwhile, I'd have to steer Hazel Marie away from him and warn her about his womanizing ways.

I looked around at Mr. Johnson, who was so woebegone as to be next to useless, then at Hazel Marie, who looked a million miles away, as she sat with her arm tight around Little Lloyd. He snuggled up to her as he watched the Weather Channel.

"I'm going to call Lillian," I said to Mr. Pickens, "and tell her we've got Hazel Marie back. I'll see how the weather is up there and, if the roads are halfway passable, I'm going to head out."

"Let me know what she says," he said, as he turned to look out of the window again.

Mr. Johnson gave me permission to use his phone and, when I got through to Lillian, it was all I could do to break in on her stream of information. Lieutenant Peavey and Deputy Daly had rung the doorbell before it was good light, looking for Little Lloyd; Coleman and Binkie had come by, worried about all of us; Sam had called three times, saying he was about beside himself not knowing where we were; LuAnne had walked over from the church after a counseling session to leave word that she'd made a doctor's appointment for Leonard, and Brother Vern had shown up on the front porch, telling Lillian that "whoever meddles in the work of those who are the called of God is doin' nothin' but danglin' over the fires of hell."

"Or something like that," she said. "He rantin' and ravin' to beat all I ever heard. You better get on back here, Miss Julia, they all goin' crazy on me."

When I told her that we had Hazel Marie and that all that was holding us up was the weather, she let out a shriek that even Mr. Johnson heard. "Them highways is still open," she told me, "I jus' heard it on the teevee. Backroads is gettin' bad, but y'all come on 'fore it get dark an' you be all right."

When I hung up, I walked back over to Mr. Pickens and gave him Lillian's weather report. "If we get started right away," I said, "we can be there before the temperature drops tonight and ices everything over. Mr. Pickens, we've just got to get home. Everything's going to you-know-where in a handbasket up there."

He gave me one of those little smiles that almost got lost in his mustache, and said, "Let me talk to Jerry a minute."

Well, a minute was all I was going to give him. I wasn't looking forward to slipping around on an icy interstate, but we had to do it.

Mr. Pickens hunkered down beside Mr. Johnson's chair and started talking to him. Mr. Johnson kept shaking his head and whispering loud enough for all of us to hear him. "Ain't no use, J. D. If I run at Phoenix, I'll just make a fool of myself. I don't wanta put my crew through all that 'cause we ain't got a chance in hell of runnin' in the top five. Not without my lucky charm, we ain't."

Well, I'd just about had enough of that, so I marched over to tell Mr. Pickens to leave him alone so we could leave.

Just as I got to them, Mr. Pickens said, "Look, Jerry, nobody but your own crew knows it's missing. Everybody else's gonna think your streak's still going. They'll stay intimidated, trust me on that."

Mr. Johnson shook his head. "I don't know, son. It's us that messes up when I don't have it."

"All right," Mr. Pickens said, "let me put it this way. We need you, and I still may be able to pull a rabbit out of a hat. You're all loaded up to go to Phoenix, aren't you?"

"Yeah, already sent most of the crew on with the backup truck, for all the good it'll do. With all the damage Bigelow did to us, I wanted them outta here. Number 17's in the transporter out there, ready to move out if anybody else came sneakin' around."

"Tell you what," Mr. Pickens said. "Instead of unloading and giving up, how about loading up Miss Julia's car and dropping us off in Abbotsville? That's not too far out of your way and, if you'll do that, I'll go on with you and find your lucky charm. If another crew's got it, they'll show up in Phoenix, right?"

"By dog, you're right!" Mr. Johnson looked as if he'd just gotten a new lease on life. "I ain't gonna find it settin' here, am I? That's where it'll be, out there where it'll do somebody some good. Come on, let's load 'er up."

"See, Mr. Johnson," I said, wanting to keep him encouraged, since it seemed the only way I was going to move Mr. Pickens was to light a fire under Mr. Johnson. "You just have to have faith that things will work out. Mr. Pickens has found what was lost for us, and he'll do the same for you. But, first, he has to get us home. And speaking of that," I went on, turning to Mr. Pickens, "just what did you mean by loading up my car? I intend for you to drive it, not ship it somewhere."

"Haw!" Mr. Johnson bellowed. "Just you wait an' see what J. D.'s got up his sleeve. I tell you, boys, my ole buddy's got tricks you ain't seen yet! Let's us get started on this, and you folks get ready to roll. Not gonna let a little sleet an' ice stop us now!"

He bounded out into the shop area, yelling and laughing and calling to Curtis. Mr. Pickens just stood there, looking pleased with himself.

"What're we going to do, Miss Julia?" Little Lloyd snapped off the Weather Channel and stood up. "They say there's another cold front right behind this one, and it's picking up moisture from the gulf. They're saying a winter weather watch is out for the mountains."

Before I could answer, Mr. Pickens put a hand on the boy's shoulder, saying, "We'll make it, and it's going to be the ride of your life. Let's go, ladies. Jerry's ready to roll."

Chapter 25

Hazel Marie and I followed Mr. Pickens through the garage and on out the back door, our breath condensing in front of us as we hit the cold air. I was astounded at what was out there, and I'm here to tell you I'd never seen anything like it. We came out into an open-sided covered space, like a two-story double carport, with what looked like one of those huge, eighteen-wheeled moving vans parked underneath. It was painted the most awful shade of turquoise with JERRY JOHNSON RACING slashed across the trailer part in bright yellow, outlined in black and white. Garish, was all I could say for it.

As if that wasn't bad enough, there was Mr. Johnson wearing a jacket that was as close to Joseph's coat of many colors as I could imagine. It was of a shimmery turquoise material, nylon most likely, although it had so many decals, patches and emblems on it that you could hardly see the background color. JR LANDSCAPING was the featured advertisement, with SK POWER EQUIPMENT, somebody's motor oil, somebody else's service station and BUCKIE'S DRIVE-IN blinding my eyes. And to add to all that, there were black and white checks running up and down the sleeves. The man was a walking billboard. And Mr. Pickens wasn't much easier on the eyes in a borrowed coat, since Hazel Marie was still wrapped up in his.

Mr. Johnson had the whole back side of the trailer laid out on the ground and, before I knew it, Curtis came around the corner in my car and drove right up on the door and stopped.

"Watch this here, Little Floyd!" Mr. Johnson bellowed, though he hadn't needed to at all, for Little Lloyd was standing right beside him, watching the undertaking with his mouth open. As indeed I was, wondering what they were doing with the only car I had to my name.

Mr. Johnson pulled a lever or pushed a button or did something mechanical and, lo and behold, the back door of the truck began to rise, taking my car with it, until it was way up over our heads.

"What," I wheezed, trying to catch my breath, "what in the world are they doing?"

"It's a double-decker transporter," Mr. Pickens said, enjoying, I do believe, my consternation. "Jerry hauls his race truck on the top deck, and they're going to put your car right in behind it. Watch, now."

When the door got to the top deck, it stopped and the driver moved my car right on inside, anchoring it good and tight. Then he rode the door back down to the ground.

"Load up, boys!" Mr. Johnson yelled. "We gonna hit the road. Hey, Miss Julia, sorry I let my Winnebago go on ahead of us. You coulda rode in style, but you ain't gonna fuss about this, I guarantee you. Might not be too legal, but just keep the blinds closed and who's gonna know? Come on, now."

Mr. Pickens took Hazel Marie's arm and helped her into the lower deck of the trailer, while Little Lloyd followed her, eager to look around inside.

"Your turn!" Mr. Johnson bellowed in my ear. "Hop on in!"

Between Mr. Pickens and Mr. Johnson, I found myself lifted up over the threshold and inside what looked like a garage on wheels. There was a narrow aisle between rows of cabinets holding every kind of tool and hose and machine you could think of. Mr. Johnson came behind us, closing and latching cabinet doors as he went.

"Keep on goin' to the front," he yelled. "I'll get y'all settled, then we'll head out."

"What is all this stuff?" I whispered to Mr. Pickens.

"Everything they need to repair or rebuild a race truck at the track. Would you believe they've got four motors ready to go if they need 'em?" He put his hand on my back as we moved toward the front.

Yes, I'd believe it. I saw enough plunder in that van to open a filling station, if you had a mind to.

About three-quarters of the way down the aisle, it took a little turn and went up two steps. We walked into a small sitting room, complete with aquamarine leather sofas built onto two sides of the space, a small table, and a wall of all kinds of electronic para- phernalia, including a television set, fax machine, telephone, computer and I don't know what all.

"My word," I said, astounded at the array before me.

"Got a satellite hookup, too!" Mr. Johnson sang out. "Refrig- erator's right under there with plenty to drink. The john's around the corner. Make yourselves at home, folks, and call me on the phone if you need anything. I'm gonna put this mother in gear and head for the mountains!"

"Mr. Johnson," I said, putting my hand on his arm as he started to leave. "Don't take any chances. That sleet's still coming down out there."

"Well, thank you for your worry, but a little sleet's never stopped me before. This here truck's got gears it don't even know about and enough tires to hold it on the road. I know you need to get home, and I'm gonna take you. And neither Bigelow's bunch nor a smokey's gonna stop us."

When he left, I asked Mr. Pickens what a smokey was. "High- way patrol," he said. Then we heard the door of the van being closed and latched, locking us inside the back side of something that looked like a circus truck, along with, according to Mr. Pickens, extra generators, engines, cool-down units, utility carts, pit carts, crash carts, tool boxes, nuts and bolts bins, body paint, oil lines, fuel lines, brake lines, springs and shocks. To say nothing of a racing truck and my car overhead, which were the only things I would recognize if I saw them.

I leaned down and looked out the window, seeing Mr. Johnson swing up into the cab. He started the motor, and I could feel the rumble of it under my feet.

"Sit here by me, Miss Julia," Little Lloyd said, "it might be kind of rough till we get on the interstate." The child was beside himself with the thrill of checking out our highly unusual conveyance.

I took a seat beside him on one of the sofas, noticing that Mr. Pickens took his right beside Hazel Marie. She was still looking down-in-the-mouth after considering the kind of men who'd been in her life. Little did she know that there was another of the same ilk sidling up to her again.

"Why," I said, rooting around on the sofa, "there're no seat belts." Then I hushed up about it, since that was clear proof we weren't supposed to be riding back there. "Hold my hand, Little Lloyd."

As the big truck pulled out from under the carport, I could hear the ting of sleet against the sides of the van. Looking out the windows, I saw sagging tree limbs, coated with ice, and began to have second thoughts as to the wisdom of our journey. But I closed the blinds as Mr. Johnson had told us to do, deciding that it was too late to back out now. And, of course, it was all for the best since getting home was what we had to do.

Mr. Pickens sat across from us, talking soft and low to Hazel Marie. She nodded now and again, occasionally giving him a sad kind of smile. I worried that he might be pulling out some of that manly charm he had so much of and which he used to get whatever he wanted. I'd seen him in action and, so far, had not seen any woman with enough immunity to resist him. Except me, of course, and I intended to see to it that Hazel Marie did, too. After he got us home, that is.

The truck lurched as it turned onto the main highway, picked up speed, and headed toward Charlotte. I hoped that Mr. Johnson was right when he said the thing could handle icy roads because, when I peeked through the blinds, there was hardly any traffic, and not a few cars and pickups stranded on the roadside and in ditches.

We were in the hands of the Lord and Jerry Johnson. I prayed to the one, and put my trust in the other.

"Mr. Pickens," I said, more sharply than I'd intended, for a sudden scary thought had occurred to me. "Have you given any thought to the fact that Wilson T. knows exactly where Hazel Marie lives and, if Bigelow can't find whatever he's looking for, he might come after her again? He and Wilson T. could be sitting there, waiting on us."

He nodded. "I've thought of it. But you said you needed to get there, so I figure we'll cross that bridge when we come to it."

I thought that through for a minute, then said, "But if you're going on to Phoenix with Mr. Johnson, that leaves us alone to deal with them. I don't like the thought of that."

"I'll talk to Peavey and some others I know. They'd like nothing better than to get their hands on Bigelow since their raid was a washout. They'll be watching out for 'em, so you'll be okay."

I nodded, reassured that Mr. Pickens was still thinking ahead on our behalf. The little room had begun to heat up, so I came out of my coat and helped Little Lloyd out of his. We had come into Charlotte by that time, as evidenced by all the stopping and going the truck was doing. The streets seemed some better, and as I peeked out the window I saw that the sand trucks were out and about, trying to make the streets passable.

About the time we got through Charlotte and back on the interstate where the riding was smoother, Mr. Pickens stood up and said, "I've got an idea to pass the time. Let me see if I can find some cards."

He rummaged around in several drawers and came out with a deck of cards and a round container that held poker chips. Not that I immediately recognized it as such, not having the gambling habit, but he announced, "Let's play some poker."

Little Lloyd was eager, surprising me that he knew how to play, and Hazel Marie hesitantly agreed. Mr. Pickens got them situated around the tiny table, wrote out what beats what on a scrap of paper for Hazel Marie's benefit, and said, "Come on over here, Miss Julia, and sit in with us. We'll play dealer's choice, but I'm ruling out strip poker, no matter what you say."

Well, I knew when I was being teased, but I had no taste for cards, especially the gambling kind. "Thank you all the same, but I'd rather watch, if you don't mind."

"Suit yourself," Little Lloyd said, doubling over with laughter, "Get it, Miss Julia? *Suit* yourself."

I smiled at Little Lloyd's quickness of mind, as Mr. Pickens grinned and rubbed his hand over the boy's head. He shuffled the cards, slapped them down in front of Little Lloyd and said, "Name your game, sport."

I made myself comfortable in the corner of the sofa, while they started their game. Hazel Marie sounded willing, but halfhearted at first, but gradually she got into the fun the other two were having. I began to doze off, lulled by the easy rocking of the truck as it made good time on the interstate. Mr. Johnson had certainly been right. So far, the heavy truck was doing just fine in spite of the road conditions. Fitting my head into the corner of the sofa, I drifted in and out of sleep, hearing bits and pieces of the game in progress.

"Hit me," Mr. Pickens said.

"Dealer takes two. Everybody in?"

"Raise you one."

"I'll see you."

"I'm out."

"Chicken."

"Let's see what you're so proud of, Mr. Pickens."

With a snap of cards on the table, Mr. Pickens said, "Pair of jacks."

"Ha!" Hazel Marie laughed. "Don't send boys to do a man's job."

Mr. Pickens picked up the cards, saying, "Loser says 'Deal, dammit, deal.' Five card stud, pairs or better to open." I heard the swish of cards and the chink of chips.

"Pot's not right," Little Lloyd said. "Oh, it's me. Sorry."

"Read 'em and weep," Mr. Pickens said. "What'll you have?"

"One," Hazel Marie said.

"Oh, me," Mr. Pickens moaned, "she's at it again."

Little Lloyd laughed. "You're really getting the cards, Mama."

Hazel Marie, sounding pleased with herself, said, "Well, you know, lucky in cards, unlucky in love. I'll see you and raise you two."

"Jesus," Mr. Pickens said. "I'm out."

"My turn," Little Lloyd said, gathering up the cards as Hazel Marie added to the stack of chips in front of her. "High-low, deuces and one-eyed jacks're wild."

I heard the snap of cards as he dealt, listened to their opens and raises and calls. After a while Mr. Pickens said, "Okay, boys and girls, down and dirty."

"See you," I heard Hazel Marie say, "and raise you three."

"Damnation, woman, what've you got over there?"

Hazel Marie giggled. "It'll cost you to find out."

Right about then, I had a mind to put a stop to the game since it seemed to be getting out of hand. But, on second thought and a quick glance, I saw that Hazel Marie was smiling for a change, Little Lloyd was paying rapt attention, and Mr. Pickens was behaving himself. I let them alone and dropped on off to sleep.

Chapter 26

I came awake with a start, feeling the truck gather itself as Mr. Johnson shifted gears. Separating the blinds with my fingers, I could see that we were just beginning the long climb up the mountain toward Abbotsville. Ice covered the sides of the road, and the trees were bent over so far they looked ready to snap. The dangerous stuff was still coming down. It would've been beautiful if we hadn't had to be out in it, risking life and limb with every turn of the wheels.

Well, worrying about it at this late date wouldn't do us any good, so I decided to call Lillian and tell her we'd soon be there. Think positively, I always say.

Using Mr. Johnson's telephone—Lord, I was going to owe him a mint—I called Lillian to announce our imminent arrival.

"If, that is," I told her, "we don't end up sliding back down the mountain. It's bad out here, Lillian, but I guess we couldn't be in better hands than a racing driver."

"What you talkin' about? Who you got drivin'? You mixed up in something you oughtn't to be again?"

"No, I am not. Don't give me a hard time, Lillian, I'm about worn out as it is. Now, Mr. Pickens and Mr. Johnson, and somebody named Curtis, a mechanic I think he is, are coming in with us so, if you don't mind, we might offer them some sandwiches or something."

"Sam'iches! They need more'n that. No, ma'am, I already got it on the stove. It'll be ready when you get here. And you better get on back here, 'cause that Lieutenant Peavy come by and say they gonna put out a warrant for Miss Hazel Marie, if she don't show up with Little Lloyd, and yo' pastor, he come over sayin' he know you don't want no new building, but he don't know you go so far as to tear down Mr. Hodge's reputation, and he think you owe the church something for doin' it.'"

I could've pulled my hair out in frustration when I heard that. I declare, every time I left town, the whole place went to pieces.

By the time I hung up, the poker game was over. The slant of the truck as it went up the mountain had the cards sliding all over the table, so we all just sat around and looked at each other. Although Mr. Pickens did most of his looking in Hazel Marie's direction, asking her if she was warm enough, did she want anything to drink, was she feeling all right, and on and on. All that solicitude would've gotten on my nerves, but she didn't seem to mind it. All I could think about was what was waiting for me when we got home.

Mr. Pickens picked up the phone and called Mr. Johnson, telling him what exit to take and giving him directions through the town to our house.

I hadn't realized that I'd been holding my breath, so to speak, until the truck leveled off as we reached the edge of Abbotsville. Peeking through the blinds again, I was relieved to see familiar landmarks, although they were considerably altered by a layer of ice. Parking lots were all but empty, except Wal-Mart's of course. There're some people who just can't stay away from that place, but not me. The first and last time I went, some old man came out of nowhere, grabbed my hand and grinned like an idiot, going on and on about how glad he was to have me there. You'd've thought he'd issued a personal invitation, when all he wanted was for me to spend my money. It beat all I'd ever seen, and I decided I could do without an official greeter and never miss it at all.

Mr. Johnson took it slow as he drove into town. It felt as if the truck was being eased along the empty streets and, when we crossed Main, I saw that the streetlights had come on in the early dark of the late winter storm.

Mr. Pickens was on the phone again, watching out the window, as he guided Mr. Johnson right to our door. Mr. Johnson pulled up on the street across from the house and parked with a whoosh of the air brakes. I looked out the side window to reassure myself that the house was still standing. After what Lillian'd told me, I wouldn't've been surprised to see one of those black-clad SWAT teams waiting for us, or some of Pastor Ledbetter's orange flags staking out my boxwoods.

Mr. Johnson and Curtis climbed out of the cab and came around to the back of the trailer to unlock the door and let us out. We gathered our coats, eager to be released from the cramped quarters. I, for one, was most anxious to see the last of long-haul trucking.

As we walked back through the aisle, sidling around the carts of racing equipment stuffed in every available space, Mr. Johnson lowered the back door of the trailer. He called it a gate, but it looked nothing like a gate to me. Mr. Pickens helped Hazel Marie down onto the street, then reached up to give me a hand.

Just as I was holding on to the side of the truck so my feet wouldn't slip out from under me on the icy pavement, Lillian came out on the porch.

For once in her life, she was almost speechless at the sight of that huge truck, its yellow running lights and red warning lights glittering in the glow of ice in the early evening. It made a picture, I'll say that for it, but I was more interested in getting in out of the slippery mess.

"My Jesus!" Lillian called, as Little Lloyd started across the street toward her. "What y'all been ridin' in? Come 'ere to me, sweet baby!"

She waited for him with open arms, having sense enough to

stay on the porch and not risk the perilous stuff herself. After almost falling when he stepped up on the sidewalk, Little Lloyd made it safely to the porch where she nearly smothered the child in her apron. Looking across and seeing Hazel Marie by the truck, Lillian treated us and half the town to another shriek of welcome.

"Stay right here," Mr. Pickens said to Hazel Marie, cocking that finger at her. Contrary to my response to his finger pointing, she smiled at him. "I'll get Miss Julia in, then I'll come back for you."

He put his arm around me, telling me to test each step, and we started across the street. I glanced back to see Curtis raise the gate with Mr. Johnson riding up with it. By the time Mr. Pickens deposited me on the porch and started back for Hazel Marie, my car had been rolled onto the gate and was starting its ride to the ground. Wondering if the little thing would be able to get enough traction to be driven into the driveway, I stood with Little Lloyd and Lillian, who couldn't believe what she was seeing, watching the experts work. I declare, there's something to be said for professional drivers because, after spinning its wheels when it first hit the icy pavement, my car responded as nice as you please to Mr. Johnson's handling of it. He drove it across the street and right into the garage.

I breathed a sigh of relief to have things, to say nothing of people, back where they belonged. Curtis closed the gate of the truck and followed Mr. Pickens and Hazel Marie up the sidewalk and on into the house, where Lillian waited to welcome them. She could hardly contain herself to have us all safe again.

"Lillian," I said, "this is Mr. Johnson and Curtis, the best two drivers, I do believe, I've ever seen. And that includes you, Mr. Pickens, since you don't know how to slow down. I declare, I didn't have any idea the streets were as bad as they are, closed up as we were inside that truck. Mr. Johnson, I thank you for getting us home without a scratch."

"Aw, hell, 'scuse me," he bellowed, as Lillian's eyes widened from the shock wave. "Wasn't no trouble. Had to make the trip anyway. But I tell you this, I'm mighty glad to park that thing. Gettin' rough out there."

The warm smell of roast beef filled the house as we began shedding our coats. And something else was filling the Victorian chair by the gas logs burning in the fireplace.

"Sam!" I cried, stopped in my tracks at the sight of him. "What in the world are you doing here?"

"Waiting for you, Julia. When Lillian called to say you were on your way, I asked Etta Mae to drop me off here on her way to another client. I've been worried about you, woman." He had his leg propped on my needlepoint footstool, and I noticed that his cast had been changed to one that came only to his knee. I tightened my mouth at the thought that the Wiggins woman might've been instrumental in his partial recovery, to say nothing of his admission that he'd been with her earlier in the day. But I admit I was glad to see him.

After introductions were made and coffee and soft drinks offered and served—I didn't keep anything stronger than cooking sherry in my house—they gathered around the fireplace, while I helped Lillian in the kitchen. Sam had clasped my hand when I'd gone over to him, asking me to sit and recount how we'd found Hazel Marie and tell him about our truck ride. But with a house full of company, I didn't have time to go over all of it with him. Besides, between Little Lloyd's excitement and Mr. Johnson's loud talking, he was getting the gist of it.

Lillian had outdone herself with all the food she'd prepared, and we loaded the table down with dish after dish. Just as I went in to call them to dinner, the doorbell rang. The sound of it brought me back to reality in a hurry. Here, I'd been so taken up with ice and sleet and trucks and Sam and Mr. Pickens hanging around Hazel Marie, that I'd lost sight of impending danger to

Little Lloyd. He wasn't safe until Hazel Marie appeared before a judge at a hearing and got a favorable ruling, which I had no doubt she'd get because I'd be there backing her up with lawyers and character references and my own personal testimony. But until that happened, those deputies could show up anytime, waving their custody papers, not caring a lick that Hazel Marie would be answering the summons bright and early Monday morning. They're so literal, you know.

I looked across at Little Lloyd, who'd been struck dumb by the sound of the bell. He sat there stiff as a board, his eyes popping open and his mouth pulled tight over his teeth.

"Little Lloyd," I said as calmly as I could, "Lillian could use some help in the kitchen."

He was up and gone in a flash. I straightened my dress, worn now for almost three days in a row, and composed myself to face a deputy looking to snatch and grab. And to throw something at Sam or Mr. Pickens if they made a move to help him.

I peeked out the window, then swung open the door, both relieved and exasperated. "LuAnne! What in the world are you doing out in this weather? Come in before you break your neck or freeze to death."

She came in with a rush of cold air, bundled up in her old fur coat, a head scarf with furry earmuffs over it and fur-lined boots. She looked like a little bear with all that ratty stuff she had on. "Oh, Julia, I'm so . . ." She stopped with a gasp at all the people in the room, who had turned to see who else was visiting.

"Oh, I didn't know you had company."

"We just got home, LuAnne. Now why aren't you home instead of running around in this mess? Here, let me have your coat."

She began to come out of all the layers she had on, whispering that she'd had to get out of the house and had come for some counseling from Pastor Ledbetter over at the church. He hadn't been there and while she waited, the time had gotten away from her and now she wasn't sure she could get home. "I'm afraid to drive in this, Julia, and I thought I'd just stay with you until the streets get sanded."

There was nothing for it but to make her welcome, though my hospitality was getting a bit strained. I took her coat and laid it on the chair by the door, wondering how I could sleep them all. Somebody was going to have to make his bed on a pallet, since it was a settled fact that nobody was going anywhere anytime soon.

"We're just about to sit down at the table. Let me introduce you, then we'll eat." Then without thinking of the consequences, I introduced her to Mr. Johnson, Curtis and Mr. Pickens as "my friend, LuAnne Conover."

After we were seated around the table, the dishes passed and plates filled, it occurred to me that there had been some unforeseen pairing up. Little Lloyd was being entranced again by Curtis's tales of mayhem on the racetrack; Mr. Pickens kept leaning in on Hazel Marie, his black eyes watching her every move so that he could hardly get his fork to his mouth; Sam claimed the chair next to me, taking the leftovers, I guessed, since the main dish in the form of Miss Wiggins wasn't there. And to my shock and dismay, Mr. Johnson had made a beeline to the place next to LuAnne, saying in his usual loud manner that good-looking women improved his appetite.

LuAnne's face was red as a beet from the attention he was giving her, as he told her what passed for a whisper, about his racing career and how he knew she'd really like being on the circuit if she ever had a mind to follow it. She kept ducking her head, taking tiny bites of Lillian's good food, and cutting her eyes at Mr. Johnson. I heard her giggle even, which is not at all attractive in someone of her age and marital status. The woman was shameless. I knew in searing detail just what she'd been missing, and it seemed to me that she was in the process of making up for lost time. I just don't have any patience for people who can't exercise a little control.

"Sam," I whispered, "LuAnne's getting herself in trouble, the way she's flirting with Mr. Johnson. You'd think she'd know better, wouldn't you? I should've made it clear that she has a husband waiting for her at home."

"A little flirting never hurt anybody, Julia," Sam said, in that tolerant tone that could run me up the wall. I expected people to act like they're supposed to, but he didn't care if they just ran wild. He smiled at me and went on, "You ought to try it sometime."

"I'd think you'd've had enough of it by this time," I snapped. "Trifling with people's feelings is just plain, well, trifling."

Sam laid his fork on his plate, looked full at me and said, "Who's trifling, Julia?"

"Well," I said, unable to hold his gaze, "well, LuAnne, for one. Maybe Mr. Pickens for another and, well, you, Sam, and you know it." I pushed my chair back, unwilling to go any further with such matters at the dinner table, and said to the others, "We'll have coffee in the living room. Lillian, let's go cut the cake. LuAnne, I'd recommend that you call Leonard and let your *husband* know where you are."

As they began to get up from the table, Mr. Johnson walked over to Lillian and bellowed, "That was about the best meal I've had in a coon's age. How 'bout signin' on with me an' go on the circuit with us? We could use somebody who can cook this good." He put his arm around her, while she laughed at his goings-on. "Teach you how to change a tire, too! By dog, I'll even put you on the pit crew!"

LuAnne made sure, though, that he didn't pay Lillian too much attention, sidling up to him and suggesting that he tell her more about his lucky charm. "It's all just so fascinating, Jerry," she said. It made me want to throw up.

Mr. Pickens came over to help Sam to his feet, giving me a

knowing smile as he did so. I declare, the man was showing himself, acting so nice for Hazel Marie's benefit. And Sam's, too, if the truth be known, because Mr. Pickens was quick to pick up on who was important to her. I determined to have another talk with Mr. J. D. Pickens, and soon. He needed to be cautioned again about leading Hazel Marie on and breaking her heart with those winning ways of his. He was entirely too free with spreading them around. Womanizers don't make good husbands. Believe me, I know whereof I speak.

I followed Lillian toward the kitchen to prepare dessert, being about fed up with all the carryings-on in the dining room. Just as I got to the kitchen door, the lights blinked, then went out.

"Whoa!" Mr. Johnson yelled, as everything went dark and people milled around, bumping into each other.

LuAnne screamed like she'd never been in a power outage before, and I wouldn't've been surprised if she hadn't latched on to Mr. Johnson. I heard her scrambling toward him. Of course, I couldn't see a thing. It was black as pitch: streetlights and the lights in the church parking lot were all out. The only flickering glow, dim as it was, came from the gas logs in the living room and gradually I could make out through the draperies the lights that'd been left on around the truck outside.

Little Lloyd was murmuring, "Mama, Mama, where are you?"

"Right here, sugar."

"My nerves are about to act up," he quavered.

"Hold on to me, sport," Mr. Pickens said, right next to Hazel Marie where I knew he would be.

"Lillian, where're the candles?"

"They's some in the desk in the living room. But I'm lookin' for that flashlight that ought to be in this here drawer," she said, as I heard her feeling around for it. "I found it."

She flipped the thing on and handed it to me. "Them batt'ries 'bout dead," she said, as the weak light beamed a couple of feet, then took a downward swoop toward the floor.

"That's a light an' a half, ain't it?" Mr. Johnson roared. "Want me to go out to the truck an' get you a better 'un?"

"This'll do, Mr. Johnson," I said, threading my way through them as they stood huddled next to the table. "No need to risk breaking your neck when I'll have candles lit in a minute."

Just as I got to the living room, feeling my way by the feeble light, a heavy hand hit the front door. I nearly dropped the flashlight.

I hadn't heard a car pull up or a footstep on the porch. In the dark of the room and the silence that always falls when the lights go out, all I could hear was the whispery sound of sleet against the windows. And that BAM, BAM, BAM on the front door.

Chapter 27

Lord, it gave me a turn. What, I mean *who*, was out there?

LuAnne gave a screech, and even Hazel Marie began to moan under her breath.

Mr. Pickens said, "Calm down, everybody."

Lillian whispered loudly across the room, "Don't answer it, Miss Julia, it might be one of them UFOs. Where you at, anyway?"

Mr. Johnson cackled. "By dog, I been wantin' to see one of them things."

Sam said, "Wait, Julia, I'm coming," as I heard his cane scrape on the floor.

I couldn't do anything *but* wait, it scared me so bad.

BAM! BAM! BAM! again, shaking the door something awful, when there was a perfectly good doorbell right at hand.

Just as I was about to get my wits together, I felt Little Lloyd brush past as he broke out of the pack toward the middle of the room, his arms flailing in the air, jittering and carrying on in an absolute panic. "I'm *scared*! I'm *scared*!" he cried, jumping high and flinging his arms up on each "scared."

Mr. Pickens moved like a flash, wrapping the child in his arms as he squatted down beside him, crooning, "Hold on, sport, hold on to me. Hey, now, you forget I'm here? Who's gonna hurt you with J. D. Pickens around?"

I heard Hazel Marie gasp like she'd been stabbed in the heart, and I knew how she felt. Anybody who'd take care of a child, well, the rest of us would be safe with him, too.

And with that reassurance, I went to the door and cracked it open. Holding the flashlight straight up so the beam would catch the face of whoever was out there before it dribbled down in a nosedive, I peered through the narrow opening.

"Deputy Daly!" I cried. "You about gave me a heart attack!"

He stood there, so bundled up in a dark coat and a cap with earflaps that I hardly recognized him. "You folks all right? Deputy Bates asked me to look in on you, and I was on my way when this sector got knocked out."

Keeping the light in his eyes, I reached behind me and grabbed LuAnne's fur coat. With one sweeping motion, I flung it across Mr. Pickens and Little Lloyd.

Mr. Pickens said, "What the hell," but he didn't sound too surprised since I was the one who'd done it. I don't think Little Lloyd noticed, so wrapped up in Mr. Pickens's arms that one more layer didn't register with him.

"Why, yes," I told Deputy Daly, "we're fine, thank you. I'd ask you in, but I know you have a lot to do on a night like this. How many have lost power?"

"The whole south end of town's been out an hour or so, and now the west end's out. Probably some trees down somewhere, but Duke Power's got crews all over the county. Uh, but another reason I come by, Mrs. Springer, is do you know whose truck that is out there?"

"I certainly do. It belongs to Jerry Johnson, who is my guest."

Deputy Daly grinned through chattering teeth. "I thought so. Saw his name on it." My goodness, he was sharp.

"Anyways," he went on, "I'd hate to give *him* a ticket, I mean, he's a racin' legend and all, but I'm gonna have to ask him to move it off the street. Too dangerous out there with everybody slippin' an' slidin' around."

I didn't say anything about fools getting what they deserved if they took a mind to drive in these conditions. Instead, I said, "I don't know where we'll put it, my driveway certainly isn't big enough. But don't worry, Mr. Johnson'll know what to do. You just run on, Deputy, and we'll see to it."

"'Preciate it, ma'am." He started to leave, then turned back. "Uh, ma'am, Lieutenant Peavey says we're still looking to pick up the Puckett boy since, you know, he's supposed to be in protective custody until the hearing. We'll be doing that as soon as things get back to normal. Pretty much have our hands full tonight, though, what with traffic lights out and folks running off the roads."

"Well, first things first, I always say."

"Yessum, me too. Y'all stay warm, now."

I closed the door, weak with relief that there was one thing that could be said for the current weather conditions. It took the mind of the Law off complaints and court summonses. All except Lieutenant Peavey, whose mind sorely needed something besides protective custody to occupy it.

"Mr. Johnson?" I called.

"I heard him. How 'bout that church lot over there?"

"Perfect. There's no way we'll have a service in the morning, so there'll be plenty of room. Now wait just a minute till I get some candles lit so we can see what we're doing. Mr. Pickens, I do believe it's time to come out from under *Mrs.* Conover's coat. It's not that cold in here."

Mr. Johnson and Curtis put on their coats, going outside in a blast of wintry air to move the truck. We watched the operation from the windows, hearing the roar of the motor and seeing the diesel smoke spume up in the falling sleet, mixed now with flakes of snow. I wasn't sure at first that the truck was going to move, as Mr. Johnson shifted gears and fiddled around in the cab. Curtis stood in the middle of the street ready to stop traffic, though there wasn't any, and guide Mr. Johnson into the church parking lot. With a lot of jerks and some spinning of wheels, the truck finally made the turn into the lot and Mr. Johnson pulled it around so that it was directly across from the house and parked neatly enough to leave plenty of room for other vehicles.

Lillian opened her mouth to say something, but I caught her eye and shook my head. Mr. Johnson couldn't be blamed for parking on a building site and running over the pastor's little orange flags. Who could see the things, covered over with sleet like they were?

By the time Mr. Johnson and Curtis came back in, stomping and discarding coats and gloves, Lillian and I had enough candles placed around the room to provide a semblance of light and warmth. Everybody gravitated toward the fireplace as the corners of the room began to cool off. Hazel Marie and Mr. Pickens took the sofa with Little Lloyd curled up between them. Mr. Pickens had his arm across the back of it, his hand much too close to Hazel Marie's neck. Mr. Johnson pulled a chair up next to Lu-Anne on one side of the fireplace, while Curtis sat beside them, his legs stretched out toward the fire. He squirmed a little to get comfortable, and looked ready to nod off. Sam sat next to the fire where he could rest his leg on the footstool, beckoning me to take the chair next to him.

I ignored him. "Lillian, let's get the kitchen cleaned up while we still have hot water."

Then, after seeing LuAnne put her hand on Mr. Johnson's and lean close to him, I said, "LuAnne, we could use some help."

She gave me a furious look, but she got up and followed us to the kitchen. We carried more candles with us and, I'll tell you what's a fact, it is not easy clearing a table in a rapidly cooling room with hardly enough light to wash a dish clean. But people had done it for centuries, so I guessed I couldn't complain about one night of it.

LuAnne and I brought plates in from the dining room, scraping and stacking them, while Lillian washed. I started hand-drying the silver, as LuAnne put things away. I'd closed the door to the dining room so we wouldn't be overheard since I'd decided to take the opportunity to remind LuAnne that she had a husband sitting at home with a disabled function, and that she ought to behave herself accordingly.

Well, come to think of it, maybe she was. But I didn't like seeing it done in my house.

"LuAnne, Lillian told me that you told her that Leonard was going to see a doctor. I hope things are better for the two of you now."

"*He didn't go!*" She threw a spoon in the drawer, slammed it shut and flopped down at the kitchen table. That was all the help we were going to get from her. I'd opened the floodgates. "He said he didn't *need* a doctor and got mad at me for making the appointment. And I did it because Pastor Ledbetter said it was my place to take care of my husband's health. Julia, I can't do it all by myself. If Leonard won't cooperate in *any*thing, and I mean *anything,* what am I supposed to do?"

She put her head down on the table and commenced to cry. I went over to her and sat beside her. "LuAnne, listen to me. I know it's hard, but consider the life of a widow or a divorced woman. If you leave him, you'll be no better off than you are now. In terms of doing without, I mean."

"Oh, Julia," she said, discounting my opinion entirely. "It's just beyond you to understand. *You* may be able to get along without the comfort of a man, but everybody's not like you."

Well, I'd known that for some little while.

I sighed and put my hand on her arm. "LuAnne, listen to me now, I'm saying this for your own good. I know you have your problems with Leonard, but you just can't throw yourself at the first man who's nice to you. It doesn't look good. And besides, Mr. Johnson's a good twenty years younger than you are."

"Fifteen!" she snapped. "And I'll have you know that age differences don't matter if two people find themselves in *tune* in other ways. Grow up, Julia. Jerry's giving me back some of my self-esteem, making me feel attractive and wanted and valued. A woman *needs* a sense of self-worth."

I just hate it when I have to listen to this modern babbling and carrying-on about self-worth and self-esteem, quoted straight out of some magazine with nothing on its mind but S-E-X. All about how to please, not your husband but your *partner,* of all things, or how he can please you or how to get in touch with your own feelings. You won't see me reading that stuff. I figured that if you have to get to know yourself through the half-educated, pseudopsychological ramblings of a freelance writer, you ought to stay ignorant.

But I said, "I know, LuAnne. It makes a woman feel good when a man finds her attractive, but you ought to remember that Mr. Johnson is a traveling man, and you know what that means."

"He's a race-car driver!"

"Truck," I corrected. "And he travels all over the country. Why, he's on his way to Phoenix now, and from there he's going on to California or somewhere. It wouldn't surprise me if he didn't have a woman everywhere he goes. He looks the type." And so did Mr. Pickens, but I didn't bring him up. He was next on my list to get a good talking-to.

"I don't care! All I care about is right now, right here! I *deserve* some consideration, considering what I've had to put up with for so long. My self-esteem is just about gone and, Julia, I tell you, I'm just about desperate. I don't know how you stand it."

Self-worth, self-esteem, I thought with exasperation, how about a little self-control? But I didn't think she was in any mood to listen to good advice.

I glanced over at Lillian, who looked awfully intent on scrubbing a pan, wondering what she was thinking. She was making out like she was deaf, dumb and blind, knowing that LuAnne treated her as if that's what she was. But I could've used some of

Lillian's common sense in dealing with someone who was displaying no sense at all.

Then, surprising me no end, LuAnne sat up, wiped her eyes with the back of her hand, and said, "Ask Lillian, if you don't believe me. Lillian, a married woman has a right to have her husband's attention, doesn't she? Even the pastor said the husband is obligated to render unto the wife her due, and it's a settled fact that I am *long* overdue."

Lillian dried her hands on a dish towel and came over to the table. "Miz Conover, I know it not my place to be giving you no advice. You been a frien' of Miss Julia's for as long as I knowed both of you, an' I don't wantta butt in on yo' troubles. But I think I might know what got Mr. Conover in the shape he in."

"Oh, please, tell me if you do. Don't hold back, Lillian, I'll take help wherever I can get it." Which I thought was a little ungracious of LuAnne to say, but then she'd never shared my high opinion of Lillian.

"Well, lemme ast you this. Do he go to the bathroom a lot?"

"Oh, Lord, yes! He's up and down, in and out, going and coming all night long till I hardly get a wink of sleep."

"Then he got prostrate trouble. I know 'cause I seen it too many times, an' heard about it, too. That's what happens when a man get a certain age, they prostrate break down on 'em an' they goes and comes one way, but they can't in another. He need a doctor to ream it out, an' he be good as new."

I wondered just how good that would be, but obviously it'd pleased LuAnne at some point.

"He won't go!" LuAnne wailed. "I begged him for the sake of our marriage, and he won't do it."

"Then try it another way," I said. "Tell him it's for *medical* reasons, not marital ones."

"Yessum," Lillian agreed. "Tell him he got to take care of that prostrate, or it dry up on him an' he won't be able to do nothin' with it. He be in the hospital then."

"Could that happen?"

Lillian and I nodded in solemn agreement of Leonard's dire prognosis, although what I knew of such things was next to nothing.

"Then I'll do it," LuAnne said, straightening up and looking determined. "I'll take him in an ambulance if I have to strap him in and buckle him down. But, Julia," she went on, giving me a fierce glance, "there's nothing wrong if I treat myself to a good time tonight. I mean, the weather's bad and the lights're out, and things are different. If Jerry wants to flirt with me, I'm going to flirt right back because I might never get another chance. And I don't care what you say."

And, with that, she flounced out through the swinging door. And came back in on the back swing. "And another thing, Julia Springer," she said, her hands on her hips. "You've got a nerve lecturing me about Jerry when you've got something worse going on right under your nose. And what I'm doing doesn't even compare. So just clean up your own house before you start on mine!"

And out she flounced again.

Lillian and I stood there dumbfounded. "What in the world is she talking about?"

"They ain't no tellin', but it don't sound too good."

"Oh, well, she's just mad, and trying to get back at me. I'll straighten her out when I have the time. Let's finish these dishes; it's getting cold in here."

Chapter 28

"I'll tell you the truth, Lillian," I said, after studying on LuAnne's outburst for a few minutes, "LuAnne's going to worry me to death. As if I didn't have enough on my plate already, she's just piling that much more on. The only good thing about it is, Mr. Johnson surely can't be taking her seriously. Fifteen years difference, my foot. She's old enough to be his mother twice over. Though I wouldn't say that to her face."

"No'm, I don't think I would either. He be gone pretty soon, so I don't 'spect she get in too much trouble."

"Maybe not, if I can keep them apart for the night. I declare, these racing people are something else, aren't they? And speaking of tonight, I've got to figure out how to sleep them all."

"You got to put some of 'em together, look like."

"Yes, and I'm giving it a lot of thought. I don't want any wandering around playing musical beds in the middle of the night. I'll just have to put people together who'll watch each other."

As we carried our candles back into the living room, I heard the clank and scrape of a snowplow on the street outside. Looking out the dining room window, I saw the bright lights of the big machine as it rumbled past, clearing a lane on Polk Street as a dump truck came behind, spreading sand.

"Looks like the sleet's stopped," I said to Lillian. "Let's hope we get power back soon. I'm getting chilled to the bone."

We went on into the living room, where everybody was still gathered around the fire. Little Lloyd had dropped off to sleep, his head against Mr. Pickens's chest and LuAnne's fur coat across his legs. Mr. Pickens still had his arm across the back of the sofa, but he'd progressed to the point of twirling a curl of Hazel Marie's hair, while he and Sam talked. There was nothing for it but to take Mr. Pickens aside as soon as I could and caution him about getting too familiar.

I forgot about that when I saw LuAnne stroking Mr. Johnson's arm. I pursed my lips and glared at Sam. There he was sitting right across from them where he couldn't help but see what they were up to, and he hadn't done a thing to put a stop to it. He looked up and smiled at me, like adulterous behavior wasn't going on in front of his eyes. He motioned to the chair beside him and said, "About time you two got in here. Etta Mae said she'd be by to pick me up about this time, so come on over here and talk to me."

"I doubt she'll be driving in this weather, Sam, regardless of the plans the two of you made. So you might as well plan on spending the night. I won't have anybody else trying to get you home, and you certainly can't walk. Now, listen everybody, there're enough beds if you're willing to sleep together."

Mr. Johnson sang out, "Got no problem with that!"

LuAnne giggled. If I heard "Oh, Jerry" one more time from her, I was going to lose my dinner.

Mr. Pickens leaned over and whispered something to Hazel Marie. I think she blushed, but I couldn't be sure. It might've been the glow from the fire.

Sam's eyes were sparkling. "Everybody's willing, Julia. Depending, of course, on how you pair us up."

I ignored their comments, as I considered my biggest current problem, which was LuAnne. With Mr. Pickens a close second.

"Hazel Marie, I'm going to put you and LuAnne in Deputy Bates's room. He won't be using it tonight." I figured that Mr. Pickens wouldn't be staging any raids with another adult in with her. And I knew Hazel Marie was a light sleeper, who'd hear Lu-

Anne if she took to stirring around. "Sam, you need lots of room with that cast and you don't need to be trying to manage the stairs. Since Hazel Marie's room is downstairs and has a king-sized bed, I'll put you there. Mr. Pickens, there's plenty of room for you in with Sam, if you don't mind."

"I don't mind, but I can think of a better arrangement."

I let them have their laugh, and went on, "Mr. Johnson, you and Curtis can take Little Lloyd's room, on the right at the head of the stairs. Lillian'll be in her usual room, and Little Lloyd can sleep with me. Is that all right, Hazel Marie?"

She nodded, rubbing her hand over the child's side, wondering, I guessed, why I hadn't put him in with her. She'd figure it out, if she paid attention to what was going on with LuAnne and Mr. Johnson.

"Mr. Pickens, would you mind taking Little Lloyd upstairs? He needs to be in bed, and I'd suggest we all get in before the house gets too much colder."

It was barely nine o'clock by the time I led Mr. Pickens upstairs by candlelight, as he carried the sleeping child. When he'd put Little Lloyd down and I'd tucked in the covers, I turned to Mr. Pickens and said, "Mr. Pickens, as your employer, I need to have a talk with you. I want you to know that I appreciate how you're lifting Hazel Marie's spirits, she was in bad need of it, but I think you might be taking your job too seriously. I don't want her to be trifled with, so you can begin to slack off a little."

Those white teeth flashed and I thought I might sometime recommend shaving off that mustache so people could get the full benefit of his smile. On second thought, he didn't need any more advantages than he already had.

"What if I'm not trifling?"

"You and Sam! I declare, I don't know what else either of you'd call it."

"Let me tell you something, Miss Julia." And he had the nerve to start pointing that finger at me. "You've got to let people do as they're going to do, anyway. Quit worrying about everybody else, and pay some attention to Sam. He can't take his eyes off of you and, if that cast wasn't holding him back, you wouldn't get two steps out of his sight."

Well, that was just plain offensive. There the man was, in perilous need of counsel himself, and what was he doing? Turning it back on me, that's what. "I thank you for your advice, but you don't know everything that's been going on. Sam is as bad as you, taking on over every woman he meets, leading them on, playing with their affections and being, in general, just too careless with people's feelings, and I'll thank you to stop pointing that finger at me."

"What?" He looked at his finger, grinned and put it in his pocket. "Well, I'm not playing around, and I don't think Sam is, either."

"You just haven't seen that Wiggins woman and the way she flounces herself around in front of him, and you haven't seen the way he acts around her, either."

One eyebrow went up. "Make you jealous?"

"No, it does not. It's just that I don't need another man who's so easily distracted. But we're not talking about me, we're talking about *you.*" I raised my finger and shook it right in his face. It was a point that needed to be made. "Listen to me now, and take it to heart. I want you to back away from Hazel Marie before she gets hurt again. I've seen you, Mr. Pickens, when you're engaged in your investigative techniques, and you just smother a woman with your smiling and your sweet words, whispering them up and making them laugh and turn red, and I'm not going to have you doing it to Hazel Marie. So let's get that straight right now."

His shoulders started shaking, and I realized he was laughing! There I was speaking as plainly as I knew how, telling him what he needed to know for his own good, and he was laughing at me.

He reached out and took hold of my finger, then he put an arm around me and said, "Miss Julia, you are some piece of work."

I declare, with that strong arm around me and that warm hand holding mine, I could've melted away right then and there. It was all I could do not to lean on his shoulder and enjoy, just for a minute, the feeling of being cared for even though I knew he was just being his usual womanizing self. But before I could stop it, while he stood there so close, smiling that warm smile, a vast feeling of loss and loneliness and, maybe, bereavement flooded my soul. If I'd met someone like him when I'd been of an age to take action, what would my life have been like? What would it've been like to've had someone with dancing eyes catch mine from across a room? What had I missed by not falling in love with a man who smiled and teased and was generous with hugs and touches? To say nothing of one with an overendowment of maleness? It didn't bear thinking about, because my time had come and gone, and all I had to look back on were too many barren years, years filled with *shoulds* and *ought to's* and hard looks and exasperated sighs. Sad and cold years, because I'd never delighted anyone the way every woman in the world delighted Mr. Pickens.

Well, it couldn't be helped.

So I disengaged myself from Mr. Pickens before I broke down and cried in front of him out of pure despairing misery.

"Come on, now," he said, his voice warm and reassuring, "let's go down before we wake that boy. I want to see you enjoy yourself for a change. You don't need to take on the problems of the world. Aren't you tired of looking out for everybody else?"

"Lord, yes. Tired to death of it, if the truth be known. But I'm the only one . . . I mean, they need me, or seem to, and nobody else. . . . Well, maybe I can try." I couldn't say anymore. I wanted him to leave so I could get myself together. I needed to have time to think things over, especially since he'd said almost the exact same words Sam had said when all this began. If Mr. Pickens and Sam thought the same way, well, wouldn't that mean that the two of them were alike in other ways as well? I mean in ways that made Mr. Pickens so aggravating and appealing all at the same time?

"You go on down, Mr. Pickens. There're a few things I need to see to up here. I'll join you in a few minutes."

He gave my shoulder a pat, smiled some more and said, "Anytime you feel things getting away from you, hon, just remember that I'm here for you."

He left then, and I was glad of it, having had more comforting than my heart could stand, being unaccustomed as it was to such sweetness.

I stood in the dark room, dimly lit by one fluttering candle, trying to get back to the here and now instead of bemoaning a past that couldn't be changed.

There was Little Lloyd, I reminded myself, a gift in my old age that was not given to many. And Hazel Marie, a sweeter woman you couldn't find anywhere, who cared for me and looked up to me. And Lillian, a rock and a bulwark against all the vicissitudes that'd come my way. And Sam. And Sam, who was always there for me.

At least, when Etta Mae Wiggins wasn't around.

Hearing the sound of a car motor on the street, I went to the window to see who could be out and about on a night like this. I always liked to know what was going on around me.

Pulling back the curtain, I could see enough in the glow of the lights from the north side of town reflecting back from the clouds to make out Pastor Ledbetter's sports utility vehicle turn into the church parking lot. I watched as the top-heavy machine managed the street well enough, but it spun and slid all around the icy lot before passing out of my view behind Mr. Johnson's truck.

"Now, what is he doing at the church this late on a Saturday night?" I said to myself, then realized that he was most likely going in to check on things, maybe to turn on some faucets. Which reminded me that I should do the same myself. There's nothing worse than frozen pipes and the resulting mess when they break.

As I turned from the window, a clanking, grinding noise coming from the other end of the street drew my attention. Peering out the window again, I saw another vehicle, this one long and low with the back end practically dragging on the pavement. Smoke billowed from the tailpipe, and the chains on the tires, one of them flapping loose against the fender, churned the sand and ice on the street.

"Well, my land," I said, astounded as I clearly made out the two-toned car as it turned into the parking lot and followed Pastor Ledbetter's tracks to the back entrance of the church. "If that's not Brother Vern, I'll eat my hat."

Chapter 29

I stood transfixed by the cold window as various thoughts flashed in my mind. Why would Brother Vernon Puckett, ranting and raving television and tent revivalist, and Pastor Larry Ledbetter, silky smooth pulpiteer of the biggest church in town, be meeting together on a stormy night? There was only one thing in the world that Brother Vern and Pastor Ledbetter could be conspiring about, and that was their need for money—the one to keep his television show on the air, and the other to build a monument in my front yard.

Certainly the session needed to know that the pastor was up to something, and it couldn't be a meeting of like theological minds. They'd run Pastor Ledbetter out of town on a rail if he invited someone like Brother Vern to occupy the pulpit. Those two had to be getting their heads together for some other reason. And I figured I knew what it was. Something had to be done, and done tonight.

Lord, when the telephone rang, it scared me out of a year's growth. I dashed to it, snatching it up before it rang again and woke Little Lloyd.

"Yes?"

"Miss Julia," Pastor Ledbetter said, assuming that I'd recognize his voice, which I did but I resented the assumption. "Do you know who parked that truck in the church parking lot?"

"Why, yes. We had to get it off the street and there was plenty of room over there, so I thought . . ."

"It'll have to be moved. The contractor's stakes have been run over, and the weight of the truck is damaging the asphalt. Do you know what it costs to repair a parking lot of that size? I'm afraid you'll have to be responsible for that expense. I don't know why people assume that church property can be used for any purpose whatsoever."

"From the looks of it, pastor, the asphalt was due to be torn up anyway, so the truck's done nothing but help you out."

"Be that as it may," he said, after a pause in which he may've been trying to decide what to bring up next, while I about froze to death waiting on him. Then, remembering his pastoral responsibilities, he said, "I hope you can keep warm until the power's back on; everything at the church is out, too. If I can help you in any way, just let me know."

"I appreciate that, but I think we're in good shape, at least for a while. It's good of you to offer, though."

Then, as if he'd decided this was as good a time as any to get any number of things off his chest, he went on, "While I have you, Miss Julia, you should know that the talk about Ms. Puckett is getting worse. I've just recently heard that improprieties have resulted from her personal associations. You and I, and perhaps Ms. Puckett herself, need to get together and see what we can do to resolve this matter."

"This matter wouldn't've come to your attention by way of her uncle, would it? Who I happen to know is over there with you right now. That man is a nuisance, Pastor, and you'd do well to keep your distance."

"He's concerned about his niece, and he's only reinforced my suspicions that all is not as it should be where she is concerned."

Well, I'd about had enough of his implications and accusations about Hazel Marie, and it struck me that he was doing some of the same kind of implying and accusing that LuAnne had done when she'd lashed out at me in the kitchen. The pastor was right; the gossip about Hazel Marie was getting out of hand.

But before I could agree to a meeting, the pastor said, "I also wanted you to know that Wilson T. Hodge got back to town this afternoon after reporting in to his office in Charlotte. He just beat the weather and he called me as soon as he got in. He shares my concern about some, uh, discrepancies in the building fund. He's going to do an audit first thing Monday which, I'm sure, will put our minds at rest. I also questioned him about Ms. Puckett, and he said he had no idea where she is, so he's obviously had nothing to do with her disappearance. I certainly don't wish any ill to befall her, but it behooves us, Miss Julia, to disconnect her name from his before the building fund drive is irreparably damaged. I think you'll agree with me on that."

In spite of the patter of sleet against the window and the chill in the room, I could feel myself heating up. "Pastor, the building fund drive is the last thing on my mind, as I've made perfectly clear long before this. Now, I don't care what Wilson T. Hodge told you, because I'm telling you that he is up to his neck in a crooked business, and he just escaped getting arrested when the deputies raided that warehouse that was in the papers."

I wanted to shake my finger in his face. "So, you listen to me and learn something. Wilson T. Hodge can lie to you all he wants, but I happen to know that he was involved with holding Hazel Marie against her will. And another thing, you ask him, just ask him, about a certain wreck he was in when he had the nerve to chase her around a racetrack. And, furthermore, I know he's in trouble with his business partner, who is also his cousin and who is as crooked as the day is long. They're both into gambling on NASCAR racing and I don't know what all else, so you'd do well to audit that building fund. And here you are, worried over a little gossip about Wilson T. and Hazel Marie, when all she's been doing is trying to get away from him. He's the one who needs a talking-to, if you ask me."

There was dead silence on the line. Then he said, "Those kinds of accusations shouldn't be made lightly."

"There's nothing light about what I'm telling you. I know what I'm talking about."

"Well, Miss Julia, it sounds to me as if Wilson T.'s perfectly pure and good intentions are being twisted by the gossip-mongers into a potential scandal. And anything that soils him, soils the church by extension. Hazel Marie's uncle has reminded me of the kind of life she's led in the past, and that sort of thing could easily hurt the reputation of even the most godly man. You see?"

Yes, I saw. I saw that he wasn't giving one thought to one of his own flock, not one bit concerned about Hazel Marie's reputation or feelings, or what she'd just gone through, courtesy of the godly man he was trying to protect. In spite of the fact that he'd been counseling her for weeks on how to be a Presbyterian. The more I thought about it, the more affronted I became. The man didn't have a lick of sense, ignoring everything I'd told him about Wilson T. Hodge and doing nothing but blaming everything on Hazel Marie.

"Well," he went on with a deep sigh, "these matters are a heavy burden to bear. We just have to do the best we can with God's help." I couldn't help but feel a stab of compassion for him, even though he'd misidentified the name and nature of his burden. But anybody who pastors a thousand-member congregation of Presbyterians deserves a little pity.

Then he seemed to collect himself and went about dashing any smidgen of pity I had left. "Now, Miss Julia, that truck out there has to be moved. I'm just before calling the sheriff and having it towed. If the owner's visiting you, tell him it must be moved immediately."

"Oh, I'll tell him, Pastor." And tell *you* a few things, as well, along with that busybody, Vernon Puckett.

I hung up the phone, leaned over the bed to see if Little Lloyd was warm enough, then went to my closet. I rummaged around until I found my knee-high galoshes with the buckles I could never fasten. I pulled them on, letting them flap loose around my shins, put on an old heavy coat and wrapped a scarf around my head.

I clunked down the staircase, looking more like a bag lady than the most generous tither of the First Presbyterian Church, for which I'd never received proper credit in the first place. I grabbed the flashlight and headed for the door, paying no heed to the sudden attention I was attracting from those around the fire.

"Julia!" Sam called out, trying to rise from his chair. "Where're you going? Don't go out there; it's dangerous."

"Hey!" Mr. Johnson bellowed. "I'll get whatever you need. Come on in here by the fire."

"Miss Julia, what's wrong?" Hazel Marie was out of her chair and coming toward me, with Mr. Pickens right behind her.

Lillian said, "You know better'n to go out in that stuff. What's got into you?"

"All of you," I said, holding up my hand, "just leave me alone. I just got a call from Pastor Ledbetter, who is over at the church with, would you like to guess? None other than Brother Vernon Puckett! And I aim to get to the bottom of a few things this very night. So I'm going and that's that."

"Hold on, woman," Mr. Johnson yelled. "If you got a bee in your bonnet that bad, I'll go with you."

"Me, too," Hazel Marie said, pulling on her coat. "I'm gonna give that fool uncle of mine a piece of my mind. He's interfered in my life one too many times."

"Well, if that's the case," Mr. Pickens said, jamming his arms into his coat. "Sam, look after things. Jerry and I'll go with these two wild women."

And out we went, the four of us trekking across the vast expanse of the parking lot, with Jerry Johnson holding on to my arm, yelling "God dog it," every time his cowboy boots slipped on the ice, and Mr. Pickens mumbling words I won't repeat as Hazel Marie tried to keep him upright. She and I had hardly any trouble getting across. That's what a full head of steam will do for you, make you so mad that you just stomp on through a layer of ice and sleet and snow like nobody's business.

We finally reached the safety of the covered area at the back entrance, which some members called a porte-cochere at church, but a carport at home. As Mr. Pickens opened the door, we filed into the interior and stood bunched up together, absolutely blind in total darkness.

"Where's the flashlight?" Mr. Pickens asked, reaching for it.

"Here it is," I said, clicking on the pitiful beam and handing it to him. "Maybe it'll last long enough to get us to the pastor's office, which is where I'd guess they are."

Mr. Johnson said, in what was for him a subdued tone—funny how a church can have that effect on a man. "Don't worry about the dark. They's likely to be some lightnin' pretty soon."

As Mr. Pickens swept the flashlight beam in front of our feet, we eased past the church kitchen on our right and came out into the echoing space of the fellowship hall. Folding chairs and tables lined the walls, waiting for Wednesday's covered dish supper.

"Lightning doesn't usually come with a sleet storm, Mr. Johnson," I said.

"Haw! It will with me inside a church. Likely to strike me dead."

That didn't warrant an answer, especially since Mr. Pickens held out his arm, stopping us, as he said, "Hold on a minute."

As we stood in the middle of the fellowship hall, I began to make out the feeble glow of light coming from the direction of the pastor's office. The low rumble of a man's voice reached us, one that I recognized as having the cadence of Brother Vern's television preaching style.

"Call out to 'em, Miss Julia," Mr. Pickens said, "so we don't scare 'em to death."

"It wouldn't be more than they deserve, to my mind." But I called out, as I struck off toward the office. "Pastor! We're coming in."

Chapter 30

We walked into the pastor's office, warmly lit by the yellow glow of a kerosene lantern and the beam of a heavy flashlight on the desk. That's all that was warm about it, though, for there was a definite chill in the air. Brother Vern looked twice his size in a quilted parka, as he stopped in midsentence and step when he saw us.

Pastor Ledbetter was sitting in his leather chair behind the desk, his eyes dark and sunken in his face. It was a settled fact that whatever Brother Vern had been holding forth on was not setting well with him. He looked stunned and, in spite of our unexpected appearance, unable to open his mouth. He just sat and stared into space. Whatever Brother Vern had been saying had clearly unnerved him. Maybe it took a preacher to get through to one of the same ilk.

Hazel Marie, however, didn't notice the pastor's stricken state. She centered in on her uncle, rushed straight at him, got right up in his face, and said, "What do you think you're doing? You're going behind my back to try to take Lloyd away from me again, aren't you? And you want Pastor Ledbetter to help you, don't you? It wasn't enough that you sent the sheriff to take my baby. You have to sneak over here in the dead of night and start telling tales in church, to turn my preacher against me! You are nothing but a sorry, underhanded excuse for a preacher, pretending to save people from their sins, when all you've ever been interested in is lining your own pockets. Well, let me tell you something. You're not getting your hands on my baby or on anything that belongs to him. Just get that straight right now!"

Mr. Pickens looked from one to the other of them, then when he realized what she was saying, he stared at her. "This is the one who filed the complaint?"

"Yes! He's claiming I'm an unfit mother!" she stormed. "And he's been trying and trying for I don't know how long to take Lloyd away from me. He just keeps on and on, making my life miserable, trying everything he can think of to get his hands on Lloyd's money."

I cringed inside, thinking it was the better part of wisdom not to announce to any single male in the world the inheritance held in trust for Little Lloyd. It was too tempting. But the damage was already done, although Mr. Pickens didn't seem all that excited by the news.

Instead, he turned a hard gaze on Brother Vern. "I've seen this lady in action, so I'd advise you to back off."

Brother Vern pulled himself up taller, got that inspired look on his face that came over him when he took it on himself to speak for the Lord. "This is first and foremost a spiritual matter of the direst consequences. It is my duty, as a minister of the Word of God and a leader of souls into the heavenly kingdom, to warn a fellow minister when he is in danger of the fires of hell. 'Brethren, if a man be overtaken in a fault, ye who are spiritual restore such a one in the spirit of meekness,' Galatians, six, one, and that's what I'm aimin' to do. Brother," he said, turning to Pastor Ledbetter, not in a spirit of meekness, as far as I could see, but in the spirit of thundering authority, as he gasped for breath. "I have come-ah to rebuke and exhort-ah, to caution and warn-ah, to put you back on the paths-ah of righteousness. Lissen to me, now, I'm-ah speaking from the Spirit-ah, put behind you the wiles of Satan-ah before you damage your soul-ah and the witness of this church-ah!"

Mr. Pickens reared back from the onslaught, and Mr. Johnson was uncustomarily quiet. His mouth was hanging open, though, as Brother Vern tore into Pastor Ledbetter.

"*What* is going on?" Hazel Marie demanded.

"Hold your peace, woman!" Brother Vern rounded on her, pointed his finger in her face and cut loose in her direction. "Hide your head in shame, beguiler of iniquity, and look no longer on the anointed of God!"

"What are you talking about?" She squared her shoulders and clenched her fists, ready to take him on. Mr. Pickens rested his hand lightly on the small of her back.

"That's what I'd like to know," I said, deciding it was time to take a hand in matters, since Pastor Ledbetter was looking more peaked by the minute. To say nothing of the fact that he hadn't said a word since we'd come in, an uncommon occurrence, in and of itself.

"This man-ah of God-ah!" Brother Vern cried, pointing the same shaking finger at Pastor Ledbetter. "Shame-ah has come upon him, through no fault-ah of his own. But," Brother Vern tempered his voice, leaned closer to the pastor and began to put on the posture of a counselor, "you have allowed it, Brother, I'm sorry to say. All, I'm sure, unawares. We never know in what form the tempter comes, do we? And he gets us in his snares before we know it, a-wrappin' and a-tanglin' us up till we don't know which end is up. That's why I come, brother, to reveal to you the vain and profane babblings of the multitude, and to warn you of the eternal peril you've got yourself mired up in."

The four of us stared at Brother Vern, trying to follow his line of thinking. No easy task, to begin with. But what he was ranting about now was simply beyond me. I couldn't figure out why Brother Vern was aiming his corrective remarks at Pastor Ledbetter. It was Wilson T. Hodge who needed the chastisement.

"Brother Vern," I said, speaking as sharply as I could. When a preacher is under the spell of the spirit, it sometimes takes a two-by-four to get his attention.

"Ah, Miz-res Springer." Brother Vern came toward me with outstretched hand. "I wouldn't distress you with this matter for the world but, since you're here, I know I can count on you as a prayer partner for the sake of our brother who's being mocked and maligned by the ignoramuses of the world."

Allowing my hand to be grasped and pressed, I said, "I'm sure our brother appreciates your concern and your prayers." I glanced at Pastor Ledbetter who looked less appreciative than anybody I'd ever seen, but I was trying to get some sensible explanation for this unlikely confrontation. "But when I pray, I like to bring out the particulars. Just what are we so concerned about here?"

Brother Vern leaned over me, frowning with a worried look on his face. "You mean you haven't heard?"

"Well, no, but I've been out of town. I'm sure it has to do with Wilson T. Hodge, though, and I'm glad for your warning about him."

"Wilson T. Hodge? You mean," Brother Vern's voice dropped to a whisper filled with dismay, "do you mean to tell me, Sister Springer, that there's *two* men that's been entangled in this? At one and the same time?"

"I don't know about two. One's all I know about, and that's a gracious plenty. Considering what he's been up to, like stealing and gambling and such as that." Wilson T. Hodge could've been guilty of every sin in the book, for all I knew.

"Stealing! Gambling! Oh, Jehovah God, have mercy!" His face suddenly red with outrage, Brother Vern rounded on Pastor Ledbetter. "You are not fit to stand in the pulpit of the Lord! Cleanse yourself, Brother, and put away the evil that's overtaken you. I come in here to counsel with you and detract you from the path that's sucked many a man of God from the paths of righteousness. I know, oh, Lord, I *know*—get thee behind me, Satan—how the wiles of a woman can tempt us and destroy us and flat-out ruin our testimony. But, Brother, you are further along the slippery slope than I recognized, and I'm calling on you to repent and renounce this woman!"

"What!" Hazel Marie shrieked. "Do you mean *me*? I'm gonna knock you nine ways to Sunday, Vernon Puckett!"

"Wait a minute! Wait a minute." I moved between them, holding up my hand. "Brother Vern, do you mean to say that you think Hazel Marie and . . . and the *pastor* . . . well, my Lord." I was so undone that I needed to sit down. I mean, I didn't have much use for Pastor Ledbetter and his worldly ways, but this was too much.

In the silence that followed, Pastor Ledbetter looked ready to throw up, sitting there with his throat working, unable to get a word out of his mouth. Mr. Pickens's eyebrows were up around his hairline, and Hazel Marie stood there gritting her teeth at Brother Vern. Mr. Johnson finally broke the silence, "I b'lieve I'm gonna start goin' to church again. It's looking a lot more interestin' than I remember."

"Now see here, Brother Vern," I recovered enough to say. "I don't know where you're getting your information, but I can assure you that adultery is not in Pastor Ledbetter's reportoire. And certainly not with Hazel Marie."

I found it a little disconcerting to be defending Pastor Ledbetter, considering the woes and constant strife of the ordinary, day-by-day dealings I'd had with him, but I'm a fair woman. He had his faults, as do most people, but this was an accusation that shouldn't be laid at his doorstep. I mean, the man was an ordained Presbyterian minister.

"Well, I'm here to tell you, Sister," Brother Vern said, irritating me no end. I hated to be called *sister,* especially by the likes of Brother Vern. "When a man of God goes a-whorin' after strange women, it ain't no stretch to figger he'll be up to something else. Then you'll get your stealin' and your gamblin', and next thing you know, he'll have a woman a-preachin' in his pulpit."

Mr. Pickens just stood there, shaking his head. Even I was taken aback at how Brother Vern's list of sins had progressed from adultery down to women preachers, taking in most everything else in between.

"I never heard of such a thing," I threw at him. "You've got your sins all mixed up, as well as your sinners." And gotten me mixed up too, if the truth be known. I'd thought the gossip was about Hazel Marie and Wilson T. and, from the looks of him, so had the pastor. But Brother Vern had just named him the culprit.

"Let's just back up here a minute," I said, intent on setting Brother Vern straight. "I take it that you've taken it on yourself to counsel *my* pastor in *my* church because you've heard some gossip about him and Hazel Marie. Is that right?"

"Not only heard it, but know it's true." Brother Vern's confidence unnerved me. I glanced at the pastor, wondering what he'd been up to, and who with, because I knew it couldn't've been with Hazel Marie. I also wondered when he was going to come to his own defense. Unless he didn't have one.

Then it hit me that he'd been counseling LuAnne Conover day in and day out and, in her current state of mind, she was as susceptible as a woman could be. Lord, the very thought of LuAnne and Pastor Ledbetter together was enough to make me queasy. But that unsettling thought had to go on the back burner; I had my hands full, taking care of Hazel Marie.

"*How* do you know it's true?" I demanded, crowding Brother Vern's space. "You've seen him with her or some other woman? Is there a witness? Tell us just how you know."

"I know because I know the woman!" Brother Vern turned, pointed at Hazel Marie and thundered, "Down on your knees, woman, and pray G-*OD*-ah to forgive you for leadin' this poor, hard-workin' preacher astray! Along with that other man you been foolin' with."

Mr. Pickens was entirely at fault for not having kept a better grip on her. Hazel Marie flew at Brother Vern like she had springs in her shoes, backing him up into the corner by the bookshelf. Screeching and screaming and raking books off the shelves onto his head, she had him cringing and cowering and scrooching up in a ball trying to protect himself from the onslaught. I'd never seen the like before, not even when she'd lit in on Wilson T. Hodge.

Mr. Pickens had her by the hips, trying to pull her away while Brother Vern kept yelling, "Jezebel! Sodom and Gomorrah!" and the like. Which made absolutely no sense.

Mr. Johnson got tangled up in the fray when he tried to help Mr. Pickens pull Hazel Marie away, so his bellowing added to the din. Pastor Ledbetter remained in his leather chair, neither concerned about nor bothered by the ruckus in his office. I wondered if the man had been struck dumb. That can happen sometimes, you know, when you think you're doing fine, then find out everybody else is pretty sure you're not.

When Mr. Pickens finally got Hazel Marie off Brother Vern and was holding her close to him for fear of what she'd do next, I walked over to her. "Hazel Marie, calm yourself down now. I know Brother Vern deserves everything you can dish out and then some. But we're going to straighten him out right now. Mr. Pickens, don't turn her loose."

"I don't intend to," he said, pushing her tear-streaked face down on his shoulder.

"Hey, Brother Whoever-You-Are," Mr. Johnson boomed as he stood over Brother Vern, "I'd keep my head down, if I was you."

"Now," I said, "Brother Vern, we need a better reason why you think your own niece and Pastor Ledbetter have been . . . well, doing what you said."

"I know," he said, edging his way to his feet, but keeping his back to the corner, "everybody's talkin' about the two of 'em. I heard it all over the county. She's over here every night of the week, closed up in this office with him, and, Miz-res Springer, it don't look good. Everybody knows what kinda woman she is."

"No, everybody does not know what kind of woman she is!" I had a surge of anger fairly close to the one that'd flung Hazel Marie across the room at him. Rumors! Gossip! Whispers! Behind-the-hand talk! And easy to believe if your mind runs that way, which Brother Vern's did. Either because he was always looking for a way to get his hands on Little Lloyd, or because he'd at some time been in the same predicament with a woman himself.

"Pastor!" I clapped my hands in front of Pastor Ledbetter's face. "Wake up! Come to! Do something! Don't just sit there like you've been poleaxed! Tell this fool what you and Hazel Marie've been doing in your office. And," I rounded on Brother Vern, "it hasn't been every night of the week; it's only been two nights a week!" Which, I guessed, if anything had been going on wouldn't've been that major a point, but it needed to be made.

"Catechism," Pastor Ledbetter gasped. His face looked wet and clammy in the glow of the lantern. "I've been instructing her in the catechism."

Turning, I said, "You hear that, Brother Vern? These two who you've been so quick to condemn have been studying the Presbyterian creed."

"It don't hold a candle to the Holy Word of God," Brother Vern pronounced. "So look not upon church tradition for your salvation. As for me and mine, we'll soak ourselves in the Bible and nothing more."

"Theology!" I said, waving it away. "I'm not getting into that

with you. This is a Presbyterian church, a creedal, catechizing de-
nomination, and we'll study whatever we want to." Well, not exactly, of course, since we had to put up with the General
Assembly.

After giving the situation a moment's thought, I said, "Brother
Vern, I think you're to be commended for your concern for a fellow preacher." Hazel Marie let out a noise that sounded like the
gnashing of teeth. "Hold on," I said, "I'm not through. But,
Brother, you went overboard and believed what you wanted to
believe. You've slandered both your niece and my preacher, leaving yourself wide open for a lawsuit that'll wipe you out and ruin
your ministry."

"Lawsuit? Did you say lawsuit?" Brother Vern was beginning to
understand that I meant business.

"Yes, and I'll underwrite it. My advice to you is to get yourself
to that judge first thing Monday and withdraw all those papers
you took out against Hazel Marie. You are dead wrong about her,
and a dozen people will testify to that fact. To your detriment, I
might add." I took a deep breath and plowed on, determined to
set him straight. "I'm telling you right now, that there's no way
you'll get your hands on Little Lloyd because your complaint
won't hold water in a bucket. I am going to have Pastor Ledbetter
and every elder and deacon in this church testify to Hazel Marie's
good name. And it wouldn't surprise me if that judge doesn't
slap you with a fine for making false accusations and stirring up
trouble."

"Well, I didn't make it up."

"I don't know if you did or you didn't, but you certainly passed
it on. And there're enough like you in this town to create a considerable amount of havoc, which is what you've done." Then I
had a flash of inspiration, recalling, in part, the Sunday School
text of last Sunday. "And Brother Vern, if you need some Scrip-
tural backup, listen to this: 'they learn to be idle, wandering about

from house to house; and not only idle but tattlers also, and busy-bodies, speaking things which they ought not.' Timothy something or other, which is the word of the Lord."

Mr. Johnson chimed in about then. "Y'all ought to sue his britches off."

Brother Vern opened his mouth, but he couldn't come up with a verse to counter mine, so he retired from the field.

He turned and headed for the door, forgetting his flashlight. Then, getting in the last word, he said, "I'll be a-prayin' for you, Brother."

Chapter 31

"Same here," I said, as he disappeared into the dark of the fellowship hall. I hoped he'd be able to find his way to the door.

Mr. Johnson seemed to be having the time of his life, as he stood with his thumbs in his belt surveying the damage with sparkling eyes. He hadn't known what he'd been missing, being unchurched as he was. Mr. Pickens seemed unable to keep his hands off Hazel Marie, patting her and rubbing her back and whispering that he'd see that her uncle never got his hands on Little Lloyd, if she wanted him to. I declare, it was a poor time for him to be drumming up business.

"Miss Julia," Hazel Marie said, turning away from Mr. Pickens and covering her face with her hands. "I'm just so ashamed, my own uncle thinking I'd do such a thing with a preacher of the Gospel. It just made me lose control of myself. I know it wasn't ladylike, but I couldn't help it."

"Get a grip, Hazel Marie," I told her. "I'm proud of you. Meekness is all well and good in its place, but it wouldn't've done a lick of good with the likes of him."

Being well acquainted with the consequences of womanly submission, I didn't want Hazel Marie to suffer from it. A woman ought to take up for herself, if you ask me.

"Well, Pastor," I said, turning to the sweating man behind the desk. He'd taken out a handkerchief and was mopping his face. "My advice to you is that you reconsider all this counseling you've been doing. It's done nothing but get you in trouble."

"I . . . I can't believe it." He shook his head back and forth, bowed over the desk. He couldn't seem to lift it up and face us. "How could anybody think? . . . I'm a *pastor,* striving to live a life above reproach. Never have I been accused of such an ungodly act."

"I guess you haven't. But you've sure done a lot of accusing, yourself. Maybe now you know how it feels."

"What's that supposed to mean?" His head finally came up, and his voice regained some of its authority. "I've never falsely accused anybody, never been a party to gossip."

Well, that just took the cake. I leaned over his desk and let him have it. "Let me remind you, Pastor, it was not four days ago, right here in this office, that you passed on gossip to me about Hazel Marie and Wilson T. Hodge. Remember that? Remember how you were so concerned about *his* reputation? And how sure you were that Hazel Marie was the cause of it all? Where there's smoke, there's fire, you said. Now, come to find out that the gossip you heard *and* passed on was not about him and her at all, but about *you* and her. Where's the fire now, Pastor?

"And I'll tell you something else," I went on, about to pop with outrage. "You're as bad as Brother Vern. You assumed the worst because you'd already decided in your mind what kind of woman Hazel Marie is. You'd already decided that if she was in contact with any man, she had to be doing something wrong. You just didn't figure it'd come back on you, did you? Her relations with Wilson T. were honorable and aboveboard, being led on by him to think of marriage and home and family values and such as that, when all the time he was up to his neck in illegal activities. But did you blame him? Oh, no, it was Hazel Marie you jumped on with both feet. If there was gossip, it had to be her fault, didn't it? Well. Come to find out, now, that the gossip had nothing to do with him. It was all about you."

"I . . . I never heard a name," he admitted, wiping his hand across his face. "I confess I never heard a name, just that it was a man of the church, and he was the only one she was seeing, so . . ." He trailed off, because the full impact hit him square between the eyes. *He* was a man of the church; *he'd* been seeing her, and seeing her by himself behind a closed door.

Pastor Ledbetter's confession was interrupted by a loud, clanging commotion in the fellowship hall that seemed to go on and on. In the midst of it, we heard Brother Vern yelling, "God bless the God-blessed luck! Dang it all, somebody help me!"

Hazel Marie headed for the door. "What's that fool done now?"

"Hold on," Mr. Pickens said, grabbing the heavy flashlight. "Don't go out there in the dark."

"Oh, Lord," I said, laughing, because I recognized the metallic sounds. "He's run into the folding chairs."

And sure enough, when I followed the light in Mr. Pickens's hand, there was Brother Vern on his hands and knees in the midst of a dozen or more metal chairs, some of them still swirling around on the floor.

"Dang it all to hell and back!" he yelled. "Who put them cussed things in the way?"

"Gimme your hand," Mr. Johnson bellowed right back at him. "I'll he'p you up. We thought you was gone."

"I wisht I was," Brother Vern gasped, standing up and brushing himself off. "I got to the door, but they's a bunch of men swarmin' around out there."

Mr. Pickens clicked off the flashlight, surrounding us with the darkness of the hall. Hazel Marie drew in a sharp breath and clutched at my arm, while Pastor Ledbetter brought the lantern to the door of his office.

"Shut that thing off," Mr. Pickens said to him in such a way that the pastor did it with no argument. Totally in the dark, in more ways than one, we all stood where we were, waiting for Mr. Pickens to tell us what to do next.

Brother Vern spoke up, "What's goin' on?"

"Don't know yet," Mr. Pickens said. Then, "Hazel Marie, you and Miss Julia ease back into the office and call the sheriff. Jerry, if you can get out from those chairs, let's go to the door and see who's out there."

Hazel Marie and I felt along the wall until we came to the office door. Lord, I'd never been anywhere as dark as that place was. We bumped into Pastor Ledbetter, who still seemed dazed by his shattered reputation. He didn't make a sound as we moved him out of the way.

Feeling around on his desk, we found the telephone and, after some more feeling and counting of buttons, Hazel Marie finally got somebody at the sheriff's department. "We need help at the First Presbyterian Church," she said, her voice quivering. "There's a gang of men out in the parking lot and we don't know who they are or what they're doing and we're scared to death."

"They coming?" I asked as she hung up.

"Soon as they can," she said. "They're all out on calls with this weather. Oh, Miss Julia, what if it's Bigelow?"

The same thought had crossed my mind, unsettling it to a considerable degree.

We heard the big door at the back of the church slam open, and a jumble of men's voices echoing in the fellowship hall. Then the whole place seemed to light up. Thinking at first that the power had come back on, I headed out of the office with Hazel Marie and the pastor right behind.

I could hardly see when I got out in the hall from the glare of headlights aimed inside. Somebody had pulled a car next to the porte cochere and switched on the brights. A group of dark figures, throwing long shadows in our direction, stood right inside the door, brought up short by Mr. Pickens and Mr. Johnson.

Just as we pulled back into the shadows, I recognized Wilson T. Hodge's voice. "She's here and we know it. They told us over at the house that she's here. Bobby's missing something valuable, and he just wants to talk to her."

"That's Wilson T.," Hazel Marie hissed next to me.

I grabbed her arm and said, "Looks like he's brought an army with him. Tell me the truth, Hazel Marie, did you take anything from Bobby Bigelow?"

"Not a blessed thing," she said, quivering beside me. "I've never even been in his house."

"Then don't let them see you. Mr. Pickens'll get rid of them." I pushed her back toward Pastor Ledbetter and whispered to him, "Take her back to the office and stay there."

Well, I couldn't just stand there, watching from afar. So I picked my way through the scattered folding chairs by the glare of the headlights until I reached the dark side of the hall. Then nearly jumped out of my skin when Brother Vern loomed up in front of me.

"Who is it?" he whispered.

"I think it's a bunch of racing men who're mixed up in something worse than racing. They think Hazel Marie's got something we think they stole from Mr. Johnson."

"What?"

"Never mind."

I left him and snuck on closer, in case Mr. Pickens needed help. About that time, Mr. Johnson's braying voice cut through the conversation by the door. "You sorry thief! Ever' sheriff's department between here and Rockingham's lookin' for you. And, Bobby, they got dead-level proof that it was you that robbed me blind. You got some gall comin' in here and accusin' a woman of robbin' you. I ought to whip your butt, boy, an' I'm just about to do it!"

"We don't know what you're referring to," Wilson T. said, in that sanctimonious way of his.

"Well, I'll tell you," Mr. Pickens said, just as calm and sure of himself as he could be. "Jerry, here, had his shop damaged and his lucky charm stolen, but you've not said what was stolen from you. If we knew what it was, maybe we could help you."

A soft, high-pitched voice from a dark figure, not much bigger than Little Lloyd, answered him. "We just want to talk to the woman. Then we'll be on our way with no harm done."

If that was Bobby Bigelow, he didn't sound or look anything like the way I'd pictured him from all the stories of his meanness. From the looks of his dark outline, he was a little, sawed-off runt, even with an overcoat on. I'd had in mind a big, rough-looking man but, from the sound of his voice, he was quiet and mild mannered. Of course, those can be the worst kind, since you expect exactly the opposite from what you're likely to get.

"Let's get this straight right now," Mr. Pickens said, "Ms. Puckett is not available to you. I'd advise you to look elsewhere if you have a problem. In fact, I'd look closer to home, if it was me." And he looked Wilson T. up and down.

Smart man, I thought, get them distrusting each other.

"He knows *I'm* in the clear," Wilson T. said. "How many times do I have to say it? Hazel Marie is the only one who could've stolen it. So I know it's her. She's nothing but a thief, and a liar on top of that. HAZEL MARIE! Come out here!"

Poor Hazel Marie'd been called an adulteress, a Jezebel and now a thief and a liar. All in one night, and I'd had enough of it. "Wilson T. Hodge," I said, coming out of the shadows into the glare of the lights. "You've got a nerve calling Hazel Marie names like that! Just get yourself on out of here. I don't know how you can come into a church, in the company of this, this criminal, even if he is kin to you. Don't think we don't know what you've been up to with him, breaking into Mr. Johnson's truck shop and tearing up everything and stealing valuable stuff and then placing bets on races you think you're going to win. And I'd like to know where you got the money to gamble like that, and I expect the pastor'd like to know the same thing. The sheriff's looking for all of you, and they'll be here any minute!" And I wished it was that minute, because I made out two more figures backing up Wilson T. and Bigelow. There was some shuffling of feet as I finished my on-slaught on their characters.

Then the door behind them crashed open, and a small, back-lit person walked in, a head of blonde hair lit up in the headlights like a halo. My heart stopped as I tried to work out how Hazel Marie could've come in from outside when I'd left her in the pas-tor's office.

So softly that I barely heard him, Bigelow said, "There she is. Get her in the car."

The two dark figures in the background blended with the small one, while Mr. Johnson yelled "Whoa there!" and Mr. Pickens plowed in swinging the flashlight.

"Wait," Wilson T. Hodge called, "that's not . . ."

"What is this! Get your hands off me!" The voice was clear as a bell, loud, demanding and mad enough to spit fire.

My Lord, it was the Wiggins woman. Of all people I could do without, she was at the top of my list.

Chapter 32

It beat all I'd ever seen. Although, to tell the truth, I couldn't see much. Just a roiling mass of people, struggling shadows, some trying to get Etta Mae out the door and others trying to keep her inside. Mr. Johnson's voice boomed out, yelling words that would've stopped anybody else in their tracks, and Etta Mae Wiggins just about equaling him in volume and vulgarity. And in a church, too. It was a wonder lightning wasn't singeing the hair of us all.

Bigelow and Wilson T. stayed on the sidelines, scrunched up in opposite corners away from the scuffle, which is pretty much what instigators usually do—start something, then stand back and watch. Wilson T. kept saying, "Wait . . ." "That's not . . . ," but nobody paid any attention to him.

I saw Etta Mae swing that big tote bag of hers against the head of somebody, knocking him into Mr. Pickens. Mr. Pickens gave him a mighty shove, sending him through the doors and out onto the porte cochere. That left the one Mr. Johnson was struggling with. Mr. Johnson pushed him against the wall and, while he was winding up for another blow, Etta Mae stepped in and did some real damage with a thick-soled boot. The poor man doubled over and started retching and moaning and gasping.

"Atta girl!" Mr. Johnson yelled, as he pushed the man, head-first, out the door. "Bring on the next bunch! Got us a fighter here!"

Mr. Pickens had Bigelow over in the corner, not laying a hand on him, but looming over him and penning him in so he couldn't leave if he'd wanted to.

Wilson T. hurried over. "We've made a mistake," he said, trying to smooth things over. "Look, let me talk to Hazel Marie. I'm sure we can straighten this out, if I can just talk to her."

"Hazel Marie doesn't want to talk to you," Hazel Marie said. I looked around to see both her and Pastor Ledbetter right behind me, standing in the glare of the lights. She looked ready to rip Wilson T. to shreds, while the pastor hung back, still mopping his face.

Seeing the pastor, Wilson T. quickly took a step back. "Larry," he said to him, "I don't want you to get the wrong idea. This is something separate from my work with your church. It has nothing to do with my contract with you. It's just a, well, a private investment enterprise with my cousin that I haven't had much to do with. It's gotten a little out of hand, I guess you could say."

"I guess you could," I said, disgusted at his attempt to clear himself. "Considering what all it's come to. To say nothing of defiling this church building by bringing such trash into it. I'll tell you this, I don't understand why winning a NASCAR race is so important that you'd be a party to hounding a poor woman to death."

Pastor Ledbetter moaned, hiding his face in his handkerchief.

Brother Vern was taking all this in. "NASCAR?" he said. "I'm a big racin' fan." Which was not a great addition to the discussion.

We heard the sound of a siren, several blocks away, but coming closer. Wilson T. plucked at Bigelow's sleeve. "You might better leave. I'll be all right. The pastor will vouch for me."

Bigelow stared at him for a minute, then jerked his arm away. Without another word, he pushed out the door and joined his men in the waiting car. It backed away from the porte corchere, taking the light with it. Then, as the driver hit the brake, it slid around in a circle on the icy pavement. We could hear the wheels spinning as it tried to get enough traction to head for the street. Two sheriff's cars turned in, light bars flashing blue streaks across the parking lot and our faces. They swerved and stopped in front of Bigelow's car, blocking it from the street. I wanted to watch what happened, because the dark bulk climbing out of one of the cars had to be Lieutenant Peavey and I would've liked to've seen him in some action that wasn't aimed at me. But I couldn't supervise everything, don't you know, and things were still happening inside.

"Larry," Wilson T. said, coming over to the pastor, "I can explain. It was all a mistake. I didn't realize what I was getting into. But it was a sure thing, Larry, although every investment carries some risks, you know that, but that building fund was just sitting there, waiting to make more than bank interest. I knew you were disappointed at the congregation's poor response, and, well, I thought a worthy investment would outweigh the risk."

Pastor Ledbetter just stared at him, so Wilson T. tried again. "We have a good start with the building fund drive, and I know you wouldn't want to jeopardize it at this point. If you'll just help me explain to the sheriff that I was a bystander, so to speak, I'll make sure the drive is successful, it's my business, after all and I'm good at it. I'll see to it that you have a beautiful new building right out there for your congregation to use and enjoy for years to come."

"Bystander!" Hazel Marie screeched. "*By*stander! You're up to your neck in Bigelow's crooked business, Wilson T. Hodge! And I'm a witness, don't think I'm not. No use trying to wiggle out of it, after what you've put me through!"

"Ms. Puckett," Pastor Ledbetter started. I could hear the placating tone in his voice, so I knew he was picturing that building rising up, brick by brick, on the corner across from my house.

Brother Vern didn't miss a trick, especially where money was concerned. He sidled up to Wilson T., listening intently to what was going on between him and Pastor Ledbetter, and ignoring Hazel Marie all together. Wilson T. ignored him, in turn, taking the pastor by the arm and leading him into a corner.

"Say you're a fund-raiser?" Brother Vern asked, following them. Then as he stumbled into a wall, "Dag-nab it! Hold on, Brother, I wanta talk to you about beefin' up my teevee advertisin'. I got my 800 numbers, and I got my direct mailin' and my phone bank, but none of it's doin' the job good enough. What's it cost to hire you? You want a flat fee or do you take a cut of what you raise? I'd like that better, that way the ministry don't lose. Wait up, now, we need to talk."

"Enough!" I yelled, surprising myself. "Pastor, there's no need to huddle up with Wilson T. at this late date. I'd at least wait till you have an audit done, by an independent firm, I might add. Hazel Marie's going to do the right thing and tell the sheriff what she knows about Wilson T. and his cousin which, when put together with what the Rockingham sheriff knows, will mean big trouble for your fund-raiser. And that's going to happen whether that building goes up, down or sideways. And I'll tell you this, Pastor, if it's meant to be built, it will be, and you won't need Wilson T. Hodge's help. Predestination's what it's called."

"I need to think about this," the pastor said. "Pray about it."

"I'm sure you do," I agreed, distracted now by Etta Mae Wiggins running over to hug Hazel Marie.

"I've been so worried about you," Etta Mae said. "I came to take Mr. Sam home and when they told me you were over here, I just had to come see if you're all right."

That just ran all over me. Why did she think she had to come out on a night like this to take Sam home? Did she think she was the only one who could look after him? I just had no use for presumption, which she had a mortal plenty of.

Then the full import of her words hit me square between the

eyes. Sam's house had no power either, and it was more than likely that James had gone home. So how was Sam going to manage by himself in the dark with a cast on his leg?

The shock of her underhanded plan to spend the night with Sam stunned me so bad that I couldn't say a word, just stood there with my nerves thrumming away.

"I'm so glad you're back, safe and sound," Etta Mae went on, ignoring the presence of everybody else. "Honey, if anything happened to you, I don't know what I'd do. You've been my idol ever since we were in grammar school. We've all been worried to death."

My lip curled when she associated herself with those of us who'd made such an effort to find Hazel Marie. I say, *we*.

"I'm fine, I guess," Hazel Marie told her. "But are you all right? Did they hurt you?"

"Oh, don't worry about me, I'm okay. I didn't know what I'd walked into, I mean, you don't exactly expect to come into a church and get attacked, do you? But I had plenty of help." She gestured toward Mr. Pickens and Mr. Johnson, who were on their way out the door to add their two cents to whatever version Bigelow and Hodge were giving Lieutenant Peavey. "Who are they anyway? Friends of yours?"

Hazel Marie started explaining who they were but, when she said "Jerry Johnson," Etta Mae squealed like a teenager. Another big racing fan, I guessed.

"You really get around, Hazel Marie," she said, with a tinge of admiration and, perhaps, envy. Of all things.

"I don't know how I get into such messes. If it wasn't for Miss Julia, I don't know what I'd do."

Thank you, Hazel Marie, I thought, for the commendation. But it didn't help much, because I was trembling all over, still outraged by the Wiggins woman.

"Well, my patient's waiting for me," Etta Mae said. "I need to get Mr. Sam home and tucked in bed. He depends on me, the sweet ole thing."

She gave Hazel Marie a quick hug. Then, bless me, if she didn't stop in the porte corchere and hug both Mr. Pickens and Mr. Johnson, thanking them for coming to the rescue. From what I'd seen, Etta Mae Wiggins hadn't needed a whole lot of rescuing by anybody. As she moved out of the light, it flew all over me again that she was heading for my house. She'd just walk in like she owned it, I knew she would. Then she'd bundle Sam up and put him in her car and take him with her to his house. And would she just get him settled and leave him there? In the dark? With no heat? Feeling his way around with a cane? By himself, in the worst winter storm we'd had? NO, she would not.

I knew what she *would* do, though. She had every justifiable reason in the world for spending the night with him. Not that *she* cared about justifying herself. Women like that never do.

I stood there in the dark of the hall, vaguely aware that Mr. Pickens and Mr. Johnson were coming back into the church. I could hear them discussing the arrests they'd witnessed, with Mr. Johnson still bemoaning his loss. Over against the wall, Wilson T. continued to whisper to the pastor as he pled for understanding. None of it made any difference to me. I had more important things on my mind. *Sam,* in the clutches of that unprincipled woman.

"Peavey's coming in," Mr. Pickens said, opening the door for him and another deputy who were there to get statements or, maybe, to arrest anybody else who needed it. By the headlights of the sheriff's cars outside, I could see other deputies transferring Bigelow and his two men to the back seats of the patrol cars. It was a most satisfying sight, to say the least.

As Lieutenant Peavey and his deputy entered the dark church, the strong beams of their heavy flashlights swept over the pastor,

Wilson T. and Hazel Marie, as well as Mr. Johnson and Mr. Pickens. I saw Lieutenant Peavey shake Mr. Pickens's hand, and heard the babble of voices as everybody tried to tell what'd been going on.

By this time, I was pressed against the wall of the kitchen, trying to determine how much danger Sam was in, and not intentionally staying out of the limelight. But that's the way it worked out. Besides, I figured the lieutenant would be in a better mood if I made myself scarce.

At Mr. Pickens's suggestion, the lieutenant agreed to adjourn to the pastor's study, where the lantern would give better light for the statements that had to be taken. As they moved out of the fellowship hall, nobody noticed that I wasn't with them.

So I stayed where I was, sick at heart over Sam's perilous situation, and no longer caring whether Wilson T. got what was coming to him or not.

This is not like you, Julia Springer. It was like a voice from out of the blue, and why not, since I was standing in a church? *Where's your gumption? Look at you: letting another woman move in where she has no business.*

Well, that did it. I'd let the same thing happen with Wesley Lloyd although, except for damaging my pride, what he'd done wouldn't've mattered a hill of beans to me. Go and stay gone would've been my response which, come to think of it, was what he'd done, with a little help from a heart attack.

I straightened myself up and pulled myself together. Sam wasn't Wesley Lloyd, not by a long shot, and Sam was worth making an effort for. So if it took a fight, then that's what Etta Mae Wiggins was going to get.

Standing there in the dark, I decided there was no profit in being the last word on proper behavior if it meant losing Sam. What would it matter if I was the one person in town who knew the *correct* way of doing things if that woman got her clutches in him? So what if some people didn't know Amy from Gloria Vanderbilt? Did I have to be the one who had all the answers? I mean, did it really matter in the scheme of things if I knew that a coffee is a morning entertainment and a tea is held in the afternoon? Who cared if I knew that open-faced cucumber sandwiches are correct in the summer and party-sized ham biscuits in the winter? And cheese straws anytime. Who cared if I knew white shoes are worn only between Easter and Labor Day, and that camellias should be planted on the southeast side of the house in our climate? What did it matter if I knew that "honor" should be spelled "honour" on wedding invitations? Or that the bride's family gives the flatware and the groom's family the silver service? Why had I ever exercised myself over people who didn't know which end was up?

None of it mattered in the face of this crisis. All that mattered now was that Etta Mae Wiggins was about to put Sam in a compromising situation, and that he wouldn't even know it until she'd sunk her hooks in good and tight. It was up to me to see that it didn't happen.

Chapter 33

I saw the flickering glow of the lantern as someone lit it in the pastor's study, heard the voices of Lieutenant Peavey and Mr. Pickens, and didn't give a rip if I wasn't in there to provide the details. I slipped out the back door, closing it softly behind me, and took my life in my hands to cross the sleet-covered parking lot by myself.

My galoshes flapped against my shins as I made my way toward Mr. Johnson's truck, looming like a behemoth between me and my house. Etta Mae was nowhere to be seen, so she'd managed the icy area without mishap. More's the pity, although I didn't customarily wish harm to anybody. But this was a special case, since she meant harm to me and mine.

As I reached the front of the truck, I steadied myself by holding on to the grill, resting while I looked across the street where Etta Mae's car was parked, and then up at my house. Blood pounded in my ears as I pictured what was going on in there in the dim light.

A shadow suddenly moved in front of me, scaring me so bad I nearly lost my breath and my hold on the truck.

"Who's that!"

"It's just me," Curtis said. "You all right?"

"Lord, Curtis," I said, gasping with relief, "you scared me half to death. What're you doing out here?"

"Got worried when those men came to the house looking for

y'all. Then when we saw the cop cars, I came out to see what was going on, and to check the truck. Want me to walk you in?"

"No. No, that's all right. You keep on doing what you're doing, I'll manage." I walked out onto the sanded street where the footing was surer, not wanting to be held up on my mission.

Halfway across, I turned around with a sudden idea of how to turn Etta Mae's attention away from Sam. "Curtis?" I called. "Are you a race-truck driver, too?"

"No ma'am, I'm a fabricator."

"That'll do. She won't know the difference. Did you see that young woman come across just a minute ago?"

"Yes ma'am. She was in a hurry and didn't stop. Went on in the house."

"She's young, single at the moment, and somewhat attractive. At least, some people think so. Would you be amenable to distracting her for a little while? You could bring her out here and show her Mr. Johnson's truck, maybe. And, although I don't usually hold with such tactics, I think a little innocent dalliance might be called for. She's quite lonely, and could use some attention."

Even in the dark, I saw his quick grin. "I'm a married man, Miz Springer. For all of three months, so I better pass if it's all the same to you."

I threw up my hands and started again for the house. At least I'd tried for an end run; now I'd have to tackle her head-on.

When I opened the front door, I wasn't a bit surprised to see the little hussy sitting on the arm of Sam's chair. It just burned me up. I ignored Sam's call to me, as I took off my coat and head scarf; this was between me and Etta Mae Wiggins.

"'Bout time you got back here," Lillian said, cocking her head toward Sam's chair. "I 'spect you about froze."

"No," I started, my mouth in a thin line as I thought that I was as far from being frozen as I'd ever been.

"Julia!" LuAnne jumped up from her chair. "What's going on

over at the church? People knocking on the door and the sheriff over there, we were worried to death. Is Jerry all right? Where is he? When's he coming back?"

"Jerry's fine, LuAnne, sit down. Miss Wiggins took good care of him, didn't you, Etta Mae?" LuAnne narrowed her eyes, not liking that at all. "Sam, you should be in bed. Lillian, let's help him up. He needs his rest."

Etta Mae gave me an innocent smile. "Oh, there's no need of that, I'll be taking him on home in a minute. That's why I put chains on my car and followed the snowplow over here. Couldn't let my favorite patient get stranded, could I?" She reached down and patted his knee.

"I'd hardly say he was stranded. Besides, he doesn't need to spend the night by himself, with neither heat nor lights."

"Oh," she said, looking at me with wide-eyed innocence, "I'd never leave a patient in his shape by himself. I'll stay with him till James gets there in the morning."

"I hardly think that's advisable. Where's your cane, Sam? You're going to bed right here."

"Julia . . ." Sam started, but I hushed him with a look. I meant for him to stay out of this.

"He needs to be in his own bed," Etta Mae said, like only she knew what he needed. "He's got his pillows to prop his cast on, and a bedrail to pull up on. He'll be more comfortable there."

"Don't tell *me* where he'll be more comfortable." I could not control the surge of anger at the little know-it-all. "And I'd appreciate it if you'd get off the arm of that chair. It wasn't made to be sat on."

She jumped up like a shot, while LuAnne and Lillian looked at me with their mouths open. It certainly wasn't like me to be discourteous, but these were special circumstances. Besides, she started it.

Sam had the strangest expression on his face while this was going on, sitting there enjoying being fought over, as it was plain to see he was doing. I could've wrung his neck.

I marched over to him, paying no mind to Etta Mae who'd edged out of my way. I sat down on the footstool by Sam's wounded leg and said, "Sam, it's bad out there, and if you don't want that other leg broken, you'll stay here tonight."

"Well, Julia," he said, taking my hand, his eyes shining from the reflection of the fire, "if you put it that way."

I looked up in triumph at Etta Mae, only to catch the edge of a smile as she turned away. Now why would she be doing that when she'd just been put in her place? But saving face is important to some people, and I didn't care how she managed it. I had what I wanted.

Knowing I could now afford to be gracious, I said, "Have a seat on the sofa, Miss Wiggins, and get yourself warm before you have to leave. I certainly appreciate your dedication to your patients but, as you can see, Sam is well taken care of."

"Yes, ma'am," she said, just as docile as I could want. You just have to stand up to the likes of her.

Footsteps sounded on the porch, as Hazel Marie, Mr. Johnson, Mr. Pickens and Curtis came in with a lot of stomping and laughing and just plain noise.

"It's over, Miss Julia," Hazel Marie said, smiling as she came over to clasp my hands with her cold ones. "Or almost over. All that's left is to get to the clerk of court's office first thing Monday and make sure Brother Vern withdraws his complaint. When he's done that, the snatch-and-grab order for Little Lloyd will be thrown out. Then all I have to do is go in and sign the statement I just made to Lieutenant Peavey about Bigelow and Wilson T. I'll have to say that Lieutenant Peavey was real happy to hear my story. He was just as nice as he could be."

"Well, make sure you get your charm back from him," I told her. "I can't imagine he'd want to keep it."

"Oh, I will. It nearly killed me to damage my bracelet." She held her arm up so that the remaining charms jangled and sparkled. "I'm so relieved, Miss Julia, because Mr. Pickens took up for me and explained everything to Lieutenant Peavey. I'm out of it now, and Bigelow and Wilson T. were arrested and put in jail where they belong."

"Taken in for questioning," Mr. Pickens corrected her, "but they'll have some explaining to do, especially after the Rockingham cops get in the act."

Hazel Marie leaned close and whispered to me, "I tried to get them to take Brother Vern in, too, but they wouldn't." She gave me a wicked grin. "I'm going to tear him up if he doesn't withdraw that complaint, and he knows it. He won't have a congregation left by the time I get through telling the world what kind of preacher he is. He won't ever try to get his hands on Little Lloyd or his inheritance again."

"That's the spirit, Hazel Marie," I said, patting her hand. "And I don't think we'll have any trouble getting Pastor Ledbetter to testify to the good home you and I've provided for Little Lloyd. And if that's not enough, we'll have Mr. Pickens and Mr. Johnson testify to your good character. Why, it wouldn't surprise me a bit if the judge turns out to be a NASCAR fan, too."

She smiled and leaned her head against my shoulder until Mr. Johnson's loud mouth broke up the moment.

"Guess we took care of them," he announced, throwing his coat on a chair. "I wouldna missed it for the world. Now, I want to shake the hand of this little gal." He headed straight for Etta Mae, a big, goofy grin on his face. "Come'ere, you little honey, I got to get you in the light so I can see what I got. Might even have to give you a great big kiss. God dog, where'd you learn to fight like that?"

Etta Mae grinned right back at him. "Fightin' off men who're too big for their britches. Like you."

Well, that just delighted Mr. Johnson, and he showed it by grabbing her up and swinging her around, putting my furnishings and general decor in jeopardy. But wouldn't you know it, and I hoped Sam noticed, she'd turned her attention entirely on Mr. Johnson. Women like that will take up with any man within arm's reach.

LuAnne didn't like it. I could tell she was fuming at Etta Mae's sudden elevation in Mr. Johnson's esteem. Even though I had no use for Etta Mae at all, I had to be gratified that she was taking Mr. Johnson's mind off LuAnne. And LuAnne could tell she'd lost out to a younger model, you could see it eating at her. Jealousy is such an unattractive trait, don't you think?

"J. D.!" Mr. Johnson cried, turning away from his current interest. "Now you got these folks up to speed, when you gonna take up my case? We got to get on the road soon's the interstates're clear if we're gonna make Phoenix. But no use me goin' if my lucky charm's still missin'. I tell you what's a fact, I was hopin' Bigelow had it and we could wring it out of him. But don't look like he does, what with the way he's been lookin' high and low."

"Yeah," Mr. Pickens said. "He wouldn't've risked coming back here if he'd had it. He'd be in Phoenix by this time instead of the county jail. No, he doesn't have it, and Hodge didn't strike me as the type to hold out for long against Bigelow. I figure somebody else got it from them and has either gone on ahead or it's still around here somewhere."

He put his arm around Hazel Marie's waist, smiled down at her and said, "I'm good at finding things, though. Just look what I came up with on my last case."

That comment didn't seem to give Mr. Johnson any particular reassurance, and I can't say I blamed him. It was a stretch to compare Hazel Marie to any kind of lucky charm, to my way of thinking. But I wasn't ready to totally discount Mr. Pickens's investigative techniques, since they'd proven somewhat helpful in

Hazel Marie's case. Although when you came right down to it, if it hadn't been for me and Little Lloyd he'd've still been looking for her.

I started to point this out to Mr. Johnson, but the lights flickered, came on, and the furnace clicked on in the basement. Everybody blinked and looked around, smiling at having our modern conveniences back at work.

Candlelight and open fires are all well and good in their place, but I could do without them in the ordinary course of events.

"Well, thank the Lord," Lillian said.

"And Duke Power," I added.

Chapter 34

In the relief of having the power back on, everybody except Sam stood up, blinking in the brighter light, glad to be able to see what they were doing.

"Lillian," I said, "let's see if we can find something to eat. A little snack before we go to bed, and before Miss Wiggins has to leave, would be welcome."

I stood up, but Sam kept my hand, pulling me back down. "Hurry back," he said.

You know, it's not always the words, it's the way they're said that warms the heart. I tried not to let it show, since the Wiggins woman was still flitting around and who knew what she'd be up to as soon as my back was turned.

"Hold on a minute," Mr. Pickens said. Then, taking Hazel Marie's arm, he said, "I want to see you in the kitchen." Cocking that finger at me, he went on, "And you, too, Miss Julia. I want you, too."

His high-handedness affronted me, but I wanted to know what he was up to now, so I followed them through the dining room and into the kitchen. Mr. Pickens didn't let loose of Hazel Marie's arm, just marched her in and closed the door behind us.

"All right," he said, frowning but trying not to smile as he stared down at her. "Let's have it."

"What?" I asked.

"It's nothing," she said, turning her face away from him. "Really, it's not."

"What?" I asked.

Ignoring me, he got right up in her face, pointing that finger at her. "Don't put me off any longer, little girl. I know you've got something."

Now how did he know something I didn't? I looked from one to the other, trying to determine what was going on.

"Come on, come on." Mr. Pickens wasn't turning it loose. "What is it and where is it?"

"Well, it's . . . ," Hazel Marie started, stopped and looked at me for help, but I wanted to know as bad as he did. "Well, it's just so ridiculous, I'm ashamed to say. I mean, I don't know why in the world anybody would want it."

"Wait a minute," I said. "Hazel Marie, do you actually have something of Bigelow's?" I couldn't believe it. Here I'd been taking up for her when she'd been accused of stealing and taking what didn't belong to her. This was a pretty come-off, if you ask me.

"No, ma'am, I don't have anything of Bobby Bigelow's." Then she ducked her head and admitted, "I did take a little something of Wilson T.'s, but nobody could call that thing valuable by any stretch of the imagination. See, Miss Julia, I just wanted to get back at Wilson T., and it was the only way I could think of. I saw him take it out of its hiding place and look at it and rub his hand over it when he thought nobody was watching. Well, I thought, you know, I thought it was a . . . well, one of those weird things that some men get fixated on, like, well, a woman's foot or her underclothes. I don't know what you call it, a feets, a fet . . . some such thing."

Mr. Pickens said, "A fetish?"

I said, "A what?"

"Something with magical powers," Mr. Pickens answered, his eyes glued to Hazel Marie, the hint of a smile twitching around his mouth.

Magical powers, I thought. It seemed to me that there was more to a fetish than that, but I didn't pursue it.

"That's it," Hazel Marie went on, "and I knew it'd embarrass him to death if anybody knew about it, him being with the church and all. I was so mad at him for taking me off and doing everything Bobby told him to do, and keeping me from coming home, that I wanted to get back at him. I was going to show it to the pastor and the building fund committee, hoping they'd run him out of town and stop putting up that building."

Well, bless your heart, Hazel Marie, I thought. She'd been thinking of me all along, and that put a different light on any of her questionable actions, in my opinion.

"Miss Julia," she said, turning to me, a look of pleading on her face, "I know it's a sin to lie and steal, but I kept trying to think what you'd do in the same situation."

Well, for pity's sake, I thought, thoroughly taken aback.

"And," she went on, looking up now at Mr. Pickens, "I knew that Miss Julia would do whatever it took to make things turn out right. But this thing couldn't be Bobby Bigelow's, I mean, he's looking for something *valuable,* for the Lord's sake. What I took from Wilson T. is not worth two cents, and I can't imagine him or Bigelow looking all over creation for it. But if it is, then they must be crazy, carrying on like the thing's a piece of gold or something."

"It's okay, sweetie," Mr. Pickens said. "Let's have it now, and I'll explain it to you."

She ducked her head and said something under her breath.

"What?" I demanded. "Look, Hazel Marie, we've been chased and manhandled and scared out of our wits because of whatever it is, and I'm tired of it all. So give it to Mr. Pickens, and let's wash our hands of it. And, frankly, I'd like to know what all the fuss is about."

"Wel-l-l," she said, her face getting redder by the minute. "It's what's left of somebody's . . . ," her voice dropped to a whisper, *"drawers."*

Mr. Pickens and I both just stared at her, our mouths open.

"Drawers?" he said. "You mean panties? Bloomers? What?"

"I don't know what it was to start with. There's not a whole lot left to tell."

"Let's see it."

"You'll have to turn around. I've got it on under my dress. Don't look."

I thought to myself he'd have the decency to step out of the room, but all he did was turn and face the door. "Go ahead," he said, and I reached over and put my hand over his eyes so he wouldn't be tempted.

I watched as Hazel Marie wiggled and twisted, reaching up under her dress and stepping out of a white elastic waistband that was rolled up on itself. You know how those things do. Then, smoothing her dress down with one hand, she dangled the ragged trophy over Mr. Pickens's shoulder.

"Here it is."

He took it, held it up, stretched it and turned it around so that I got more of a look at it than I wanted. The whole back end of what was once a pair of some man's underdrawers was gone. But hanging in the front was the unfortunate remnant of what had to be a placket. You know, the place of access.

"I hope that thing's clean," I said.

After letting me have a good look and taking one himself, Mr. Pickens leaned against the door and commenced laughing his head off.

"What's so funny, Mr. Pickens?"

"Oh, God," he laughed, straightening up and wiping his eyes. Then he sobered up right smartly, turned to me and said, "No wonder Bigelow risked arrest to get this back. We're messing with serious stuff, here." And he doubled over, laughing again.

"I can't imagine what's so serious about the thing. It's just a rag, not even fit to polish silver with. Get hold of yourself, Mr. Pickens."

"If it's what I think it is, you better believe it's serious." He turned to Hazel Marie. "No telling how many people'd give their eyeteeth to get their hands on this, these, whatever they are."

"Oh, for goodness sakes," she said, waving it away. "Who would want such a thing, except idiots like Bigelow and Wilson T.? You wouldn't believe how careful Wilson T. was with it. He kept it all folded up in a velvet bag, treating it like it was the crown jewels or something."

She stopped, because Mr. Pickens had another laughing fit. He finally got himself under control, taking an inordinate amount of time to do so.

When he was able to speak again, he said, "How'd you get it away from him?"

"It wasn't hard. While we were at the racetrack in Rockingham, Bobby was so mad at Wilson T. for letting me get to a phone so many times that he was hardly speaking to him. And Wilson T. was following him around, trying to get back in his good graces, so I was able to find the bag. I took that thing out and put it on under my dress. Then I wadded up a handful of Kleenex and stuffed that in its place. Bigelow and Wilson T. were so busy fussing with each other and trying to get that race truck to run, they didn't even know it was gone. Well, until I was gone, too."

I stood there about ready to start tapping my foot. All this upset and turmoil for a pair of ragged shorts, it was more than I could comprehend.

"Well, I want to know why in the world everybody is so interested in a pair of worn-out underclothes," I said. "If Wilson T. and Bobby Bigelow needed some kind of magic fetish, they could've just torn up another pair. I tell you, the state of the world these days is just deplorable, what with one thing and another, and here grown men are running all over creation trying to find a pair of used boxer shorts. I'd've thrown those things away a long time ago, if it'd been me."

"This?" Mr. Pickens dangled the ragged thing in front of our eyes again, in spite of the fact that I'd seen all I wanted to of them. "This is Jerry's lucky charm."

"*That* thing?" Hazel Marie's eyes nearly popped out of her head, and mine weren't far behind. "You mean, that's what he's been looking for, and I had it all the time?"

I backed up to a chair and took a seat. Here, I'd had in mind a medallion or a rabbit's foot or a gold charm like Hazel Marie'd dropped all across the state. And all the while it'd been a piece of his intimate apparel.

"Thay Lord," I said. "I guess I don't understand the racing mentality."

"It's different, I'll say that for it," Mr. Pickens said, his mustache twitching again. "Look at these things. He's worn 'em so long, there's hardly anything left." He started laughing again, holding his hand over his eyes and shaking his head. "I know one driver who'll wear only a certain pair of shoes, and another who shaves a special way on race day. Another one has to pat the hood of his car three times before he gets in it. But Jerry . . . Jerry has his lucky shorts."

"One thing I'd like to know," I said, "does Mr. Johnson wear that rag by itself or does he put on a whole pair along with it?"

"You'll have to ask him, Miss Julia. I'm not sure anybody knows and, in spite of your curiosity, I'm not about to ask him."

"Oh, my goodness," Hazel Marie said, "he's going to be so mad at me."

"No, he won't," Mr. Pickens assured her. Then folding the rag carefully, he slipped it in his pocket. "Let's go tell him; then tomorrow, when I meet with Peavey, I'll make sure Bigelow and your boyfriend know Jerry's got it back. That'll change some odds, I expect."

Hazel Marie glared at him. "Don't you start on me again about any *boyfriend*."

Mr. Pickens smiled at her, those black eyes shining. "Ex-boyfriend?"

"Not even that. He was just the only one available at the time."

As Mr. Pickens said something to the effect that somebody else might be available, I was thinking the less of her for trying to disclaim her earlier interest in Wilson T. Hodge. Then it came to me that she was most likely telling the truth. I knew she'd never been as enamored of Wilson T. as he'd been with her, which is as it should be, but she'd seemed so agreeable to his attentions that I'd thought it was just her way. Some women are born knowing that playing hard-to-get attracts men, who always want what they don't have.

Then it hit me that she might've been trying to please me, hooking up with a man of the church who had nice manners and a steady job and the preacher's respect.

I turned away from them, hoping the two of them wouldn't notice my momentary dismay, because it came to me that Hazel Marie had been looking for the so-called *decent* qualities in a prospective husband, without a thought in the world for whether she liked him or not. Just the way I'd done with Wesley Lloyd—looked on the outside and ignored what my insides were telling me.

If there's one thing I've learned, it's this: It doesn't matter how good a man appears to be, if you don't feel a little spark you'd be better off hightailing it away from him. One way or the other, it's not going to work. I don't mean that the marriage won't last. It can if you're of my generation, brought up to put up a front. And it could last if another man didn't come along to create an internal combustion. Like Mr. Pickens was wont to do. Or Sam.

"Now, Hazel Marie," Mr. Pickens said, just as serious and straight-faced as he could be, "I'm a little worried about you, seeing how you got so attached to men's underclothes. I wonder if I could interest you in some of mine?"

"Mr. Pickens!" I couldn't believe he'd be so forward.

Hazel Marie was equally shocked, but she quickly recovered as a smile spread across her face. "They'd have to be in better condition than that thing."

"Hazel Marie!" I gasped.

Neither of them paid me any attention, standing there looking at each other and smiling all over themselves.

"Sweetheart," Mr. Pickens said, as if they were the only ones in the room, "everything about me is in A-one condition. Trust me on that." Then he put an arm around her and drew me close with the other one. "Let's go tell Jerry to get ready for Victory Lane."

Chapter 35

Hazel Marie came to a stop in the dining room. "I don't think I can face Jerry," she whispered. "I mean, all this time I've had his lucky charm, while he was so worried about losing it. I just feel terrible."

"Don't worry about Jerry," Mr. Pickens said. "He'll be so happy to get it back, he won't care about anything else. In fact, he's liable to grab you up and give you a lip-smacking kiss." Mr. Pickens smiled at her. "Then I'll have to shoot him."

"Mr. Pickens," I said, "we're not going to have any of that, I'll tell you right now."

"Well," Hazel Marie said, a little smile playing around her mouth, "I think, if it's all the same to you, I'll just run up and check on Little Lloyd. So I'll be out of the line of fire from either of you."

She looked up at him again, and they stood there smiling at each other. Remember that spark I was talking about? Well, there were any number of them arcing between those two right there in my dining room. The whole situation should've made me uncomfortable, but it didn't. It made me walk on past and look for Sam.

He was standing by the fireplace, balancing himself with his cane. Waiting for me, I'd like to think. But whether he was or not, I went to stand beside him and take his arm. Staking my claim, so to speak, in case Miss Wiggins had any lingering ideas. Mr. Pickens and Hazel Marie had warmed me up to a fare-thee-well, and I wanted to share a little of it with Sam.

"Jerry," Mr. Pickens said as he came in, interrupting the whispering going on between Etta Mae and Mr. Johnson, "Got something for you. At least, I think I have. Recognize this?" He pulled the rag from his pocket and dangled it for us all to see.

Mr. Johnson came off the sofa in one bound, yelling, "My lucky charm! How the hell, oops, sorry folks, where'd you find 'em? J. D., I swear, buddy, you're the flat-out best there is!"

Well, that just polished Mr. Pickens's ego that much more, something he didn't need, what with his own high estimation of his abilities. He stood there grinning, so pleased with himself I could hardly stand it. Not that I don't believe in giving credit where it's due, but it just did me in that he'd figured out Hazel Marie's part in the mess before I could get around to it. Maybe he was as good as he thought he was, although I had my doubts considering how much help he'd needed from me.

"I'm good," Mr. Pickens said, in that smug way of his, "and that's a fact. But I had some help and I don't mind admitting it."

He walked over to me and had the nerve to point that finger in my face. "This is the one who kept me on the trail. Wouldn't give me a minute's peace, 'what're you doing now, Mr. Pickens?,' 'let's get busy, Mr. Pickens,' 'quit foolin' around, Mr. Pickens.' I swear, Miss Julia, if you'd take over my business, we'd make a million a year. How about it?"

"Oh, Mr. Pickens," I said, somewhat embarrassed by his teasing and the fact that everybody was laughing because, I suspected, they knew what he said was the truth. But somebody has to take over to get things done. "You're doing fine by yourself. But if you ever feel yourself getting slack, just come on over and I'll set you straight."

"You'll be seeing a lot of me, don't worry about that. I'm

counting on help from you and Sam," he leaned down and whispered, "with Hazel Marie, and don't you start on me, Miss Julia, about leading her astray. I'm about to strain myself just getting her attention."

Sam started laughing, then he slipped an arm around me right there in public. "Tell you what, J. D., I'll help you get what you want, but I need some help getting what I want."

"You two," I said, pretending I wasn't pleased and hoping at the same time that Etta Mae was taking note. "I don't think either of you needs anybody's help. Except both of you could profit from keeping your eyes on the prize you want, rather than letting them wander to anything wearing a skirt. Just look at that, would you, and take a lesson."

I nodded toward Jerry Johnson, who'd hung his lucky charm around Etta Mae Wiggins's neck. That ugly placket hung down on her bosom like a pendant. Just the most vulgar thing you could ever hope to see, what with her prancing around showing it to everybody.

"You about raced the bottom outta these things," she said, laughing up at Mr. Johnson.

"I sure have," he bellowed, the sound waves echoing around the room. "My ex-wife got so mad one time that she threw 'em away. I had to go dig 'em out of a Dumpster, nearly fell in, too. They been washed and bleached so many times, they're about eat up. But they still work. Man, do they ever! Phoenix, here I come, I'm gonna lap everybody, goin' wide open, and end up cruisin' Victory Lane! See if I don't!"

In spite of all the bragging and flirting they were doing, I was pleased to see them carrying on with each other, since it was plain that Mr. Johnson was no longer giving a thought to LuAnne. Just as I'd predicted.

But LuAnne was just as bad in her own way as Etta Mae Wiggins. She'd turned her attention to Curtis, and the poor man's eyes were searching desperately for a way out, as she talked and hung on his every word. I had a good mind to send Mr. Pickens for Leonard, just to see what she'd do when he walked in. I declare, people act in the strangest ways when the lights go out.

But I was so content with myself, the way things were working out, that I decided to let her enjoy a little thrill. Even if Curtis wasn't appreciating it. It wouldn't hurt him to be nice to a needy woman.

Just for the evening, you understand. Tomorrow was another day, and I'd have to see to it that things got back to normal. I'd have to make sure that Leonard got himself reamed out, or whatever had to be done to him, so LuAnne would leave both me and Pastor Ledbetter alone. She needed to tend to her own knitting or, who knows, with all that counseling she'd been getting from the pastor, the next hot rumor would be about the two of them. And that'd lift the town off its hinges.

And speaking of the pastor, I intended to see that the building fund drive was stopped dead in its tracks. We didn't need a big activities building. Especially right in front of my eyes. That money could go to foreign missions or, even better, to home missions that could always use the help. And if the pastor wouldn't see it my way or, heaven forbid, if he spoke up for Wilson T. Hodge and got him off, I'd just get on the telephone to the session and the deacons and the Sunday School superintendent and the Women of the Church and go through the church directory. What I had to pass on to them wouldn't be gossip, it would be flat-out undeniable facts. There is a difference, you know.

As for Brother Vernon Puckett, the less said of him the better. But you know me, I didn't intend to let him fade into the woodwork only to pop up again when we least expected him. Twice now, he'd tried to get his hands on Little Lloyd, because that child's trust fund is an ever-present lure, blinding him and leading him on to the most outrageous acts of underhanded deceit and deception. I wondered if I made a quiet, but minimally generous, pledge to his television ministry, he'd leave us alone. I don't mind paying somebody off, if I get my money's worth.

But to more current problems. I'd have to watch Mr. Pickens and see how he conducted himself. If he was truly interested in Hazel Marie and, more important from my viewpoint, she was truly interested in him, I'd see to it that those black eyes of his stopped their wandering ways. I wasn't about to let her heart be broken, and I intended to make that clear to Mr. Pickens in no uncertain terms.

And speaking of broken hearts and the fickle men who caused them, Sam had some proving to do, himself. And the first thing he had to do was get rid of Etta Mae Wiggins. I didn't care if she was planning to meet Mr. Johnson at the NAPA 250 at Martinsville the same weekend as the Goody's Body Pain 500, whatever any of that was, that they'd been whispering about, I knew how handsome and attractive Sam was to women. If he as much as smiled at her, she'd be all over him again. What woman wouldn't?

Well, Hazel Marie and I would just have to make up our minds to watch our men. I hated the thought of that, although I will admit to the thrill of victory when I'd snatched and grabbed Sam away from Etta Mae Wiggins. A woman ought to be able to trust somebody. But if you happen to care about a man who can't help but draw other women to him, like Sam and Mr. Pickens, why, I guess you just have to be on your guard all the time and protect them from themselves.

"I think it's time we were all in bed," I announced. Then, as gracious as a winner should be, I turned to Etta Mae. "Miss Wiggins, you shouldn't be driving this time of night, so I'll offer you my bed. Of course, Little Lloyd's already in it, but he's a good little bedfellow. I'll rest down here on the sofa."

Sam drew me closer and said so that only I heard him, "I'll keep you company."

I looked into his kind eyes and smiled before I could help myself. I didn't give a thought to how it would look, even to somebody like Pastor Ledbetter who was so concerned about the proprieties that he couldn't see what he was stepping in himself. Feeling Sam's arm tighten around me, it didn't enter my head to worry about what people would say. After all, who would know and, at our age, who would care? They'd probably think we couldn't manage anything anyway.

But what they didn't know wouldn't hurt them, because I had in mind making a few victory laps myself and, from the looks of Sam, I didn't think he'd need a pair of ragged undershorts to keep up with me.

Miss Julia is back in her third outing,

Miss Julia Throws a Wedding

(available from Viking)

Miss Julia, the feisty Southern heroine, is delighted to hear that Deputy Sheriff Coleman Bates and attorney Binkie Enloe have finally decided to get married—but not so delighted to hear they plan to tie the knot at the courthouse. Miss Julia decides to organize a *proper* ceremony. Many hilarious hurdles fall in her way, however, in this wacky, warmhearted tale of not-so-gracious living.

"You're getting married?" I repeated.

"I finally got her to say yes," Coleman said, looking down on her. He'd make about two of her, she was such a little thing. "Took me forever to do it, too."

Such a handsome young man, I thought, as I had many times before. And Binkie, that tiny ball of fire who could hold a jury spellbound and bend an Internal Revenue agent to her will, was transformed by the glow of happiness. It was a wonder to me why they'd waited so long, but I wasn't about to look a gift horse in the mouth.

"Well, it's not a moment too soon, I must say. And nobody's happier about it than I am."

"I'm real happy about it," Little Lloyd said, his eyes rarely leaving Coleman. "But I thought y'all were already married."

"Things're not always as they seem, Little Lloyd," I said, glaring at Hazel Marie over his head. But her attention was fixed on the happy couple and she didn't notice. Which was just as well, since she already knew where I stood as far as her own less than acceptable situation was concerned.

"Oh, I can't wait to tell J. D.," she said. "He'll be thrilled."

"Let's hope so," I said. "And let's hope that he takes a lesson from their example. Now, you two," I went on, turning to Binkie and Coleman, "what are your plans?"

"Quick and easy," Binkie said. "We just wanted you to be the first to know, Miss Julia. Coleman and I met the first time right here in your living room, remember?"

Of course, I remembered. She'd come in out of a thunderstorm, soaked to the skin, and Coleman'd been lost as soon as he set eyes on her.

"When is it?" Hazel Marie asked. "Have you set a date?"

"Next Friday, at the courthouse," Binkie said. "And we want you all to be there."

"Oh, no," I said, gasping with dismay at such an unseemly plan. "You can't do that! Binkie, what're you thinking of? Your folks won't stand for it, even if they have retired to Florida. There're too many things to do to get ready for a wedding—ordering and addressing invitations, picking out your dress, reserving the church, planning the reception, selecting your china pattern, and I-don't-know-what-all."

Binkie waved her hand, dismissing the best part of any young woman's wedding. "We aren't going to worry with all that, Miss Julia. My folks're not in good health, and they're not able to travel. So we're going to do it without all the trimmings. Just cut to the chase, huh, Coleman?" She gave him a friendly nudge with her elbow.

Lillian grinned. "Sound like to me the chase already over."

"It better be," Coleman said, giving Binkie a squeeze. "I've been after this woman so long, I thought I'd never catch her. It can't come too soon for me."

"Well, Coleman, the groom should be eager; that's only right and proper. But, Binkie, a bride deserves a big church wedding, a dress with a long train and bridesmaids and flowers and all your friends celebrating with you. Queen for a day. Well, for longer than that with all the weeks of planning you'll need. You just can't have it at the courthouse in a week's time. Why, you wouldn't have any memories, much less any wedding pictures."

"Well, I know, Miss Julia," Binkie said, looking down at her lap and then up at Coleman. "But we're both busy, and my workload is just so heavy. I can't take the time. . . ."

"I have to take her when I can get her," Coleman broke in with a smile. "And besides, we've been, well, keeping company so long, as you keep reminding me, Miss Julia, that we don't think it'd look right to have a big church wedding."

I certainly appreciated Coleman's sensitivity to my feelings on the subject, and his careful wording of what everybody in town knew, namely, that they'd jumped the gun some time ago. In such cases, though, the best thing to do is just ignore the facts and go ahead and do what has to be done. Although I'd draw the line if Binkie wanted to wear white.

Still, I was dismayed at the thought of a hastily arranged and hurriedly accomplished civil ceremony without benefit of clergy, so I said, "I can't believe you'd want to do it at the courthouse; you need a minister at the very least. And you can keep it small. An intimate wedding would be lovely and perfectly suitable. You wouldn't need to use the sanctuary; you could have it in the chapel. It's perfect for a small wedding. Oh, Binkie, I just can't stand the thought of you two taking a few minutes between making a will and making an arrest to run down to the courthouse to get married."

"I don't know, Miss Julia," Hazel Marie chimed in. "It sounds real romantic to me."

Of course, in her situation I guessed it would, since any sort of ceremony would be better than what she was getting. And if she could've gotten Mr. Pickens as far as the courthouse, even I would've been willing to forego the blessings of the church.

"It got to be next week?" Lillian asked.

"Yes, because the following Monday and Tuesday're the only time we can get a long weekend together," Binkie told her. "I can't take off any longer, with all the cases I have pending. But that's honeymoon enough for now."

4 · ANN B. ROSS

"Oh, my word," I said, leaning my head on my hand. "Coleman, you've got to do better than that. You're both going about this the wrong way. You ought to be making some memories that'll carry you through the years and the bad times. Not that I think you'll have any bad times, but you never know. And if you have a lovely wedding to look back on, it'll certainly help."

"I understand what you're saying, Miss Julia," Binkie said. "But we either do it next weekend or it'll have to wait until fall. And neither of us want to do that. And as far as even a small church wedding is concerned, with my schedule, I just don't have the time to make all those arrangements."

Lillian said, "Miss Julia got the time."

No one said anything for a minute, as the grinding of gears of another loaded truck pulling up across the street and two dozen voices shouting directions made us all cringe. When Lillian's words had a chance to sink in, a smile spread across my face. I jumped up from my chair, marvelling that I hadn't thought of it, myself.

"Why, of course! That's what we'll do! Binkie, Coleman, you've got to let me do it. Why, it'd be no trouble at all, would it, Lillian? It's the perfect solution!"

"Oh, say yes," Hazel Marie said, looking as excited as I felt. "Miss Julia is so good at organizing things, and I'll help her. I'd love to help; it'll be so much fun, and you wouldn't have to do anything but show up."

"She's right, Binkie." I pushed my case hard, wanting so much for this young couple to get a good start in life. Even though they'd pretty much already started. "I'll make all the arrangements, if you don't mind having it at our church. I know everybody over there and I can get things done. Oh," I stopped, remembering that Pastor Ledbetter was out traipsing around the Wailing Wall or the Dead Sea or some such thing on a tour of the Holy Land. Wouldn't you know he'd be gone right when I could've used him. "Well, our senior pastor's halfway around the world and won't be back in time. Ordinarily, it wouldn't matter a hill of beans to me where he was, but this is certainly an inconvenience."

"Pastor Petree is here," Hazel Marie reminded me. "He may be an associate, but I think he's a full-fledged minister in spite of it."

"Well, I guess he'll have to do. Now, Binkie, just say the word and we'll get you married in style. You won't have to do a thing but pick out your dress."

"Well," Binkie said, looking up at Coleman. "What do you think?"

"Up to you, honey," he said.

"Oh, please," Hazel Marie said. "Let us do it."

"Well, if it won't be too much trouble. . . ." Binkie was trying not to smile, but I could tell that she was pleased. And why not? Every young woman wants a wedding to remember, so I determined in my heart to do the best I could with what I had to work with. Although who ever heard of putting on a memorable wedding in a week's time?

"Wonderful!" I said, pacing now in front of them as one plan after another went through my head. "Binkie, I declare, if you could possibly give us two weeks. All right, all right, we can do it in one. It won't be much, but it'll be something. Now, I know young people these days like to do everything together, you know, pick out their invitations, their china pattern and such but there's no time for that. You'll just have to let me have a free hand. On, my, invitations should go out at least four weeks before the wedding, and they should be engraved. Well, it can't be helped. Start your list, Binkie, and you, too, Coleman. We'll invite by phone. It may not be the correct thing, but it'll have to do. Besides, we're not inviting Amy Vanderbilt, so our etiquette doesn't have to be perfect." I stopped in mid-pace, thinking of the wedding I could've put on if they'd given me enough time.

"Binkie," I started up again, "you'll need to pick out your china pattern. And your silver and crystal."

"I've got all of mother's. She wanted me to have them when they moved to Florida."

"Good. She has lovely taste, and that's a few less things to worry about. But you need to go out to Belk's and get on their bridal list, and anywhere else that you want people to shop for you. If they're going to spend the money, they might as well get what you want."

"Hold on a minute, Miss Julia," Coleman said. "This is sounding pretty complicated."

I gave Binkie a long look, trying to read her feelings, and what I saw was a rosy flush on her pale face and a sparkle in her eyes. I knew I was right to push this, because every bride deserves all the attendant festivities at least once in her life, although I knew a few who'd done it more than once. I'd even heard of one twice-divorced woman who'd gone down the aisle in full white regalia with four bridesmaids behind her. An example of the worst possible taste.

"Coleman," I said, "here's the first lesson for you. Pick out your groomsmen, order your tuxedo—although you really ought to own one—and the flowers for your bride, pay the preacher, plan the honeymoon, and leave the rest to us. Oh, and show up on time. That's all the groom has to do."

"Yes, ma'am," he said, then pulled Binkie closer to him. "What do you say, sweetheart?"

"I don't know how you're going to do it," Binkie said to me. "But I guess it could be fun. At least, let's make it fun. Not something dreary and formal, with all that traditional rigamarole. I don't want us to get carried away with trying to do everything by the book. Something small and simple and happy will suit us fine. But, I warn you, Miss Julia, I can't be much help; my schedule next week is so full I get tired just thinking about it."

She was telling the truth, for I noticed as she was speaking that she'd begun to look a little green around the gills. Lord, there was nothing worse than a bride getting sick right before the wedding.

"You ought to be gettin' some rest," Lillian said, frowning at her. "You an' Coleman, neither one, don't get enough rest, an' you don't eat right, neither."

"You ought to listen to Lillian," I said, nodding in agreement. "And I want you to put everything out of your minds, and leave it all to us. We'll get it done, and done right. Oh, I wish there was enough time for me to give you a party, a tea or something, and I know your friends would like to give you a shower. Although, I'll tell you something your mother'd tell you if she could. Don't encourage showers; suggest a luncheon instead. People'll give you nicer wedding gifts if they don't have to buy half-a-dozen shower gifts beforehand. See, this is the kind of thing I can help you with."

"There's just one thing," Coleman said, and he pointed his finger at Little Lloyd. "*You* have to be in it, bud."

If the child had smiled any wider, his face would've split wide open. He nodded, too overcome to speak.

"Thank you for wanting to do it, Miss Julia," Binkie said, leaning her head against Coleman. "But please don't put yourself out; I just want to get it done."

That was Binkie all over. She'd always had a mind of her own, and it was usually different from what you'd expect from a girl raised as well as she'd been. Why, she'd even refused to make her debut at the Governor's Ball in Raleigh when she'd been the only girl in Abbotsville to've been asked. It'd nearly killed her mother. But Binkie had me to reckon with now.

"It's settled then," I said. "So don't give it another thought."

"Uh-oh," Coleman said, as he fiddled with some little attachment on his law enforcement belt. "Use your phone, Miss Julia?"

"Of course. You know where it is. Now, Hazel Marie," I said, as Coleman headed for the kitchen phone. "You're just going to have to make the sacrifice and put off your move until this wedding's over. I'm going to need you, and Little Lloyd, too. In fact,

I'm not sure I can do it in this short amount of time if you're not here to help me."

"Wel-l-l," she said, her eyes darting around. "I guess I could. I mean, it's only a week, so maybe J. D. won't mind."

I could've cared less whether Mr. Pickens minded or not. This wedding was having added benefits, as far as I was concerned.

As Coleman came back into the room, he said, "Binkie, Miss Julia, sorry to break this up, but I have to go. They're calling everybody back on duty—a little problem at the jail. Come on, sweetheart, I'll drop you off and get on down there."

"Wait, wait," I said, as Binkie got up from the sofa and followed him to the door. "We have to discuss, oh, I don't know what all, a million things. Come to dinner tomorrow night, and we'll get it all done then. And bring your invitation lists and, Binkie, both of you need to ask somebody to stand up with you. That's the law, you know; you have to have two witnesses."

They were on the porch by that time, but Coleman turned back. "Lord, Miss Julia," he said with a teasing smile, "if the two of us don't know the law, I don't know who does."

FOR THE BEST IN PAPERBACKS, LOOK FOR THE

In every corner of the world, on every subject under the sun, Penguin represents quality and variety—the very best in publishing today.

For complete information about books available from Penguin—including Puffins, Penguin Classics, and Compass—and how to order them, write to us at the appropriate address below. Please note that for copyright reasons the selection of books varies from country to country.

In the United Kingdom: Please write to *Dept. EP, Penguin Books Ltd, Bath Road, Harmondsworth, West Drayton, Middlesex UB7 0DA.*

In the United States: Please write to *Penguin Putnam Inc., P.O. Box 12289 Dept. B, Newark, New Jersey 07101-5289* or call 1-800-788-6262.

In Canada: Please write to *Penguin Books Canada Ltd, 10 Alcorn Avenue, Suite 300, Toronto, Ontario M4V 3B2.*

In Australia: Please write to *Penguin Books Australia Ltd, P.O. Box 257, Ringwood, Victoria 3134.*

In New Zealand: Please write to *Penguin Books (NZ) Ltd, Private Bag 102902, North Shore Mail Centre, Auckland 10.*

In India: Please write to *Penguin Books India Pvt Ltd, 11 Panchsheel Shopping Centre, Panchsheel Park, New Delhi 110 017.*

In the Netherlands: Please write to *Penguin Books Netherlands bv, Postbus 3507, NL-1001 AH Amsterdam.*

In Germany: Please write to *Penguin Books Deutschland GmbH, Metzlerstrasse 26, 60594 Frankfurt am Main.*

In Spain: Please write to *Penguin Books S. A., Bravo Murillo 19, 1° B, 28015 Madrid.*

In Italy: Please write to *Penguin Italia s.r.l., Via Benedetto Croce 2, 20094 Corsico, Milano.*

In France: Please write to *Penguin France, Le Carré Wilson, 62 rue Benjamin Baillaud, 31500 Toulouse.*

In Japan: Please write to *Penguin Books Japan Ltd, Kaneko Building, 2-3-25 Koraku, Bunkyo-Ku, Tokyo 112.*

In South Africa: Please write to *Penguin Books South Africa (Pty) Ltd, Private Bag X14, Parkview, 2122 Johannesburg.*